THE HUNGER & THE HUNTED

THE HUNGER & THE HUNTED

A NOVEL

C. LINDSEY WILLIAMS

To Meredith and Jessica,
Thanks for restoring in me a smidgeon of hope.
You have no idea…

To Nick,
The show must go on.

"There are few things more powerful, or more intoxicating, than knowing there is someone who desires you utterly. And if it is illicit, secret, forbidden, that makes it all the more exciting."

—AUTHOR UNKNOWN

MAIN CHARACTERS

Geoffrey Scott Cameron, 45
- Founder & CEO; Cameron, Boone, Covington & Associates
- University of California, Berkley (BS Economics); Stanford University (MS Finance)
- Married, 19 years
- Three children: Lucy (16), Brooke (13) and Scott "CJ" (10)
- Residence: Tiburon, California
- Hobbies: Coaching sports, fast foreign cars, skiing, hiking, international travel

Susie McMillan Cameron, 42
- Wife of Geoff Cameron
- Stanford University (BS History)
- Loyal spouse and uber-mother
- PTA Chairperson; National Charity League executive board
- Residence: Tiburon, California
- Hobbies: Yoga, fitness, philanthropy

Meredith Gabrielle nee Luchaisse Edmonson, 30
- Cheer Instructor, Dance Teacher; Grand Junction Union High School
- Julliard Institute of New York (BFA, Dance); NYU (MA Education)
- Wife of Robert "Bobbie" James Edmonson
- Married, 4 years
- No children
- Residence: Grand Junction, Colorado
- Hobbies: Piano, photography, backpacking, outdoor adventure

Robert "Bobbie" James Edmonson, 30

- Head Football Coach, Granite High School Grizzlies
- Southern Colorado Community College (AA Sports Management)
- Graduate, Grand Junction Union High School
- Husband of Meredith Edmonson
- Residence: Grand Junction, Colorado
- Hobbies: Body building, deer hunting, archery, spectator sports

Nicolas George, 45

- Chief Operating Officer; Cameron, Boone, Covington & Associates
- Trusted friend, business partner and confidant of Geoff Cameron
- UCLA (BS, Economics); USC Marshall School of Business (MBA)
- Single
- Residence: San Francisco Downtown
- Hobbies: Event Planning; Travel; Bridge; Poker

Jessica "Jess" Riley Stevens, 34

- Manager, Sunset Gardens Senior Housing
- University of Colorado, Boulder (BS Psychology)
- Best friend of Meredith Edmonson
- Single mother of one daughter: Jasmine (14)
- Residence: Grand Junction, Colorado
- Hobbies: Hiking, cross-country skiing, apre-anything

TABLE OF CONTENTS

LONG BEFORE

VALENTINE'S DAY, 1998

GEOFF TOOK SUSIE TO DINNER, AND AN OVERNIGHT STAY, AT A romantic lighthouse station/Bed & Breakfast in the middle of Oakland Harbor with spectacular views across the Bay to the city skyline of San Francisco. It was an especially warm night, and they dined outdoors under the stars. Susie looked magnificent. She was wearing a dress that had an ever-increasingly-rare plunging neckline that exposed a generous glimpse of soft skin along her inner breasts, and she was particularly flirty. Happy to be free of motherhood for the night, Susie felt a bit nostalgic for those early years of dating and marriage—and the freedom to have uninterrupted conversation, verbal foreplay and sex.

As the night unfolded, Geoff waited until desert to present Susie with a surprise gift. It was wrapped in pink chiffon with a darker pink bow. The box was no larger than a small book. He quietly and secretly pulled the box from under the table, and slipped it in front of her. The card said simply, "I Love You So Much. Happy Valentine's Day!" Susie couldn't imagine what Geoff had bought her. After all, it was their tradition to not buy gifts, but rather, to select a cache of funny and thoughtful cards to be presented on the night with often playfully insulting and/or suggestive comments. They had already exchanged cards. But, a gift was extraordinary and quite unexpected. He still remembered the deep breath she took, and the swelling of her breasts, as she contemplated how she was going to open this beautifully wrapped treasure.

As she loosened the ribbon and bow from the box, the chiffon seemed to slip to the floor. Susie opened the box, and was at first surprised to see that there was, in fact, another felt box inside. She looked up at Geoff's face and caught his adoring eyes staring into hers. "Go ahead," he said softly. "Open it."

She opened the second box slowly. She could see jewelry, but a small envelope fell out onto the table. She immediately snatched it. She slid her finger inside the envelope, and broke the red wax seal. She pulled out a piece of heavy bond paper, and as she began to read, Geoff said smiling, "Sorry. I'm not too good with Power-Point or Desktop Publishing." Susie didn't reply. She kept reading and a tear slowly fell across her left cheek, caressing it. When she looked up at Geoff, her eyes were pools of adoration. "There is no one on this planet who could possibly deserve you," she almost whispered. "How in the world was I so lucky to have captured your heart?" she wondered. Embossed on the paper, was the following message:

To My Valentine,
When you wear this,
And feel its touch against your heart,
Think of me.
I will always be with you. Only you.
I love you.
Geoff

Geoff got up from his seat, and came around behind Susie, and nuzzled her neck softly kissing the very bottom of her ear lobe. The illicit gaze down her neck, and deep down the front of her slightly open dress, aroused him. He pulled the long Sterling silver cable necklace from the velvet jewelry box. It had a loop at one end, and placing it around her neck from behind, he carefully fed the other end though it. Still behind her, he let gravity feed the cool wispy loose end down between her breasts. He kissed the back of her neck this time, and slowly returned to his side of the table.

The waiter quietly placed the Picasso of deserts in front of each of them: A molten Grand Marnier soufflé sprinkled with dark chocolate flakes. A small glass of aged port was delicately placed next to these final creations. No more words were spoken. Geoff and Susie took a few half-hearted nibbles at their desert, and finished their port.

"Why don't you head back to the room while I take care of the bill?" he said. Susie got up, turned around and pressed herself into Geoff's waiting arms. He could feel her soft and aroused breasts on his chest, and smell the familiar scent of her.

She whispered, "Don't be long; I miss you already." And with that, Susie slowly extricated herself from Geoff's arms, and with a wink, was gone.

PRE-GAME WARM-UP, 2011

BOBBIE REACHED BACK INTO THE CENTER CONSOLE OF HIS TRUCK. He was still parked at the far end of the parking lot with his back to the school. After all, a playful handful of a cheerleader's ass had been the highlight of his day so far, and he looked forward to getting shit-faced drunk and fucking his wife.

He pulled the pill bottle from under the empty beer cans, and screwed off the safety lid. Two small pink pills fell into his hand, and he realized how much he resented having to take Viagra. What was wrong? He was still quite young, and yet he often had a problem getting an erection. Clearly, he was not emotionally attached to his wife, and sex was only a conquering for him. Was that it? Or, was he drinking too much? He had heard that mixing Vitamin V with booze would neutralize the effect.

He popped the pills into his mouth, and washed them down with his fourth beer. Shit. He had to piss. Bobbie almost fell out of his truck, and walked to the front bumper and turned around towards the bushes. He fumbled with his zipper and swore loudly as he tried to untangle his flaccid penis from his underwear and jeans. As his urine began to flow, slapping on the curb and dirt in front of him, he shivered and allowed his head to tilt backwards. He closed his eyes and enjoyed the immense relief.

"Everything OK, Coach?" Carlos, the evening security guard called out.

Bobbie, snapping to, urgently shoved himself back into his pants, peeing on himself. "Motherfucker!" he hissed. "Yes, everything fine here, my man. Just had to take an emergency piss. Do you need tickets to tomorrow's game?"

Carlos called out without hesitation, "Absolutely! Do you have extras? Enough for my wife and kids?"

"Sure," Bobbie called back. "Pick them up at my office in the morning. And, if I forget, talk to Pat, my hot assistant. She'll get you all set up."

"Muy bueno, Senor Edmonson, muchas gracias!" And with that, Carlos disappeared into the night.

Fuck, now he had to wait around for another 15 minutes or so to let his pants dry out. He climbed back into his truck. It was now 10:30, and his little wifey-poo would be upset again about how late he was, and that he, again, ruined dinner, blah, blah, blah.

"Who gives a shit anyway," he thought to himself. "She has to understand my priorities. So, if she gets her little panties in a bunch, refuses to put out, and wants to just lie there and take it like she always does, so be it. Fuck her."

Bobbie reached back into the center console and felt around for the brown paper bag. He pulled it out and carefully removed the syringe and an unmarked bottle of clear fluid. After drawing the liquid to the three-quarter line, he removed the needle from the bottle and held it towards the dark sky. He snipped the syringe with his thumb and pointer finger - removing any trapped air. He then placed the syringe on the dashboard, and looked around for anyone who might be lurking at this late hour in the high school parking lot. Not seeing anyone, he scooted to the passenger side of the cab. He undid his belt and lowered his jeans and still-damp underwear to his knees. Carefully grabbing the syringe off the dashboard, Bobbie leaned to his left, and plunged the needle deep into his right buttocks, and slowly released Human Growth Hormone into his bloodstream.

He waited a few seconds before pulling up his pants and fastening his belt. He was getting hungry and horny. It was time to head home to his food and his little fuck bitch—as he called her privately to his friends.

He turned on the ignition—the supercharged V-8 engine roaring to life. ZZ Top was blaring on the radio with one of his favorites: "Legs." He turned down the music slightly, backed up, and aimed for the parking lot exit. His butt was sore, his stomach growled, and he could feel his dick hardening. And, God, he needed another drink. "Ho-ward bound!" he called out the open window to no one. As he stomped on the accelerator, his truck peeled out onto the boulevard.

● ● ●

It was dark when Bobbie pulled up the driveway. No lights were on in the house except for a table lamp in the living room and a dim light from his bedroom. He found the front door locked, and fumbled for his keys to open it. They fell on the ground and he swore. No lights, a good beer buzz, a sore butt and damp, sticky, pants made the task of picking up his keys a bit more challenging than it should have been—let alone getting the right key in the dead bolt.

The house was humble by every social and physical standard. How ironic given Bobbie's outsized ego, rock-star town status and muscular build. It was all they could afford at the moment, but Bobbie planned on demanding a big raise after the season. Two bedrooms, one bathroom, a small kitchen with a beer-stocked fridge and a ready microwave, and a family room with a large flat screen TV used mainly these days for sports and reviewing game films. The family room also had a small round table and chairs for eating, and an over-stuffed, and over-used, couch. He was honestly embarrassed, and hated coming home to it more with each passing day.

There was nothing but silence in their bedroom, but he would be waking her up soon enough. He still needed a little time to dry off, and reload. He opened the fridge and grabbed a beer by the neck and yanked it out. He rummaged around in the top drawer by the sink - neither trying to be quiet nor hiding his frustration by not immediately finding the bottle opener.

"God DAMN it! Either buy us a few fucking bottle openers and leave them where I can find them, or buy beer with screw-caps! Seems simple enough, right?" Bobbie roared back over his shoulder. "Fuck this," he said, "You are so fucking useless."

With that, Bobbie slammed the bottle back into the fridge and headed for the cupboard above the cutting board where he kept his hard booze. He stopped to get a tumbler and dropped two large ice cubes into the glass. After retrieving a bottle of Jack Daniel's, he poured himself a generous serving that floated the cubes, and sat on the couch in the darkened room. Only a small light in the kitchen lit the room, and he could hear the crackling of the electric wall heater. He took a swallow of his Jack, waited a few seconds and took another. The liquor warmed him, and he put his head back on the couch.

It had been an hour since he had taken his Viagra, and he was hard and ready. His mind was catching up, too. He couldn't wait to wake up his little fuck bitch and give her a pounding. After all, tomorrow was a big game, and as always, he needed some relief. He would eat his microwaved pasta and chicken afterwards.

As he finished his Jack Daniels, he sucked on the remaining ice cube while he closed his eyes. "This is going to be even better tonight," he imagined. His erection felt like it would burst from his now-dry pants—the pleasure of anticipation almost unbearable.

As he moved to the bedroom door, he placed his ear next to it and listened. Silence.

Bobbie opened the door, and peered into the dimly lit room. The bedside table lamp was emitting a low romantic haze. His eyes widened. The bed was perfectly made. Meredith was gone.

PART I

THE HUNGER

1

GEOFF

"**L**IKE MOTHER'S MILK," GEOFF CLOSED HIS EYES AND SIGHED AS both he and Steve, the bartender, laughed. The Grey Goose dry martini slipped, ice cold, down his throat. Then, he heard a roar above him.

The Denver Broncos had just scored a touchdown on a long pass from Peyton Manning late in the first quarter. This got everyone's attention as this was a rare Thursday night football telecast, and the home-team Broncos were playing the hated 49ers. The first score of the night, but it certainly wouldn't be the last.

Geoff had just concluded a grueling three-day meeting diving deep into the operational and leadership details of Hudson Environmental, LLC—a company Geoff's firm, Cameron, Boone, Covington & Associates was under contract to finance under terms so favorable to CBC that it almost seemed unfair. Certainly, there were surprises uncovered in their sleuthing at Hudson's headquarters in Grand Junction, but Geoff, and his trusted and experienced internal team of diligence experts, found little to alarm them. And, what they found they could fix, but first, Geoff would use as leverage to sweeten the deal for CBC. All in all, it had been a very successful three days.

There was another roar. The 49ers had fumbled the ensuing kick-off, and the Bronco's had recovered the ball deep in San Francisco territory. Bummer. Geoff Cameron lived in the San Francisco Bay Area in the small quaint town of Tiburon—across the Bay from the City and from the 35th floor office of Cameron, Boone, Covington & Associates. He was a huge 49er fan. In fact, he had season tickets. He used them to entertain clients of his firm, but particularly enjoyed treating his son, Scott, to a spirited day at Candlestick Park—the 49ers storied, but aging, home field. His mind continued to wander back to his home.

．．．

He had met his wife, Susie, at Stanford when she was getting her Bachelor's in History, and he was completing his Master's in Finance. The two of them made a smart, good-looking couple. She: blond, 5'9", creamy pale skin, with a lithe, sporty figure. He: 6'3", thick, wavy, longish, salt-and-pepper hair, tan lean body, blue eyes and in very good physical shape. They would make beautiful children together—so everyone said.

They were married in Palo Alto in a small, private affair attended by their immediate families and close friends. He was 24 and she was 21—young by today's standards, but they were in love with their whole promising future in front of them.

After honeymooning in nearby Carmel, they came back to the Bay Area, found a small apartment in the Marina District of San Francisco, and Geoff embarked on an entry level job with a local private equity firm founded by Stanford alums who took a liking to his GPA and street-smarts. Susie, found work at the local library—which was perfect for her as she had dreams of one day going back to school to get her law degree.

Those early years were brimming with hope, anticipation, happiness and passion. Most nights, Susie would get home by 5:00 PM, and have an inexpensive dinner fixed and a bottle of cheap wine ready for when Geoff arrived—sometimes very late. Susie was happy and unbothered by their late nights as they were both moving together towards their dreams. Geoff was thrilled being involved in so many business deals greedily absorbing everything he could learn and using his finance degree to benefit his career.

Dinner was always filled with excited conversations covering everything from their jobs, their friends, their families and serendipitous flirtations that usually led them to the bedroom for passionate sex. In those early years, both were physically hungry for amorous adventure. Their bodies molded well together and easily; their lives rhythmically moving together toward a shared future of dreams fulfilled. What memories…

．．．

Steve was back, and Geoff realized he was neither listening to the game nor to the bartender. The reminiscing of his early years of marriage, warmed him. But, these days, he couldn't wait to get back to Tiburon and enjoy the enthusiastic welcoming by his three kids and his deliriously loving Labrador Retriever.

"Shall I shake you another?" Steve asked.

Geoff realized that his first martini glass was drained. "Sure," he said. "But, after this one, cut me off. You know what they say about martini's?"

"What's that?" replied Steve.

"They're like women's breasts. One is not enough and three is too many." Both Steve and Geoff laughed heartily at the joke Geoff frequently told—particularly when he was with an appropriate audience: like Steve, a complete stranger. He was beginning to feel the effects of the vodka in those wonderful deep-dish, v-shaped, glasses.

The television emanated with what seemed like a prolonged din of crowd noise. The Broncos were driving again. What set them apart was an un-assailed confidence born out of four successive winning seasons and a Super Bowl appearance. Not only were the players experienced and talented, but they also possessed exceptional leadership. The entire enterprise, and the loyal Denver fans, believed they could win every game, and the team executed their on-field performance each week with that same spirit.

Geoff let the cocktail onion crunch in his mouth. Wasn't he, and his firm, just like the Bronco's? CBC was at the height of success, and the partners and employees all knew it. They saw deals often before they hit the market—either because they were brought to them exclusively, or their dream team of talented analysts had uncovered the opportunistic details that led to a take-over or outright purchase led by Geoff and his partners. And, here he was, in Grand Junction of all places, doing what he loved best: tidying up the remaining details of another smart deal.

The TV roared to life again, this time with a resounding groan, as a field goal attempt by the Broncos sailed wide right, and the 49ers took over on their own thirty-eight yard line. Maybe this game wasn't going to end so predictably. How fun to be in a strange city, enjoying martinis, after a successful business week, and enjoying your favorite team take on the local powerhouse! Oh, how he wished he could be at the game with his son, CJ.

● ● ●

Scott "CJ" Cameron was 10 years old, and loved—actually adored—his father. In so many ways, Scott reminded him of himself when he was that age. The two of them were inseparable whenever Geoff was home. Geoff loved to coach his son's soccer and baseball teams, and Scott was a talented young athlete who earned his teammates' and team parents' respect. He was a starter and contributor, and was especially proud that his dad was the coach of both teams that won easily and often.

CJ was born in 2004 as Susie and Geoff's third child. Geoff, particularly, was thrilled to have a son after joyously raising his two older daughters, Lucy and Brooke. Those girls were his world, and yes, they had him wrapped (as in: around their little finger). But, he longed for a son with whom he could share all of his outdoor passions, his love of competitive sports as well as teach him to be a man. It didn't take a lot of coercing to convince Susie to share Geoff's middle name as his son's first. So inseparable were these two from the very start that Scott started to be called Cam (a logical shortening of the Cameron Family name), or Cam, Jr.—hence, CJ. And, CJ stuck.

Geoff and CJ loved to watch football together, and while college football was exciting, it had too many teams to capture young CJ's attention. He loved the Pro's and particularly the 49ers. His dad had bought him a 49er uniform when he was quite young, and CJ slept in it for almost two years. Also, in his room was a signed 49er helmet by Joe Montana—perhaps the franchise's most famous and adored player. Geoff had paid $22,500 at a charity auction for the enshrined headgear, and had it in his private office—that is until Scott "CJ" Cameron was born. And, from the day he and Susie brought Scott home to Tiburon to take residence with his parents and sisters, that helmet sat on a credenza, overlooking Scott's bed, as a sentinel of protection, and a not-too-subtle symbol of a future full of promise, adventure and sports.

• • •

Steve stood to the side while he placed the second martini glass in front of Geoff being careful not to block his view of the game. The glass was frosted fresh from the freezer; an olive and onion already placed on a fresh skewer settled deep in the vessel. Steve rattled the shaker with prolonged vigor, and finally when his hand was going numb with cold, he poured the Grey Goose slowly over the "vegetables" until the glass was precariously full with a delightful film of ice chips floating on top. Geoff lowered his lips to the glass while it still sat on the table to sip off the top layer of liquid heaven so he could pick it up without spilling.

The vodka had already produced that sensational first internal washing of the brain that allows equal amounts of euphoria and contentment. But, Geoff was quietly embarrassed as he had momentarily lost track of the game. As Steve fetched a menu, Geoff settled back into watching his 49ers. Unfortunately, time had slipped somewhat from his attention, and the half-time program was on with an array of network critics and ex-coaches and ex-players dissecting every critical move that both teams exhibited in the first half. What was the score, for heaven's sake?

The halftime exhibition reminded him of his two girls, Lucy and Brooke. They, too, had both enjoyed the enviable gift of beauty, and in their respective ways, excelled: Lucy in modern dance, and Brooke as a budding cheerleader herself; although, junior high school can hardly be considered breaking into the big leagues.

The girls were born three years apart. After Lucy was born, her proud mother and father took to parenting with a flourish. Susie had all-night feeding detail while Geoff played the role of important back-up providing unquestioned support when he was home and giving Susie well-deserved breaks and quiet time. They loved their daughter so much that each quietly and privately wondered how they could love another child with such depth. Most parents struggle with this, but for Geoff and Susie, it was acute. It was why they waited for over two years to even think about having another child.

As the girls continued to grow, the emotional time and energy of child-rearing began to take its toll on Susie. She was often exhausted when Geoff came home, and was ready for the hand-off the minute he walked in the door. And, while Geoff cherished this time, he too was often emotionally and physically depleted after a long day of working on deals. But, Geoff knew how Susie had spent the day: around child-talk with little, or no, adult interaction, and importantly, with children that brought complete unpredictability to her world of order and tidiness. So, he frequently took the girls off her hands and took them on a neighborhood walk with his "traveler" of chardonnay in a paper cup. Meanwhile, Susie could prepare dinner and watch TV without interruptions, and psych up for the daily homecoming of daughters and husband from their walk.

Fifteen years later, he loved everything about his life: providing for his family, being a great dad to his three kids and the everyday routine of home. Hell, he even looked forward to yard work—making that home by the water even more attractive to the envious passersby that often stopped and wondered what the house was like inside—and who was lucky enough to live there?

● ● ●

Steve was back with his dinner salad. Geoff hadn't remembered ordering; must have been the martini's. Steve said, "The world's best prime rib is on its way: medium rare as you demanded and a twice-baked potato with extra sour cream. You must be happy about your 49ers! Glass of wine with your salad or with your dinner?" Steve was asking. Without taking his eyes off the screen, Geoff replied, "No thanks. Not now, anyway."

A minute later, Denver scored, and the crowd in the restaurant and those huddled around the bar, erupted. It was a fun, relaxed, festive evening—even if Geoff's team was losing. He was now happily engrossed back into the game amongst a rowdy, enthusiastic, but friendly, crowd. It was sure to be a tense final 10 minutes of a very exciting contest between rivals.

But then, something grabbed Geoff's attention through the ever-increasing volume of Thursday night's patrons. He wasn't sure what he heard, but then he heard it again: a woman's voice.

"You are not from around here, are you?" He looked to his left and hesitated for a moment.

"No, I am not. How could you tell?"

2

MEREDITH

SITTING NEXT TO GEOFF WAS A STRIKING, RAVEN-HAIRED, WOMAN; he guessed she was in her late 20's or early 30's. She had a smile every bit as stunning and similar to the actress, Julia Roberts, and she was clearly enjoying this little introduction. She had big brown eyes and her skin was buttery smooth and the color of mocha. Her personality was inviting, happy, carefree - and seemed a little flirtatious. Not that Geoff was really noticing. He snapped back to the question at hand. "OK, so…how do you know I am not a native Grand Junction'er?"

She smiled and said, "You have all your teeth."

With that, Geoff choked on his martini, and helplessly laughed and coughed for what seemed like a very long time. She laughed, too, and put her hand lightly around his waist, and offered, "Can I get you some water? Obviously, the soft drink you are enjoying here is not agreeing with you."

Geoff recovered quickly, and for the first time, deliberately turned away from the football game. He was curious about who this person was, and was instantly drawn to her friendliness and warmth. He paused long enough to catch his breath and really observe whom he was speaking with. She was very cute, but her smile was something else.

"You into the Bronco's?" he asked

"Who are they?" she smiled in reply.

"Oh, they are just your every day, Super Bowl-winning, league-dominating, local team from your home state. That is, of course, if Colorado is your home state." Geoff offered, "And, you have the most beautiful smile—with all your teeth, I might add. You must not be from here either."

"Oh, *THOSE* Bronco's!" she laughed. "Actually, I know all about them. And, no, I am not from here either—at least initially. I moved here from New York City five years ago in search of work, to be honest. Landed a job at a local high school teaching dance and cheer for pennies an hour. What a great career for one who graduated from the Julliard Institute. Married a local boy who works as a football coach for a competing high school. You now have my life's story. What's yours?"

Geoff was now getting interested in this woman, and the easy conversation that was unfolding. "Well, if you want to know the truth, I am a builder; a builder of businesses. I search for struggling companies that need my firm's expertise, and money, to fix them. We buy them, fix them and sell them. Simple as that. Wife; three kids; dog; house in the 'burbs. Sorry if this is all terribly boring."

Geoff was now assessing the woman that was sitting next to him at the bar. Stunning in an exotic way. He suspected that most women wouldn't call her beautiful, but most men would find her sexy, approachable and captivating. Her hair was long and rich with slight red tints through those thick black locks. She was dressed conservatively enough. She didn't seem to be out on the prowl for some action. She was wearing a soft leather jacket over what looked like a fitted blouse. She wore tailored black jeans and ankle boots. She was probably around 5'3". And although she was sufficiently covered in a conservative outfit, he could tell she had a nice figure—this struck him particularly unusual for a dancer. But it was her smile and friendliness that drew him in to this conversation.

And it was that smile that was now asking another question, "Tell me more about your business. It sounds so challenging yet with so much opportunity to travel and meet interesting people."

"Like you?" Geoff smiled.

"I'm not that interesting."

"You are to me."

She blushed slightly, but it went undetected.

"Care to join me for a quick bite of dinner? I would like to hear more about you, and life 'on the farm' here in Grand Junction—and how your life has changed since moving from the Big Apple."

She replied, "Well, I guess so. My husband is out of town at an away game. He travels a lot this time of year. Goes with the territory. Football coach widow. Dinner would be very nice and completely unexpected."

"You'll have to order rather quickly as my world-famous rib-eye is due here any minute."

As fate would have it, Steve returned this time with Geoff's dinner.

"Can you hold that for a few minutes?" Geoff said. "This young lady is going to have dinner with me, and I am hoping she'll join me for a cocktail beforehand. Can you bring us an additional menu?" Steve already had the menu in his other hand, and placed it on the bar in front of them.

"Of course," she replied. "I'd love to have drink. I'll have a vodka gimlet."

Turning to Geoff, Steve inquired, "And, for you, sir?"

"Think I will have another Grey Goose, with just a twist this time. You know what they say about martini's, Steve." This time it wasn't posed as a question, but rather a confirmation that the evening was unfolding in a very unexpected way.

"Right." Purposely hiding their secret, he said, "Shaken not stirred." He then added, "How about those 49ers of yours? Quite a come-from-behind victory. Sure quieted the bar scene here."

"How did my 'Niners do it?"

"With literally seconds left in the game your quarterback threw a risky pass— deep and down the throat."

The mystery woman replied, "Not being that much of a football fan, sounds like a game with a happy ending I might have enjoyed watching. That must have been quite a score."

Geoff laughed once again. Surprised by his complete lack of interest in the final minutes of such an exciting game, he turned back to the warm smile next to him that had attracted him. He held out his hand. "I don't even know your name, and I already know your life's story. AND, I have invited you to share my bar and have dinner with me. How rude! I'm Geoff—with a G."

As she reached out her soft hand and slid it into Geoff's, she smiled and nodded. Coupling it with hers, she said, "I'm Meredith—with an M."

3

BOBBIE

THE WHISTLE SHRILLED SO LOUDLY THAT IT CAUGHT EVERYONE'S attention across the entire football field. Even the assistant coaches flinched whenever that piercing shattered the afternoon air.

"Conner, get the fuck over here you shithead faggot!" yelled Head Coach Robert "Bobbie" Edmonson. "Is that any way to hit the receiver?"

Conner was scared to death of Coach Edmonson—or just "Coach" to the players, staff, administration, press and frankly to the entire Grand Junction community. Every player and coach was scared of him. Everyone. But, parents loved him. The community adored him.

"I tackled him right after he caught the ball, Coach," Conner replied with his eyes looking back at the field.

"I want you to crush that motherfucker and smash his face into the ground. Then I want you to grind your elbow into his side while you push him hard against the turf using his lifeless body to help you get up. If he stays on the ground, for even a moment, I want you to stand over him as though you have just slaughtered your worst enemy."

"Coach, this is just a practice, and Johnny is my teammate," argued Conner.

"You ARE a fucking faggot! Time for you to go shower up and head home to mommy. She'll likely pamper your sorry ass, and give you your dolls to play with. Sure as hell they ain't no G.I. Joes."

"But, Coach, if I hurt Conner, he can't help us in the game Friday night," Conner again protested.

Bobbie lunged for the kid and grabbed ahold of his facemask and tugged hard on it until they were literally face-to-face. Coach Edmonson's could feel the heat in his face - now misshaped by Conner's own facemask as he tried to climb into the boy's helmet. "You want to play on a state championship football team? Or do you want to join the Chess Club?" Bobbie was now hissing and spraying spittle through the facemask.

Conner was silent. He could feel the tears starting to boil into his eyes—not sure whether they were from rejection, anger, embarrassment or just plain humiliation in front of all of his friends and teammates.

"You're done. Go home to mommy and suck your fucking thumb."

With that, Bobbie pushed Conner violently to the ground. He blew hard on the whistle, and the scream of the shrill caught everyone's attention. But, he had to blow it a second time to get the action on the practice field to fully stop. The boys, and coaches, turned and stood at attention.

"This practice is over," Bobbie ranted. "All players and coaches: meet me in the locker room in 15 minutes for a mandatory meeting. Freshmen: pick up all the on-field equipment, and stow that shit where it belongs. Now, get your asses in gear."

* * *

Bobbie was seething. He literally couldn't wait to lay into this latest group of pathetic players. As he saw it, there was no way this team was remotely close to winning a league championship—let alone the coveted Colorado State title. And, the only way to toughen them up was to rough them up—both physically and emotionally. Hell, it was how he always got what he wanted out of people: fear and intimidation.

Bobbie marched into his office adjacent to the locker room and slammed the door. He sat at his desk and placed his face in his hands massaging his temples in particular. After a few moments, he crashed his fists onto his desk overturning an old beer stein that held pencils and pens and launching a shot glass that had held paper clips. The litter was now all over his desk and floor.

"Mother FUCKER!" he growled through clenched teeth.

The job was clearly getting to him.

* * *

Six years ago, when he was named head coach of the Granite High Grizzlies, no one expected much. A former star running back, and high school heart throb, Bobbie had returned to his alma mater after injury shortened what he hoped would be a stellar college career leading to the pro's. He never made it past junior college. His grades, his size and then his shredded knee, ended any hope of a scholarship to a major football power. There were no offers. None.

So, here he was coaching the Grizzlies. It had all started well enough when, in his first year, they won as many games as they lost—quite an accomplishment for a rookie coach and a one-horse team that had a losing record the past eight seasons. Bobbie brought hope that year, and a little pride back to the community. People started coming out for the games on Friday nights and filling the stands for the first time in decades.

Those early years were fun, he had to admit. He was an "all in" coach that demanded excellence and discipline from his entire team and staff. He had the backing of the faculty and, importantly, the parents. The community rallied behind the team, too, and many of the local businesses donated significantly to buy new uniforms, new equipment and to fund the remodel of the locker room facilities. Everyone in town knew Bobbie simply as "Coach," and he reveled in his new-found celebrity.

The second year the team went 9-7 and just missed the regional play-offs. Year three, the Grizzlies were 12-4 and were on a roll having won their last eight straight games. Their quarterback was injured early in the first quarter of their first playoff game in more than two decades, and although the team fought hard, they lost badly to their rival, the Silverton Bullets. Bobbie swore that would never happen again—not on his watch. Two straight State Championships followed where the Grizzlies only lost one game over those two years. Coach could do no wrong, and was adored and embraced everywhere he went in town.

It was after his fifth season (or maybe during it), that he became obsessed with his self-image. Winning had built his ego systematically. He worked out daily, and was certainly in excellent physical shape, but he looked in the mirror constantly and tried to imagine how his fans saw him—particularly the women and girls that were ever present in his life. Sure, he was handsome in a rugged, manly sort of way, but he longed to be idolized for his prowess on the field as well as his swagger around town. His wife didn't count. She had to idolize him. Hell, he paid $20 for that marriage license, and anyway she was married to the hottest ticket in Grand Junction.

But how this morphed into a personal struggle started innocently enough. Still smarting from the loss of his quarterback a few years ago, and recurrent injuries to many of his star players, Bobbie, always trying to find that "edge" to get his players well and back on the field in the shortest time possible, sought answers. For a high school team from a small town, the roster was limited, and the loss of a key player or two—even for a few games—could wipe out his season and his growing celebrity.

• • •

Bobbie stepped from his office, still red-faced, and walked into the heart of the locker room, and his team. The room quickly quieted. Bobbie stood on a bench and prepared himself for the message he was going to deliver to his team.

"For the last two years, many of you have shared the exhilaration and pride that goes hand-in-hand with winning two successive Colorado State Championships. You worked your asses off. You developed discipline. You looked after each other. You were tougher physically than your opponents. And, you were more determined."

A player in the middle of the locker room yelled, "Yeah!" And, the team cheered.

"Shut the fuck up!" screamed Bobbie. "Out there today on the practice field, I witnessed a cancer that had to be removed. A weakling, who if allowed to be in your midst, would have weakened you, too. There is no place on this team for a player who is not willing to give a 150%. To repeat two years in a row as State Champions is a feat that has only been accomplished once before us. To win a third consecutive title has never been done. Every season, every game, every play gets more and more difficult for us. Why? Not because we have sustained a few injuries; not because we have a smaller front line on both offense and defense, not because our competition is better. It is simply that every season, every game, every play, each of our opponents is out to bury us; beat the champions; belittle us in front of their fans—and in front of ours. Their will to win is bigger than ours. So, we have to fucking be meaner, angrier, tougher, more ferocious and more committed to winning than they are. Whoever and wherever 'they' are. If there is any one of you who is not 150% committed to our Grizzly Nation, to the legacy of excellence we are creating, to the pride of Colorado that we are…leave now; you know exactly where the door is."

Bobbie waited for 30 seconds in what seemed like 5 long minutes. No one dared budge. He scanned his audience and made eye contact with virtually every player.

"Make no mistake about what happened today. That pussy Conner was a tumor in our ranks. He wouldn't hit hard; he wouldn't strike to hurt; and, he sure as shit wouldn't have been a valued teammate to you: the Grizzlies—the pride of our great state. Winning teams hit hard and take it hard. Get angry! Get your fucking Grizzly jaws bloodied! And back down to no one!"

The chant started slowly but grew quickly to a deafening crescendo: "JAWS, JAWS, JAWS, JAWS, JAWS, JAWS, JAWS!" The team was now in an excited frenzy.

Bobbie blew his whistle twice quickly to get everyone's attention once again. He continued, "Now each one of you put on your letterman's jackets, grab your things, head out and rest up for tomorrow's big game against the Silver Bullets. Remember what they did to us several years ago? Go to bed and dream of squeezing the holy shit out of them—not silver from their bullets, but blood from their scrawny throats."

The team gathered around him in the center of the pack. He raised his clenched fist into the air, and every player crowded in to join the construction of the traditional pyramid of arms. Bobbie yelled, "'Grizzlies' on three; one, two, three…"

The team shouted, "GRIZZLIES!" and a large cheer shot out, and high-fives were exchanged generously.

With that, Coach Bobbie Edmonson dismissed his team weary that tomorrow's game was going to be a lot tougher than he, or his team, could expect. They were going to lose.

4

SUSIE

SUSIE DIDN'T THINK MUCH ABOUT GEOFF BEING GONE THESE DAYS. He was enormously busy buying and selling companies, and was on the road in what seemed like an endless calendar of business trips. She no longer asked him where he was going. She was too busy with the kids, and when he was gone, she had to manage the entire household all on her own. She was not resentful in the least, just constantly tired and drained. If she wasn't engaged in her personal chauffeur service shuttling the kids and their friends to and from school, activities, sports, play dates, sleep-overs and so much more, she was chairing the weekly PTA meetings, planning and shopping for endless meals, managing the affairs of the local chapter of the National Charity League, picking up the house, supervising homework efforts and trying with considerable effort to find time for herself.

Time for herself involved an almost-daily visit to the gym (Mondays, Wednesdays and Fridays) and Yoga (Tuesdays and Thursdays) while the kids were in school. Forget weekends—they were just too hectic.

Susie was in great shape. Heck, she was thin and pretty as a small child, and grew into a lean, tall beauty that seemed to only improve with age. She didn't put on weight like other expectant mothers, and was in the gym within days of childbirth. She always had the top-of-the-line running stroller, and in those early years, jogged daily around Tiburon while her nanny looked after the household.

When she was young, Susie was the envy of her friends—thanks mostly to her beauty and the attention she attracted from boys. Her friends weren't jealous, however, as Susie was probably the nicest person in her class, and her good looks never seemed to affect how she looked at herself and others. She was free, in a way, to look forward in her life accomplishing great things without the burden of being a plain person—always primping, always attending to make-up, always shopping for attractive, figure-flattering, clothes. She looked great in a pair of jeans and a t-shirt, and was simply stunning in a dress. But, she handled all of this with an ease and grace rarely found in a teenager and later as a budding adult. She had loads of close friends, and she never had to vie for popularity.

Susie graduated Summa Cum Laude from her high school in San Marino, California—a WASP'y community of affluence and privilege in the northern suburbs of Los Angeles. Not an athlete, despite her height and build, Susie preferred to spend her free time on Student Counsel as representative of her classmates and volunteering at the nearby Halfway House for abused mothers and children. To no one's surprise, she was Homecoming Queen in her senior year, and in addition to a 4.4 GPA, Susie was the lead in the school musical and was Secretary of the Student Body. She applied to all the typical Ivy League schools, and on a whim, threw in an application to Stanford University in Palo Alto, California—where she was accepted along with all the rest of her college applications. She enrolled in the fall as a pre-law history major.

Once in college, her popularity continued. She pledged Pi Beta Phi, and was named pledge class president. She certainly worked harder academically at Stanford than she had ever studied in high school, but after two B's in her first semester of her Freshman year, she never again received anything but A's.

Boys came just as easily in college as they did in high school. They were always showing up around the sorority house looking for Susie and her friends. But unlike those early teen years, there was alcohol, drugs and sex. Susie certainly wasn't a prude, but she didn't drink much or do drugs of any kind. She found the boys' advances largely unwanted, because she was hit on so many times that she found it all a nuisance and a bit comical. Her friends, on the other hand, craved the attention of the cute guys, and talked endlessly amongst each other about their sexual fantasies. They spoke openly about their exploits and failures of the prior nights' parties.

Susie lost her virginity as a senior in high school, and to her, it was nothing special. It was something to get over with, and stop worrying about. She had briefly dated a good-looking, and nice-enough, guy named Brad who was on the swimming and water polo teams. They had gone to the prom together, and like everyone else, ended up at a house where the parents were out-of-town. They drank a fair amount of alcohol, and ended up in a room downstairs—both knowing that "it" would be very quick and rushed. But, Brad was no virgin, and knew what to do. Although he was a bit awkward in his haste, he was at least gentle. He was quick to come, but it was far from romantic, and left her personally unsatisfied. But, it was over quickly and she at least now could say that she was no longer a virgin.

Once in college, Susie got laid—often. The pattern seemed the same for most encounters. She was pursued aggressively, pampered extensively, taken to the nicest restaurants, wined and dined, and taken to the nicest hotels for love-making. Oddly, orgasms weren't her thing. She was chased so often and aggressively that sex held little appeal for her, and if she was honest, she faked most of her climaxes. She was sure that when she met the right guy that things would change for her. And, due to her endless stream of male suitors and unlimited sexual opportunities, she had an almost non-existent fantasy life. Unlike her friends and sorority sisters, who were always hoping, wishing, planning, imagining, and scheming, Susie almost never masturbated. Her puritan mother taught her it was "dirty," and her father never dared approach the subject of sex—yet alone venture into the taboo subject of auto-eroticism.

Susie never let her social life interfere with her studies. She knew when to lock herself in her room or to steal away to the library for what seemed like endless hours of studying. But she was a good sister to her Pi Phi sorority, and enjoyed the academic break that parties and social gatherings afforded. And, it was at one of these fraternal functions that she met one Geoff Cameron.

5

GEOFF

GEOFF SPIED HER FROM ACROSS THE ROOM. TAN, BLOND, TALL, athletic-looking and engaged in a very energetic conversation with a mixed group of students. He couldn't tell if the talk was serious, political, religious or "newsy," but he sure intended on ordering a drink at the adjacent bar (an old warped card table covered with booze, beer and cheap wine) and entering into this discussion—if, for no other reason, than to introduce himself to the blond gazelle.

Geoff excused himself from the two girls he was talking with and stepped over to fix himself a drink. Their stare followed him as he slowly made his way between students who were getting happier and louder by the minute.

When Geoff reached the bar, he picked up a typical red plastic cup seen mostly on as a goal of sorts for the most popular of college sports: Beer Pong. After fisting the cup full of ice, he poured a generous portion of cheap vodka into the cup and topped it with a Red Bull float. After taking a swallow, he came up behind his life-long friend, Nicolas George, who was visiting from LA. Nick was attending USC where he was getting his Master's degree in Business Administration. Taking his vodka in his left hand, Geoff swung his arm up and around Nick's head, and in an affectionate reverse hug, used his arm-lock to pull Nick backwards so that he could whisper into his left ear.

"So, my friend, when, exactly, were you going to introduce me to your new friends—especially Miss Talkative across the way?" Geoff let go of his mock attack.

Nick brightened up immediately, and smiled easily. "Say, Geoff, we were all going to call you over to join us, but you seemed like you were preoccupied seeking carnal knowledge with those two doctorate candidates," Nick said loudly so that all in his group could hear. Everyone in Nick's small circle laughed.

He continued, "I love your friends! Much more interesting than I thought they would be. Stanford students actually have a personality!"

Geoff replied, "You need to get out more often: see the world—or at least get out of La La Land and visit a few more out-of-the-way places. That way, you will find that EVERYONE is smarter and more interesting than you and your Trojans! What's a Trojan anyway? DON'T answer that! You obviously need to get far off-campus, and off the grid, to get a real education!"

The group laughed and started playfully attacking USC, and taking a few shots at Nick. Geoff jumped in and introduced Nick in a much more formal way than he was sure that Nick had done on his own.

"This, my friends, is Nicolas Wentworth George. Nick to you and me. Nick and I met in grammar school at the age of 8, and we have been best of friends ever since. We have spent our still-young lives getting more into trouble than getting started—let alone getting ahead. Our stories are legendary—if only in our own minds. We laugh at our own jokes, and we are building a library of nefarious adventures and hijinks so that we never run out of material for story-telling—even if it is just between the two of us. Maybe I'll write a novel about it someday.

"On a much more serious side, no one is brighter, more trusted, more orga-nized or more detail-oriented than Nick here. Self-described as OCD-gifted, Nick calls himself the Doctor of Detail. I would literally put my future into his hands. I am sure that we will be working with each other once we free ourselves from these shackles of higher learning. And, knowing how observant and curious Stanford students are, you ladies have probably noticed that Dr. Detail here is quite easy on the eyes, and has an engaging personality. Must be in short supply at USC which is why he visits here so much! Please…get to know him, but handle him with care."

Geoff looked across the circle and made eye contact with the tall blond. He smiled and she smiled back. Taking that as an invitation, he excused himself, walked around to her, and introduced himself.

"Sorry about the lengthy intro to my buddy. Thought you all ought to know whom you were hanging out with. Absolutely great guy, that Nick." Geoff then extended his free hand, "Hi. I'm Geoff Cameron."

"I'm Susie McMillan; nice to meet you. And, yes, he is a great guy, but surely is 'GU' for all the smart pretty girls at this party. Maybe he should go introduce himself to the obvious party-crashers you were talking to earlier. A long-distance relationship with either of those two bimbo's will likely be a one-night stand eight miles from here."

"GU?" Geoff inquired.

"Geographically undesirable," Susie deadpanned.

She hesitated, but then continued, "I've never run into you before. You seem older—not in a bad way of course—just, well…older; more mature."

He responded, "That is your first mistake. I'm not a boring old man! You obviously are blind and your personality radar needs adjustment."

"I'm actually in to older men, and I hope I never insinuated that you were boring!" Susie replied.

Geoff asked, "How much older do you usually find men that you are attracted to?"

"Five to ten years. They just seem so much more secure and experienced—in a worldly sort of way. Maybe I have a daddy complex or something," she explained.

"OK, my penalty shot coming right here: How old are you?" Geoff inquired. And then added, "And, how old do you think I am?"

"THAT is certainly an inappropriate question—especially coming from someone as seemingly mature and worldly as you. Let's just say that I can drink legally, barely. You must be five to ten years older than me, or I wouldn't be standing here giving you the time of day," Susie smiled.

"Let's just say that an undergraduate degree at Berkley, an East Coast upbringing with all the parental expectations and my round horn-rimmed glasses have all conspired to give you the wrong answer. When you graduate, don't bother applying for "Guess Your Age" role at the circus!"

The two talked for almost 45 minutes about all the superficial stuff young un-introduced couples give and take from each other: where from; family; major; why Stanford; favorite classes and instructors; currently dating, etc.—and the fact that Geoff was only three years older than Susie. The din in the room was not subsiding. The corner they had found did nothing but act as an echo chamber. Finally, Geoff said, "Can I refill your glass? Maybe it will help our hearing—and my manners."

Susie simply said, "I would enjoy that. But, I would prefer a far quieter place, with a table to sit at, fine spirits that will limit my hangover in the morning, and a glass, not plastic, to sip from. Your choice. Your treat. You asked my age."

And with that, Geoff found Nick, gave him the keys to his apartment and told him that he was on his own for the rest of the evening. Nick warmly gave him a bro-hug, and said he would see him in the morning. "I already ordered you two a cab. You have a reservation waiting at the Quincy in 30 minutes. Quiet back table; away from the crowd; away from the kitchen; and away from the bathrooms. Just as you like it." He added, "Be careful my friend: she is smart, very perceptive…and very into you!"

Geoff winked at Nick. "Thanks Good Buddy. What would I do without you? You are always there to look after me: saving me from myself. See you either very late tonight or in the morning for a large cup of coffee and a detailed debrief."

And with that, Geoff grabbed his leather jacket and scarf. He found Susie coming from the living room with her Gucci purse and cashmere coat. He noticed nothing but her regal demeanor—and the quick glance she gave to her watch.

He offered his arm and she grasped it behind the elbow as she had been taught as a debutante at her parents' National Charity League. As they walked out front to catch their cab Susie noticed he was wearing nice shoes and a sporty watch. She smiled to herself. Good breeding.

The cab arrived just as they emerged from the sorority house. Opening the door, Geoff let her in and made sure her dress was lifted out of the way of the door before he closed it. Running around to the other side of the cab, Geoff jumped in, closed the door firmly and said to the driver, "Quincy's on Fifth, please." As the cab pulled away, Geoff took Susie's hand in his, and they started their journey together.

6

BOBBIE

IN THE OFF-SEASON BETWEEN HIS FIFTH AND SIXTH YEARS, BOBBIE was introduced to Spencer Miller—a weaselly character that operated in the shadows of society. He worked for a lab in San Diego that specialized in pharmaceutical solutions to injury rehabilitation. But, it didn't stop there. Spencer had at his disposal pharma solutions to a lot of different things—including HGH to bulk up his "kids" to prepare them for the games each week and presumably prepare them physically to play in the Big 10, Pac 12, or whatever elite team would recruit them. Winning seasons, and winning kids, led to more winning celebrity, donations and recruitments.

Their first meeting occurred after a particularly close game with a school in their league with a losing record and a long history of poor performances. The Grizzlies had won, but only after a last-second field goal had given them the one-point margin of victory. Bobbie was not sure if he was furious that his team could hardly beat a bunch of patsies, or that two of his standout players were still on the bench recovering from minor injuries that, in his day, any player worth their mettle would have played with. After his players had raced into the visitors' locker room, Bobbie stayed on the field to prepare his post-game comments. Someone nudged Bobbie on the shoulder and thrust a card onto his clipboard.

"You should have slaughtered those guys," a long-haired, ruddy-faced, stranger was saying to the coach who had not yet registered the intrusion. "Too bad you had good talent sitting out the game. They hurt?"

Bobbie, seeing the card flipped onto his clipboard and hearing the inquiry, turned slowly around to see a character that he immediately dismissed as a loser. Perhaps he was a relative of one of his players.

"Who are you?" Bobbie inquired.

"Spence Miller; Doc Spence Miller to you."

"You the home team physician?"

"One of them," he replied.

"Why are you so interested in our team, then?"

"Because, I have watched your progress with the Grizzlies over the past several years. You are to be congratulated. You have built that pathetic school football team into a winner—a State Champion at that. But your success is not sustainable; not in a small market like Grand Junction. Too small a pool of students to recruit with only four high schools. But, I can help," Spence was saying.

"Listen, Dr. Miller—or whatever the hell your name is," Bobbie chided. "I am a bit busy here. Why, again, would the team physician of one of our opponents be interested in helping out a competitor in its own league?"

Spence smiled. "I am not the team physician. Let's just say that I am a consultant that is working on improving the competitiveness of their offensive and defensive players on both the front lines. You have to admit your team had a heck of a time getting around them. In fact, you almost lost the game—a game you should have won by a big margin."

"I know, I know, I know. But, you haven't answered my question as to why you might want to help out the Grizzlies. And, I am now overdue in my locker room to address my players and coaches. Get to your point," Bobbie said as he stooped to pick up his sweatshirt.

"I need to make a living. And, as I mentioned to you, I am connected to your opponent tonight, but more as a consultant. Let's just say I assist, as a freelancer, with their physical strength and injury recovery. God knows every coach could use that kind of help. But, for a team like yours to sustain the level of expected excellence, you may need my help maybe more than anyone in this here part of the country. Not only is your offensive line undersized to properly protect your quarterback, but your two hurt players should have recovered by now and be helping your team demolish the opposition. I doubt you are going to win many more State Championships at the rate you are going. Even the lesser teams in your league are catching on, and bulking up," Spence espoused.

Bobbie had no choice but to cut him off. "Listen, thanks for the tips on how to win games for the Grizzlies. I don't need your help, Doctor...?"

"Doc Spence. Spence Miller. The Dispenser." He winked, but Bobbie didn't catch it.

"I'll keep your card, Doc, in case I'm interviewing for assistant coaches, mind-readers, or arm-chair quarterbacks," Bobbie laughed as he turned to head in for his team meeting.

"Speaking of quarterbacks, a shame yours was on the bench tonight. If I was helping you, he would have been playing. And, I suspect you would be having a different kind of post-game pep talk in five minutes."

● ● ●

Coach Edmonson ignored the comment and headed straight into the locker room. When he arrived, his players and coaches were waiting; their travel bags stuffed and sitting in a pile waiting to be loaded onto the team bus. Everyone stood and cheered when Bobbie entered. "Grizz-lies! Grizz-lies! Grizz-lies!"

"Shut the fuck up!" yelled Bobbie. "How in the hell could you almost lose to that team? They are lower than scum, and you let them dominate you on the line, in the backfield and on special teams. Their offensive line man-handled us, and we could not even get one sack of their quarterback! I would certainly not be cheering this victory if I were you. It was embarrassing. In fact, I will be seeing all of you, coaches included, in the weight room at 6 AM sharp tomorrow morning to work your asses into better shape. Anyone who doesn't show up doesn't play, or coach, next week. Understood?"

And turning to his two injured players sitting together on plastic chairs against the wall with their crutches next to them, he added, "This goes for you two pussies, too. You will lift with the rest of the team. I expect you back in the line-up by next week—hurt or not."

Swiveling back to his team, he said, "I was embarrassed out there tonight. This should have been an absolute crushing. Instead, I fucking had to pull every trick out my hat to give us a chance. The only player who deserves any praise tonight is Justin. Thank God you have a great leg and a sense for direction. Otherwise, you sorry sacks of shit would have lost another game you shouldn't have. Now, get the fuck out of here, and get on the bus. See you in the morning. At 6. And, don't be late, or you will be adding 100 push-ups to your morning. I have nothing more to say."

With that, Granite High's head coach spun around, and the business card he had been handed, dropped on the floor. He picked it up, looked at it longer than he should have, and shoved it into his pocket.

7

CONNER

HE BURST INTO HIS HOUSE THROUGH THE FRONT DOOR, AND slammed it behind him. Corey, his mother, spun around and caught a glimpse of her son as he bolted up the stairs. Conner had been crying. What? It was too early for football practice to be over.

She left her dinner preparations on the stove, and quietly walked up the stairs. She softly placed her ear to his door, and she could hear the sobs. What was all this about? Conner was never this upset. In fact, it seemed that he was enjoying school for the first time in years. And, being on the football team had boosted his self-confidence. He had made a lot of friends on the team: friends that would look after him.

She knocked softly on the door. No answer. She knocked again. "Conner, can I come in for a sec?"

"Go away! I don't want to talk to you."

This surprised Corey, as she had a particularly close relationship with her son. "Well, since you are home early, we can eat at 7. Your father will be home soon."

"I'm not hungry! I just don't want to be bothered. Go away. Please."

That last 'Please' got caught in his throat. What had happened? Corey thought she ought to call Coach Edmonson, but then thought how busy he must be preparing for the game. She would talk to Conner later that evening or at breakfast tomorrow. Worst case, she would call the mother of Conner's friend, Johnny. Johnny was a wide receiver on the squad, and had befriended Conner. Their friendship grew over the first summer of high school as they lived in adjacent neighborhoods. They shared some of the same classes, and were inseparable. Surely, Johnny would know what happened, and would tell his mother.

But, Corey would have to call later in the morning from her work, and she hoped the two mothers would be able to connect. She had no choice. The call would have to happen at a break in her preparation for trial as the lead prosecutor in a highly publicized sexual harassment case. Corey hated creeps and assholes—particularly those that preyed on innocent women and children. She had a sterling reputation as a tireless preserver of victim's rights. She had never lost a case, and, at worst, had negotiated large financial settlements to keep the victims—her clients - from the embarrassment of testifying. She would win this case, she knew, but nonetheless, she prepared like a tigress—as she always did; never taking anything for granted.

But, she and her husband went to bed that night not having the opportunity to speak with their son. Conner never came out of his room. His music blared late into the night. And, their hearts ached.

8

MEREDITH

THEY LAUGHED THROUGHOUT DINNER. NEITHER COULD EXACTLY explain the connection, but the chemistry flowed in both directions. They had shared enough of their backgrounds to realize just how different their worlds were, but this just added to the mystique of the evening and their attraction to one another.

Geoff loved people, and initially, his personal interest in Meredith was purely plutonic. But as the evening lingered on, and the martini's turned to fine wine, Geoff's personal interest slowly grew more personal.

The football game was now over, and Steve cleared the dishes from the bar top.

"God, that was the best prime rib I have had in a long time," Geoff exclaimed. "The juicy red center and the crispy outer crust were perfect. Add the stuffed baked potato, and feather-light Yorkshire Pudding, and you have all the makings of a last supper."

Meredith questioned, "What do you mean by a last supper?"

"Well," Geoff explained, "I love to learn about people by asking provocative questions. I use this technique when I am hosting a gathering of folks that are largely strangers to each other. Each person can ask any question of their choosing, and all around the room, each has to answer honestly—ending with the inquirer. Then the next person can ask their question, and around the room it goes, again."

"And...so what does that have to do with the Last Supper"

"Not THE Last Supper, but A last supper—as in, 'If you were on death row, and you could have anything you wanted for your last supper, what would it be?' You would be amused at all the different answers, and learn a bit about each person."

"So, you would have the prime rib dinner you had tonight?" Meredith asked.

"No, actually I would want a thick slab of meat loaf, a simple salad of butter lettuce, onion, bacon and chopped hard-boiled egg, and a baked potato loaded with extra sour cream, chives and bacon. Martini's to start, for sure, and a glass or two of Napa Valley Cabernet. Did you learn anything about me?"

She thought for a moment and said, "Yes, I think you are a very settled and happy person that came from a loving family that enjoyed simple pleasures. How am I doing so far?"

"Just about nailed it. Maybe not quite as settled and happy as you might think, but you are warm—moving to hot." Geoff returned the question to her, "So, what would you like for your last supper?"

"Semen." Meredith deadpanned.

For the second time tonight, Geoff choked on his beverage—laughing. "Semen? Really? Why in the world would you say that?"

If it was possible to laugh at yourself and cry at your life, Meredith was at that ironic moment. But, she gave little away. She smiled, and looked Geoff directly in his eyes, and as she spoke a tear slipped from her left eye. "I would only want my last meal to be meaningful."

Taken by the pathos of the moment, the honesty of her answer and the instinctive urge to take her in his arms and comfort her, Geoff slowly raised his right hand, and with his thumb, gently wiped the tear, and its path, from the soft skin of her cheek.

She didn't ask Geoff what he might have learned about her. The tenderness of that unexpected moment spoke volumes. She lowered her face, and then started to laugh freely. "You either think I am a hooker or one fucked-up human being."

Geoff didn't reply to her comment. Instead, he reached over and lifted the Chardonnay bottle from the ice bucked Steve had left for them on the bar, and put two fingers of that golden wine in each of their glasses. Then he said, "Hey, next question—that is if you are up for it."

"Up for it? Hell, I'm all in! Do I get to ask the next question?"

Geoff mockingly lifted his left hand to his chin giving the appearance of deep consideration, and replied, "Only if you stay true to the premise of the game, and ask good, provocative, questions. Based on your answer to my first question, I'm guessing you'll have no problem coming up with appropriate ones yourself. Try me."

Meredith thought for a minute, then asked, "What is the one thing you admire most about your spouse, and what is the one thing you would change in your spouse?"

He seemed a bit surprised at the question, but carried on by replying, "My wife is the perfect mother to our children, and an exceptional manager of our entire household. I'm not sure I would have the patience to deal with all the juvenile conversations and the myriad of teen-related angst and anger. She is an UBER-Mom in all aspects."

"And what would you change?" Meredith asked.

Geoff looked at Meredith and said, "I'm not sure I know you well enough to answer that one, but because I don't know you at all, it's maybe easier."

"You know me well enough to know I want semen as my last supper!" she laughed.

"OK! OK! Right you are. Well, how do I say this? Susie is kind of a-sexual. I'm not sure if it is because she was abused as a child, had an Elizabethan upbringing that declared that sex was bad, or if she is so beautiful that she never developed a healthy fantasy mind, but she simply does not want to be intimate. Sex to her is work and a major inconvenience and an interruption to her life. She never wants to talk about it, either. I guess I would want Susie to be amorous, adventurous and open to a bit of erotica—or SOMETHING!"

"TMI!" laughed Meredith.

"Your turn," said Geoff.

"Well, my husband, Bobbie, is the head football coach for one of the high schools here. The program is very successful, and we get quite a bit of attention around town—the proverbial big fish in the small pond so to speak. He's great at what he does—probably too great—and like your Susie, he is very good looking. See how much we have in common?"

"So, what is it exactly that you like best about him?" Geoff probed.

"His success, mainly, I guess."

"That wasn't the deep answer I thought you'd give me. I'll give you a 'pass' on that one. How about the one thing you would change?"

Without hesitating, Meredith replied, but her eyes looked through Geoff off to some distant spot behind him. "He's a brute, and an abuser of drugs and alcohol. When he gets drunk or high - or both - he can turn into a monster. He's especially unstable during the football season when the pressure of performance is amped up. He stays out late, God knows where, and comes home and often abuses me."

"I'm so very sorry, Meredith," Geoff said softly. "I didn't mean to unsettle you with this stupid game of mine." He wanted so badly to hold her in his arms and comfort her.

Looking now directly into Geoff's eyes with moist eyes of her own, yet a smile, Meredith said, "Hey. This was my question. Chill out. I didn't mean to bring this whole amazing evening to a crash-and-burn."

She punched him lightly on the shoulder and said, "Your question!"

"Are you sure?' he replied.

I'm sure, but take it a little bit easier on me—now that you know so much about me. NOT!"

The two spent the next hour probing each other with simpler and easier questions: most-watched movies, favorite books, etc. But then this question from Geoff, "What is your favorite song and by what artist?"

Meredith took a sip from her wine. They were on their second bottle by now, and it was nearly empty. There was chemistry. Two-way. No doubt. They both felt it, but remained guarded.

Meredith said, "'I Need You Tonight,' by INXS. I just love the urgency of the lyrics and the primal nature of the beat. But, it's an older song. I'm going to cheat. I have to confess that I also love Country and Western. There's a song by Lady Antebellum. I don't remember the title, but it's about two ex-lovers who, in the middle of the night can't keep their minds off each other and wish the other would show up. I think it's called 'I Need You Now.' Shit. Sounds like a theme, here. It's not meant to be anything. Maybe I'm getting a bit drunk."

With that, she laughed. "'I Need You Tonight' and 'I Need You Now.' Maybe we should move on to your answer."

Geoff, who was also now feeling the warmth and lack of inhibition from the alcohol, stated, "'Take It Easy,' by the Eagles. No contest. It's the best song ever recorded. It has two of the most memorable lines—for a guy anyways. The first is: 'It's a girl, my Lord, in a flatbed Ford, slowing down to take a look at me.'"

Meredith blurted, "See how much we have in common? You love C&W just as much as I do!"

"I didn't know the Eagles were Country," Geoff laughed.

"Well, they are, and I am mightily impressed with your musical range of appreciation!" Meredith intoned. "So, what was the second line in the song that you love so much?"

"I'm truly catching a bit of a buzz here, but maybe it will give me the courage to turn that Eagles' line into our final question of the night," Geoff said. "What time is it anyway?" He looked at his watch. "Holy crap! It's 1:30 AM!"

Meredith laughed and said, "I have nowhere to go tonight and no dorm room police to check me in. My husband's on a road trip with his team and is not due back until late tomorrow afternoon. You?"

Geoff replied, "My flight is due to depart at 9 AM, but I suppose I'll need to sleep off this wonderful night. I'll have Nick, my COO, make arrangements to hold the plane until later in the day."

"You mean, rebook on a later flight," she said.

"Well, sort of." He let the comment slide. "Now, where were we? Ah, yes, the most provocative question of the night: straight out of my favorite song from my favorite Country and Western band. But I am seeking a serious answer here."

Geoff looked right at Meredith, and asked, "How do you find a lover who won't blow your cover? They are so hard to find."

They took each other in for what seemed like a full minute but, in reality, it was only seconds. She leaned into him so that they were just inches apart. "Take me home, will you?" she whispered. "I've had lots to drink, and I would feel a lot safer with an escort."

Geoff felt the bottom of her breasts brushing the tops of his hands, and his breath quickened.

"Sure," he said. "But, you haven't answered the question."

Meredith got up from her barstool, and grabbed her coat. "I'm headed to the girls' room. Meet you out front?"

"Sounds like a plan," Geoff replied.

As she left for the bathroom, Geoff looked back at her. He couldn't help it. She was beautiful in a very sexy sort of way, and he hadn't had so much fun with a woman in, what, years? Decades? He was clearly feeling his resolve melt.

"Steve, can I have the check?" Geoff called out to the bartender.

Steve walked over and placed the bill on the bar. $378.76. Geoff placed his American Express Black Card on top of the bill and Steve picked it up and processed the charge. It didn't take long. Geoff and Meredith were the last ones in the restaurant.

Steve returned with the paper slips to sign, and Geoff filled in a $100 tip. "Thanks for all the great advice tonight. The food was excellent, the martini's outstanding, the wines first-rate, the service world class and the confidentiality extended towards my new friend and me especially appreciated."

Steve smiled and said, "Yessir! Happy to help you integrate so easily into Grand Junction living. Hope to see you again next time you are through town." Then he lowered his voice and said something that sobered Geoff a bit. "Be careful. She is absolutely delightful and clearly interested in you. Her husband has the reputation of being a very dangerous prick."

"Thanks," Geoff responded. He looked Steve in the eye and said, "Forewarned is forearmed."

Steve then added, "You have no idea."

Meredith appeared back at the bar, and had a broad smile on her face. "What's with you two?! Can we leave now?"

Geoff said, "We were just wrapping up some high finances here."

Meredith asked Steve, "Can you call us a cab or an UBER if they're out this late?"

"No need." Geoff interrupted. "My driver's out front."

9

BOBBIE

BOBBIE PACKED UP HIS THINGS AND HEADED FOR HIS TRUCK—A Chevy dual-axel raised monster. He threw his gear in the back, and literally climbed in the driver side door. He sat back and closed his eyes for a few moments. Then, he opened the center console and pulled out several objects: a 16-ounce Budweiser, a bottle of pills and a syringe. He left the handgun there.

After popping the top of the beer, he raised it to his lips and pulled almost half the can of liquid down his throat. He was still in the parking lot of the school, and drinking on campus was a clear violation of school rules, but fuck the school—and the rules. He was Coach, right? He, and he alone, had brought notoriety back to the Grizzlies, and everyone in town, and every parent, stood in awe of him. He took another hard swallow, put his head back on the headrest and allowed his mind to wander away from football for a rare respite from the pressure he felt every moment of every day of each football season.

His mind took him to the high country of Montana where, in the off-season, he would track and kill elk and moose. He rarely used a rifle for such sport. He far preferred to hunt with a bow and a quiver of arrows. He hunted alone. It was the one place where he could act out the violence inside him preferring to call his prey his enemy. And, he particularly liked wounding his enemy, and using his considerable tracking skills, find the incapacitated animal—still breathing and eyes bulging in fear—and taking that final shot that threw the creature into a brief and uncontrollable fit of jerks and spasms. It was almost sexual to see life ebb away at his hands, and have his prey eye him in abject horror as it lay paralyzed on the ground, knowing, in those final split seconds of life, it had been fatally defeated.

Winning in football was uncannily similar. Assess your prey by studying it and analyzing its strengths and weaknesses. Put a game plan together as to how to identify its soft underbelly and wound the beast. Track your enemy to its weakness, and always fire the first shot. The more unexpected the attack, the better. Wound first; never try to finish off your enemy at the outset. Much more personal reward to toy with your enemy as a cat plays with a mouse before beheading it. Bobbie never liked running up a big lead in the 1st Quarter for all the same reasons. He wanted his players to experience the wounding, the tracking, the toying, during the game—always in control awaiting the planned death strike in the 4th Quarter. Each time the Grizzlies approached the game in that manner, and a victory secured, the boys ran off the field feeling like invincible *men* ready to practice harder, prepare longer and kill again.

"Hey, Coach!" squealed a girl's voice from across the parking lot. Bobbie quickly squashed the empty beer can and shoved it into the center console. It was hard to make out who it was, but as the girl approached, he realized it was Gabby, one of the cheerleaders. He jumped out of his truck, and walked over to greet her halfway to avoid any questions about what he might be doing in his truck. She gave him a hug, and gushed, "We have all been like practicing extra hard so that we can like be really good for tomorrow's game against Silverton!"

Bobbie took her by the shoulders in a very firm grip, and ogled her from top to bottom. The beer was just beginning to warm him, and he could feel his inhibitions washing away. "My God, you're cute! How in the world will all you cheerleaders be anything BUT good with all that practice and natural beauty. And you, Gabby, are particularly beautiful."

Gabby blushed and realized Bobbie still had his hands on her while he spoke. And while not at all experienced in such things, she felt a stab of anxiety that she was out here alone in a dark parking lot with Coach Edmonson holding her shoulders and looking directly into her eyes while they spoke. His eyes were glassy and he also smelled of something that she thought was beer.

"Thanks, Coach. Just thought I would wish you and the team good luck." And with that, she twisted quickly out of his grasp wondering if she was totally over-reacting. Was this uncomfortable personal encounter all a part of her imagination? She had little direct experience to draw upon for comparison.

As she started towards her own car at the far end of the lot, Bobbie implored, "Gabby, hey! One more thing."

She stopped and turned around, and fighting off her nerves, walked back to the Coach. He said softly, "You know, you remind me of a young fawn. So beautiful, so innocent, so spry, so leath. What a great cheerleader you are. You really stand out. You are growing into such a striking young woman—I mean physically. Show it off a bit more tomorrow; I mean, all of you girls. It will get our players more fired up, and we need the extra testosterone flowing - if you know what I mean. Do you know what I mean?"

"I think so," she said. "I'll tell the girls."

"Just don't say it came from me. Make it your own idea, OK?" Bobbie again placed his hand on one of her shoulders, but this time softly. He looked into her eyes again and said, "The boys will thank you, and they will all be lining up to ask you girls out to the Formal. The girls should thank you, too."

"Sure," she said, "and, good luck, again, in the game tomorrow." She then turned to leave once more.

This time, Bobbie said, "Atta girl," and reached down to pat her on the butt, but instead cupped his right hand on her ass. She didn't react, but rather broke into a run towards her car. Like an elk into the woods.

10

GEOFF

AS GEOFF STARTED FOR THE DOOR, HE OFFERED HIS ARM IN A POLITE, but warm gesture. Meredith took it in both hands. A cool breeze met them as they exited from the restaurant. Football season brought cold nights and invited huddling for warmth.

Twenty yards down the street, stood a Lincoln Towne Car. Immediately, upon Geoff and Meredith appearing on the street, the engine came to life, the headlights flashed twice, and the car briskly moved to pick them up. A young man emerged, and opened the door. "Good evening, sir," he said. "Back to the hotel?"

Geoff responded, "Let's drop off my associate to her home, then you can drive me to my hotel."

"Please, no," Meredith intoned. "Under the circumstances, and being my hometown, I insist on seeing you to your hotel first."

"OK then. Thank you very much. You can drop me off and then drive my business associate back to her home, and make sure she gets safely in."

"Yes sir."

Meredith jumped in first, and the driver closed her door. Geoff and the driver then walked around to the other side of the car and Geoff climbed in next to her. The car was already warmed, and the engine was running. The driver slipped into his seat and looked into the rear-view mirror. "We'll be at your hotel in about 13 minutes. Do you prefer the privacy glass?"

Geoff said, "Sure. Thanks."

And with that, a humming sound emanated from the middle of the car, and a sheet of dark glass rose between them and the driver compartment. "What in the world is that?" Meredith exclaimed.

"Privacy glass. The driver can neither see us, nor hear us, unless I alert him using the intercom."

Meredith laughed. "I see," she said as she turned in her seat and looked at Geoff. "So, he can't see what I am seeing: a wonderfully handsome man with charm, warmth, wit and smarts sitting next to a woman blushing in his presence?"

"That's right. He isn't…"

Meredith cut him off. "And, a man with a terrific sense of humor and a very kind heart."

They sat looking at each other not saying much more. Geoff let the warmth of the alcohol, the car and Meredith's presence envelop him.

"Geoff," she continued, "I'm married."

"I know that," he replied. "You told me all I needed to know back at the bar playing our little question game."

"No, no, it's not that. Your last question. I'm giving you an answer to your last question. 'How do you find a lover who won't blow your cover? She's so hard to find.'" Meredith went on, "You see, each person has to have as much to lose. They both need to be happily married with a life too good to ruin. They also need to respect each other, and trust each other. But that respect and trust comes with time—time lovers rarely afford each other."

"But didn't you say back at dinner that you were married to an abusive brute?" Geoff inquired carefully.

"I'm not talking about me, but giving you an answer to your game. You asked a question, and I am answering it. Truthfully. The way I see it."

Just then, the car came to stop, and the engine was idling. Geoff leaned forward and pressed the intercom button. "Driver, are we at my hotel?"

"Yes sir," came back at them from the speaker in the roof.

"We'll be just a minute," Geoff said.

"Yes sir."

Geoff turned to Meredith, their chemistry clearly creating a moment. He took her hands softly in his, and lightly rubbed his thumbs over the back of her small fingers. He sat there for a minute, and not looking up at her, but rather at their intertwined hands, said, "I can't tell you how much I have enjoyed the total freedom of happiness I have experienced with you tonight." He looked up, and their eyes locked. "You have made me laugh and smile; you have made me forget every worry; you have been a complete breath of fresh air in my stagnant world. You have made me want to see you again. I want to get to know you better. All of you."

Geoff let go of her hands, turned and opened the car door. He stepped outside into the cold air, stopped, and put his head back into the cabin, and said, "How do I get a hold of you?" But, he was speaking to an empty passenger seat.

He felt a hand slip around his arm. "I'm easier to catch than you think," she laughed.

Startled, Geoff spun around, and stood facing Meredith. She had not put her coat back on, and he was staring down now at her wonderful smile and soft cleavage that now bore ample goose bumps. If she noticed, nothing was said. She said with a shiver, "Hurry, let's get inside!"

Perhaps it was the alcohol; perhaps it was the chemistry; perhaps it was his newly-realized loneliness; perhaps it was the excitement; perhaps it was because they were both married and had much to lose; perhaps it was simply the moment; but, whatever it was, Geoff reached down and grasped her hand and they ran to the lobby door.

Once inside, they let go of each other, but were laughing. Once at the elevator, Geoff hesitated before pressing the call button. He made a living—a damn good one—at making key strategic decisions at the right time. He would look back in the years to come and say that this moment, and the decision he was making, would alter his life irreversibly in the most wonderfully exciting, and the most tragically devastating, ways.

Meredith felt his hesitation. "I'm only walking you to your room—making sure that you get to your beauty sleep without incident." It was hard to hide her smile.

He reached around her, and called for the elevator. They stood in silence, but the moment came soon enough. The far-right door chimed, and opened softly. They walked in, and Geoff pressed the PH key for the penthouse 24 stories above them. The doors slowly, and softly, slipped together. Meredith turned and joined Geoff, first with her arms inside his coat - and then placing her head against his chest. Geoff's heart was racing, as was his mind, but he was lost in the moment— literally breathless. He didn't speak. Meredith turned her head up towards his, and offered her soft and inviting lips to him. The elevator was racing skyward, and the next decision had to be quick. He lowered himself to her, and without uttering a single word, softly brushed his lips against hers. The sensation of her mouth was forbidden and unforgettable. He lingered, lightly nibbling at her upper lip—first on her right; tracing the very tip of his tongue tickling her lip across to the other side of her mouth; nibbling the soft flesh of her left. Meredith's legs were weak. She had never been kissed with such restrained passion before.

The elevator chimed, announcing the arrival at their station: the Penthouse. It was hard to break their intoxicating moment, and they were forced to do so by the opening door. They tore themselves away from each other, their hearts racing. They stood there for a minute, but soon Geoff raced his hand between the now-closing doors, and they responded by re-opening.

Geoff and Meredith said not a word, but stepped into the penthouse lobby. It was now 2:15 AM, and there was not a sole awake to their knowledge. In fact, there may not have been anyone else willing to pay the Penthouse rate for a midweek stay. Geoff had not seen anyone else there the entire time of his business trip. He was leaving tomorrow.

Meredith again came to him, and put her arms around his shoulders—her hands behind his head with her fingers running through his thick wavy hair. She simply said, "I want you." Geoff was aware that as Meredith stood on her tiptoes to stretch her arms up to reach his neck, her legs were split and she was rubbing against his right leg. He was aware that he, too, was getting excited—the growing urgency pressing against her, too.

"Oh, God, Meredith. I want you. I know you can feel it, too. But, I need to process all of this. I don't want this to end, by the way. I'm just confused—in a good way. I need to go to bed," Geoff said, his voice trailing, "Alone."

Meredith didn't move but seemed to hold tighter—not in a threatening way, Geoff instinctively felt, but in a resigned, almost sad, sort of way. She didn't speak.

He leaned down and kissed the top of her head. Speaking through her hair, he said, "I want to see you again. How do I get a hold of you? I only know you as Meredith, and you only know me as Geoff. I think it's best we keep it that way, Mrs. We-Both-Have-As-Much-To-Lose."

She kept her head against his chest, pulling back only to reply, "I have a friend named Jessica Stevens. She works at Sunset Gardens Nursing Home. She is the manager there, and is 100% trustworthy and discrete. You can find me through her. How do I find you?"

Geoff replied, "You can't. But, trust me, I will reach out to you in the next few weeks. I plan to be back in Grand Junction before the month is out to close this deal I am working on. Otherwise, if this deal drags on, I will make arrangements for a rendezvous at a different time and place."

"But how will I know? If it's a different place, I'm not sure I can get there. I don't have much money. What about…" Meredith stopped.

Geoff now had her by the shoulders and he was pushing her gently away so that he could look her directly in the eyes. She could feel her tears welling again. He said simply, "Jessica Stevens. Sunset Nursing Home here in Grand Junction. I'll find her. Believe me. I'll find you. Trust me."

They stood there for a few seconds in silence. Geoff was acutely aware that their entire encounter and conversation—all in the elevator and Penthouse lobby—were uninterrupted and private. He reached for the call button and pushed. The elevator, having no other passengers at that hour, on that night, opened immediately. As they both stepped into the cab and the doors closed behind them, Geoff asked, "May I escort you back out to your car?" This time there was no reply. The embrace was immediate and heated. Their mouths found each other's, and the kissing had more urgency and passion. Geoff had his hands behind her head, but moved his right hand down Meredith's neck and slowly felt his way over the top of her silk blouse until he caressed her left breast. She gasped. The elevator ticked away floor-by-floor as if a timer on two sticks of TNT. She could feel the sweet hardness of his erection on her leg, and moved slightly sideways so that the pressing would be in her crotch. The connection was electrifying, but all too brief, as the elevator slowed abruptly.

Geoff and Meredith peeled apart as the doors opened, and in a few precious seconds, frantically pushed and pulled their disheveled clothes back in order the best they could. Meredith quickly moved out the door towards her awaiting car that she could plainly see outside the front doors. She stopped and turned around, and her look changed. She seemed to possess an urgent hunger and a pleading desperation. She mouthed the words, "Call me."

• • •

The doors to the elevator closed. Geoff turned around, and put his forehead against one of the walls. The silence was welcoming. What had he done? This was incredibly stupid. He was happily married. To Susie. He had wonderful kids that he adored. Lucy, Brooke and CJ. He was Founder and CEO of CBC—one of the most successful, and reputational, international private equity firms. He was playing with fire. '…a lover who won't blow your cover.' Crap.

Geoff exhaled and pulled himself back into reality. The elevator wasn't moving. What? What was happening? He then realized that he hadn't pushed the button for his return trip to the Penthouse. That broke his mood, and he laughed—although nervously.

The elevator climbed, and Geoff paced the entire way up—exiting when the door opened at the Penthouse. He slipped out and headed for his room—unaware of the little black bubble in the high dark corner of the elevator that had captured his journey. Actually, all three of them.

11

GEOFF

I T MUST HAVE BEEN THE ALCOHOL, BUT GEOFF AWOKE IN DARKNESS
with a sweat-soaked t-shirt and a pounding headache. At first, he tried to clear
his head to remember exactly where he was. Not unusual for a world-traveler;
disorientation in the middle of the night was common. It had happened so many
times before. Geoff looked around the room, and slowly pulled the curtains back
on the fog that shrouded his memory, and looked at the hotel clock on his bedside
table. 4:51 AM. He had only been asleep for a few hours at best.

Sitting up, he swiveled to his right and put his feet on the floor. Geoff massaged his temples, and ran his fingers through his long hair sweeping it back away
from his throbbing forehead. His first thought was that he needed a haircut badly.
He would text his assistant, Rose, in the morning and get that scheduled soon
after he returned.

He stood up and headed into the bathroom. He found his bottle of Excedrin
in the side pocket of his shaving kit, and meted out three pills that he swallowed
together with a handful of tap water.

His head clearing now, he thought about his flight back to the Bay Area, and
what time he needed to be ready to depart the hotel for his ride to the airport.
Not being the best on detail, he fortunately had two trusted confidantes who
were brilliant at arranging his schedule and his often-complex business dealings:
his assistant, Rose and Nick, his Chief Operating Officer—whom he used for
the more confidential and complex dealings of the Firm. He had called Nick last
night to change the flight plan and delay the departure of his aircraft.

Not sure that he got his late message last night, Geoff walked back and sat on the side of his bed and checked his messages on his private mobile phone. Sure enough, Nick had picked up the message and confirmed that the new ETD (estimated time of departure) was 11:30 AM. The driver would pick him up at the hotel lobby at 10:45 AM—plenty of time to get him to the airport, get the aircraft loaded and depart Grand Junction on time.

Grand Junction. That's where he was! It was all now flooding back to him. Jesus, was he glad that she wasn't there in the room with him. What was he thinking? What was her name? M. "Meredith with an 'M,'" she had said. Holy shit. What WAS he thinking?

As he lay back onto his bed, he rolled the memories, now freshening, back into his consciousness. He first remembered her look. The smile, the hair, the butter-brown skin, the soft cleavage. But, it was the joy he had experienced in being with someone so responsive to him. Her interest in what he was doing. She laughed easily and heartily at his jokes. She was so completely present for their time together. Each of them wanting to learn more about the other. There was an unexplained and completely unexpected chemistry between them. And yet...

Geoff thought of his kids at home and Susie. What a terrific family he had. So complete. So proud he was of their accomplishments, their happiness and their love for him. He thought of their beautiful craftsman house on the water in Tiburon—one of the most picturesque and desirable communities in America. Funny, he thought of mowing the lawn when he got home, and cleaning up the gardens, too. Susie had said there had been a storm that week, and the yard was a mess. He couldn't wait to get home, spend some quality time catching up with Susie and hearing about CJ's latest games and the girls' exploits. A good night's sleep, and waking up with no sweats or headache, would lead directly to his Saturday morning coffee and a day of satisfying yard work. A smile came to his face as he rolled over and pulled the covers up to his chin. This was going to be a great weekend; he couldn't wait to get home.

Meredith. M. What in the hell was he thinking?

As he closed his eyes, he could feel the aching in his head subside. He drifted quickly into a deep sleep.

12

JESSICA
MEREDITH

MEREDITH COULD HEAR, THROUGH A DISTANT HAZE, THE SOUNDS of footsteps overhead that both awoke her and confused her. Where was she? As she rolled over, her face brushed against rough fabric, and she flinched. What? Her eyes opened slowly staring inquisitively into a cushion of earth tones. As she pulled her head back, she realized she was sleeping on Jessica's couch in her apartment. It was a feeling of relief for several reasons. One, she was comfortable there - as she had spent many a night in her best friend's living room. Two, she was away from Bobbie—not having to deal with the trauma of recent verbal and physical abuses. Three, she was "home" safely after drinking so much the night before.

Jess was Meredith's best friend here in Grand Junction. They had befriended each other soon after Meredith arrived from New York when they each were eating dinner at local restaurant alone. Well, Meredith was alone and Jessica was with her then 12-year-old daughter, Jasmine. It was Jasmine that originally attracted Meredith to their table. Meredith was taken by the delightful conversation mother and daughter were sharing as well as the daughter's good manners. Meredith commented to Jasmine how cute she was, and also how impressed she was at what a fine young woman she appeared to be. A conversation struck up between Jessica, the girl's mother, and Meredith. They have been "besties" ever since.

A single mother, Jessica scraped together all she could—working long hours at her job at a senior living facility—so that she could provide for her pride and joy. They called each other the Jess and Jazzy Show and were inseparable. Often, during Meredith's frequent visits, she felt like she was an intruder—spoiling precious time between Jess and Jazz, but was accepted like family. Jazz often calling Meredith "Auntie M" - after the Wizard of Oz. They spent a lot of easy time together and the bond grew quickly. Meredith spent many a night at Jess' both when Bobbie was traveling extensively for football and also when things got rough in Meredith's marriage—which seemed more and more recent over the past six months.

Meredith could smell the coffee in the other room, and when she got up from the couch, she was shocked to see that it was already 10:30 AM. Jess had left the coffee maker on, on purpose, Meredith was sure, so that there would be hot coffee for when she arose from the dead. She was dressed in a nightshirt and her panties, and hadn't remembered getting undressed last night. Leave it to Jess to look after her in such condition.

She held the steaming mug in her hands and warmed herself. She went back to the living room, pushed aside the familiar blankets and sat on the couch taking a cautious sip of her brew. The heat radiated through her chest as she sat back and tried to piece together the night before.

She remembered the man in detail. He was tall and very good-looking with longish, wavy, salt-and-pepper hair. He was dressed well, but casually (if you could call it that)—formal for around these parts: tailored slacks, pressed shirt, leather coat, cashmere scarf, shoes that clearly were too expensive to be from around here, and a gold Rolex watch with a white face and Roman numerals. And that smile! Yes, all the teeth were there. White teeth. Straight teeth. Teeth that made up an easy smile that beckoned her to be intrigued by him. A smile, no doubt, that peaked her curiosity about this stranger in her favorite restaurant, and drew her to make conversation with him. A smile that warmed her, and ultimately enticed her.

Jeff. No, GEOFF—with a G. How could she forget? What was his last name? Shit! What was his…last…name? Then, it came back to her. No last names. No dramas. No guilt. No contact. Think! Every detail…THINK! The monogram. What was it?

What she remembered was the connection. The easy way in which they spent time talking and laughing and sharing. It was like they had known each other for years. But they didn't, did they? Time passed so lightly. She felt safe. She felt whole. She felt free to be the person she hadn't been since moving to Colorado. She laughed. And, she had allowed herself to cry softly—her tears brushed away by a very caring and understanding man. She felt trust.

As she relived the prior night, Meredith was completely overwhelmed by the feelings of gratitude for the fate that had landed in her lap. Bobbie was travelling today with the team, and her not going home last night assured her that he wasn't going to be able to abuse her. And she didn't have to answer to him until he was home—hopefully with another victory. That would calm him. She had been over-whelmed with a completely irrational and emotional decision to spend money they didn't have on drinks and dinner at Grand Junction's nicest restaurant—a place where she doubted that anyone would know her. A treat to herself. She had put on some of her clothes that made her feel like her days back in the Big Apple, and dabbed her favorite perfume on her wrists and touch between her breasts. She headed out the door with nothing in mind except treating herself to the quiet gift of peace - and no obligations to herself, her job, or God knows too, her husband.

The night had unfolded quickly in her mind, and Meredith struggled for every little detail. She had left the restaurant with him hoping for an invitation to his bed—even brilliantly devising the strategy to walk him to his room. OK, so he probably saw right through that, but they did go to his hotel first. They had a driver. A new Lincoln Towne Car; she hadn't seen it around Grand Junction before. Privacy glass. What? And then, the arrival. She had slipped out of the car so quickly to meet him. And, the journey to his room.

Meredith put her nearly empty coffee mug down on the small table to the side of the couch. She put her head back on the cushions and closed her eyes. The ride up the elevator was a rush; very full of anticipation and excitement. Did he feel it, too? The brushing of noses; the intimate touching of cheeks—and that first kiss. She could still feel his lips on hers. Soft, slowly traversing her upper lip, his tongue traveling back across the same lip—this time just barely inside—stopping at the edge of her mouth, and almost unperceptively, he nipped at her - more with his lips than his teeth. Meredith shuddered now as she did the previous night. The taste of him still fresh in her mouth and on her mind.

In her memory, the night continued…The more urgent kissing. The passion glazing their eyes. His hand behind her head: stroking her hair and then on her bare neck exploring her skin as though freshly peeled. His hand roaming back around to her exposed plunging neckline, and then…slowly, gently, lightly, mov-ing down to her breast. The way he ever-so-delicately teased her nipple. God…

A loud bang from upstairs brought her back from the memories of last night. It must be the neighbors upstairs doing housework or something. Meredith looked at her watch. It was now 11:30, and Jess might be coming home for lunch soon to see after her friend. It would be just like her. Even though she would have to wear her clothes home from last night, Meredith wanted to shower. She knew that she could use the master bathroom as Jess had always insisted. Jazz had her own bathroom, but her shower left a lot to the imagination—certainly not in a condition for guests—and certainly not, in Jess's humble opinion, ever for Meredith. So, Meredith headed to Jess' room.

The master bathroom was large by apartment standards with a walk-in shower that had a built-in seat, and two shower heads: one from the ceiling for rain and the other a classic wall-mount that had various settings for rinse and massage. Meredith turned on the shower, and pulled her nightshirt over her head. She stood in front of the full-length mirror and looked at herself. She was lucky, she thought. Her breasts were medium-sized and firm. She had small pink nipples that had a home on the higher side of her mounds—proof to her, and the world, that her tits were real (not that she had anything against plastic surgery) and special. She had a small waist and a small, round and shapely, butt. Lucky indeed.

The steam was now filling the room, and Meredith slid off her panties. She entered the shower, and switched the faucet to "RAIN." First holding her hand out making sure the water was the right temperature of hot, she allowed herself the joy of moving slowly under the water and feeling the tepid liquid as it poured over her head and down her body. She closed her eyes. The water was sensual; her body sensitive—made more so by her immediate memories. She meditated on the water feeling almost every drop concentrating on the movement of the water from her head, slithering over her shoulders, cascading between her breasts, gliding down her stomach, and erotically, across her velvety smooth crotch. She pumped a generous handful of soft soap into her palm and began to apply it to her neck—massaging it deep into her sore muscles. The soap flowed, along with the water, down her chest and across her now-aroused breasts. She soon found herself meditating on the water flowing down her back. She slowed her mind to cherish the water as it flowed down between her shoulder blades, swooping across the small of her lower back and into her ass. She turned a bit, spread her legs and bent slightly over allowing the warm liquid to enter her crack more deeply. Her breath quickened and she was aware that her breasts were noticeably swelling and her nipples hardening.

Meredith switched the faucet back to "SHOWER" and the rain ceased, but a strong outpouring of water spewed from the fixture. She first stood under it enjoying the firmness of the water on her neck and shoulders. But, the sexual meditation of the earlier rain brought more pleasure to her imagination, and she could feel a tightening in her lower abdomen. She adjusted the shower head to spray directly onto the seat in the shower and in a more focused stream. Meredith then turned around and let the water flow strongly on the front of her upper torso. She thought of Geoff as she did this, and mentally replayed his caresses - and the soft, yet passionate, kissing. Adjusting herself, and spreading her legs, she allowed the sensation to enter her. Deep within her lower stomach she could feel it starting. The pulsing. The waves. The rushing and receding. Starting slowly. Building. Bigger. Faster. She focused on the water. Her body. Slippery. The pleasure. The kiss. Her cupped breast. The nibble. The pulsing suddenly turning to convulsions of now unstoppable pleasure. Meredith allowed the orgasm to overcome her; consume her totally. She whimpered and bucked quickly and uncontrollably for several seconds—finally moving out of the stream and crossing her legs to avoid any more stimulation.

She couldn't stand; her legs felt like jelly. Finally, Meredith was able to get up and stand under the water as it again pounded onto her shoulders. Slowly, she reached out and turned off the water gathering herself—still breathing heavily; recovering. She grabbed for her towel, and dried herself. She felt wonderful and refreshed. As she stepped out from the shower and settled in front of the sink to brush out her hair, she heard sounds from the kitchen.

"Jess? Is that you?" Meredith inquired a bit too loudly.

"Sure is, girlfriend!"

As Meredith emerged from the bedroom, Jess was making a large salad with loads of fresh vegetables. "I thought you might drown in there," she laughed.

"Nope, not me. I'm a real water girl, remember?" Meredith happily replied.

"Well, get dressed and come join me. You have some explaining to do, young lady!"

"Explaining?"

"Yes. I want to hear all about last night."

Meredith grabbed her clothes and went back into Jess' room to change into her outfit from last night. After she had herself largely put back together, she emerged into the kitchen.

Putting two large bowls of salad on the table along with some sparkling water, Jess stopped and looked Meredith in the eyes. "Well…?"

All Meredith could muster at the moment was a deep sigh. Then she said, "You absolutely won't believe this. So, sit down, shut up and try not to interrupt me."

13

GEOFF

LATER, THE MORNING AFTER HIS UNEXPECTED DINNER WITH MERE-dith, Geoff was greedily enjoying his third cup of coffee. The morning was cool and overcast, and the forecast had predicted showers for early in the afternoon. Geoff was waiting outside his hotel and couldn't help but look up and study the clouds forming overhead. It was getting darker, for sure, and there was no question foul weather was approaching. He loved extreme weather, but not when he flew. It always made him a bit nervous, and he couldn't put his finger on the reason why. Flying never bothered him when he was younger, but when he got married and had children, the fear crept in: the thoughts of not seeing his kids grow up and the resultant inability to be a part of their lives. He shook his head quickly and pushed those thoughts aside as he always did.

He looked at his watch and it was 10:45 AM. It was exactly then when the hired car pulled up and stopped in front of him at the curb. "Mr. Cameron?" the driver asked as he jumped out of the car and headed straight for Geoff's bags.

"Yes, that's me," Geoff replied.

The driver opened the rear passenger door to the black Escalade and let Geoff in—closing it once Geoff was settled. He ran around to the back, and loaded the luggage. As soon as he was back in front, seated and had fastened his seat belt, he turned around and enquired, "Headed to Private Aviation, correct?"

"That would be great. Thanks."

"We'll be there in fifteen minutes. Privacy glass?"

"No thank you; not today," Geoff said. He couldn't help but remember last night, and the ride with Meredith to his hotel. The privacy glass had been a new experience for her—a novelty that allowed them to continue to get know each other better. That was an understatement.

"…before the weather sets in," was all Geoff heard, and he realized his mind was elsewhere.

"Pardon me?" Geoff said.

"I said, you are lucky, and you'll get out of Grand Junction before the weather sets in," the driver remarked.

Geoff replied, "I sure hope so. The pilots should have re-filed their flight plan, and pre-checked the plane so that we can depart immediately."

"Yes sir. As you know, the private aviation building is tiny and is across the airport from the main terminal. I'll have you at the front door in 10 minutes."

Geoff didn't reply. He pulled his iPhone from his pocket and opened it, using the fingertip encryption, to access his email. He addressed his first note to his COO, Nicolas George.

> To: nick.george@cbc.com
> Subject: Debrief
> Date: October 24, 2014 at 10:53 AM MST
> From: geoff.cameron@cbc.com
> En route to airport. Thx for arranging later time change. U R best. C U AM office tomorrow 4 full debrief.

Next, he texted Susie.

> To: Susie@camfamily.com
> Subject: Late Departure
> Date: October 24, 2014 at 10:55 AM MST
> From: geoff.cameron@cbc.com
> Got delayed this morning, but boarding soon. Should be home late afternoon; not going to office. How are the kids? Dinner tonight? Want to go out, or BBQ at home? Let me know. XOXO Me.

He hesitated. Did he even want to suggest dinner at home? They hadn't had a real "date night" in quite some time, and the thought of a nice dinner out, and some long-overdue intimacy, was what he really craved. The kids' busy schedules, and Susie's attentiveness to them—along with her myriad of school, community, fitness and charitable work—didn't do much for her libido. As a result, their sex life had waned. Geoff did all he could think of to keep that fire burning, but increasingly, he felt a failure. He hit "Send."

The Escalade came to a halt, and Geoff looked up, surprised to see that they were already at the airport. The driver stopped the car, and exclaimed, "We're here."

He then jumped out of the car and ran around and opened Geoff's door. He remarked, "Private Aviation. I'll see you inside with your bags, sir." He waited until Geoff had stepped out of the vehicle, then closed the door and headed to the back of the car and activated the rear lift gate. He extricated Geoff's luggage and personally walked them in to the building setting them down by a small counter in the front room.

The Private Aviation "terminal" was a small, low-slung, modern structure standing alone at the far end of the Grand Junction airport. It was made up of a well-appointed reception room complete with plush furniture, a stocked bar, a credenza adorned with fresh snacks of pastries and fruit and a large flat screen TV—today, turned to the Weather Channel. Behind the reception area was a small office that had large windows looking out to the tarmac as well as a plethora of communications equipment. And, there were two bathrooms.

On the other side of the building, there were eight aircraft parked: six turbo-prop planes of various makes and sizes, a helicopter and a glistening new Gulf-stream 550 corporate jet. The G550, as it was affectionately called by everyone who knew anything about "flying private," was the flagship of corporate jets. It was developed by General Dynamics' Gulfstream Aerospace unit in 2004 as an upgrade to their previous superstar, the Gulfstream V. There have only been about 600 of the planes built and sold world-wide, and with a base price tag, before adding luxury options, of $61.5 million, it's hard to imagine anyone, other than the US Military and a few Middle East sheiks, owning one.

The G550 sat fifty paces from the back door of the Private Aviation building. It was idling with the front passenger ramp lowered. Michael Parrish, the chief pilot, was walking around the outside of the aircraft making his second thorough exterior inspection. He was dressed in the approved uniform for all transportation personnel who worked for Geoff and CBC: khaki pants with a dark brown belt, matching brown Cole Hahn penny loafers, and a blue professionally laundered and pressed shirt bearing the unmistakable logo of the Firm. That same logo was displayed proudly on the tail of the parked Gulfstream—as well as on the other jet, and two helicopters, that CBC owned and frequently flew to all corners of North America and beyond.

Geoff approached Mike and startled him, calling out, "Change your name!"

Mike whirled around, and stood at attention crisply replying, "Nice to see you, sir. Welcome aboard."

What a name for a pilot: "Parrish"! But, Mike was Geoff's favorite. He had hand-picked Mike to be his chief pilot soon after he was hired as one of four, full-time, on-call, pilots of Cameron, Boone & Covington. Nick was meticulous in selecting the Company's pilot candidates pouring over hundreds of applicants, and putting the ten finalists through exhaustive capability testing and background checks before offering employment to any of them. Mike quickly earned Geoff's respect and admiration with his professional, no-nonsense, approach to flying. And when transporting Geoff, he always insisted on a co-pilot and a well-present-ed cabin attendant.

"How's our bird?" Geoff yelled above the spooling engines.

"She's checked, re-checked, fueled, primped and ready for service, sir," Mike replied. "The final flight plan was just filed to reflect our current planned departure, as well as a new route heading southerly over the Rockies to avoid the leading edge of this storm. I know how you hate to be jostled about back there," he said pointing his thumb over his shoulder at the back of the plane.

"The rest of the team aboard?" Geoff asked.

"Yes sir. Most boarded 30 minutes or so ago, but don't think they are com-plaining...yet! All accounted for. Four in total; five including your good self. Stephanie has them set up with pre-flight refreshments, and it seems the mood is very good. Beats Coach Class on United!"

Geoff put his hand on Mike's shoulder, and reached out and shook his hand. "Thanks, Mike. I can always count on you. Glad to be in your care. Now, get us airborne and home to San Francisco, Captain!"

Mike saluted.

Geoff turned around and headed for the extended ramp that led to the main cabin. He took a step up, stopped, and turned around. "Oh, and one more thing: change your name!"

Geoff laughed, and Mike managed a quick smile. "Yes sir."

And with that, Geoff Cameron, president of Cameron, Boone and Covington turned and navigated the final few steps up and into the G550—the symbol of the extreme success of his firm—and, coincidentally, his pride and joy.

14

SUSIE

SUSIE WAS QUIETLY FURIOUS AND FRUSTRATED. SHE WAS CAUGHT, once again, in bumper-to-bumper traffic driving her oversized Chevrolet Suburban Denali to the baseball field in Oakland where her son, CJ and his team, were playing against a very talented opponent in their league. She had a load of girls in the back who were shrieking at the top of their lungs expelling the latest gossip of who was seeing who, and who had done what to who, and who had received invitations to the upcoming prom. They were now yelling over the top of one another, and Susie could barely make out the gist of what they were saying, or trying to say, to each other—let alone concentrate on the road in front of her. CJ was playing shortstop, as he always did, and was the lead-off batter today—making it even more important that they made it there on time.

The girls had reluctantly agreed to come along as Susie had no choice. Geoff, CJ's team coach and primary transportation for his son's sporting events, got tied up in Colorado this morning and had to delay his flight home—and in so doing, couldn't drive CJ to the game. Once again, this left her to juggle her schedule and be the miracle worker. Also, the coaching duties were left to the assistant coach who all the boys disliked, and the parents despised.

CJ was disappointed, too. He loved his dad, and was very proud that the he was the son of the head coach. He especially liked making his dad proud with his exceptional playing—on the field and at home plate. As the season unfolded, Geoff made most of the practices and virtually all of the games.

But today, CJ took the team bus, and was in a huddle with the other boys, surrounding the assistant coach minutes before the umpire yelled, "Batter up!"

when Susie ran up to the bleachers, red-faced and out of breath. She had forgotten her folding chair that made sitting in the bleachers bearable in the car in the far-off parking lot. She was welcomed by the other mothers and a few dads, and was immediately questioned about the whereabouts of the boys' coach.

"Oh, Geoff had an early morning meeting today in Colorado and couldn't get a flight back in time," Susie answered. "He's been putting together a large transaction there, and as you all can imagine, his time is not his own."

The parents nodded their understanding, but turned towards the field when the umpire called for the coaches to meet at Home Plate to exchange line-up cards. The kids were all in the dugout in their uniforms ready for the start of the game, and the parents were relaxed and ready, too—except for Susie who was still decompressing from her chaotic ride across the city with a full gaggle of giddy teenage girls.

Somewhere along the journey to the baseball field, Susie had received a text that annoyed her. She wasn't sure why, but it did. It was from Geoff, and he was delayed in Grand Junction. Along with giving an estimate of when he would be home, he wanted to know if she wanted to go out to dinner or stay home. Out to dinner? What? Doesn't he know that she has had a very long week, alone, taking care of everything? He didn't even mention the baseball game. That struck her as unusual, but then again, his deals were intermittently complex and all-consuming. "I guess he just assumed I would be there to support CJ at his game while at the same time shuttling the girls to wherever they wanted, or 'needed' to go," she mused. Her thoughts continued, "You're damn right he's taking me out to dinner—and not someplace fancy. Mexican in the village will be just fine. Then, home to chill."

Susie was interrupted by some shouting. CJ was already at second base, and the umpire had called out his teammate on strikes—angering the parents. "Jeez, did I miss my son's at-bat?" she grappled.

The rest of the game unfolded as it had begun: Susie so consumed with her schedule that she was on her smart-phone almost the entire time, and paid little attention to the game. The girls' planned activities and how she was going to be able to get them to where they needed to be—let alone manage a life for herself, continued to perplex her. The house was at least clean and picked up—thanks to Martha, their long-time nanny and housekeeper. What would she do without her? She had so much more on her plate, and felt constantly overwhelmed. The National Charity League was in the midst of planning their annual fund-raiser—a masquerade black tie affair—and Susie was in the thick of that, too. The gardeners needed to plant the annuals in the gardens surrounding the front of the house, and she hadn't had the opportunity to get to the nursery to pick them out and schedule the delivery. "This has to be done this weekend," she thought.

The time passed quickly, and Susie barely recalled the events of the narrow loss. CJ had played well, that she knew. But the rest of the players, and the game they played, were a blur. She said her good-bye's to the other parents, collected her daughters and their friends, and found CJ horsing around with some of his teammates. They all walked the long distance to the far end of the parking lot and loaded into the Suburban. CJ sat up front with his mother while the girls held court in the back. It was a quieter ride home; the girls finally exhausting themselves of all the iterations of the social hive of their school, and CJ was tired and a little moody about the loss.

Susie turned on the radio to her favorite Alternative Rock station, and headed back to Tiburon. She didn't even want to think about Geoff at the moment. He was just another entry onto her "to-do" list for the day. Dinner at home? Or out? Either way, she would need to prep: either go to the store and acquire all the dinner fixings and make dinner; or, get home, shower and dress, and apply make-up and be ready to be up-beat, attentive and cheerful. Neither sounded at all good to her. It was going to be Mexican, damn it. That simple.

She stopped at the stop light, and noticed that the car was much quieter. She looked over her shoulder and all the girls were just sitting back there talking calmly to each other as though they had rung out all they could ascertain for the day. CJ was asleep with his head against the window—his mitt as a pillow. Susie turned right at the freeway entrance, and again waded into the miasma of cars and trucks of a Friday late afternoon commute. Friday nights should be fun, but lately they represented an unwelcome gateway into the unstructured phalanx of activities that now made up her weekends. She exhaled, settled back into her chair, and with all her concentration focused on what lay ahead of her, headed for home.

15

GEOFF

GEOFF DUCKED HIS HEAD AS HE BOARDED THE AIRCRAFT. ONCE inside the cabin, a cheer went up from the four teammates who had been working long hours poring over all of the details of due diligence for this latest acquisition target.

"Sorry I'm late, y'all," Geoff said with surprising sincerity. "I had several last-minute calls, and each required some focus, home office assistance and a bit more negotiation. Think we are all good now with our progress on this purchase. I hope Stephanie here took very good care of you."

They all seemed to respond in the affirmative at once talking over one another. Each was delirious to be able to fly back on the company plane—particularly this beauty. Stephanie smiled and said, "I think we have the restless natives sated for the time being. I made sure they were watered and fed."

Stephanie had been with the Company for four years. She was always cheerful and ready to please whomever she came in contact with. She was 31, tall at 5'9", blonde, attractive of course—both physically and by personality, and could be a bit flirty. Her responsibilities were loosely tied to hospitality, and she could tend bar, organize meetings and parties, and often filled in as receptionist if needed. But, her real passion was going on these trips and acting as hostess extraordinaire - whether it be as a flight attendant, on-site travel concierge or Geoff's personal assistant filling in for Rose who didn't like to travel or be away from home. Steph loved to travel, and being single, she would gladly choose to be away from the office for as long as she was able. She reported to the COO, and it was rumored that she and Nick were perhaps having an affair, but if that were the case, neither let on in any way. Both were single, and other than there was a legal reporting structure that could get them both in trouble, everyone turned a blind eye to the purported relationship.

Captain Parrish came on the PA system.

"Ladies and gentleman. This is your captain, Michael Parrish speaking. Joining me up front here at the controls is your co-captain, John Bartlett. Together, we will assure you of a safe and fast flight back to the Bay Area.

"Let me be the first to welcome you to CBC1—our newest plane and the flagship of the Cameron, Boone and Covington fleet. You are on a Gulfstream 550—the largest and most luxurious private aircraft of its type in the world. We will be flying back to San Francisco at an altitude of 49,000 feet at a speed of Mach .880. At that altitude and speed, we will have you back on the ground in time for your afternoon office chores." A loud groan went up. "Please be seated in one of the twelve seats at the front of the cabin and fasten your seatbelts for takeoff. The seats are facing forward, but they swivel. It doesn't matter if you are facing forward or backward. Once airborne, I will notify you when it is safe to move about the cabin—meaning that you will be able to unfasten your seat belts and move back to the comfortable chairs and tables behind you. There are two spacious bathrooms in the main cabin for your use during our flight. If there is anything that we can do to make your flight more comfortable, please see your CEO, Geoff Cameron." Laughter…"Now, please make sure you are buckled in—and hold on tight."

And with that, the G550 slowly taxied into position, and radioed the control tower for permission to depart Grand Junction. The engines spooled up to a high-pitched whine, and the brakes were released. All were facing forward, and as the plane rapidly came to its take-off speed, the G-forces pushed them strongly back into the plush cushions of their seats. Within only a few moments, CBC1 tilted its proud head to the sky and rocketed into the clouds.

Once airborne, and released from their seats, Geoff's employees dispersed to occupy the large leather lounge chairs that made up the rear "living room" of the plane. Steph got to work fixing drinks and preparing some exquisite finger food for her small cadre of guests. She worked at the Company side-by-side with all of them, and in fact had seniority over two of them, but she treated them all as royalty. That was her charm, and she loved playing the role as their in-flight hostess.

Further aft, behind a locked door at the rear of the "public" cabin, was the Executive Suite complete with a small office, bedroom, and a full bathroom with shower. This was only used by Geoff, Nick and the rare VIP that CBC was trying to impress or placate. The only executives that could authorize the use of the executive suite were Geoff, his two partners and Nick. Geoff would never consider entering that space in front of his fellow employees. He wanted always to be viewed as one of "them"—all part of an integrated team of professionals that were separated only by their job responsibilities. He was adored for this, and all but the travel and transportation personnel, were on a first-name-basis with him. The Company's other jet had an interior just as lush—just smaller. The main cabin of the other aircraft doubled as office, sleeping quarters and lounge.

As the G550 soared across the Rockies high above the incoming storm, Geoff put his head back and closed his eyes. So many thoughts churned through his head. He immediately focused on the deal at hand, and the valuable work his team had executed. They had uncovered several areas of vulnerabilities that enabled CBC to renegotiate several key terms of their purchase agreements. And the company that they were acquiring was an organization that could be bought at a low price with residual areas to trim costs making a huge "paper profit" that would please his investors and partners. He truly loved hunting down these vulnerable targets; companies that had grown progressively weak due to clear oversights, comfort and complacency.

Then his mind wandered to last night - and Meredith. He couldn't shake the thought of her. The smell of her, the feel of her, the heart of her, her humor, the carefree conversations, the mysterious sadness within her, the connection, the chemistry between them. Magnetic. "That's what it means," he thought.

Geoff opened his eyes, stretched and got up. He made his way back to the lounge area of the plane and took a seat amongst his work family. Holding court, he asked each one what they enjoyed most about this trip—and importantly, what they had learned that would make them even better as professionals at CBC. They joined together in a spirited discussion that took on both business and personal perspectives, and each felt a strong affection for their leader.

Mary, their whip-smart Finance Manager, asked Geoff, "Say Boss, you excited to be going home? We all live vicariously through you, by the way. I think I speak for most if not all in the Company, that we all want to grow up and have such a wonderful home life as you do."

Geoff blushed. Certainly, no one would interpret his reaction to anything but a reaction to a deeply personal question. "You bet I am!" Geoff replied. "Unfortunately, I missed CJ's baseball game today chasing this deal, but I can't wait to see him and my two girls tonight when I get home. And, I think Susie and I will have a date night tonight. It's so important for you all to set aside some one-on-one time with your spouses or partners to constantly reconnect. Relationships should be joyous, spontaneous and fulfilling, but they are also hard work. Never forget that, just like here at CBC, anything worthwhile is worth putting your all into. You will only get the best, by giving your best."

Charles, an analyst on the Finance team asked, "How long have you and your wife been married?"

"Nineteen amazing years. Three kids that are the pride and joy of my life. Susie is a better partner than anyone on this earth deserves. She is the CEO of our home, and pulls off probably the most complex roles of leadership that I have ever witnessed. I wouldn't want to change places with her for all the tea in China. Well maybe all the tea…"

Everyone cracked up. They were rapt by the honesty of their boss. How many other firms could they work at where they could have a "fireside chat" with their CEO in the lounge of a private jet (not just *any* private jet), sipping champagne and sharing this type of intimate conversation? Each in their own way, thought it and felt it. Even Geoff. At that moment, those employees would rather be nowhere else on the entire planet—and working for no other company. Geoff had created this remarkable environment of teamwork, trust and family values—and enormous, second to none, success.

The captain came on to the PA system again, and asked everyone to return to their seats for their decent and landing. He added the following surprising news, "During our flight west, I am sorry to report that the San Francisco International Airport has reported a thick marine layer, we know this as fog, has smothered the airfield. As a result, the air traffic controllers have closed all but one runway for landing aircraft placing long delays and an abundance of flights into a holding pattern over the City. Fortunately, we have been able to alter our flight plans and land, with priority, in Oakland across the Bay. Your COO, Mr. George, has arranged for the Company's fleet of limousines and town cars to meet you plane-side on the tarmac to gather your good selves, and your luggage. Your CEO, Mr. Cameron, has arranged for those limo's to take each of you immediately home to your families and friends."

There was a big cheer followed by lots of clapping, high-fives and spirited conversations mixed with laughter.

As each of the passengers found a seat and buckled their seat belt, Geoff stood and added, "In each vehicle, there is a bottle of Napa Valley Chardonnay for your spouse or partner to enjoy with you this evening—unless, of course, you want to consume it early. I'll never tell. That secret is in the vault." More laughter…"Understanding that most of you have your cars at the office, I have instructed your drivers to be on call for you in the morning to take you back to the office to fetch your vehicles—whenever you get up—and whenever you want to make that trip. Thanks, again, for all you do for CBC. I value you all more than you will ever know. Your contributions are a big reason we are so successful here. I hope you have enjoyed this important journey."

Geoff sat down as the four employees whooped their appreciation and genuine love for the man who stood as an example of everything they all hoped to grow up to be one day: successful business CEO, remarkable human being, and a father and husband extraordinaire.

Again, he allowed himself the luxury of putting his head back and closing his eyes. This time, he could only see Susie. Amazing Susie. He couldn't wait to get home, open a bottle of fine wine of his own, and pour a glass for each of them. A long, hot shower, and putting on some fresh clean clothes would be the precursor to their dinner in town. He could visualize her in her fitted pants, silk blouse, scooping neckline and dangly necklace. He couldn't wait to hold her, kiss her and later, make love.

He quickly opened his eyes and looked out the window as the runway in Oakland gathered up to meet them. The bump and squeal of the tires alerted them that they were almost home. The talking in the cabin got louder as each was happy to be heading to their loved ones and the weekend ahead. As the plane taxied to the Private Aviation terminal, Geoff could see the line-up of black vehicles with each of the drivers in their CBC uniforms of khaki pants and logo-embroidered blue shirts, standing at the ready to receive them. A surge of pride overtook him, and he smiled.

As the G550 came to a halt, and everyone got up to leave, Geoff shook every hand and thanked them again. As they disembarked down the stairs, they were met by their two pilots, in Company uniform, who also bid them farewell. Geoff was the last off the plane. Mike and John met him, too, on the tarmac.

"Thanks, guys. Great flight. John, maybe next time you will be in the left seat, and Mike will be your slave. Anyway, John, your last name creates a whole new level of increased confidence!"

They all laughed and shook hands. Mike added, "Don't worry, Chief, I'll be making the long flight back to San Fran in the morning as soon as this fog lifts. We need to reunite this bird with her siblings at the Company hanger. They are getting jealous."

"Tell them not to be so put out. There are numerous exciting, and once-in-a-lifetime, trips ahead to places we have never been to explore uncharted territory.

The fleet will all be called to duty, and will all play an important part of carrying us to our future."

Both Mike and John saluted in unison. "Yes sir!"

And with that, Geoff's personal driver, Frank, approached them and grabbed the last bags remaining by the plane. "Mr. Cameron, welcome home. How was your trip?"

"Great, Frank. Thanks for asking. All good. Worthwhile for the whole team. But, I am bushed, and anxious to see my wife. And, I have a thirst you could scratch. Home, please!"

"Privacy glass this afternoon?"

"No thank you. But, could you put on some easy listening tunes—low volume?"

"Not to worry; I know your favorites. We'll be "wheels down" in Tiburon at Chez Cameron at 4 PM latest—if traffic cooperates."

Geoff climbed in the back of the black stretch BMW 7 series and lowered the seat-back tray. Frank closed the door and walked around to the driver's seat as Geoff logged in to his personal phone and along with a myriad of emails and text messages, he saw several messages from Susie.

The BMW pulled away quietly, and some gentle jazz flowed into the spacious back seat. Frank knew not to talk unless addressed as Geoff used his time in the car for calls or answering emails. His business could wait for a moment while he checked in with Susie.

The four notes that followed in succession outlined, in unnecessary detail, just how hard her day, and her week, had been. In fact, her whole time managing the family—"alone" - had been "beyond comprehension." While Geoff was off "galivanting around the US having fun with your minions," she had had zero time for herself, and was looking forward to Geoff getting home.

"Tomorrow, I am headed out for some serious retail therapy. May not come home. Need you to look after the kids. Both the girls and CJ have plans, so put your driving cap on. The yard needs work and I have a list of things I need you to do around the house. It has been neglected."

The next note read, "Too tired for going out tonight. Just leaving for CJ's game with four screaming girls in the back seat. Sure wish you could have wrapped up your meetings earlier as planned. I'm exhausted."

The last note read, "CJ lost, and the team missed their coach. Traffic supposed to be horrible. The red oil light came on today in my car. What does that mean? Too tired to worry about dinner. I'll leave that up to you. I do NOT feel like going out. Get the picture? Maybe you can stop on the way home and pick something up. Kids are all going out with friends, so it's just us. Should be home by 6:30 in time for the mad child exodus. Is Frank driving you? Maybe he can hang around and drive the kids to their friends' houses? C U soon."

"God. Well, I guess we're not going out tonight," Geoff rolled these spousal texts, around in his mind. "I'd rather be back in Grand Junction working on my deal," he thought.

"Frank?"

"Yes sir?"

"Can you stop by Whole Foods on the way home? I need to pick up a few things for dinner."

"Not a worry, sir."

"And, what is your schedule this evening? Can either you, or one of the other drivers, be able to drive my kids to their friends' houses at around 7?"

Yes sir. I can do it for sure. Margaret can keep my dinner warm until I get home. She loves to eat with me, and we love to watch game shows together. Thanks to our recorder, we have them all lined up to watch whenever I get home. I'll call her and let her know."

"Thank you, Frank. And, thank Margaret for me, too. I've got you on special triple-time tonight with a generous tip."

"No need for that, Boss. You are the most generous person I have ever worked for. It is a pleasure to be of service."

Geoff went back to his emails, and found a refuge from his mixed emotions. It was so much easier, and at times enjoyable, to deal with the rigors of work than to deal with someone who didn't seem all that excited to see him. But, he tried to put himself in Susie's shoes and understand the non-stop chaos that teenagers wrought on a single parent and their often bedraggled and weakened psyche. She was special, and if the truth be known, he would much rather be out on the road, doing deals then schlepping teenagers and dealing with their fragile egos.

Geoff exhaled and his emotions calmed as he worked through email after email. He had made a dent for sure, but had a long way to go when Frank pulled up to the Whole Foods in his neighborhood.

In the meat section, Geoff got a couple of thick filets. He added some fresh broccoli even though he really didn't like to eat it himself, he knew Susie loved it. He added a couple of large Russet potatoes, and an extra carton of sour cream. He knew they had butter and seasonings at the house as well as some great wine. He retrieved a carton of French vanilla ice cream and containers of strawberries, raspberries, blueberries and boysenberries, and he headed for the check-out counter.

When Geoff got back in the car after packing the grocery bags into the trunk, he sat back and stared out the window as Frank pulled out of the parking lot. On the radio was "I Need You Tonight," by INXS. It took a minute for the song to register. "…there's something about you, girl, that makes me sweat…" The beat was urgent and catchy. It then struck him that this was one of Meredith's favorite songs. He tried to listen to the remaining lyrics, but the song was over. He'd have to download the song; note to self.

Soon, the BMW was pulling up to the front of the Cameron Residence at 101 Bayfront Drive, Tiburon, California. Frank helped with the luggage and the groceries, and asked if he could come back at 7 PM to shuttle the children.

"Not an issue, Frank. Thank you again for being so flexible."

"No worries, sir. See you back here at 7." And with that, Frank left.

Geoff put the groceries away, and marinated the steaks. He scrubbed the potatoes and washed the broccoli. He then went upstairs with his bags, and unpacked. He put his laundry in the large wicker basket in his closet, and his dry cleaning in a separate joint bin he shared with Susie. He then stepped into a hot shower, and let the hot unrestrained stream work its magic on his neck and shoulders. He was so glad that he secretly had removed the water restrictor from the showerhead! When he had done it, it had made him feel more than a bit guilty as he was so honest with everything that he did. But that quickly passed with the onset of the deluge. He really looked forward to this guilty pleasure every day, and every time, he stepped into his shower.

After drying off with a thick soft towel, Geoff quickly brushed back his long wavy hair and brushed his teeth. He threw on some deodorant and even though he left the day's stubble for Susie (which she said she loved), he patted on some of Susie's favorite after-shave. He felt refreshed.

After throwing on some comfortable jeans, a button-down shirt with rolled-up sleeves, and some casual shoes, he went downstairs and opened a bottle of Silver Oak Napa Valley Cabernet. He poured himself a generous glass, and after swirling it robustly, he raised it to his nose and he inhaled deeply. Beautiful. He took a sip, then another. Without putting on a coat, he walked outside across the front yard to the sidewalk and turned around. He spent the next few minutes studying his magnificent home—a house he had never dreamed he would ever be able to afford.

16

TIBURON

A GREY AND WHITE CRAFTSMAN, THE HOUSE STOOD OUT ON THE pointe as a classic beauty. It boasted 7,165 square feet, five bedrooms, a massive great room, formal dining room, a home theater, game room, study, walk-in wine closet that held 2,000 bottles and a kitchen to die for: it, alone was 900 square feet and had two of everything—two ovens, two dishwashers, two sinks, two refrigerators. It had an oversized island that served as a gathering point for casual evenings, but doubled as a staging area for large, more formal parties. The house also had a massive butler's pantry that had enough storage and counter space to support any gala event serving 100's of guests. It, too, had a full adornment of appliances. The bedrooms were large and each had their own luxury bathroom. But, Geoff and Susie each had their own bathroom attached to the master suite—each with their own shower, toilet, sink and vanity. Susie had a bidet in her bathroom. The master suite took up a large portion of the northern upstairs, and Geoff and Susie had designer, walk-in, closets. About the only thing that they shared was a hamper for dry cleaning and professional laundry—and their California King bed.

Geoff took another sip of his wine, and turned to face the unobstructed view of San Francisco Bay and the city skyline in the distance. He took a deep breath of that magnificent pure ocean air, and just stood there for a minute to absorb the beauty. He loved the tranquility of it all, too. But tonight, he couldn't spend precious minutes to himself. He wanted to make sure that dinner was well underway by the time Susie and the kids arrived.

As he turned and headed back to his front door, he noticed that the grass needed cutting and edging. It had certainly grown a bit shaggy, and Susie was right to point out that it required attention. She had always badgered him about letting their professional gardener mow the lawn, but Geoff found a Zen-like peace, and welcomed exercise, in his weekly garden work. It kept him grounded and happy. He would get to it tomorrow between transporting the kids around to their activities or Sunday at the latest.

17

GEOFF

THE DOOR BURST OPEN, AND THE SUDDEN NOISE STARTLED GEOFF. The shrill of the girls' voices—a mixture of laughing, and talking—spilled into the kitchen from the garage. Lucy and Brooke, along with their two friends, bounded up to the large center island to survey the work that was clearly in progress.

"It smells so good in here, Daddy," chirped Brooke. "What are you making?"

Geoff pulled his apron over his head, and put it down on an adjacent chair. "Before I give away all my cooking secrets, I demand a hug from my babies!"

Brooke came running over and threw her arms around her dad's neck. "Hi, Daddy! I missed you so much! Where have you been?" It didn't seem she wanted to let go, so Geoff, still hugging his younger daughter tightly, picked her up and twirled her around.

"I was in Colorado working on another business deal. But, I missed you all to the moon and back! Did you go to the game to see CJ play?" he asked.

"Yeah, we had no choice. Mom made us go 'cause she said she didn't have time to drive us home after school," Lucy interjected.

Lucy was the oldest of the Cameron kids. She was in high school, and sported a fully-blossoming teenage attitude complete with indifference, impatience and more-than-occasional profanity. There were some good moments still, but they were getting increasingly few and far between. Geoff handled her with a light-hearted sense of humor that seemed to frequently annoy her—and her mother even more. Susie had little patience for Lucy these days, and their bitter vocal battles were almost a daily occurrence.

"Hey, young lady, give your dad a hug!" Geoff invited. Lucy came over and gave him a stiff hug and a peck on his cheek.

"Mom is being such a bitch today!" Lucy hissed in his ear.

"Easy now, Luce," Geoff replied. "I'm sure your mother is stressed and has had a very busy day."

"You're just saying that to protect Mom. She has been like on my case all day. She is so annoying." And, with that, Lucy disappeared quickly from the kitchen and bounded upstairs with her friend, Natalie. Geoff could hear, "Hi Mr. Cameron!" as the two of them evaporated from the scene.

"What are you, making?" Brooke asked again.

"Oh, a little something for your mom and me. I know she is tired, and would like to stay home tonight and chillax. So, I stopped at the store on the way home and picked up a few of your mom's favorite things. Basically, steak, baked potatoes and veggies."

"But, what smells so good?"

Well, you are probably smelling the sautéed onions. I threw some extra garlic and butter into the concoction. Don't tell your mom about the butter, OK?" he laughed.

"Your secret's safe, Daddio!" Brooke smiled widely. "I'm running up to change and pack. I'm spending the night at Elaine's house. We've rented a couple of scary movies."

"Elaine, did Mrs. Cameron speak to your parents to make sure it was all right for Brooke to come over?" Geoff inquired.

"Yes, Mr. Cameron. It's all set. Mrs. Cameron called."

"Mom always does!" Brooke added. And, with that, the two of them scurried up the stairs, too.

Brooke was two years younger than Lucy, and still in junior high school. She was still the sweet, caring and loving child she had always been. She was easy-going and self-motivated. That didn't mean that she didn't get upset by the occasional bullying that went on in all middle schools, or get into trouble from time-to-time, but on the whole, she was a dream child—at least for now.

Geoff turned and lowered the flame on the onions, and checked the marinating steaks. He was washing the broccoli when Susie came in carrying a number of bags and shouting over her shoulder, "I know you're tired, Scott, but I need you to get all your things out of the car, and get upstairs and into your shower. Don't forget to put everything away and throw your dirty laundry into the hamper."

Geoff looked over his left shoulder and smiled. "Hi, Honey!"

Geoff could hear his son's muffled voice a long way off in the garage. Susie stopped, put her things down on the floor, and without acknowledging Geoff's greeting, she turned and went back from where she came.

"Hurry, Scott! You don't have much time. Jimmy's parents will be here in half an hour to pick you up." Susie raised her voice louder and called, "Did you hear me?"

"Yes, Mom!" Geoff could feel CJ's eyes roll back, but he was actually, at 10 years old, too young to have learned that disrespectful trick yet. He'll learn from Lucy soon enough.

"Hi, Dad!" Scott called out as he dropped everything on the kitchen floor, and ran up to his dad, jumped high in his arms and wrapped himself around Geoff's neck." He held on for a long time. "We lost today, but I got three hits: two doubles and a single! Where were you today?"

Geoff always hated missing any activities his kids were involved in, but CJ's baseball was special. Geoff was the coach of the little league team, and he knew this father-son bond wouldn't last forever. And today, in particular, it stabbed him with what felt like an arrow through his heart, but Geoff covered it well.

"I got held up in Colorado. I had some meetings that ran late this morning, and then we had bad weather landing in San Francisco so we got diverted to Oakland. I'm so sorry I missed our game."

"That's OK, Dad. You're coming tomorrow right?" Scott asked.

"Wow, I forgot! Two games in a row! Yes, of course! I will be there for sure," Geoff responded. Susie wanted to go shopping tomorrow, so he wasn't sure how all the kids were going to get everywhere, and what role he was going to play in the shuttling. And, as Geoff put Scott down, he asked, "Do you know what time your game is tomorrow?"

CJ took off for the stairs at full speed. As he turned the corner and disappeared out of sight, Geoff heard him yell, "No!"

Geoff took stock of the moment, and had to smile. Those three kids meant everything to him. The wild unpredictability was fun, and he loved seeing his kids grow up before his eyes. Too soon they would all be gone, and the excitement would be over. The evening pick-ups and deliveries would land his kids at their three friends' houses, and he was happy that he had arranged for Frank to come back at 7 and drive his girls to their destinations.

"God DAMN it!" yelled Susie. She had just come back to the kitchen and tripped over CJ's baseball glove and bat that he had left on the floor. "Scott! You come down here, NOW, to get your stuff which I asked you to take to your room!"

No reply.

Geoff could hear water running and suspected that CJ might already be in the shower. More likely, though, the girls were getting ready for their sleep-overs, and they were the ones in the shower. CJ was probably already distracted and in his own young-boy world. In any event, the rooms were far away from the kitchen, and upstairs at the far end of the house, that it was highly likely none of the kids could hear any calling from the kitchen. Susie had wanted to put in an intercom system when they built their dream house, but Geoff had nixed the idea as they were so far over budget that an intercom seemed a waste. Tonight, it would have been helpful.

"Can I fix you a drink, or pour you a glass of wine?" Geoff asked brightly.

Susie didn't reply. She leaned over and picked up Scott's things and headed briskly out of the kitchen. Geoff caught her, and gently held her arm. She took a deep breath, and turned slowly to him. "Sorry," she said. "Yes, a glass of wine would be lovely. Thanks, Honey."

He poured her a glass so that she could take it with her leaving him to the business at hand. Geoff returned to the sink and finished washing the broccoli. He then poured himself another glass of Cabernet, and headed out back to light the barbeque. He stopped at the back door to turn on the lights and water features that both spit jewels of water into the pool and allowed their man-made stream to flow with the easy sound of a babbling brook. He strolled past the sparkling pool and jacuzzi that were beautifully lit, and the thought crossed his mind that he and Susie had never skinny-dipped in their pool together. Maybe tonight?

He lit the barbeque, and headed back towards the house. He stopped again to enjoy the view back into the large windows of his home. He could see shadows moving frantically upstairs, and saw that Susie was back in the kitchen. He remembered a Country and Western song that said something about "the best view at my house is the front porch looking in." He wasn't sure of the lyrics, and he was in his back yard, but the meaning was the same, nonetheless. He lifted his glass and smelled the earthy aroma of a dark forest, blood-red plum and blackberry. Then he savored another sip of his wine. It was smooth and tasted great. He felt great. How could he not?

Geoff came in the kitchen to fetch the steaks. "When are you going to tend to the yard? Cj's game is at 10 AM tomorrow, and you need to be there by 8:30. The girls need to be picked up sometime in the morning, too. Can you call the parents and find out what timing is best for them? I'm out-a-here at nine at the latest. Tomorrow is the first day of the summer sale at Neiman Marcus, and I want to get a few new dresses for our trip to the Bahamas."

Susie was at the Viking stove checking the pre-heat temperature settings that Geoff had entered for the potatoes. He came up behind her, and put his arms around her waist. He softly kissed her on the back of her neck, and whispered into her ear, "It's really nice to be home; great to see you, Honey."

Susie didn't flinch. She opened the top of the steamer and checked the broccoli. "Remember, I don't like my vegetables soggy."

He turned her around, and still holding her waist, looked into her eyes. "Hey," he said. "Hey. I am here to pamper you, feed you, water you, and wait on you hand and foot. Please exit my workspace and leave me to my pampering. You are welcome to join me at the barbeque, or you can stroll upstairs and draw a bath. But either way, you are entitled to relax and let me take care of you. And, hey…it's really nice to be home, and it's great to see you, Honey."

Susie softened and smiled. "OK, OK. I get it. Thank you. Nice to see you, too. How was your day? How was your trip?"

Geoff pulled her close and hugged her tight. "How about helping me out by being my able, and sexy, assistant chef by grabbing those steaks while I check on the potatoes? I'll steam the broccoli when we come in with the steaks."

Susie turned to the far counter breaking Geoff's hold. "Sure!" she said. "Actually, why don't you cook while I set the table?"

"The table is already set—in the library." This is where Geoff and Susie used to escape the kids for their secret love-making. It was at the far end of the ground floor, and not in the children's flow. The floor to ceiling books in the mahogany cabinetry muffled their sex and laughter. Geoff tried to remember the last time they had tried anything there, but couldn't.

He checked the timer, and the potatoes still had 30 minutes to cook. "Join me outside," he said as he picked up the platter with the two thick filets. Susie followed him out, and walked with him to the barbeque.

"The pool sure looks nice," she said. "It'll look a lot better when the lawn gets mowed and the rest of the yard picked up."

Geoff ignored the comment. He'd learned to ignore a lot over the years. He knew he was an exceptional provider, and yet he couldn't seem to avoid ridicule and criticism. It always seemed worse when he got home from a trip—as though resentment had been boiling up while he was gone, and she just needed to get it off her chest. Come to think of it, it occurred to him that she was this way before he left on a trip, too. In either event, he had learned to swallow hard and just not respond. It saddened him to see her so unhappy.

"How about a swim after dinner and after the kids are all gone?" Geoff threw out.

"What? A swim? What do you mean, 'after the kids are gone'?" Susie responded with an edge to her voice. "Is that all you think about?"

"What do you mean?" Geoff asked. "All I asked you was if you wanted to go for a swim later. Or a jacuzzi. The pool temp is set at 80 degrees and the jacuzzi is at 103 degrees. We never use the pool."

Susie snorted and said, "No thanks. I'm not a pool girl. I think I will take a shower after all." And with that, she headed back to the house.

Geoff lifted the lid to the barbeque, and put the steaks on the grill. The meat sizzled and the smoke rose to the sky. He could hear the water of his pool and creek, and see the steam rise from the jacuzzi. He was on his third (or was it fourth) glass of the Silver Oak Cabernet. He wondered what Susie would wear to dinner. He fantasized about her in a low-cut sweater top with no bra. Perhaps she would put on a short skirt and wouldn't wear panties either. He couldn't help but get excited at the thought. Maybe he could entice her into the pool after all. OK, maybe the jacuzzi.

Geoff's phone rang. He looked at his iPhone and the Caller ID read, "Frank—Driver."

"Hello Frank," Geoff answered.

"Good evening, Mr. Cameron. Just to let you know I am out front. I'm quite early, but wanted to make sure I was on time."

Care to come in for a snack or a water, juice or soft drink?" Geoff asked sincerely.

"No thank you, Mr. C. I'm happy to wait out front until your kids are ready," Frank said.

"You only have the two girls and their two friends. Two stops close by. I really appreciate you're being available on this Friday night."

"Don't give it another thought; it's my pleasure to serve, Sir."

Well, thanks again, Frank. I'll let the kids know you are here."

Geoff flipped the steaks to their other side. "Perfect," he thought. "These are going to melt in our mouths."

He then grabbed his phone again, and texted Lucy and Brooke. "Frank in front ready when U R. All go same car. I'll pick U up tmrw 1 PM. Love U!!!" He watched for the activity upstairs although he couldn't hear anything, but soon the house was still.

While he was at it, he texted CJ. "Clean room before leaving pls! I'll pick U up 8 AM tmrw at Jimmy's. I'll have your uniform glove bat. Love U!!!"

"What did they do before cell phones?" Geoff thought. "It is easier to communicate with my kids via texting than talking to them. And, they respond. Quickly. And, usually without drama. Upon reflection, it had become easier to communicate—texting - with his wife. "Talk" when you want to - when you want to—with some forethought.

Then he sent a note to Susie. "Dinner almost ready. Kids on their way out. Heading in with steaks. Tossing salad. Come dressed for dinner." He added the winking Emoji, and smiled.

● ● ●

The table was set with their fine china, silver and best glassware. A candelabra was aflame with three flickering white spires matching the white linen tablecloth. A new bottle of Caymus Special Selection Cabernet was open, and decanted, on the table, too. The first course of tossed green salad with fresh chopped vegetables and garlic croutons was already set at their respective places, and the main course was in the kitchen, in the warming drawers, ready to be served. But, no Susie.

Geoff walked to the wide staircase and called up in the direction of their bedroom. "Honey, dinner's served!"

"O—K!" Susie yelled back—a little to forcefully.

Geoff was seated alone at the table in the study, and he had soft music playing in the background. He sipped his wine, and savored the new flavor of this freshly opened bottle. He was feeling a little frisky and amorous. As he waited patiently, he let his mind drift back to just last night and his evening with Meredith. God, was she something else? Cute, funny, interesting, captivating, intriguing and very sexy. Her creamy dark skin was what especially captured his memory tonight; although, their kiss still lingered on his lips, and he could remember, with clarity, the feel, taste and smell of her.

"Hi," Susie said as she came into the study and sat before Geoff could get up, as he usually did, to properly pull her seat out and seat her. "The salad looks nice."

She was in a pair of comfortable jeans and an old pull-over turtleneck sweater. Her wet hair was pulled back in a ponytail, and she wore no make-up. Geoff actually felt over-dressed in his blue jeans, loafers and pressed dress shirt.

18

SUSIE

"**G**EEZ, CAN'T WE GET A LITTLE MORE LIVELY MUSIC? IT'S LIKE A funeral parlor in here!" Susie exclaimed. And with that, she got up and changed the music to New-Age Rock and turned up the volume.

Once the main course was served, Susie continued with her articulation of her week. How hard it was. How tiring. How lonely. How mundane. How infantile. How overwhelming. How exacerbating. How thankless. "How was your trip?" she finally got around to asking.

Geoff, as usual, understood the nuance of the question but didn't take the bait. "First of all, it was a lot of work, and I think in the end, quite successful. I'm guessing we all averaged 16-hour days. Meals we had brought in to the hotel conference room where we were all working on our due-diligence. I made a few visits to the home office where I could meet with the principals and have some questions answered. We ate every meal together, usually with yellow pads by our sides as we continued to evaluate the unfolding opportunity."

Geoff looked up and saw that Susie was on her iPhone texting. He stopped talking and remained silent for quite some time while Susie continued to text. She finally looked up. "Sorry; had to text the kids to make sure they got to their friends' houses safely."

"No worries," he replied. "And…?"

"Yes, they're all safe. Sorry, you were saying?" Susie added.

Geoff hesitated, and took a slow deep breath. "Not sure where I lost you."

"You were saying something about 16-hour days."

"Right. Yes; well; we worked long hours and ate all meals together. And, I believe this will be looked back upon as an especially successful, and life-altering, trip. I was so knackered on the last night that I went to a local restaurant, had dinner at the bar and watched our 49ers pull a last-minute upset of the Denver Broncos. Lots of locals, and they were especially vocal—but respectful and kind to their guest."

Geoff could tell that Susie wasn't really listening to what he was saying, and for a quick second, he thought of saying something completely off the wall such as, "...and the bull testicles I had for dinner screamed at me when I bit into them!" but he didn't want to lose any control tonight, so he continued asking questions about their kids and the past week.

They were through dinner and desert in pretty short order. Geoff thought Susie loved the ice cream desert with fruit and orange liquor drizzled over the top, but she didn't say so—just kept talking, but finished it completely.

"I'm exhausted," Susie exclaimed as Geoff got up to clear the dishes. "I'm going to bed. I've got a big shopping day tomorrow."

"Why don't you head upstairs and get undressed? I'll do the dishes, and come up and join you in about twenty minutes."

"Let me at least help you clear the table," Susie said.

Geoff headed to the kitchen with his hands full of dishes, and settled at the sink with warm water and dish soap. Susie finished clearing the table in the study, and headed upstairs without saying so.

Geoff loaded the dishwasher, washed and dried the remaining pots and pans, and put them all away. When he reached their bedroom, Susie was already in bed with the covers pulled up to her chin. He quickly undressed and slipped into the bed beside her—spooning her from behind. As he wrapped his arms around her, he knew instantly that she was sealed up in her matronly flannel nightgown. They had not made love before he left, and he calculated that it had been eighteen days since they had last had sex.

He moved his hands slowly over her back, massaging her shoulders, then her neck, then lowering his hands to the small of her back. As he continued to rub her back, he tried to slowly and seductively pull up her nightgown. It didn't take long. Susie pulled away from him and exclaimed, "Jesus, Geoff! Can't you keep your hands to yourself? You just walk in the door, and all you want to do is fuck me. You don't give me three seconds to get used to you being around the house again."

He was stunned. "What? WHAT? Getting used to me being around the house again?" he brooded silently. The evening had not turned out as he thought it was going to. Skinny dipping. Who was he kidding? The table in the study. Sure. A low-cut sweater. No panties? Get real, Geoff.

There was silence on the other side of the bed. Geoff got up and went into his closet where he put on his pajamas and came back to bed. Susie hadn't moved. He climbed back into bed, crawled over and kissed her lightly on the cheek. "I love you, darling," he whispered.

He then rolled back to his side of the bed, and lay there staring up towards the ceiling. He replayed the events of the night—and the day that had preceded it. He thought about all three of his kids, and how lucky and happy he was to be their father. Then he drifted off to sleep. And dreamt of Meredith.

19

BOBBIE

BOBBY'S KNEES WERE KILLING HIM. HE WAS SHAKING AND WAS DRIP-ping wet. His head pounded. His mouth felt as if it were full of cotton that belied the amount of fluid that had passed from his stomach to the toilet—well, some in the toilet anyway. He could feel the waves of nausea gripping him again. He leaned his head inside the bowl, and his mouth involuntarily thrust open expelling a torrent of rancid air and a dribble of vomit. The spells of dry heaves were prolonged and painful. He thought he might suffocate or pass out. He gagged again, gripping the toilet as though that action might somehow deliver him from the worst of the spasms. But, as he sunk his head once again, and his stomach convulsed for what seemed the fiftieth time, his eyes bulged and the pressure forced water from there, too. He took a few deep breaths. "Is it over?" he thought?

Bobbie had been kneeling on and off all night. The nausea had overcome him soon after he collapsed into bed at around 2 AM. After finding her gone, he had tried to reach Meredith several times on her phone, but she didn't answer. He hadn't noticed that her car was gone from their carport. And when he checked after discovering his wife went missing, he exploded - punching his fist through the fiberboard wall through to the family room. His anger had boiled over as pain shot threw his knuckles and wrist.

"Where are you, you fucking bitch?" Bobbie roared. "God DAMN you to hell."

Bobby removed his fist from the wall and went immediately back into the bedroom to look for clues. He was a great deer and elk tracker, but he had never worked his talents on humans. Tonight he would start. He couldn't tell immediately that anything was amiss. The room was clean, and everything seemed in its place. Her purse was gone, but that was all that he noticed at first. He didn't know why, but he looked under the bed. Nothing. He checked the closet. Nothing. He checked the bathroom. Nothing. Fucking cunt. NOTHING!

His wrist throbbed and he went back to the liquor cabinet and removed the top from the bourbon bottle. He gulped two large mouthfuls, and wiped his mouth with the back of his hand—his good hand -the same one holding the bottle, spilling a stream of brown fluid on his shirt and the floor.

"FUCK YOU!" he yelled, and with that, threw the bottle with his full force at their flat-screen TV. The bottle shattered into a million pieces—shards of glass and spangles of bourbon raining down in a wide semicircle covering most of their family room. The flat-screen was cracked in such a way that a Black Widow would be proud. There would be no more sports and entertainment in the Edmonson house for a while.

He was seething. He was too drunk to recognize his explosive temper had materially grown out of control since he started seeing Doc Spencer.

Where the FUCK was she? He looked up at the ceiling, clinched his fists and yelled at the top of his lungs. No words; just a guttural explosion. Then he headed back to the kitchen for more self-medication. This time: vodka.

Bobbie had finally had enough. The room was spinning, his throbbing hand was now radiating up to his elbow and he was hyperventilating. He staggered his way back into the bedroom and collapsed on the bed. He immediately passed out. He regained partial consciousness about 45 minutes later.

He awoke dreaming that he was drowning. Bobbie had never learned to swim, and he had frequent nightmares of being under water looking up through the oscillating murky water to the blue sky just out of his reach. He always awoke in a panic gulping air as though it was his last breath. This time, he was actually drowning in his own vomit. He was face-down, and every time he struggled for precious air, he sucked bile into his lungs. Panic struck him. He rolled to the side of the bed not sure where he was headed or why. He just needed to move; to live; to breathe. As he slithered off the bed onto the floor, his mouth jerked open, and the vomit poured forth in a vicious stream. He kept crawling. He didn't care. He was dying. He squeezed in a little air, coughed and retched again.

When he next regained consciousness, he was lying on his side on the bathroom floor. He took quick note of his surroundings, including the vomit there, too, and this time, reached up and put his head in the toilet and began an endless ritual of survival that would last until the morning.

• • •

Bobbie pulled himself up off the floor, and looked at his watch. Shit! It was already 9 AM, and he would again miss his office hours. Then it came to him that tonight was the bus ride to Silverton, and tomorrow was the big game against the Bullets. There would be a small cadre of parents attending, but he had insisted that all players travel together, and stay together in the motel provided by the home school.

He headed into the kitchen to grab a handful of aspirin, and when he turned the corner, he literally stopped and gaped. The room was as he left it, but he tried hard to remember what had exactly happened. All he could piece together was that Meredith was gone, and he had been self-medicating. There was broken glass with shards everywhere. The flat screen was shattered. There was a hole in the wall, and overturned furniture.

"Fuck it," he whispered to no one. "She can deal with it whenever she gets home. Fuck you, you little cunt. That will teach you a thing or two about sneaking out on me." And with that, Bobbie began to head to the bedroom as he was disrobing.

As he was pulling his shirt over his head, his bare feet sank into a cold chunky sludge that oozed between his toes. "SHIT! What in hell's name?" He yanked the shirt from his head and looked down, and in vile repulsion, realized he had stepped into his own vomit. "I need to fucking get out of here," he exclaimed. The overwhelming smell of his stomach contents made him gag. As he quickly surveyed the room, he saw that the bed was soiled just like the floor. He pulled the sheets together in a ball, and flung them on top of the pool on the floor. "Don't say I don't do anything for you, bitch."

He turned on the water, and while he waited for it to get hot, he took Meredith's towel, and wiped the bathroom floor, the toilet, the sink and the wall. He then folded it and placed it back on the towel bar.

When he was dressed, Bobbie packed a small overnight bag making sure he had a change of clothes for dinner tonight, and his game-day uniform: black slacks and shoes and his Grizzlies team shirt and hat. He packed a warm jacket and a sweatshirt in case the weather turned ugly. He inspected his medicine cabinet, and grabbed a bottle of aspirin, his general toiletries, and a baggy of pot. He left the unmarked vial of HGH and the surringes, as he had just injected yesterday in his truck. But, he snatched his clear bottle of multi-colored pills that included recreational opiates and his Viagra. "You never know," Bobbie smiled. That cracked him up.

Bobbie made his way to the front door crunching on glass as he went. "Hope the bitch is wearing shoes," he thought. "Then again, I hope she's not." He closed the door behind him. He locked it, too. And although he could give a shit about most of the crap in this house, he loved his gun and his hunting bow with the razor-tipped arrows. When the high school playoffs ended in about a month, it would be hunting season, and he planned on taking a full week off to hunt alone in the wilderness of the Rockies.

Throwing his gear in the back of his truck, he headed towards Grand Junction High School: home of the Grizzlies, and a destination that held an unexpected surprise.

20

GEOFF

NICK HAD NO IDEA WHAT GEOFF WANTED TO DISCUSS THIS MORN-ing. He had texted him early, and wanted to have a private meeting in the CEO's office at eight. Coffee would be ready. Nick always looked forward to these meetings, because they were largely enjoyable due to the long-term personal and trusted professional relationship they shared. Nick considered their relationship as far closer to a friendship than to a boss/subordinate one. It was because of this, that he went out of his way to make sure every detail of every assignment was just as Geoff wanted and expected—and then some. Today would be no different.

Nick put his coffee down and sat back in his chair. He was clearly surprised at Geoff's request. He was having a bit of difficulty processing what Geoff was saying to him. "You need to find her, and make sure that she, and she alone, gets this message."

Nick added, "Her name is Jessica Stevens, right? And you said she works at a senior living facility called Sunset Gardens in Grand Junction?"

"That's it," Geoff replied. "Make sure she gets the envelope. I want to make 100% sure that the Jessica Stevens you are handing this to, is the intended Jessica Stevens. Understood?"

"Absolutely crystal," Nick said. "I will confirm that there is only one Jessica Stevens residing in Grand Junction, and then insist on a positive ID. When do you want me to make contact?"

"Today."

"Shit, Geoff. I have a full…"

"I'm only asking if you can make contact today, but you can make the visit as it suits your schedule this week. I need you to pick up additional due-diligence materials at our potential acquisition there anyway, so the side trip shouldn't pose much of a problem. This is personally important. You can take the G4."

Nick exhaled. "Geoff, I can easily fly commercial. United has a commuter flight out of Denver to Grand Junction three times a day."

"No way," Geoff replied. "You will fly private as you will be on official company business. Also, to keep your identity a secret. And, I need you back here ASAP running our operations—not out waiting on the TSA, the weather and the whims of commercial travel. For this little side-trip, it is extremely important that once you make contact, and confirm her identity, that you give her this." And with that, Geoff pulled an 8 ½" x 11" envelope. On the front was printed,

> Jessica Stevens, Manager
> Sunset Gardens Senior Living Centre
> Grand Junction, CO
> Personal & Confidential
> *To be opened by addressee only.*

Nick was quiet. After a sip of his coffee he asked, "So what's up with this Jessica girl?"

Geoff sat forward on his chair leaning on his desk, hands clasped. He made unblinking eye contact. "Not much. This is a personal matter—not family. Personal only to me. You have always been my trusted confidante, and this is why I can only put this little errand into your hands. This detour stays in the vault, understood?"

"I will throw away the key, Geoff. Rest assured. You know this."

Geoff laughed. "Of course. Thank you, Nick, for assisting me with this little mission."

Nick stood and placed the white envelope into his portfolio. "Thanks for the coffee; I have a few calls to make."

Geoff stood, too, and came around the desk. They shook hands ending with their usual bro-hug.

Yes, they were close, and shared an unspoken trust in each other. They were soon to become far closer—and that trust, tested.

21

JESSICA

IT WAS 2:45 PM, AND JESSICA LOOKED AT HER CALENDAR. DAMN IT. She was hoping to leave early today and pick up Jazzy at school. Instead, a man had called, and insisted on meeting her personally. He wanted to tour the facility, and get some detailed information. He was flying in from out of town, and the personal inspection was important as he was making an emotional decision for his mother who lived in Grand Junction. Jess had agreed to the meeting even though she had tried to lay him off on one of her subordinates. He was persistent and insistent.

She arose and headed for the bathroom as these tours often dragged on for far longer than the scheduled 60 minutes. These were emotionally charged decisions for all involved, and Jess was particularly good at assessing the parties and selling the facilities, the personnel and the services at Sunset Gardens. She had been working there for eight years, and held almost all the important positions. The tenants loved her, and she couldn't help but spend every spare minute mingling with her "homies" as she liked to call them. She would pop into Arts & Crafts, sit at the jigsaw puzzle table, join a card game, roll out a yoga mat, pull ping-pong balls for Bingo, help serve meals—and just be there for frequent hugs and chatter. Yes, she was very good, and her Sunset Gardens Senior Center was always full with a waiting list. That list she humorously called "LOFI: Last Out—First In" as in when someone died, the first on the waiting list would be admitted.

As she returned, she rounded the corner into her office and was startled to see her assistant speaking with a tall, attractive, middle-aged, man whom she presumed was her 3 PM appointment. "Oh, hi, Jess…"

Jessica replied, "I was just asking Mr., uh?"

"Morrison. William Morrison," the man replied.

"Yes, right. I was asking Mr. Morrison if he wanted some coffee or a water."

"Thank you very much, but I am fine," he said shifting his gaze to Jessica.

"Ok, I will leave you two. Jess, just let me know if there is anything you need."

"Thanks, Rox. Will do." And, with that, Roxanne left the office, and Jessica walked up to this handsome, tan, dark-haired man, broke into a warm smile and extended her hand. She said, "Jessica Stevens. It's nice to have you here for a visit, Mr. Morrison." And motioning to a plush armchair added, "Please have a seat. I am anxious to find out about your mother, and to accompanying you on a tour of our little resort."

Nick quickly took stock of Jessica. Very nice woman. Not athletic, but solid. Dirty blonde hair. Seemed sincere, efficient, capable. "What in the hell is Geoff up to with this woman?" George thought. The secrecy around this meeting led Nick to believe that Geoff was having, or contemplating having, an affair with her. But in his mind, it didn't add up. She was certainly cute, and he could see Geoff, if he were single, taking her for a spin in the sheets—but worth risking Geoff's marriage to drop-dead beautiful Susie? He decided to get right to the point of his visit.

He turned around and walked over to the office door and closed it. He didn't sit. Instead, he said, "My name isn't William Morrison. You can call me Nick. You can say I'm a friend of a friend."

Jessica became instantly worried, and the look on her face betrayed her.

"Please. You have nothing to worry about, Jessica Stevens." Nick said softly and kindly. "I have come simply to deliver a package to you—nothing more. But, first, I have to ask you for a picture ID."

"I'm sorry Mr. Morrison—or whatever your name is—I'm going to have to ask you to leave." And, Jessica arose.

Holding up his hand, Nick froze Jessica for a few precious moments. Opening his portfolio, George pulled out the white envelope and showed it to her. She looked down and read the cover.

"Please, Ms. Stevens. I mean you no harm. You are safe with me. I'm sorry about the false pretenses under which this meeting was arranged, but it was very important that I meet with you in person and in private. In fact, I do not know the contents of this letter—only that I have been asked by my boss to deliver it to you, and only you. I am also not to witness you opening the envelope. You will do so, hopefully in private, after I am gone. I am guessing you are who you say you are based upon the fact that your name plate, name badge, parking stall and car registration all confirm that you are indeed Jessica Riley Stevens. The picture you have posted on Facebook and LinkedIn also match the woman I have the pleasure of being with. However, I need to have a photo ID confirmation before I can leave this with you," Mr. George said as he again showed her the envelope.

"OK," she replied. "Thanks for the clarity. Let me grab my purse; I'll be right back."

Jessica walked to the door, and opened it walking directly over to Roxanne's desk. "Hey, Rox, will you grab my purse for me?"

Nick could hear the request.

But very quietly, she whispered, "And, call security ASAP. Please hurry."

Roxanne picked up the phone and dialed security while at the same time she reached behind her desk and into the cabinet that held both their purses. She purposely stalled fumbling with the bags as though the straps were tangled.

Security was trained to not answer any phones, but when dialed on this particular line, to move quickly to the originating phone extension. Within a minute, two uniformed officers arrived at Roxanne's desk, and together with Jessica they walked back in to confront the man who now stood with his back to them looking out the window.

"Mr. Morrison, Nick, William, or whoever you are, I have to ask you to please leave. Now."

Nick spun around, and his eyes widened. Jessica stood in front of the two uniformed men, and never lost eye contact with her intruder. The men took a step forward, and Nick raised both hands.

"Not to worry, boys," he said to all three of them. "I'm on my way. Thank you, Jessica, for the tour and the hospitality." She said nothing.

And with that, Nick turned around, grabbed his portfolio from the desk and walked calmly past Roxanne's workstation—stopping to thank her, too. He was escorted to the front door, and walked out to the street, all eyes on him, as he was punching something into his cell phone. In seconds, a black limousine pulled up at the curb. The driver jumped out, and closed the passenger door behind this mystery man. In seconds, the black car, with tinted windows, sped off.

• • •

One of the security guards asked, "Ms. Stevens, you OK? You want us to file a formal report or call the police?"

"No. Thank you, no. I appreciate how fast you guys got here. I'll be fine."

And, with that, Jessica went back to her office, telling Roxanne to hold her calls and visitors, and closed the door behind her. She put her elbows on her desk and buried her face in her palms—slowly massaging her temples. "What the heck was *that* all about?" she uttered to herself. She'd had some weird days before, but this one gave her pause. Her phone rang.

"Jess, it's Rox. You OK?"

"Geez, Roxy, you're the second person to ask me that in the last 15 minutes. I sure think so. That guy didn't actually want a tour, he wanted to give me a mysterious envelope. Nothing was adding up, so I had you call security. Thanks for watching my back. Just need a bit of time to re-group, and then I'll head out to see Jazz."

Jessica started to pack her things and organize her office. As she was collecting some vendor files from the long table against the far wall, she stopped. Holy shit…the envelope. He must have forgotten to take it with him during all the commotion with security. She irrationally thought about running after him, but he was long gone—she had seen to that personally. There was no return address. "Oh well," she thought. "I'll think about what to do with it later." She shoved it into her briefcase, and left to meet Jazzy at their apartment.

22

NICK

NICK WAS MET AT THE AIRPORT BY MIKE PARRISH. AS CDC'S CHIEF Operating Officer, Nick was always very happy to see the Firm's Chief Pilot. No one had more experience, training and loyalty than Mike. He took his job seriously and professionally; yet, he had a very pleasant personality. He took and followed orders without questioning, and no job was too small or big for him. Nick was especially proud as he had chosen him from hundreds of applicants. He was trained and licensed on all of CDC's aircraft except the helicopters. Geoff paid him twice the industry average.

Nick climbed aboard the Gulfstream V. "It's just you and me today, Mr. George," Mike said as he gave him a salute. Mike was dressed, as always, in the CDC "uniform" of khaki pants, pressed light blue shirt with the distinctive CDC logo, and dark brown loafers and belt.

"Aye, Aye, Captain," Nick responded as he headed up the stairs into the aircraft's main cabin

Mike climbed aboard, too, and spent the next 15 minutes completing all his internal pre-flight inspections from the cockpit. He had already circled the aircraft on foot twice studying every detail of the plane's exterior.

Nick was deep in thought when Mike stuck his head into the cabin. "All set for take-off. Buckle up and hold on. Buzz me if you need anything at all. We'll be back in San Fran by 6:30. Weather is clear the whole way."

"Thanks, Mike. Will do." And with that, Mike turned back into the cockpit but left the door open as he frequently did when he was flying with just Geoff and/or Nick. Both enjoyed a cockpit visit occasionally once airborne.

As the engines spooled up, and the aircraft slinked away from the private aviation terminal, Nick pulled out his cell phone and typed the following:

From: ngeorge@cbc.com
Subject: Mission Accomplished
Date: October 28, 2014
To: gcameron@cbc.com
Have DD docs & personal delivery successful. Almost arrested. ETA 1830. C U tomo.

He hit SEND. His message, and the Gulfstream V, lifted to the sky.

23

JESSICA

Jessica fumbled with her keys with her arms carrying her briefcase and take-out Chinese food. She opened the door to find Jasmine hard at her studies with a mountain of books and papers spread out across the kitchen table.

"Can you help me, baby?" Jessica pleaded as a bag started to slip from her grasp.

"Sure," was all Jasmine said in a very quiet, uninterested, tone. She didn't move.

The bag of Sweet and Sour Pork and Orange Peel Chicken fell to the floor, and Jess yelped, "Damn it!" But, Jasmine didn't flinch. She just leaned forward to erase a note and turned up her music—completely in her own world.

Jasmine was fourteen, and very much the sassy, brassy teenager that Jessica had feared she would grow up to be. Headstrong and righteous, combative and indignant, Jazz reminded her of herself when she was her age. But, Jazz was self-confident and driven—unlike her father who had walked out seven years prior, leaving them penniless. He left to "discover himself" studying Eastern Religion at a Buddhist monastery. Jess spent an extraordinary amount of time raising Jasmine by herself. She could put up with a little hormonal rage now and then in exchange for the smart, independent woman Jazz would soon become.

Jessica turned the oven to "Warm," and placed the small containers on the shelf inside. She went to the fridge and opened a bottle of Chardonnay and poured herself a generous glass, and sat on the couch in the family room—the same one Meredith had slept on just the other night. She put the glass to her lips and let the cool liquid quench the anxiety of that afternoon. Before long, her glass was empty, and she was feeling the initial glow of the wine. She got up and poured herself another serving. She looked over at Jasmine, and she was head-down into her homework. Jess could hear the music from her daughter's ear buds all the way across the room. Then, she spied her briefcase, and remembered the envelope.

She got up from the couch, and collected her things and headed upstairs to her bedroom. There, she removed her work clothes and hung them up in the walk-in closet. She slipped on some sweats and headed over to her desk where she had left her wine. Seated, she thought hard about the events of a few hours ago: What did he want? Who *was* he? Why the mysterious meeting? Who could possibly want to give her something so secretive? Why the picture ID? Did he leave the envelope on purpose, or was it an oversight? Did this have something to do with her ex? And if so, what was this—another round of dividing up what they didn't have? The divorce and property settlement had long ago been finalized. A reconciliation?

She enjoyed more of her wine, and she had to admit the curiosity within her was growing. Jess looked over at her briefcase, and got up. She first went to check on Jazz, and halfway down the stairs, found her exactly where she had left her: at the dinner table studying through some very loud and pulsating electronic music—with her showing no signs of hunger or wanting to be interrupted. So, Jessica turned around and headed back upstairs.

Once in her room, Jess closed the door and pulled from her briefcase the white envelope addressed to her. She placed it face-up on the desk next to her wine glass. "Private and Confidential." "To be opened by addressee only." Well, she was the addressee, and there was no one here to look over her shoulder to spy on the contents. She took the last swallow of wine draining her glass. Then she picked up the envelope, twirled it around several times, taking stock of its weight and shape, then held it up to her lamp. Still, she could detect nothing. So, she slipped her finger under the flap, and slid it along the length of the envelope giving life to its contents and pushing air from her lungs.

Jess reached in and grabbed its contents, and pulled out another sealed envelope with its back to her. Without thinking she flipped it over, and printed on the front read:

MEREDITH
Personal and Confidential
To be opened by addressee only.

What? Meredith? What in the world? Could this have something to do with her chance dinner last week with the stranger? Jessica's mind started to wander.

Then, the shrill voice from her daughter downstairs broke the trance. "Mom! I'm starving! When are we eating?!"

Jessica jumped to her feet and when she opened her bedroom door, she could smell the rich aromas from the now-warmed Chinese food. "I'll be right down, Baby!" Jess yelled back. But she was sure Jazz couldn't hear her.

She returned to her desk, and picked up her phone. She quickly brought up Meredith's line, and thumb-typing with experienced and practiced speed, she wrote: "Call me Urgent". Then she hit SEND. It wouldn't be the last time…

• • •

Jess and Jazz sat at the cleared-off end of the dinner table, and spooned Chinese food onto their plates. They were both having seconds. The spicy food tasted delicious, and both were unexpectedly hungry. And, while Jazz was drinking a Coke, Jessica finished her bottle of wine. They talked about school, and boys, and pimples, and Facebook, and the usual teen dramas. Jess was very good at keeping the conversation going even though her 14-year-old answered in short, clipped, answers, and was constantly looking at her phone and texting a myriad of supposed friends. Jess knew this was age specific, and the behavior would pass with the years, but she worked hard at keeping her annoyance in check. She drew the line, however, at rudeness and lack of respect; high on the list was eye-rolling and attitude. Thankfully, that wasn't present tonight.

This time, it was Jess' phone that pinged. She picked it up from the table and looked at the screen. It was from Meredith.

"Good time to call?"

Jessica replied, "Give me 5; I'll call U".

Then she looked up at Jasmine, and said, "You want any more food?"

"Nope," came the reply

"No, THANK YOU," Jessica corrected.

And with a small eye-roll Jasmine replied, "No THANK you."

Jessica smiled and cleared the table of their wrappers, plates and glasses, and headed upstairs. "Holler if you need anything, baby," Jess said as she passed. There was no reply; the earbuds were already plugged back in and the volume as strong as before.

24

MEREDITH

SHE TURNED UP HER STREET, AND FOUND IT EERILY DESERTED. What was she expecting? It was mid-afternoon, Thursday, and most everyone was at work. Grand Junction was a largely blue-collar working community after all, and the hours of 8 to 5 meant something. But today, many of the locals were heading out of town for Silverton to go see the biggest game of the season. For the team, its coaches and parent supporters, it was an overnight, due to the distance, but given the rural nature of their state and the league in which they competed, this was not unusual.

Last night, Meredith had not wanted to go home, and so had crashed at Jessica's. Bobbie had objectified her one last time, and she was tired, and frankly frightened, of Bobbie's recent behavior. He certainly wasn't like this when they had met. Meredith, though, was determined that enough was enough.

There was no note at the house, no phone call, no text, no email. Meredith just didn't go home, but it was premeditated. She had with her a change of clothes, toiletries and make-up. She was sure Bobbie would be out late that night as he usually was before a game, and would come home drunk again. And, while he would be mad, Meredith knew he would pass out, and the big game would soon erase his anger. They would deal with her little unannounced night away when he got home and was much calmer. If necessary, she would sooth him with apologies and a blow job. That always worked.

Bobbie was busy with his boys getting them psyched up for the big game, and would leave with them on the team bus. This was the biggest game of the season so far. The Grizzlies wanted to avenge their only loss last season to the hated Bullets, and a victory would secure their third straight league championship and send them to the regional finals. Meredith never traveled with the team even though their cheerleading squad was partly her responsibility. She doubled as the dance teacher at nearby Grand Junction High, and to make ends meet, taught private lessons in town.

Meredith turned her eight-year-old Ford Explorer into her driveway, and parked in the carport. She unloaded her bag and purse, locked the car and headed in the side kitchen door. She inserted her key in the doorknob and the door clicked open. She leaned down to pick up her things when the stench hit her. What on earth? She stood up and looked into the kitchen. It was a mess. Empty beer cans on the counter, and even an overturned whiskey bottle.

She cautiously, and slowly stepped inside surveying the unimaginable scene. She couldn't quite process what she was taking in. Were they robbed? It sure looked that way, except the smell of vomit, urine and booze overwhelmingly hinted that a robbery was not likely the culprit.

Without picking up a thing, and walking very cautiously, Meredith made her way into the Family Room—the crunching under her feet, unsettling. There she saw the smashed flat screen and the broken beer bottles. There were open bags of chips and half-eaten frozen burritos both strewn on the table and littered on the floor. She moved to their bedroom.

What greeted her was a scene straight out of the Exorcist. Pools of dried vomit seemed everywhere, from the bed, to the floor, to the walls. A ball of sheets sat in one of those puddles. A half-drunk bottle of vodka tipped precariously on the bedside table. God, it was hot, too. The window heater was turned up to 90, and the whole room felt like it was melting. She instantly felt nauseous, and put her hand to her mouth covering her nose. Meredith gagged as she hurtled back out to the kitchen. She caught her breath, and tried her best to regain some semblance of composure. "Not in here," she thought as she headed directly for the door leading outside to the fresh fall mountain air.

It took her twenty minutes to calm down and assess the environment that she found herself in. Meredith paced around the yard thinking. Bobbie had been treating her with increased hostility and irritability recently. She was sure he had a drinking problem, but he always drank more to relieve stress during the football season, and that got worse during the playoffs. It would subside as each athletic year came to a close…until preseason practice commenced. But, this? Maybe she was to blame. Bobbie had the weight of the world on his shoulders. The school, the parents and community at large had now turned to expect winners of the

Grizzlies—no…State Champions, every year now. Perhaps she wasn't being the understanding and supportive wife she needed to be.

Turning towards the carport, she saw something on the ground. As she approached, Meredith couldn't quite make out what it was, but saw that there was some writing in the earth in front of where she usually parked her car. As she knelt down, she saw the word "CUNT" scrawled haphazardly in the dirt. And, next to it, was a hypodermic needle.

Meredith dialed the police, but after two rings, hung up. Shit. She had to clear her head and think about this. Don't do anything rash. She then called Carlos, the security guard at the school. Like her, he had a second job to make ends meet. He had a janitorial service in town, and a small crew of hourly workers that he could call on to help with unexpected challenges.

"Carlos? This is Meredith Edmonson. You know, from school?"

"Oh yes, Mrs. Coach! How are you? I mean, uh, hello!" he said a little uneasily.

"Carlos, I need some help, and I need you to keep this a secret, OK?" Meredith pleaded.

"Sure. What can I help you with?" Carlos was now serious.

"It seems some kids broke into our home, drank our liquor and made a mess of the place—including smashing our TV. I saw Bobbie, er, I mean Mr. Edmonson, as he was leaving for the game this afternoon. It's just too much for me to handle. And, Bob, I mean Mr. Edmonson, will be so angry if he comes home to find his house all torn up. Can you come over as soon as possible and professionally clean the house from top to bottom?" Meredith was almost pleading.

"Well, yes, Mrs. Edmonson, I might be able to get some guys over to your place, but I am on my way to the big game myself. Coach got me some tickets, and I am halfway to Silverton as we speak. When do you want a crew there?"

"Tonight at the latest. It will take hours to clean, disinfect and straighten everything up. I want the house spotless when Mr. Edmonson arrives home tomorrow after the game."

"Let me make a couple of calls and get back to you, OK?"

"Sure, Carlos. Thank you. Let me know, privately, how much I owe you. I owe you more than your fee, by the way. And please, do not tell Mr. Edmonson."

"Don't worry about a thing, Mrs. Edmonson. I'll take care of it." Carlos hung up.

Meredith waited a few seconds before she, too, hung up. She bent over and picked up the syringe and brushed her foot over the writing by the carport. She took off her sweater and wrapped the sleeve around her face inhaling deeply before rushing back into the house. Once inside, she rushed to each room opening windows and turning off the room heaters. She then made her way to Bobbie's weapon closet. It was locked, but she knew where the key was in his top dresser drawer. The stench overcame her again, and she hastily made her way back outside once more.

She was shaking now—not sure if it was the cold or whether she was in shock. Probably, a little of both.

Her phone rang. It was Carlos. A crew of four men would be there within the hour. Meredith thanked him profusely, and then asked him, again, to keep this strictly between them. He said, "Of course. I have also told my men to not mention anything about this project. In fact, none of them know who you are." Meredith found that hard to believe that anyone in town would not know Coach Edmonson, but she had no choice but to trust Carlos.

She took another deep breath and headed back in. She fit the key into the exterior padlock and swung the door open. Inside, were Bobbie's two rifles—both with hunting scopes—and his real treasure: his hunting bow—which also had a scope - and a large quiver of razor-tipped, barbed, and blood-stained arrows. She shook her head, and closed the closet door and locked it. She then went to her dresser and pulled out a new change of clothes.

● ● ●

Meredith got in her car, and drove three country miles to another dead neighborhood. She pulled over and stopped by a brown, thirsty, weed-choked, lot and rested her forehead on the steering wheel. The tears came easily. In waves. She allowed herself to feel the depths of her sadness ripple up from her chest and convulse her. The sobs were un-abating. She didn't care. She had held it together for so long, but now the truth of her pathetic life, trapped here in Grand Junction, rocked her soul. Meredith felt there was nothing left—just emptiness, loneliness and hopelessness.

"How, in God's name, did I get myself into this situation?" she thought. She thought back to her interviews with the school, and the people she had met. How many years ago was it? Six years? Seven? It was the only job offer she had received, and although it was a far cry from the fast-paced and exciting world she knew in New York, she accepted the position because she needed the money. She planned on working in Colorado for five years, and then move back to the Big Apple—or another big city—in a role far better suited to her degrees in Dance from Julliard and Education at NYU—and far more exciting. But, what she hadn't planned on was meeting the local head football coach, a whirlwind romance and marriage.

Sitting up now, she put her head back against the headrest and closed her burning eyes. She tried to pull the memories of last Thursday night back so that she could once again roll them around in her mind. Who was this man? He couldn't stop asking questions about me. Not just superficial me, but *me*—who I was, what I loved, what passions made me tick. We talked about our joys, our fears, our likes and dislikes, and how we saw the world. "Come to think of it, I think we talked mostly about MY joys, fears, dislikes, etc. I don't recall much at all about him," Meredith thought. What was it about him that I remember? He was really good looking, older. He was clearly successful. But, more than anything, he was present with me. He took the time to listen, and ask, and comfort, and have some very light-hearted moments. Was that it? It was so light hearted. She couldn't remember the last time she had felt this way. And that kiss. And the embrace…it had felt so natural.

The sadness came back to her as the reality of her life hit her again. Here she was, sitting in her vehicle, crying, in a one-horse town, married to a bastard whose entire ambition was to get a promotion to a junior college football program—or worse, get a raise and stay here. Meredith took another forced breath, followed by another. She looked in the mirror, and was appalled by what she saw: a tragically sad woman whose vulnerable eyes projected her complete unhappiness.

It was then that her phone beeped with a new text message. It was from Jess.

25

JESSICA

JAZZ HAD GONE TO BED, AND JESSICA AND MEREDITH SAT ON THE couch that would later tonight be Meredith's bed. Jess had opened another bottle of wine, and the two of them perched themselves across from each other, legs folded underneath them. Jess had spent twenty minutes comforting Meredith when she had first appeared at her doorstep. The tears returned with Meredith - having not the willpower or the desire to stop them. Just seeing Jess seemed to break the dam. But, she was calmer now; emotionally exhausted.

Jessica told Meredith about her day, and about the stranger that came for a visit. She described the man, and Meredith couldn't remember seeing anyone like him in town. But, she was happy to hear a story that took her mind off her ransacked house, and her catastrophic marriage. But, as the story continued to unfold, Meredith became more intrigued with what was in the envelope.

"Jess, what have you gotten yourself in to?" Meredith asked.

"Well," Jessica replied as she reached behind the couch and pulled out the original white envelope, "maybe you can tell ME?"

Jessica handed the envelope, addressed to her, to Meredith. The look on Meredith's face was utter surprise. She hesitantly reached for the envelope, took it and placed it in her lap face up. Jess had reinserted the contents. Turning it over, Meredith reached in and drew out the inner envelope. She read the cover. Nervously, she slowly unsealed it.

"Wait," Jessica interrupted. Meredith stopped. "That is addressed to you, and it is quite clear that it is confidential and personal. How about I go fetch us something to eat, and let you read this alone?"

"No way, Jess. You are my best friend, and you have always been there for me. We have no secrets. In fact, I am not sure I could open this alone."

And with that, Meredith opened her envelope and pulled out a typed note. She silently read—and re-read—the note several times. She shook her head slowly back and forth—her eyes staring straight down to the floor.

"Holy shit," was all she could think of to say.

26

MEREDITH

M,

If you are reading this, then my friend and associate, Nick, was successful in delivering this to your contact, Jessica, at Sunset Gardens, and she, in turn, was successful in delivering it to you. Nick is 100% trustworthy, and is extremely reliable. I am sorry if his visit in any way upset your friend.

I cannot keep you, or our wonderfully carefree evening together, out of my mind. You are so full of life and joy, and you sparked in me a very warm fire that has brought a long-forgotten smile to my face. I remember vividly holding you in my arms, and the feel of you next to me. And, I just can't shake the sweet, soft, taste of you.

I would like to see you again. If this is not possible, I completely understand; it's a lot for me to ask. But, there is so much more of you that I want to explore.

Come with me on this unexpected journey…

G

PS: If you want to connect, please set up a new and anonymous, untraceable, email address, that only you will be able to access, and send it to me at gquest100@hotmail.com. Do not sign your name.

PPS: I have never done this before, and I am very nervous (being 100% honest).

• • •

Jessica sat there quietly respecting her friend's obviously intimate moment. Then she got up and went to the kitchen to refill their wine glasses.

"I felt it, Jess," Meredith said too quietly for Jessica to hear. She was breathing heavily now shaking her head. She dropped the note to the floor, and grabbed an overstuffed pillow and pulled it to her chest. Resting her cheek on the side of it, she laid it down on her lap and closed her weary eyes. The next thing she felt was the warmth of Jessica sitting next to her, and her hand massaging her shoulder.

"Hey, babe…you OK?" Jessica spoke softly.

Meredith didn't raise her head at first. She nodded into the pillow. After a few seconds, she raised her head up and looked at Jessica. "I think I am dreaming. Both nightmare and fantasy. At the same time. No one would ever believe that the things that happened to me today, all happened to me—all…in…one…day." She said it without emotion, and she said it directly to Jessica—even though her eyes seemed focused far away. The note remained on the floor, face down.

Finally, Meredith sat back, and still clutching the pillow, said, "How about that refill?"

Jessica laughed, and that seemed to break the mood for both of them. Meredith started to laugh, too—softly. "God. Help me!"

Jess leaned over and picked up the two full glasses, and gave Meredith's to her. "So, girlfriend, you going to let me in on your little secret?"

Meredith picked up the note from the floor, and handed it to her friend. She watched the changing expressions as Jess read. When she was done, she looked up and they locked eyes.

27

SUSIE

WEEKS HAD PASSED SINCE GEOFF HAD FIXED HER DINNER. HE LOVED to do that for her, she knew, but he really wasn't that great a cook. She winced with every bite knowing that he had used too much butter, too much salt, not enough organic vegetables and was careless about preservatives. "How in the world am I going to keep this figure?" she said aloud. "The girls at spin class are going to start looking at me funny."

She didn't know exactly why she reacted this way. She was almost resentful. Her therapist said it was a childhood thing. "You know, it all comes back to your upbringing," she would say. "You are too obsessed with your health. But, this shouldn't result in these kinds of feelings. You must be allowing some other Freudian unhappiness boil to the surface."

Susie did her best to mask her growing unease. Geoff traveled a lot, and he never seemed to have enough time to take care of the job list she prepared for him while he was away. He said he loved yard work, and being her handyman, but the lawn always needed mowing, and you know, a rake would be a good thing to use now and then. The kids made her feel like a very unappreciated hired driver. She was constantly exhausted. Get up in the morning. Get dressed. Give Rosanne instructions on grocery shopping and what menu's to prepare for the day. See the kids off to school. Run over to spin class or yoga—depending on the gym's schedule. National Charity League meetings followed by another boring lunch out somewhere with one of her dozens of girl friends. That would take her to pick-up duties and shuttling the kids to their activities: baseball practice for CJ, and whatever the girls were up to on the day. There was hardly enough time for her weekly manicure, facial and hair appointments.

What happened to her dreams of becoming a lawyer? Having a life of her own, and a professional identity? Those early days of being a librarian while studying for her GMAT's were so full of promise. "I busted my tail at Stanford to be a home-bound, housewife?" she mused frequently.

She was so busy these days, and Geoff was always off gallivanting around the world "doing deals," staying in 5-star hotels and dining out at the nicest restaurants. At least that's what she thought. He called and texted several times a day. And, he always came home so happy to see her and the kids. He treated her the best he knew how. It just didn't feel to her that she was getting the most out of her mundane life. The unhappiness often gripped her, but she willed it away.

And, he always wanted to have sex with her before he left on a trip—and particularly when he got home. Didn't he understand? He was off having the time of his life while she was tied to this house and the kids. She only wanted to have sex when she felt particularly close to him—usually when they were away at a resort, by themselves, without the distractions of his work, or of the house or parenting.

Susie particularly liked the combination of being on Geoff's arm, in very public settings, wearing the expensive necklace or bracelet he seemed to often surprise her with. She loved being the envy of every woman in the room. Yep, those nights she would happily put out for him—even if she really wasn't in the mood. Hell, she could fake her orgasms like the best of them.

●　●　●

Susie was sweating heavily, and was out of breath. She wasn't sure she could go on, but she was in the front of the class with her Spin instructor in front of her and most of her classmates behind. If she gave up, she would be embarrassed and humiliated. So, she slowly let up on her pace and kept her head down.

The pounding beat finally stopped, and the Spin master told everyone to reduce their speed, pedal slowly and take five minutes to cool down. Relief at last!

"Hey, Susie, nice article on one Mr. Cameron!" exclaimed a voice directly behind her.

Susie turned around and saw two rows back that snooty bitch, Rhonda; Rhonda with the fake smile and tits. She was married to a real estate broker, and always seemed to have the latest Mercedes, the newest clothes and dirt on someone. She appeared to live to absorb gossip and pass it along to anyone who remotely cared.

"What article?" Susie inquired.

Oh, just the New York Times. Front page, Business Section. He's a hottie—that husband of yours."

"I didn't know that the two of you had met," Susie replied dryly.

"We haven't. But, I'd like to some day. His picture was splashed on the front page with the article. Let's just say I wouldn't be climbing over him to get to my husband!" Rhonda broke into a hearty laugh. "I'd keep a close eye on him if I were you."

"Seems like all I have to do is keep him away from you," Susie smiled. She wanted to add, "But he wouldn't be interested in some cheap trick like you." But she kept her socially trained mouth shut.

Rhonda carried on loudly so that all near them could hear her saying, "Article says he is one of the pre-eminent venture capitalists in America, and even speculated that your—I mean, the Company's—net worth was in the tens of billions. *Billions* with a B. What are you doing here hanging out with us common folk?" There were a few chuckles.

Susie was at a loss for words. On one hand, she enjoyed rubbing Rhonda's face in her affluence, but on the other, she preferred to keep their wealth a relative secret. "Can you email me a copy of the article? I would love to read it. Geoff, and his company, are in the press a lot these days, and he didn't mention that he was interviewed by the New York Times."

"Sure," Rhonda replied. "I'll get it to you today. Say, when are you going to sell that dump in Tiburon, and move in with the real movers and shakers in Atherton?"

Susie had just about had enough. Unfortunately, people like Rhonda neither had a muzzle nor a filter, so Susie replied, "Oh, thanks for the real estate advice." And knowing that her husband was a sleazy residential agent, she added, "We love Tiburon just fine. And, if we ever decide to move to the sleepy, land-locked, confines of Atherton, where acreage and hedgerows define families, we will definitely call a broker." Implied in the statement was that it wouldn't be Rhonda's husband. But Susie said so with a light smile and a laugh. Rhonda was so clueless.

Later in the afternoon, Susie's phone chimed indicating a text message. It was from Rhonda. Attached was the scanned New York Times article, and the photo, with a brief message that said, "The HUNK of 5th Ave!"

Susie took some time to study the picture. At 45, her husband was certainly in his prime. She knew the photograph well; it was the stock shot the public relations firm had arranged and promoted. But, it showed Geoff at his best with a serious expression, gazing off into the distance, wind blowing his thick salt-and-pepper hair back off his handsome face as though he were piloting an America's Cup sloop across Australia's Sydney Harbor. The wrinkles at his eyes showed an equal bias for laughter as seriousness.

The article was just as flattering. While largely talking about Geoff's firm, CBC, and the recent rumors surrounding his company's latest quest: the acquisition of a medium-sized petroleum cleansing firm, Hudson Environmental, based in Colorado, it also touched on Geoff's personal life. This surprised Susie as Geoff was militaristically careful about keeping his family out of the press. It didn't say much, but while answering an inquiry as to what drove him to be so successful, it quoted Geoff as saying, "My family is everything to me. They are the sole reason I work as hard as I do. When I die, I want to be remembered, not as an internationally recognized businessman, but rather as a cherished dad to my kids and dedicated husband to my spouse."

"I wonder why he never mentioned this to me?" Susie thought. "I guess I'm going to have to get him laid tonight," she smirked. "If I'm lucky, that will only take a few minutes."

28

BOBBIE

IT WAS SATURDAY, EARLY EVENING, AND THE RAIN HAD HELD UP. THE game was now late in the Third Quarter, and the Grizzlies were taking their vengeance out on the seemingly defenseless Silverton Bullets. The score was 45-0; yet, Bobbie paced the sideline like an uncaged lion. In equal measure, he was shouting instructions to his boys, berating the referees, insulting the opposition and flirting with the cheerleaders. Clearly, Bobbie was in his element.

A year ago, the game was a nail-biter, and the Bullets handed the Grizzlies their only loss of the season. While it didn't steal the league championship from Bobbie's Granite High, it was an embarrassing loss at the Grizzlies' home field that smashed his ego and threatened, at least in his mind, the negotiations for a renewal, and extension, of his coaching contract.

There was suddenly a time-out called by the referees, and both coaches were called to the middle of the field for a conference. The players were asked to retreat to their respective sidelines out of earshot.

The Head Referee for the game, Eldon Banks, spoke first as he addressed Bobbie saying, "Coach Edmonson, Coach Norris here wants to call the game on account of his players' safety. Many of their starters are banged up pretty good, and their second and third string players are too small to face your team safely."

"We will forfeit the game," Coach Banks said as he held out his hand to Bobbie to shake. "Well played."

Bobbie looked at the outstretched hand, and turned and spat on the ground. "Like hell you will," he said as he lifted his gaze to meet that of the opposing coach. "Last year, you embarrassed us at our home field, and while the score was close, we played every down until the clock determined the game was over. Now, you want to deprive my boys of the revenge they so definitely deserve?"

The opposing coach was calm and professional when he replied, "Bob, I'm not asking for your permission. I'm telling you that I am calling the game right here and now—for the safety of my players. If you do not want to shake my hand, that's up to you. But, YOU are depriving your boys of a moment of sportsmanship that your teams have, over the years, sorely lacked."

Bobbie moved threateningly closer to Coach Banks. The referees, who were largely weekend volunteers, didn't move to separate them. "You know what? The reason your team is made up of a bunch of faggots is because you are such a pussy. Wouldn't it be a novel idea to teach these boys how to be men? Let the game continue."

Coach Banks, took a step back, and was calm as he replied, "This game, both on and off this field, is…"

He never saw the punch coming. The crack on the side of his jaw was sickening. The Bullets' head coach's eyes rolled back into their sockets, and he twisted slightly and fell forward—Bobbie stepping aside to avoid contact with the falling body. Coach Banks toppled like a ragdoll, face first, striking the turf with his forehead, and lay motionless on the ground. The referees stepped in and bear-hugged Bobbie pulling him away from the heap on the ground. But it was, as everyone in the stadium realized, too late.

Players and coaches from the Silverton bench ran to assist their fallen head coach. As Bobbie struggled free out of the grasp of the referees, he strode towards his bench with his right fist clenched and held high. His uncontrollable outburst was witnessed by a stunned and silent audience in the bleachers, but his team, in unison, cheered and ran towards their coach surrounding him with raised helmets, chanting, "Grizz-lies! Grizz-lies! Grizz-lies!"

The cheerleaders, unaware of the full impact of the situation, faced the crowd and commenced one of their favorite cheers: "Blood makes the grass grow! Grizz-lies! Grizz-lies! Blood makes the grass grow!" The relative silence in the stands only made the girls yell louder and try even harder to get the parents and guests fired up.

The public-address announcer informed the crowd that the game had been forfeited, and the victory had been conceded to the Granite High Grizzlies of Grand Junction. The Grizzly spectators were now fully animated with a miasma of jubilation, shock, inquiry and gossip. Bobbie gathered his team around him on the field, as was customary after each game, for the post-game pep-talk. "We…

are…the…CHAMPIONS!" Bobbie yelled. A big cheer arose from the circled players. "You earned this with your hard work, your hard nose, your hard hits and your hard playing. Let this be a lesson for ANYONE, or ANY team who dares challenge the Grizzlies: your jaws will be bloodied! And we will rip you apart piece by piece!" The boys started chanting again, "JAWS! JAWS! JAWS! JAWS!"

"OK, boys, time to shower and celebrate! Everyone…to the locker room!" Bobbie demanded; his smile wide. The cheerleaders were still leading cheers for the parents that lingered after the game—many of whom had hotel rooms and were staying over to celebrate together - driving home in the morning.

As the boys cheered and cleared the field and ran for the visitors' quarters, Coach Eldon Banks was being assisted off the field by two men who looked back over their shoulders as the Grizzlies dispersed. They wanted to get a good look at the man they intended to have arrested and sued on behalf of their school and coach. But that man was paying no attention to their side of the field. In fact, he was heading over to the stands to join the post-game rally.

A huge cheer erupted when Bobbie strode up to the fans. He raised both arms in the air, Rocky Balboa style, and let out a huge "whoop" which lathered up the crowd. The band was playing the team's fight song for the fourth time, and the fans were lapping it all up.

Then, the band grew silent, and after everyone had quieted, the band started in on Granite High's alma mater. Bobbie stepped up to the line of cheerleaders, found Gabby and landed next to her. He put his arm around her waist placing his hand a little too close to the top of her butt. She turned in surprise, and when she saw the coach, broke into a joyous smile. "Congratulations, Coach!" she squealed—the band drowning out her words.

As they sang, everyone swayed back and forth singing at the top of their lungs. The swaying allowed Bobbie to move his hand lower on Gabby's backside, and either she didn't feel it, or she didn't care.

Up in the stands, a relative stranger lurked near the top row somewhat removed from the throng of excited parents. Dr. Spencer Miller, D-Spencer to his "friends," surveyed the scene keenly. He had witnessed the mid-field altercation. The concern he felt was problematic. For the past year, he had been supplying the team, through Coach Edmonson, Human Growth Hormone to bulk up the key physical players—specifically the linemen on offense and defense, and the linebackers. Their coach had requested an extra allotment for his injured players so that they could recover more quickly. But, it soon became evident that Coach Edmonson was using the drug himself. He was bulking up with unnaturally shaped muscles, and was doing nothing to hide his new physique. In fact, the small, tight, t-shirts he wore could well have been a neon sign flashing arrows at his chest. But, what worried Dr. Miller the most was the irrational and volatile personality that Coach Edmonson was exhibiting.

Football practices had been filled with outbursts, and even unprovoked violence, witnessed only by his players and coaches—except when Doc Spencer secretly visited. But, it was today's game, and the game-ending fight, that worried Dr. Miller the most. Going nuts in such a public setting, coupled with his new body and persona, would lead even the most inexperienced observer to deduce that the coach was juicing with HGH.

He would have to cut him off. As the celebrations continued, Dr. Spencer Miller turned and quietly exited the stands and headed for his car.

● ● ●

The alma mater was coming to a close. The band finished with a resounding crescendo and everyone turned to high-five, or hug, their neighbor. Bobbie turned and embraced Gabby—placing one hand behind her shoulder blades, and the other on the small of her back. He drew her tightly to him so that her ample young breasts pressed against his chest. He whispered in her ear, "Hey Gabs, come by my room tonight after the team dinner, OK? I have a surprise for you to give to the girls, but I want it to be given to them by you, the Cheer Team Captain."

Gabby blushed, and said with an abundance of enthusiasm, "Sure, Coach Edmonson! What time?"

Bobbie replied, "How about coming over twenty minutes after the bus drops everyone back at the motel? And, Gabby, remember: don't tell anyone about our little surprise."

"OK! Cool! Thanks, Coach! See you later!" And with that, Gabby was off chasing after her friends who had already headed for the team bus to be there when the players emerged from the locker room.

Bobbie finally turned around to jog off the field to join his players in celebration. He had his speech ready. As he turned, he was surprised by a man, not thirty feet away, holding up his iPhone obviously snapping a picture. At first, Bobbie thought this must be an adoring fan, but Bobbie knew all the parents, and didn't recognize him. "Can I help you?" Bobbie said with a sharper edge in his voice than what he intended.

"Nope. Just getting your picture is all," the man replied. "For our lawyers."

"Fuck you!" Bobbie blurted. "Your fucking coach started the entire alter-cation. He made inciteful comments that were personally injurious to me, my team and our community. Go ahead and fucking sue me you little maggot piece of shit!"

The stranger turned, without saying a word, and walked off. There were sirens in the distance.

● ● ●

The team dinner was a wild affair with the compulsory food fight, toasts, cheers and unabated yelling, laughter—and if you were a parent or coach, drinking. Bobbie spoke glowingly about his team, the upcoming State Championship play-offs and the support he felt from all the parents and the entire Grand Junction community. He was liberal with his praise, and just as liberal with his drinking. He was having a particularly good time. He knew that with this victory, he would be insisting on a new, lucrative, five-year, no-cut, contract. And, the school—if they wanted to keep someone as talented as he was—would have to pony up the big bucks. It was his time.

He rose to his feet once again and silenced the room as best he could. "I just want to send a shout-out to our fabulous cheerleaders!" The room erupted again, and Gabby beamed as she looked towards the coach catching his eye. "You girls are the heart and soul of Grizzly Pride, and your spirit has lifted us all season long! Please know that you had a lot to do with our winning the League Championship this year!" Bobbie raised his left hand in the air and yelled, "Let's hear it for our cheer squad!" The room returned to its pandemonium and raucous celebrations.

Bobbie slipped away from his table after this latest toast, and went to the bathroom where he shut himself in the far stall—the stall clearly marked for handicapped users. Fuck the cripples. Reaching into his jacket pocket, he pulled out a baggie of colored pills. The booze he'd been drinking brought forth an almost uncontrollable laugh that he tried to stifle. Reaching into the baggie he grabbed a pink pill, his Viagra, and contemplated taking a yellow Percocet—a prescription pain medication that he used recreationally, but decided against it. He needed to be lucid enough to address the team before boarding the bus, and to be able to talk coherently on the way to the hotel. After that, he didn't care. He also checked his bag of pills for the little white ones. Bingo. There were four of them. He would only need one. He placed the Viagra on his tongue, and swallowed it without water.

Bobbie's phone pinged. He was sitting on the toilet with his pants still but-toned up, and he stood, reached into his pocket and looked at his phone. A text. Meredith. "Heard you won. Congrats" was all it said.

"Congrats? ConGRATS? Is that all you can think to say?" Bobbie said under his breath. He kept mumbling, "Gee, this only means a big promotion, a new house, and a new life for us. Maybe, just maybe, you'll want to thank me for all I have done for you. The way I like to be thanked."

The door to the bathroom opened, and one of the Grizzly players stuck his head in saying, "Coach? You in here? The bus is loaded and we all want to leave." The door closed. Bobbie didn't respond.

When he was alone again, Bobbie got up and stuffed his baggie back in his front pocket. He looked at his phone again, and without responding, tucked it, too, into his jeans. "Bitch," was all he could think to say. Without knowing why, he turned around and flushed the unused toilet. He washed his hands at the sink, and headed out to join his peeps. A smile came to his face. Gabby.

29

GEOFF

IT WAS MID-WEEK, TWO WEEKS AFTER NICK'S TRIP BACK TO GRAND Junction. Geoff had set up his new private email account with a secret password known only to him: 1003in2014!—the date he and Meredith had enjoyed their chance meeting. But, although he checked the email every day—sometimes several times a day—there was nothing. With each passing day, Geoff second-guessed himself. It started with a surprisingly emotional self-evaluation of his morals and his marriage. What in the world had he done? What was he thinking? Those same questions he had asked himself as he lay awake in that Grand Junction hotel suite. Susie had done nothing wrong to deserve this betrayal. Now he had sent a hard-copy message to a complete stranger with whom he had had a brief emotional affair with. Nothing had happened, but still…

As the days and weeks passed, he largely forgot about his encounter. He was enormously busy at work, and CBC was in the process of evaluating eight new opportunities. He had been to London, New York and Atlanta—rarely sleeping. He loved chasing opportunities, and his recent travels had been exciting. If only Susie appreciated him more. "What would it take for her to greet me when I came home, and actually be legitimately happy to see me?" Geoff wondered.

• • •

Tonight, Geoff had arrived home early—for him—at 6:30 PM to barbeque for the family. When he walked in from the garage, he noticed that Susie's Range Rover had a slightly dented rear bumper. He came in the back door, and was greeted by a platter of fish and chicken thrust at him. He grabbed the plate from his passing wife. "You're late. Here's our dinner. You better hurry up and light the barbeque."

Geoff had just landed two hours ago after a grueling three days of negotiations on the disposition of one of their underperforming assets. The meetings had gone well, but Geoff was road weary and exhausted. He put the platter down, and slowly walked to the front hall, took off his overcoat and hung it in the large coat closet. He then returned with a smile on his face, and walked up behind Susie as she stood stirring something on the stove. He slipped his arms around her, and gently hugged her. He kissed the back of her neck softly, and took the large spoon out of her hand. He turned her around so that they were facing each other. Still holding her around the waist, he looked into her eyes and said, "Hi, Baby. It's great to be home. Thanks for preparing dinner."

Susie allowed herself a hint of a smile. "It's nice to have you home for a change, too," she replied. "Now, go light that fire, or we will be eating at midnight."

"Of course," Geoff said. He leaned forward to kiss her on the lips, but Susie was on the move already and had turned. The peck landed on her cheek. She stopped, looked at him with a smirk, and patted him twice on the chest and nodded. She leaned back and pecked him on the lips.

"I know what you are thinking. Don't get any ideas," she dryly intoned, and turned around and started stirring whatever it was she had going on the stove. "God, he's going to want to have sex again," she thought. "I just got him laid a couple of weeks ago."

Just then, he heard footsteps pounding overhead, and the loud shrieking voices of his daughters shrieking almost in unison, "Daaaaaaaaaaaaaddy's hoooooooooome!" They came bounding down the stairs and tore into the kitchen—each grabbing him with arms around him and peals of laughter.

"How was your trip? Where did you go? Did you get to fly on the small jet? Did Mom tell you about hitting the post with her car? Did you hear that CJ drove in the winning run at his game? Can you help me with my homework?" The questions were fast and furious—and delightfully welcome. He missed his kids especially on these weeks when he was away a lot. He felt like he was missing their entire childhood.

He gave them both a hug together and each one their own special hug before Susie interrupted them. "Enough girls. I need your Dad to barbeque our dinner. Don't distract him; he needs to pay attention to the grill or we will have our usual charcoal-crusted, overdone, meat. I'll call you when dinner is ready. Now, get back to your homework."

Geoff, letting go of his girls said, "It's so great to see you. I've missed you and your mom. I'm glad I'm home," making eye contact with them both. "We'll call you when I am done burning up our dinner!" The girls each laughed and kissed him on the cheek, and they skipped their way back upstairs to their respective rooms.

Geoff went over to the large island in the middle of the kitchen, and opened the bottom drawer that held a variety of odds and ends. He fetched out his apron and slipped it over his head. He struggled a bit trying to tie it in back, but·Susie was oblivious to his challenge. He finally got it fastened tying a knot instead of a bow, but nevertheless was pleased with his triumph. He grabbed the platter on the counter, and headed out to the barbeque.

Once there, he reached into the outdoor refrigerator, and pulled out a nice bottle of Chardonnay which he opened on the spot. Pulling a wine glass from the cabinet, he poured himself a glass, swirled it and took an immediate sniff from the top of the glass. It smelled great.

He lit the fire, and instead of heading back into the house, he stayed outside with his wine and his cell phone. It was a good time for him to reflect on his trip, and answer any new emails that had come in during the past hour. He grabbed his wine glass and his cell phone and powered up the screen. It was then he saw it. A little envelope icon. This one in the unusual bottom right position on his screen. His breath caught in his throat. His reflex reaction was to look back towards the kitchen. "That was foolish," he thought. "I am so far away from the kitchen that no one inside would know if I were here or not—let alone see if I am reading an email. And, who cares? I am always reading email, everywhere." The guilt he felt was palpable, and his heart was racing. He looked once more towards the kitchen, then, touched the envelope icon. It asked for his password.

> From: mquest99@aol.com
> Subject: It's Me
> Date: November 14, 2014 at 7:42 PM MST
> To: gquest100@hotmail.com
> G,
> So wonderful to get your note. Jessica gave it to me unopened. She's a great friend. But, she did call the security guards on your delivery boy! Who are you, really? James Bond? ☺

Can I start by saying that you have totally tipped my world upside
down? How was it possible for you to just appear in my life the way
that it happened? And to think that I stopped in that night just to get a
quick bite to eat. I can hardly stop thinking about our time together.
Yes, I would love to see you again.
My next question (be 100% honest!): But how?!
Your "unexpected journey" is unexplained…
Sorry it took me so long to reply. I think I have been in a state of
self-inflicted shock.
Please write me back. Hurry.
M

Geoff read and re-read the note numerous times—alternately looking up at
the stars above him, and staring into his wine glass. He felt flush; his heart was
racing, and for the first time in his adult life he felt something akin to being
naughty. But, the excitement, and the urgency to reply, were spinning his mind.

"Geoff!" came Susie's voice yelling from far away as she popped her head out
the back door. "Don't burn the chicken! And you sure as hell better not scorch the
fish. I like there to be a bit of moisture left in mine!" She popped right back inside.

He snapped his head up to attention. "Shit!" He breathed as he looked at
the grill expecting to see black smoke billowing skyward. Instead, he stared in
relative disbelief at the platter which still stood on the counter with the raw meat
untouched—and uncooked. He turned down the fire on the grill and took the
spatula and laid each piece carefully out to cook. He picked his phone back up,
and immediately texted Susie. "Don't worry; slow cooking; being xtra careful." He
then logged back in to his special secret account, and read, again, the note from
Meredith.

30

GABBY

GABBY WAS MORE THAN A LITTLE BUZZED. SHE HAD SECRETLY MET up with a few other cheerleaders and a number of players in one of the boys' motel rooms, and they had had a few beers and some tequila shots. The mood was rowdy. The Grizzlies had just won their biggest game of the year, and many of the boys and girls in the room, including Gabby, were seniors soon heading off to college or work. They weren't just feeling like adults, they were LIVING like adults—free and uninhibited. The laughter and shouting was getting louder, and none of the kids thought much about toning it down. The motel also housed parents and school staff, but they didn't care. They were having their own parties

Gabby looked at her watch. "Shit! I'm late!" she exclaimed, but no one seemed to hear. She moved over and sat on the arm of the couch next to Lily, her roommate for the night. "Hey, Lills. I'm going out for a bit to get a surprise for everyone. I may be a little late, OK?"

Lily looked at her with an expression of surprise. "Where you going, Gabs? We're having so much fun here. It's going to get wild!"

Gabby put her arm around her friend's neck, and spoke into her ear, "You can't tell anyone, 'kay? Coach Edmonson has gotten a surprise for all the cheerleaders, and he wants me to come by and pick it up. I don't know what it is, or anything. Don't know if we are going out to a store. Anyway, I'm already late. Don't worry about me, and don't tell anyone, 'kay?"

Lily hugged her without getting up from the couch. As one of the boys handed Lily another beer, Gabby slipped out the door and headed for Coach Edmonson's room.

• • •

There was a soft knock on Bobbie's door. He looked at his watch; 10:47 PM. He got up, and opened the door. Gabby stood there, still in her cheerleader outfit—the letters GHS in gray and blue across her ample chest.

"Gabby! Come on in," said Bobbie warmly. He stood aside so that Gabby could enter.

"Hi, Coach! Great game!" was all that Gabby could think of to say as she came in and stood at the middle of the room. She waited for Coach Edmonson's reply feeling a little awkward.

"Thanks, Gabby. You sure did one hell of a job today, and we all so appreciate the spirit that you girls showed tonight—and frankly, all during the season."

Gabby blushed feeling very happy, and if the truth be known, she was feeling very grown up and appreciated.

"Come on in and sit down," Bobbie motioned to the couch. "Would you like something to drink?" As Gabby sat on the couch, Bobbie moved to the counter in the kitchen, and grabbed two glasses out of the cupboard. He filled them both with ice. "Well?" he repeated.

"Sure. Do you have a soft drink? A Coke or something?" Gabby answered.

"Gabby, I want you to listen to me, OK? You are eighteen years old, old enough to fight in a war and vote. You can smoke. Pot. You are legally an adult, and can do anything you want to do, right? It is legal to drink at eighteen in almost every other country in the world except this stupid country of America. You following me?"

Gabby fidgeted looking down at her hands; she was unaware that she was wringing them. "I'm only seventeen, Coach," she replied without looking up.

Bobbie walked over to her, and placed his hand under her chin and lifted it up so that they were looking at each other. "Gabby, you are old enough in my book. You are a beautiful young woman. Emphasis on 'woman.' I can tell that you have already been drinking, too."

Gabby looked away saying, "I'm so sorry, I'm so…"

"Gabby, look at me." She lifted her gaze to meet his eyes. "I won't tell anyone, OK? And to prove it, let's have a drink here. It will be our little secret, OK?" Gabby remained silent. Bobbie poured himself a generous portion of bourbon into one of the glasses. He picked it up and swirled the brown liquid around in his glass, smelled it by inhaling deeply and after sighing, took a healthy sip. "What can I fix for you?"

Gabby felt more than uneasy. Her instincts were telling her she was in the wrong place at the wrong time. But, she did like Coach a lot, and he was getting a gift for all of her friends. He was really cool, too. He had always been nice to her—albeit a little "handsy" and flirtatious. But all boys treated her that way. She had gotten used to them staring at her tits or her ass. If she was being truthful, she loved the attention.

"How about vodka and Red Bull? Do you have that?" she found herself saying. But, as soon as it was out of her mouth, she felt so grown up—and frankly excited.

"No Red Bull, but I do have Coke. I can mix that with vodka or rum. What do you think?" he said.

"Vodka. I'll have Coke with Vodka, thanks."

Bobbie poured a small amount of vodka into a glass, and from the fridge retrieved a can of Coke. Popping the top, he filled her glass. Handing it to her, he said, "Stir that with your finger."

She did as she was told, and put her finger into her mouth to clean it. That simple gesture aroused Bobbie, and he could immediately feel a tightening in his jeans.

"Hey Coach, can I use your bathroom?" Gabby asked.

"Sure. It's in my bedroom. Sorry if it is a little dirty."

Gabby took a swallow of her drink, and said, "Thanks Coach, I'll be right back." She stood and walked through the doorway to Bobbie's room. She looked around as she headed towards the bathroom. She noted his duffle on the bed with clothes strewn haphazardly around it. She also noticed a syringe on the bedside table. That surprised her, but she had to pee, and was not thinking straight anyway. She still had a good buzz going, and she was looking forward to finishing her new drink. She quickly forgot about the needle.

Gabby pulled her panties down to pee, and sat. She immediately shrieked as the cold wet toilet rim met her flesh. It took her a second or two to realize what had happened.

"Everything OK in there?" Bobbie called.

She stood straight up, and grabbed some toilet paper and wiped the back of her legs. "Gross!" she thought as she reached around and lowered the toilet seat.

"Yeah, I'm fine!" she yelled back. "Be right out!" Gabby sat on the seat and peed. As she did so, she inspected her panties for any traces of blood. She had, on a couple of occasions, been catatonically embarrassed to find out that her period had started—soiling her clothes so that others could see. Ever since that last episode, she checked herself religiously with each visit to the bathroom.

Bobbie couldn't imagine what had startled Gabby, but his mind was working quickly on other matters. He reached into his front pocket, and pulled out his baggie. Quickly he rummaged through it until he found one of the little white pills. He pulled it out, looked at it, smiled, and said quietly, "We are going to have so much fun tonight, my little Gabby."

He dropped the pill into her drink.

31

MAIL

GEOFF TURNED HIS ATTENTION BACK TO HIS PHONE. HE LEANED against the counter so he could keep an eye on his barbeque while he typed.

> From: gquest100@hotmail.com
> Subject: Hi Ms M
> Date: November 14, 2014 at 6:54 PM PST
> To: mquest99@aol.com
> Question: What are you doing right now? I'm outside at my barbeque burning our dinner.
> Answer to your question: Leave our next meeting up to me. I plan to be in the area to close my deal next week. You free? Let me know if you can get free to meet for dinner or…?
> G

It didn't take but a second or two…

> From: mquest99@aol.com
> Subject: Q & A's
> Date: November 14, 2014 at 8:58 PM MST
> To: gquest100@hotmail.com
> Thinking of you. Do you still look like I remember you? God, I hope so! Hahaha

Not sure about next week. Football season here, and my husband is a
HS coach. He's very busy, and may be traveling. Stay tuned. You have
flexibility?
M

Geoff smiled. And shook his head.

From: gquest100@hotmail.com
Subject: Flexibility
Date: November 14, 2014 at 7:03 PM PST
To: mquest99@aol.com
Some. But will need some notice. Let me know.
Shit! My fish is on fire!
G

By the time he had flipped his fish and chicken, there was another note for
him to open.

From: mquest99@aol.com
Subject: Burn Baby Burn
Date: November 14, 2014 at 9:05 PM MST
To: gquest100@hotmail.com
Will advise on date(s). Save some fire for me. 😢
M

32

GEOFF

GEOFF COULD HARDLY BELIEVE HE WAS ENGAGED IN ALL OF THIS. HE felt like a kid again. If he was being perfectly honest, being pursued by such an alluring younger woman was flattering. He hadn't felt this way in a very long time. Certainly, not with Susie. He was lost in thought when he heard Susie yell, "Hey! I can see the flames from here!"

Geoff instantly snapped back to reality and jumped to the barbeque. He flipped the chicken and fish over again, but unfortunately, the food was already blackened. He could salvage the mess, he thought, by only cooking the meat for a short time on this side, and scraping the black tops when Susie wasn't snooping. Yes, it will be a little on the overdone side, but possibly OK.

"Got it! No worries, babe! Just getting the grill marks on the food like you like it!" Geoff called back. But, by then, Susie was back in the kitchen. Rosanne was off tonight, and Susie, therefore, had to do everything.

Geoff did his best to scrape the chicken, but the fish was too soft. He turned off the fire and placed the meat on the platter—covering it with foil to keep it warm. He brushed the grill to clean it, and lowered the lid. When he got indoors, he asked Susie, "You want me to call the kids?"

"Sure, if you want to," she replied. Then added, "Goddamnit, Geoff, you burned the food." She had uncovered the meat and it didn't take much to realize that Geoff had indeed tried to cover up his mistake. "What in the hell were you thinking out there? Never leave the grill unattended; I've told you that a million times!"

"I didn't leave the grill. I was deep in thought about our deal in Grand Junction. It's supposed to close next week, and there are lots of things still to do. I guess my mind wandered a bit."

"A BIT?!" she replied with a sharp edge to her voice. "Maybe you shouldn't cook when Rosanne isn't here. Actually, maybe you shouldn't cook at all. Jesus."

Geoff ignored the barb. He walked to the foot of the staircase in the front entry, and yelled up, "Kids! Dinner!" He heard the rustle of feet coming from multiple areas upstairs.

CJ came down first. "Smells great, Dad! I'm starving! What's for dinner?"

"Barbequed chicken and fish," he replied as the girls followed down the stairs closely chasing their younger brother. They all turned and headed to the great room where the table was set, and their dinner was waiting.

CJ was already diving into his food when the rest of the family arrived. Susie reached over and grabbed his arm as it was poised to shovel another spoonful of rice into his mouth. "CJ! You are not to start eating until everyone is seated and the hostess—that means your mother tonight—lifts her fork. Now stand up and seat your sisters, and when you sit down, put your napkin in your lap, and wait for everyone to be served. When I lift my fork, you can start eating."

Looking at Geoff she said, "When did your children stop practicing their table manners?"

Geoff always found it amusing when their kids did something extraordinarily good, it was "our children"—as in "Look what *our* son, CJ, did today!" Or if they did something bad as in tonight, "Look what *your* kid did…" He smiled.

Then Susie added, "Your dad burned the food…again…so just try to carve around the black bits." She said so without looking up from her plate.

"Sorry kids, I got a little distracted. Hope it's edible."

"Mine's great!" Brooke exclaimed.

"Mine, too!" CJ added.

"Thanks, Dad, for cooking us dinner tonight. It's delicious!" Lucy said looking back and forth between her mother and father—clearly sensitive to the jab her mom was delivering.

Susie spoke up, "Well, isn't it nice to get all the recognition for the cooking when all you did is barbeque the heck out of the meat? Any 'at-a-girl's' for your mom?"

All the kids chimed in, at once, in a cacophony of compliments and thanks for their mother. She just kept her head down, and worked on cutting her chicken. "This is a bit tough." She put the bite in her mouth, and as she was chewing she said, "And, dry."

Geoff remained quiet and seemed deep in concentration.

"Penny for your thoughts?" Susie asked.

Geoff didn't hear her. "Geoff!" she said loudly.

"What?" Geoff looked up.

"You are really distracted tonight. Please rejoin your family!" Susie scolded

"Sorry." Pulling his head up, and looking at each of his children, Geoff said, "As I mentioned earlier to your mother, kids, I am close to closing an important deal next week, and I am working on a lot of moving pieces to the puzzle. I have to fly to Colorado next week, and I may be there four or five days. I'm just a little distracted is all. But, CJ, I will be there for your game Saturday." He continued, "So, let's go around the table, and let me know what your favorite thing that happened to you today—starting with Lucy."

. . .

The dinner went much better once Geoff became present. There was a lot of laughter, and Geoff enjoyed learning about his kids' school classes and activities. When dinner was over, he cleared the dishes, and moved to the sink to rinse and load the dishwasher. Susie didn't bother to help, but that was OK, because Geoff enjoyed this quiet time. Tonight, in particular, he had lots on his mind.

He was halfway through the pots and pans when he felt two arms reach around him and hands enter each of his front pockets simultaneously. Geoff tried to turn around, but Susie held him tight. "Thanks for your help with dinner tonight," she said in a quiet voice that he could barely make out over the running water.

Geoff was momentarily stunned. Having Susie make such an unexpected gesture of lighthearted intimacy was very much out of character for her these days. His mind had been completely engrossed elsewhere. "Women have an uncanny sixth sense when it comes to their partner's soul," Geoff thought. Is it possible that Susie was on to what he was feeling and planning? Impossible. Right?

He quickly dried his hands on his apron and reached behind him, and grabbed her ass and pulled her even tighter to him. "You're welcome. Sorry I overcooked the main dish—again."

Susie laughed and said, "Yeah, buddy, OK. Don't let it happen again! I'm heading up to bed. See you upstairs." And, with that, she pulled her hands free from Geoff's pockets and quietly left the kitchen.

. . .

When the kitchen was clean, he turned off the lights, checked all the doors to make sure they were dead-bolted, and headed upstairs. Susie was already in bed, asleep. He went into his study, closed the door behind him and sat at his desk.

Geoff loved his office. Susie called it his man-cave. He had a large desk, highly organized, with two walls of bookshelves that kept the hundreds of books that he had read. He particularly liked reading biographies about successful business leaders and military strategy. Also, high on his list, were books on failed companies and real-life tragedies. He philosophized that he would rather learn from others' mistakes rather than learning those lessons "the hard way."

The other wall of his office looked out across the blue water of San Francisco Bay. He loved watching the comings and goings of the sailboats, and the slow and powerful freighters hauling their containers to the docks and on to the market. At night, the twinkling of the city lights reminded him of a diamond necklace. Tonight, he thought of a diamond necklace draped across Meredith's neck.

He picked up his phone and accessed his secret account. For the next hour, he sat at his desk and re-read the emails, and fantasized about this mystery woman.

Meredith. With an M.

33

GABBY

ABBY WOKE UP IN HER MOTEL ROOM. IT WAS DARK, AND SHE HAD no idea what time it was. She was nauseous. Her head throbbed and the room was spinning. She tried to remember what happened last night, but could only focus on getting to the bathroom. Her roommate, Lily, was fast asleep, and Gabby hoped she wouldn't wake her with her retching.

When she got up from kneeling on the floor, she realized that under her sweater, her bra was up over her breasts. "That's weird," she thought as she made her way back into her bedroom. But, she was not thinking clearly; she knew that much. Sleeping in her clothes could do that, she figured.

"What happened last night?" she thought as she slowly crawled back into her bed feeling physically brittle. She was still in her cheerleader outfit—never a good sign to be in bed with the clothes you wore the night before. She racked her brain to try to clear the cobwebs so she could think, but there was simply no recall. The last thing she remembered was leaving the little party, and saying good-bye to Lily. But where was she going? Fatigue and the toxins in her body easily overcame her, and she fell into a deep sleep. It wasn't until Lily was shaking her awake at 8 AM the next morning, did the fog begin to clear. But, not entirely.

"What happened to you last night?" Lily asked. "Coach Edmonson pounded on my door at around one, and when I opened the door, he had you in his arms. You were passed out. He said he found you in one of the hallways near his room. He made sure you were breathing and OK, then brought you here. He said he knew you had been drinking, but promised me he wouldn't tell anyone. He's really cool. We loaded you into your bed, covered you up and you were out until you got sick a little later."

Gabby rubbed her temples, and looked around the room. "I must have gotten totally drunk last night. What was I drinking?"

"We were doing tequila shots in Johnny's room, remember? That was after a few beers. You then got up and whispered to me that you were going to see Coach about a surprise he had for the cheerleaders. That was the last I saw of you," Lily said.

Gabby tried hard to remember. It just wasn't clear. "A surprise?" she asked almost to herself. She shifted on the bed; her crotch hurt. She seemed to be looking back deep into the recesses of her mind. "I was going to see Coach Edmonson?"

"Yep; that's what you said last night."

Gabby got up, and went to the bathroom. She leaned over the sink and cupped her hands filling them with water. She washed her face hoping the cold water would sober her up. When she came back into the room, she said, "I can't remember a thing. That's freaking me out. Don't let me drink that much again, 'kay?"

Just then, there was a soft knock on the door. Lily got up to answer it, and when she opened the door, Coach Edmonson was there. "Good morning you two," he said. "Checking up on our cheer captain. How you feeling, Gabby?"

"What happened last night? Do you know, Coach?" Gabby asked.

"You came to my room to pick up these," Bobbie said handing her a brown bag. "These were meant for each of the girls as my thanks for cheering us on all season long."

Gabby opened the bag and saw six little boxes, each one with a different name on it. "Go ahead, open yours," Bobbie said.

Gabby rummaged around in the bag until she found hers. She fetched Lily's box, too. "Is it OK for us to open them together?" Gabby asked.

"Of course," Bobbie said with a smile. "But why don't you open them after I leave. I just wanted to check up on you, Gabby. You were passed out down the hall from my room, and you had dropped the bag with the gifts in them. I went out to get some fresh air and luckily found you. I know, at this age, you all are experimenting with alcohol. It's important to learn your limits. I think this is part of growing up, and part of your education. I don't think anyone else saw you, and no one saw me carry you back here. So, let's just keep this between us, OK?"

Gabby was overwhelmed with appreciation. "Thank you, Coach, so much. You are the best," was all she could think of to say.

"I would hope someone would look after a daughter of mine in the same way. You are so welcome," he said with a wink. "The bus leaves in an hour or so. Don't be late." Bobbie turned and left the room.

Lily immediately tore open her little box, and inside was a dainty gold charm bracelet with a small football attached to it. "So thoughtful," she said smiling. Gabby opened her box, and found the same gift. They strategized as to when they would give the other girls their gifts, and decided that the best time would be when they got on the bus so that Coach could enjoy seeing the girls opening their packages.

Gabby got up, and said, "Mind if I shower first?" She was really sore. The only thing she could think of was that she must have bruised herself when she passed out. But her crotch? It was now burning.

She went into the bathroom and closed the door. After turning on the shower, she started getting undressed. Her sweater first; then her bra. She slipped off her pleated cheer dress, and went to remove her panties. "What?" She stopped. What was wrong, here? Her panties were on backwards. And, inside out. "Huh?" There was blood on them, too. But in the rear, not in the front. Nothing made any sense. "How could this possibly happen?" she thought hard.

Gabby climbed into the shower, and let the hot water sooth her. She let the caressing liquid rinse her head, and flow down her body. She sensed an odd feeling of being cleansed. It felt as if dirt and grime were being washed away down the drain. As she enjoyed her shower and started to recover, she parted her legs and peed. "Ow!" she flinched. The burning was painful. Did she have a yeast infection? She sure hoped not. Not sure why, but she looked down to watch her pee go down the drain. It was then that she saw blood.

34

BOBBIE

BOBBIE DROVE INTO HIS DRIVEWAY. THE BED OF HIS MASSIVE pick-up truck was strewn with bags of football gear, coolers and his duffle. Meredith's car was in the carport. He was extremely nervous about seeing her. He couldn't imagine what the house looked like inside. And, being honest, he couldn't conger up what her reaction was going to be when he walked in the door.

He pulled his truck in beside Meredith's car, and started pulling the coolers out of the bed, and emptying the water and ice onto their brown lawn. He was leaning over the side rail grabbing his duffles when he heard Meredith's voice. "Home sweet home. Put your stuff away, and then we are gonna have a talk."

Bobbie turned around, and with a big smile on his face, said, "We WON, Baby! Woo-hoo! Did you hear?"

"I heard," Meredith replied. "That's really great. But, I want to talk about *us*, this house and our future."

"Sure, Baby. We are going to celebrate TONIGHT!" Bobbie slung his bags over his shoulder and headed for the side door where Meredith was standing. Holding his bags in his left hand, he threw his right arm around Meredith's shoulder. He winced in pain, and stopped short.

"That from the fight?" she asked.

"Man, good news travels fast," he replied more than a bit surprised that Meredith had already heard about the altercation with the other coach from the night before. "He was a total dick. And he insulted our team. I had no choice. Anyway, we beat the shit out of those pussies. Third straight league championship. All good for us. I'm going to shower, then let's get shit-faced and celebrate, OK?"

"I'm not drinking tonight," Meredith answered.

"What?" Bobbie responded, surprised.

"After the last time you got drunk, you abused me. That is never going to happen again. Take your shower, we have lots to talk about."

Bobbie smiled. "You bet we do, Baby. The superintendent has asked me to see him Monday morning. Finally, I will get the raise that I have earned. And, we will get the house that you have always wanted."

"Well, first you have to pay for the damage that you did to our *current* house. I had to call a professional crew to clean it. The TV is smashed, and the carpeting has to be replaced. What is with you these days?" Meredith stammered.

"Forget about this piece of shit. It is in our past. Think three bedrooms, picket fence, enclosed garage." Bobbie was exuberant. "Fix me a bourbon, will you Mer. I am in the mood to celebrate—not talk."

Bobbie walked right past her, and went straight into their bedroom. He was amazed at how clean the house looked and smelled. The bed was made, and he immediately thought about fucking Meredith hard tonight. Maybe he would do it from behind, again, just like the other night.

He pulled a few things out of his duffle, and tossed his dirty clothes on the floor. As he undressed, he pulled his pills out of his pocket. Opening the baggie, he grabbed a Viagra and choked it down. He then moved to stand in front of the mirror as he removed his underwear and sleeveless t-shirt. He stared at his reflection admiring his ripped physique. He turned left then right, and even flexed in a forward crab pose watching the veins bulge in his arms and chest. "No doubt," he said to himself, "I am a god."

When he emerged into the family room, he had put on a clean pair of jeans, and had pulled on a turtleneck that was probably two sizes too small. Other than his sore right hand and wrist, he could not be feeling any better. "Where's my drink?" he asked.

"Bobbie, we need to talk, and I want to talk to you while you are sober."

"Fuck that!" Bobbie yelled. "I have been slaving away for three plus years putting this piddly little football program on the map. I have gone out and busted my butt for you so that you can finally have that fucking little dream house you have always been wanting. I win the League Championship for the third year in a row, and come home expecting that you will actually be excited for me. For us. I have my big meeting Monday with the Super, and all you want to do is talk. Well, fuck that. I'll just have to celebrate alone."

Bobbie strode into the kitchen and poured himself a stiff drink. Bourbon over ice as he always liked it. "Well, now that there isn't any TV, I guess we can get naked and fuck before dinner. What do ya say?"

"Sorry, Bobbie. Not tonight." Meredith was resolute.

Bobbie snarled, "You unappreciative bitch!" And, he drew his arm back across his chest, and flung his backhand at her face. She let out a frightened yelp, and cowered. He never made contact; stopped just short of her right eye. Then he started laughing.

"Come on Meredith, can't you take a joke?" Bobbie was saying. "I would never hurt you. You are my wife. I am doing all this for you, Baby. Come on, let's sit down and have a drink together. We can talk."

Meredith looked at him as though she was looking at a complete stranger. "Wouldn't hurt me?" she said. "Really?!"

Bobbie had already had enough "talking." He got up, went back into the kitchen, poured himself another full glass of iced bourbon. He stood at the sink while he downed it in two gulps. He tossed the empty glass into the sink. It was a miracle it didn't break. Without another word, he went back into the bedroom, grabbed his team letterman's jacket, and walked right past her. As he threw open the kitchen door, he belched loudly. Meredith heard his truck door slam, and the engine fire up. He yelled out his window, "Well, if you don't want to celebrate with me, someone else sure as hell will. Later!"

The tires ripped the gravel free from the driveway as he jammed his foot on the accelerator. The truck fishtailed badly - barely missing their mailbox. And in seconds, he was gone.

35

MAIL

GEOFF'S WAS ENJOYING THE LATE NIGHT VIEW FROM HIS HOME office when his phone pinged. It startled him. Susie was asleep. He fumbled for the mute button, and set his phone to vibrate. He looked at his phone, and he caught his breath. It was M.

From: mquest@99aol.com
Subject: Thinking of You
Date: November 15, 2014 at 1:12 AM MST
To: gquest100@hotmail.com
Could use a friend right now. Miss the comfort of our time together. I have an overwhelming need to be held. Someplace safe. With you.
Could be free next Friday and Saturday nights. State football playoffs next weekend. Hubby traveling.
Any chance of seeing you? Fingers crossed.
M

Geoff closed his eyes and tried to concentrate. All he could see was Meredith, looking up at him, lips parted, soft smile, beckoning. Here was a woman who really wanted to be with him. God, that felt good.

From: gquest100@hotmail.com
Subject: Pack a bag
Date: November 14, 2014 at 11:25 PM PST

To: mquest99@aol.com

Me too. I'll plan on being in the area next week to close my deal. Not much notice, but it should work out. Let me know ASAP if you can't make it. Plan on being picked up at around 2 PM Friday. Returning Noon Sunday. Good so far? How flex are you re getting yourself to a secret meeting point?

Excited to see you…

G

From: mquest99@aol.com
Subject: Bags Packed
Date: November 15, 2014 at 1:34 AM MST
To: gquest100@hotmail.com

Yes, yes, yes and yes…Tell me where and when. Will get time off. I can hardly breathe.

M

From: gquest100@hotmail.com
Subject: Details to follow
Date: November 14, 2014 at 11:39 PM PST
To: mquest99@aol.com

Time zones messing me up! It's LATE for you! Sleep well. Look for details forthcoming. Need oxygen, too.

G

From: mquest99@aol.com
Subject: Forthcoming
Date: November 15, 2014 at 1:45 AM MST
To: gquest100@hotmail.com

The only thing I hope to see forthcoming is YOU! Sorry, late night pun. Question: What should I bring to wear? Be 100% honest!

M

From: gquest100@hotmail.com
Subject: Nothing much
Date: November 14, 2014 at 11:47 PM PST
To: mquest99@aol.com

…and mountain casual. You got that, right?

G

From: mquest99@aol.com
Subject: Not Much and Casual
Date: November 15, 2014 at 1:49 AM MST
To: gquest100@hotmail.com
Got it.

M

Geoff logged out of his secret email and texted Nick to meet him at the office at 7:30 for morning coffee and a new assignment. The quick response surprised him not a bit. Nick would be there.

"What's the topic?" was Nick's only inquiry.

"Personal. See you manana, partner."

36

GEOFF & NICK

GEOFF SET HIS ALARM FOR 5 AM, AND HEADED TO BED PLACING HIS phone on the bedside table. He could hear Susie's deep breathing. He undressed, and went to his bathroom to brush his teeth. When he returned, he climbed into bed—feeling more than a little guilty. Was he doing the right thing? Clearly, no. But, he had set things in motion. He could always abort the mission.

Climbing under the covers, he slid over next to Susie and cuddled - putting his arm over Susie's midsection just below her breasts. Immediately, she rolled away from him. She was offering nothing tonight—except her back. An occurrence that was becoming more and more routine with every passing year. All he had wanted was a reassuring cuddle.

He closed his eyes, and started to think of how he was going to disclose, and include, Nick in this little character detour. Before he knew it, his alarm was going off.

● ● ●

Geoff and Nick left the office and walked to Fisherman's Warf to get a real coffee from the Italian Café and to secure some important privacy. They brought their coffees to an outdoor table. Nick had his laptop. The weather was brisk, but not raining. The heat lamp and the coffee warmed them.

Geoff started, "Nick, what I am about to ask you to do is beyond the scope of your job, but you are the only one that I trust completely. You can turn me down with zero repercussions. Please think this through before you say anything in response, OK?"

"Go on," Nick said. "Does this have anything to do with one Jessica Stevens?" He winked.

"Not quite," Geoff replied. "Stop me any time you don't want to hear any more."

Nick nodded, took a sip of his coffee and encouraged, "Continue."

"Her name is Meredith. I do not know her last name. And, she does not know mine. I want to keep it that way for as long as I possibly can—forever if possible."

"Impossible, but go on," Nick smiled, interested.

"I met her on my last trip to Grand Junction. Chance meeting at a restaurant. We just clicked." Geoff did not want to admit he met her at the bar. He continued, "She and I—I just can't explain this—had a unique evening together and it became clear that we each had chemistry for each other."

"Did you sleep with her?" Nick asked straight away.

"No. No, we didn't. But, let's just say we connected on a very deep level. More emotionally than physically." Geoff stopped for a moment, took a sip of his coffee and looked out across the Bay. He continued looking back catching Nick's eye, "We've been emailing for the past couple of weeks."

Nick sat up and said, "Hold it right there, boss. Do you realize how dangerous that is? If Susie had any inkling something was going on, all she would have to do is turn on your computer and look at your mail. You'd be toast. Burnt toast."

"I'm not that stupid," Geoff was shaking his head. "I set up a private email account and secret password. I had Meredith do the same."

"Glad to hear, but if this is to continue, you need me to set you both up with an encrypted mail so that only the two of you can decode each other's messages. You can't be too safe."

"Not bad advice from a single guy," Geoff laughed—more from relief that the conversation was being accepted, not necessarily the assignment, yet.

"Well, when you're juggling multiple girlfriends," Nick winked. He continued, "So tell me about this Meredith. Is she hot? She better be, because you're smoking hot wife is no throw-away, if you know what I mean."

Geoff took a moment to gather his thoughts, then said, "I am really attracted to her. That's all I can say." Geoff's voice grew quieter. "We had such a great connection. She listened to me. Laughed at my jokes. Asked me endless questions about my work, and how I thought about things. Asked my advice, and seemed genuinely appreciative of my responses. She smiled at me all night. God. That smile. It's so hard to explain, Nick. It was as if I was somehow important to her. And, I couldn't help but feel the ache in my heart. I haven't felt important at home in such a long time, and I can't tell you how painful that is for me. Here was this beautiful woman—so different in almost every way from Susie—leaning on my every word, so engaged in our discussions. I found the more we talked and laughed, the more I wanted to spend time with her."

"You sure you didn't 'drink her pretty'?" Nick was actually serious now. "You know what they say about having the Ten-Two Disease?"

"No, what do they say?" Geoff inquired.

"What's a ten at two AM is a two at ten AM." They both cracked up. A bit of the tension left the conversation.

"No. I mean, yes. I had loads to drink. And, a rare hangover in the morning. But, Nick, I can only explain the lightness of the night with her. Our emails have taken on the same personality. I'm beyond curious."

Nick asked with a smile, "Has she sent you a picture? You know? A little reminder that assures you that she was not a 2 at 10?"

"Nope. And, I don't intend to ask her for one. I remember her for her cute and engaging personality, smile and heart." Geoff again was lost in thought. "That's enough. Plenty enough memory for me."

"OK, boss, I'm all in. You can trust me with everything. I'm flattered that you think enough of me to share this part of your life with me. But, I have to say, that your protection is my highest priority, and I have to get your agreement that if I feel that you are in any personal or physical danger that I can tell you, and you will do as I say. That is the condition I will put on this arrangement. Agreed?"

Geoff nodded looking down at his empty cup. He then lifted his head and met Nick's eyes. He extended his hand, and they shook. "Thanks, Nick."

The next words out of Nick's mouth were, "Let's, as a matter of urgency, get your emails encrypted."

"No argument. I'll give you my private email address and password. I'll send Meredith a note to confirm that you will do the same for her—and that you are to be trusted. I already told her that when you almost got arrested," Geoff said.

"What about this Jessica woman?"

"According to Meredith, she has the same level of trust with her that I do with you."

"Well, that would be saying a lot. I hope that relationship doesn't end up being the weak link in all this. It's probably the one thing I cannot control," Nick instructed.

Geoff could only nod.

"I need a beautiful executive home in Aspen for the weekend. I can't risk staying at a hotel. Someplace where they can privately land the Ranger (Geoff was making reference to the Company's Jet Ranger helicopter). Two trips. I want to be there and settled in the house when Meredith arrives. The pilot is to know nothing about his passenger, and he is to ask no questions of her, understood? You can brief him as you please." Geoff was getting very intense.

"Geoff. Leave this to me. I promise that every detail will be looked after, your safety and identity concealed, and the only thing you will need to worry about is when Meredith enters your home and closes the door behind her. In fact," Nick continued, "I will be hiring a contract pilot who knows neither you, or anything, or anyone, other than what I choose to brief him on. You good?"

"Thanks, Nick. You are the best. What would I do without you?"

"Well, let's not think about that, OK? We need to get back to the office. We both have loads of work ahead of us."

Geoff nodded and immediately jumped to his feet. "Thanks, Nick. I am in your hands."

He replied, "I sure hope you, I mean we, can keep a lid on this. One crack and it could spell doom for you, your reputation, your marriage, your family, this company—everything. This Meredith, she must be something very special for you to roll the dice like this. I can't wait to meet her one of these days."

"Look, Nick. I am only meeting her for the weekend. We'll see. As you say, it could have been an alcohol-fueled one-night fantasy. The 10-2 Disease. Thanks, again, for being complicit with this crazy messed-up friend of yours. Feels a bit like our days at Stanford and USC."

"Not quite," was all that Nick could think to say as he chuckled. He thought, but didn't say, "Yeah, but you are now married with three great kids, you're 45 years old in the prime of your life, head up one of the top global financial institutions, and have an enviable business and personal reputation. She's fifteen years younger than you are. Are you fucking...out...of...your...mind?"

They headed back to work.

37

BOBBIE

IT WAS 9:50 AM MONDAY, AND BOBBIE WAITED OUTSIDE THE SUPER-
intendent's office. His appointment was for 10 AM, and he was early—and
ready. He had worn his new jeans and a fresh Polo shirt in the school's colors.
He had practiced his presentation numerous times in front of the mirror, and
couldn't help but smile. This was going to be a meeting that would change his
life. He had worked so hard for it. Should he ask for the $150,000 salary right
away? Or, should he demand his earned 5-year contract that would start a little
lower, say at $120,000 and grow $15,000 per year—averaging $150,000 over
the next five years? He had his clipboard with him so that he could take notes
of their offer.

The door opened, and the superintendent, Don DeLatore, stepped out, and
said, "Come on in, Robert. Please have a seat." The formality struck Bobbie as
very odd, but what the heck—they would soon be putty in his hands.

Bobbie entered the office, and was instantly surprised to see Charlie Fredricks,
Granite High's principal, and Janet Jacobs, the District's human resources manager. They were arranged in a semi-circle along with a stranger Bobbie couldn't
place, facing a lone chair that he correctly guessed was for him. This all seemed a
little strange at first, but then Bobbie relaxed as he realized that to negotiate such
an important contract, all these players would need to approve the terms.

Superintendent DeLatore spoke first. "I think you know everyone here, Robert, except Hugh Preston. Hugh is the District's contracted attorney who handles
all personnel matters." Bobbie smiled and reached out and shook Hugh's hand.
Hugh was expressionless.

"Man, they sure brought the big guns to this meeting," Bobbie thought as his enjoyment of the meeting was growing by the second. "I didn't think it would be THIS good!" He shook everyone else's hand in succession around the circle greeting them by their first names. They all sat.

Hugh started, "Let me begin by congratulating you on a terrific season on the football field, Robert. The results over the past several years have been impressive, to say the least." Bobbie could feel his chest swell, and he was hoping not to blush. He was actually fidgety.

"Thank you, Mr. DeLatore," Bobbie responded. "The boys worked real hard for the League title this year, and we are very prepared to compete successfully at the State play-offs starting next week. The younger ones are looking forward to the years ahead as we defend our Grizzly pride." This was going to be good.

The group seemed to shift in their chairs. Hugh continued. "Robert, Charlie wanted to say a few things."

The principal cleared his throat, and looking up said, "Coach Edmonson, the School has received a complaint of harassment from one of your players. A Conner Lockhart. The complaint outlines a string of abuses you have inflicted on the players, but specifically outlines an afternoon of humiliation inflicted on him in front of his teammates. Do you recall the specific incident? We certainly want to hear your side of the story."

Bobbie was stunned. He tried to clear his head. And, awkwardly, buy some precious seconds to recall the incident and provide the most professional response. "No, actually, I don't. You hired me to build the greatest football team in the State. To do so, I place demands on these boys that are at times very tough on them. We are all teaching them to become men. Conner is a puss...oops, sorry, Janet. I mean he wasn't putting in the same effort as the other boys. If I allow a weakling on the field, he would put in danger the well-being of all the other players. At very least, we would lose games. At worst, there would be injuries." Bobbie tried hard to remember exactly what he had done to Conner that afternoon. He remembered he had sent him home with some tough talk to make an important example for the other players.

"Football is the toughest of sports, and I am sorry if my methods are hard on some of the players. But, it is our job to weed out the weak. These are life lessons for these kids. And, you want, and deserve, a winning football program here, and I have delivered that to the school - for you and all the community. I don't think I deserve this kind of interrogation. Frankly, I thought we were meeting to discuss an extension of my contract."

They all looked around at each other. The principal spoke. "Coach Edmonson, a harassment suit has been filed in State Court naming Granite High School, the Grand Junction School District, and you, personally, seeking actual and unspecified punitive damages. The suit has been brought to court by Corey Lockhart, Conner's mother, who is one of the most successful sexual harassment lawyers in the State of Colorado. Can I ask you another question?"

The heat was moistening Bobbie's collar, but he was trying his best to act cool. He shifted in his chair and said, "Anything you like." Bobbie noticed that the lawyer in the room rarely looked up, but never stopped writing.

Janet Jacobs, the HR manager interrupted. "The night after the game in Silverton last week, what did you do after the team dinner?"

Bobbie was shocked. "What? What do you mean 'What did I do after dinner?'"

"Exactly, what did you do from the time you finished your dinner to the time you joined the bus for the ride home in the morning?"

"What is this all about?" Bobbie's voice was raised.

Hugh Preston, the lawyer, spoke next. "Well, Mr. Edmonson, you have been accused of some very serious matters—crimes actually—and we wanted to get your side of the story. That is only fair. This is a voluntary meeting and you can leave at any time. No one is holding you here. But let me remind you that we are, at this stage, on your side here—all of us being accused of wrongdoing. We need to assess the risk, and formulate a strategy to defend the District and Granite High School—and by extension, you.

Bobbie was incredulous. "Crimes? *WHAT* crimes? Is this about my silencing that good-for-nothing coach at last week's game? He insulted me; he insulted our players; he insulted the school; he accused us of unfair competitive practices; and, he threatened me. I had every right to def..."

Hugh broke in, "Actually, no, Mr. Edmonson, there is nothing in the complaint that addresses that altercation, but I am finding this story endlessly fascinating. You have been accused of harassment and physical injury to one of your football players: one Conner Lockhart; and rape, non-consensual sex with a 17-year-old minor, providing alcohol and drugs to a minor, and unwanted fondling of a minor all relating to a Jane Doe—her name can't be released publicly, but for our confidential purposes we are talking about a Gabrielle Perkins, whom I believe you know as the head cheerleader on the Granite High cheer team. And, finally, there is a further suit filed on behalf of three players, not previously mentioned, that alleges you required that they use illegal performance enhancing drugs—specifically Human Growth Hormone. They all are threatening to testify that you injected them personally. All of these offences allegedly occurred on school property—or at officially sanctioned school events—placing the school, and the school district, directly into legal jeopardy."

Bobbie's face was flushed. He sat there absorbing the enormity of the moment. With gritted teeth, he said, "That is all complete bull shit. That fucking coach of the Bullets is behind all of this, isn't he? What an ass hole."

"Please watch your mouth," Janet implored. "This is neither a locker room nor your private residence."

Bobbie stammered on, "And Gabby? You have GOT to be kidding me! She came to my room, drunk, and passed out. She was attending a room party where they must have been doing shots or something. But, she came to my room and collapsed. I picked her up and carried her back to her room. No FUCKING good deed goes unpunished in this place."

Hugh spoke next. "Mr. Edmonson, we are only advising you of the accusations. Of course, you are innocent in a court of law, and with us, until proven guilty. We are only here to assess risk on behalf of the school and the district. But, we are recommending that you hire your own attorney to properly defend yourself against these accusations that you say are false. Because if you are found guilty, you will be subject to penalties including court awarded damages, and likely imprisonment. It would also go without saying that these offences would appear on your permanent record, and you would be listed, for life, as a sex offender. I doubt there would be a school or university in the land that would hire you."

Don DeLatore spoke next. "But, Robert, to be fair to you especially, the District needs to conduct a full investigation into the matters at hand here. Therefore, effective immediately, we are suspending you, with pay, for the next 90 days while we conduct that investigation. You are to leave the premises immediately after this meeting, and you are not allowed on campus, or at any Granite High School, or Grand Junction School District, event."

Bobbie was silent. His face hardened, and he stared at each participant in the room one-by-one. "I see," he said. "And the game this weekend? Are you saying I can't coach the team in the State playoffs?"

The lawyer said, "Yes. That is exactly the type of event that you are banned from attending. And, there has been a restraining order filed in the local court requiring you to have no communication whatsoever with your accusers, and you are required stay at least 100 yards away, you would know that distance, right?…from each and every one of them. This restraining order extends to the

Granite High School campus, the accusers' family members and all faculty of Granite High."

Hugh extended to Bobbie a handful of papers that were copies of the complaints as well as the restraining orders. Bobby leafed through them, although it was clear to all, that he wasn't fully absorbing the enormity of what he was holding. "Who's going to coach the team this weekend?"

The principal answered, "Your assistant head coach, John Bossick. He has not yet been notified as we wanted to meet with you first. We intend to notify the coaches, players, students, faculty and the parents this afternoon."

Bobbie nodded.

Handing Bobbie another piece of paper, Janet Human Resources Supervisor said, "This is your copy of the statement that will be released later today." It read:

MEMO
For Immediate Release
November 18, 2014
To: Granite High School Faculty, Students and Parents

It has come to our attention that there are serious, but unsubstantiated, allegations of misconduct concerning our football and athletics programs. We take these allegations with the utmost of concern, and have launched an internal investigation into those allegations. We are in the process of interviewing all named affiliated participants.

Effective immediately, Coach Robert Edmonson, has agreed to take a voluntary paid leave-of-absence to assist us with the investigation. No contact between Coach Edmonson and the students, the faculty, staff or parents is allowed during this investigation.

As for the upcoming playoff games, Coach John Bossick, will act as Interim Head Coach.

In conclusion, we take the behavior of our school community—encompassing all members—as the highest of priorities here at Granite High as well as the District at large. We will report to you regularly, and with transparency, as to both our findings and any resultant actions we plan to take.

Please feel free to contact Janet Jacobs (303) 283-5002, the Grand Junction District Human Relations Director, with any questions or concerns. Importantly, please notify her if you are aware of any inappropriate behavior by staff, faculty, students or community members, or if you have information that you feel might be helpful to our investigation.

Sincerely,

Don DeLatore, Grand Junction District, Supervisor

Janet Jacobs, Grand Junction District, Director of Human Relations

Hugh Preston, ESQ; Oppenheimer, Rhodes and Preston, LLC.,
   Grand Junction District, Legal Representative

Charles Fredericks, Granite High School, Principal

Bobbie got up from his chair without asking if the meeting was over. His face reddened as he stood. He started for the door, but then stopped. He turned to face them all. "Fuck you. Fuck all of you. I'm going to hire a lawyer, all right, and I am going to sue the shit out of all of you for false…What the fuck do you call it? Who gives a shit. You are ruining my career, and you will pay."

He flung his papers in the face of the superintendent catching him completely by surprise. Don received a paper cut across his nose, but didn't notice it until he felt the blood trickle across his cheek as he stooped to help the others pick up the loose leaves.

Bobbie had to get to his office. He needed to think things through privately. He marched to the door saying nothing, flung it open, stormed out, and with a backhand pull, slammed the door behind him. Bobbie looked up and stopped dead in his tracks. Two, uniformed and armed, Grand Junction sheriffs were waiting for him. Each man stood immediately as Bobbie exited the office, and both carried a very serious expression—as well as a weapon. The door reopened, and Principal Fredricks stuck his head out saying, "These gentlemen have been instructed to escort you directly off campus. If there are any personal items in your office you wish us to send you, please contact Janet, here, and she will assist in getting them sent, or delivered, to you. And, Robert," he continued, "we all want to get to the bottom of this just like you do. Look at this as a paid vacation."

Bobbie was livid, and he jerked around so forcefully that one of the officers instinctively reached for his gun—but kept it holstered. All the surrounding staff was in shock as to what was happening before their very eyes. The sheriffs subdued Bobbie and walked him out of the building and, in silence, to his truck. There were three additional police cars in the lot to make sure the coach would exit the school as instructed.

Bobbie climbed in his truck, started the engine, revved the motor, but was cautious as he departed the school grounds. He was being followed.

38

MEREDITH

MEREDITH SAT AT HER DESK BY THE WINDOW AT HER OFFICE. IT was Tuesday, November 18—three days after last hearing from Geoff. It was cold out - freezing in fact, but the population was waiting for a warm-up. The weather reports were forecasting unseasonably temperate days toward the end of the week followed by a late weekend blizzard. The trees in the courtyard were bare, and the grey skies added to the scene that certainly couldn't be lifting the spirits of the residents here, and it wasn't lifting hers either.

Bobbie had come home Monday night drunk as a skunk. But something was different about him. He usually bounded in, boisterous, and ready for a cocktail, dinner and more. But that night, he had come in wild-eyed and angry. He had already been drinking—a lot. Said he had been with his buddies at their favorite bar, Pistol Whipped Willy's…"strategizing." He wasn't making much sense. His words were slurred and he was rambling. Meredith could make out something about an altercation of some sort at Bobbie's work; something about him being too tough on his players. He also stammered something about going hunting. Monday morning, he had left for school early with boundless energy, and was looking forward to his meeting with the "higher ups" to discuss a contract extension. Clearly, something had not gone according to plan.

That night when Meredith came to the bedroom, Bobbie was passed out across the bed with his clothes still on. He was snoring loudly and stank of bourbon. She quickly and quietly changed into some sweats, grabbed her pillow and made her way back out to the couch. She had been sleeping there a lot lately.

When she awoke Tuesday, Bobbie was not in the house. When did he leave? She hadn't heard him. He didn't respond to her texts. His duffle was gone, and so, too, were lots of his clothes. When she checked the hunting closet, she found his bow, quiver, and arrows missing. When she called Granite High to speak to her husband, the office administrator only said that Coach Edmonson was away and not due back for several weeks. What? She wouldn't volunteer anything further. "What about next week's playoff game?" Meredith asked.

"I'm sorry, Mrs. Edmonson, that's all I am authorized to say," was all that came out of her earpiece.

Meredith hung up, and was still for a moment. She nodded her head as though to understand something. Then she exhaled deeply, and finished putting her lunch into a brown paper bag. Grabbing a bottled water from the fridge on her way out, she locked the house and went to her car. There was a note on the windshield held there by the wiper.

She loaded her things into the car, then pulled the note free. It read, "Going hunting. School says I'm abusing my players. They put me on leave—at least paid. Not coaching the play-offs. Fuck them. I'll get even. Back Sunday night. –Bobbie".

39

MAIL

MEREDITH'S PHONE CHIMED, AND SHE SNATCHED IT QUICKLY OFF her desk expecting a text from Bobbie. But it wasn't her usual email. What she saw, froze her.

> From: gquest100@hotmail.com
> Subject: I'm Local
> Date: November 18, 2014 at 10:34 AM MST
> To: mquest99@aol.com
> I'm back in GJ closing my deal. I feel so close to you, but so far away.
> You still free this weekend? Please say yes!
> G

Meredith shook her head crazily as to clear cobwebs. She closed her eyes, and took two deliberate deep breaths before returning her gaze to her screen and re-reading the message. It had been a crazy 24 hours. Now that this little playful fantasy and flirting was turning into a reality, should she dare? Bobbie was very unstable and unpredictable these days. What would he do if he came home early and found her not at home? Or worse, caught her running off with another man? She shuddered. But, he was gone. Unreachable. Hunting in the back-country. And, very out of the picture—at least until Sunday. She realized her hands were shaking when she tried to type a response.

> From: mquest99@aol.com
> Subject: Can't Breathe

Date: November 18, 2014 at 10:40 AM MST
To: gquest100@hotmail.com
Yes! Hurry! Rescue me! Need to be back Sunday afternoon latest. Where are you meeting me? When? So excited…
M

Meredith hit "send." Oh crap. The reality was hitting her. What should I wear? What should I bring? I don't know where we are going! He did text "mountain casual." He also said, "nothing much." Shit. Do I remember what he looks like? Meredith started to become anxious and to panic a bit. Her phone chimed.

From: gquest100@hotmail.com
Subject: Rendezvous
Date: November 18, 2014 at 10:51 AM MST
To: mquest99@aol.com
There is a resort south of you by about 50 miles. It's called Gateway Canyons. You know it? On Hwy 141. Park in the lot as far away from the street as is possible, and come to the lobby with your bag. Friday. 2 PM. Does this work?
G

This time, Meredith didn't hesitate. She thumb-typed her reply.

To: gquest100@hotmail.com
Subject: Can't wait that long
Date: November 18, 2014 at 10:53 AM MST
From: mquest99@aol.com
Do I know it? It's only the nicest, coolest, place within 1000 miles. You have great taste. Now I am getting nervous. I've never stayed there; didn't think I ever would. 3 days too long for me to wait! Can we meet for a drink tonight? Same place as before?
M

This time, there was no reply. Meredith paced her office, and went out for a walk in the frigid, gray weather. Did she say too much? Will he want to meet for a drink? Why hasn't he replied? Now, she was sick with worry.

• • •

It was hours later when her phone started ringing. It startled her. Her workday had been a disaster. Not being able to concentrate, Meredith had gotten little done. She grabbed her phone, and looked at the Caller ID: Jessica. "Hey Jess! I was just thinking of calling you. We need to talk. What's up?"

Jessica replied, "Oh, nothing really. Jazz is out tonight at her father's, so I was wondering if you wanted to catch a quick drink on the way home?"

"Better than that. I think I may be free for dinner. I was hoping to catch up with an old friend, but I haven't heard back. Can I let you know last minute?"

"Sure. But let's plan on meeting at the Grand Hotel lobby bar at 5:30, OK? If your dinner materializes, you can leave from there. Sound good?"

Meredith was, for a moment, stunned. The Grand. That is where Geoff stayed last time he was in town. Likely, that is where he was staying again.

"Hey, Meredith! You still there? Hello?"

"Sorry, Jess. Yes. That'll work perfectly. See you there at 5:30."

Meredith hung up, and looked at her watch. It was a little after 4:00. She got up and went to the bathroom where she took a look at herself in the mirror. Clearly, she was not prepared to see Geoff in this daggy outfit. Whether he could meet her later for drinks and dinner, or if they had a chance meeting in the hotel lobby, she needed to go home, change and put on some make-up. She threw some things together in her backpack, and slung it over her shoulder. On the way out, she stopped by the front desk of the PE Department, and logged herself out. No more classes today, and no appointments. Good. Gayle was on duty, and clearly not paying much attention. Meredith startled her when she said, "See you tomorrow, Gayle; I'll be in early."

Gayle almost swallowed her gum. "OK, Mrs. Edmonson. See you tomorrow."

Meredith loved the relative freedom she experienced at Grand Junction High School. Her credentials, and her work ethic, were impressive for a high school dance and cheer coach. The kids loved her, and she had an easy relationship with the parents—unheard of according to her peers. She was between sports as her school football team only won two games this season (and not in the playoffs), and basketball was weeks away from their season—after the Christmas break. She taught Dance on Mondays, Wednesdays and Thursdays, and volunteered at the one dance studio in town on most Saturdays. And, everyone knew she moonlighted at Granite High with their cheerleaders. No one questioned her schedule or what she did. She could come and go as she pleased.

• • •

Meredith was home putting on some mascara. She had been stressing about not hearing from Geoff, but had decided that a fun night out with Jess was just what she needed. However, she thought it was likely she would run into him at some point in the evening, so she was purposely deliberate in combing out her hair—pulling it back into a cute raven pony tail with a black ribbon that matched her leather pants. She threw on her silk blouse last after dabbing a hint of her favorite perfume, Allure, on her wrists, behind her ears and between her breasts. She grabbed her keys, her coat and her scarf, snatched her clutch, and headed for the door.

Getting into her old Explorer, she started the engine and turned the heat to "high." She then pulled down her sun visor to have one last look in the mirror. She needed to add some lipstick. Just then, she heard a dull chime, and realized her phone was in her purse. She lunged for it—knocking it off the seat onto the floor. "Shit!" she yelled to herself. Fumbling with the clasp, she got out her phone and stared at the message.

> From: gquest100@hotmail.com
> Subject: Swamped!
> Date: November 18, 2014 at 5:22 PM
> To: mquest99@aol.com
> M,
> So sorry to be "off the grid" this afternoon. Last minute troubles with the closing. Working late tonight. Trying to get this wrapped by Friday. Crazy. Will be with my team all this week. I keep smiling when I think of you. 2 PM Friday…Can the clock move faster? Are we really in the same city right now?
> G

Meredith smiled, and again shook her head. Crazy, all right. She decided to not tell Geoff where she and Jessica were meeting. She didn't want to affect his concentration; he needed uncluttered mental space to get his deal done. And selfishly, Meredith didn't want anything to interfere with their weekend.

> From: mquest99@aol.com
> Subject: Score
> Date: November 18, 2014 at 5:31 PM MST

To: gquest100@hotmail.com
Concentrate, and get all your work wrapped up, so that you can score big on this deal, and feel sated this weekend. I won't text again (even tho I'll really want to!). See you Friday at 2!
M

Within seconds, this reply chimed:

From: gquest100@hotmail.com
Subject: Score?
Date: November 18, 2014 at 5:33 PM
To: mquest99@aol.com
Very funny, "punny" girl! Hahaha
G

Meredith sent a quick note to Jessica letting her know she was running a little late. Jess instantly replied that she had a great table at the back of the bar where they could "talk." Meredith put her phone down on the passenger seat, and headed out to The Grand.

40

SUSIE

THE DAY BEFORE HIS TRIP TO GRAND JUNCTION, SUSIE COULD TELL that Geoff was unusually distracted. He said it was because this deal was taking too long to close, and he questioned whether it would be worth it when the two companies finally met at the closing table. He was headed out for a longer trip than usual, and didn't plan to be back until Tuesday, the 25th. He would be missing another of CJ's games. It was rare for him not to be home on a weekend, but he said he had to go to New York immediately after Grand Junction. He wasn't sure the Colorado deal was going to get done in time, and it didn't make sense to fly back to San Francisco and turn around a day later and fly back across the country to New York. A waste of his time and jet fuel he had said.

Susie had watched him pack for this trip. By now, she was an expert on what he usually took with him, and she was surprised to see him pack some very expensive casual clothes. "Too smart for backwater Grand Junction, and too casual for sophisticated New York City," she thought at the time. She had urged him to bring a couple of ties and a suit, and both his surprise at the suggestion, and his quick agreement, registered strangely with her. Why hadn't he thought of it? So unlike him. She let it pass.

That night, she fixed him his favorite dinner: meat loaf, baked potato and a simple green salad. He could have her for dessert. As the night unfolded, Geoff was unusually subdued.

"What's up, Honey?" Susie inquired once they were seated.

"What do you mean?" Geoff looked up; a fork of meatloaf in his right hand.

"You seem unusually distant this past week. Is everything OK at work?"

"Of course. I'm just busier than I have ever been. Deals are taking so much longer, and the negotiations are getting so much tougher. I'm sorry if I have been distracted lately. I guess I'm getting a bit overwhelmed, and feeling the need to get back out on that baseball field with CJ," he said seriously.

"And back in the yard, too," Susie deadpanned. The dig hurt a bit, but Geoff let it pass as he always did.

"You're right, Sus. Maybe we need to finally hire a gardening team to keep up with the yard. I'm OK with that…so long as you let me mow a lawn and trim a hedge here and there." Geoff was smiling now, but it wasn't an easy expression—Susie could tell. She decided to change the subject.

They spoke about the kids and the busy week they all had ahead while Geoff was gone. Susie knew every detail, and was particularly concerned about Lucy. She was a tough teenager, and her social status was all she focused on—that, and her image in any reflective surface. Geoff just nodded his head and laughed. "That's why you are so good with them, Hon. You're a girl; you understand them. Don't you remember when you were their age?"

Susie shot back, "Yeah, well, when I was their age, and I talked back to my mother, my daddy would slap me across the face, and send me to my room."

Geoff ignored the comment, but added, "That was a different generation. Our parents weren't as clued in as we are today about raising kids. We have to be bigger than that."

"Bigger than what?" Susie challenged. You're never here—well, not as much as you used to be. You don't even know what I am talking about. Lucy is growing up right under your nose, and…I'm sorry Honey. I didn't mean to jump on you. It's just that I feel like I am doing this parenting thing all on my own these days, and you are getting busier every year."

"Don't you like being a parent?" Geoff asked sincerely. "You always said that the kids were your life. Yes, they are getting older, and their social lives are blossoming, but we are also privileged to have assistants that few other families can afford. We have a housekeeper, a driver on call, a cook when necessary, and soon a gardener!" Geoff winked.

Susie calmed herself. "You're right. I love the kids, and being in their lives. I love this house, and being Mrs. Geoff Cameron. Believe me, I do. It's just so overwhelming at times. When do you get back Tuesday? Brooke has a dance recital at 4:00."

Geoff said, "Not sure. Depends when my meeting is over. If I can leave the City by noon, with the time difference, I can make the recital easily. I'll make every effort to be there."

Geoff cleared the dishes after dinner, and straightened up the kitchen. He stopped in to say good night and good-bye to each of his kids. They were all working on homework at their respective desks. Of the three of them, only Lucy was on the phone. He was sure it started with a math problem, but quickly transitioned to boys and the upcoming dance. He couldn't help but smile. He loved his kids.

When he got to his bedroom, Susie was already in bed waiting for him. He undressed and slid in next to her. He was surprised to find she had nothing on. He turned off the light and rolled over to embrace her. She said quietly, "Well, hurry up; I'm tired, and you have a long day tomorrow."

The sex was uninspiring. When it was Susie's turn for pleasure, she rolled over, climbed out of bed and walked into the bathroom. Geoff could hear her washing herself. She came back to bed with her flannel nightgown on, kissed him on the cheek and snuggled deep under the covers. There was never a bad orgasm, Geoff had to agree, but his real joy was a deep-seeded desire to please his partner. That was not happening of late. He loved his wife. And, he adored his family.

Dinner tonight had been delicious. But his dessert was half-baked.

41

GATEWAY CANYONS

COLORADO STATE HIGHWAY 141 IS AN UNDULATING RIBBON OF asphalt that runs southwest out of Grand Junction, uninterrupted, for 114 breathtaking miles of some of the most beautiful vistas in America. It is, at once, hard to conceive the unfolding scenery on the ground while the heavens above are painted by the hand of God, Himself. The spring with its wildflowers, and early summer with its green pastures, are sublime, but fall is special: it pours itself out across the valley floors in splashes of orange, red and yellow at every turn—over every ridge.

But this was winter, 2014, the buttes were impossibly draped in powdered sugar from an early snow. The valley floors were brown, but water flowed easily down canyons and cracks, and on this particular weekend, the weather was to warm noticeably—high pressure blanketing the region—and there would be more melting ahead of a strong cold storm expected late Sunday.

Fifty-four miles south of Grand Junction, on State Highway 141, rests Gateway Canyons Resort. Nestled below the grand palisade of rock that shades it and protects it, the resort sprawls out in unobtrusive clusters of five-star luxury amidst some of nature's grandest creations. Wildlife abounds, and humans share, almost guiltily, the surrounding Eden with the other creatures and flora of the Canyons of Gateway.

42

MEREDITH

MEREDITH WAS NERVOUS. SHE KEPT HER EYES ON THE ROAD AHEAD, looking for black ice. It was midday, and her temperature gage read 49 degrees. Her intuition told her that she had nothing to worry about, but something deep within her alerted her senses. She didn't like to drive in winter. In New York, she had the advantage of public transportation. But, not here. And, certainly not *way* out here. She had only been down this road once—many years ago in summer. She remembered it as strikingly beautiful, but Bobbie was driving, and she was a bit car sick. He was racing his truck and wouldn't slow down. They were on their way to meet some of his friends to camp out.

Meredith's anxiety only increased as she looked at the clock. She didn't want to be late. She had taken way too long to pack—having been unable to decide what to bring. Mountain casual. OK, she did that well enough, but to dress for dinner? She had packed two of her favorite outfits: a floor-length dress, slit up the leg to her thigh with a turtle-neck top, but sleeveless. Her second outfit was her tried and true leather pants that she coupled with a gray silk top. Her bag sat on the seat beside her. She hadn't planned on the extra time to drive in cold, melty, conditions, and the combination of the clock and the road were working against her.

Finally, at 3:10 PM, Meredith rounded a corner, and there stood the arched entryway to the Resort—the words "Gateway Canyons" etched on a nearby sand-stone monument. She turned into the parking lot, and as instructed, pulled all the way to the rear, and parked under a bald pepper tree. Her heart was racing—so hard in fact, she thought she might be sick or perhaps pass out. She waited for a few seconds and gathered herself before she turned off her motor and climbed out of her Explorer. The sun shone brightly, and she pulled on her sunglasses before fetching her bag. She glanced back at her vehicle one last time—worrying if it would be noticed by anyone who could possibly know her, and who could impossibly be way out here on this winter weekend.

But, the real feeling she was experiencing was one of letting go from a safety net. Walking away from something she knew well, something familiar, towards an extreme unknown. She could feel her resolve start to ebb away, and she slowed down as she approached the lobby entrance—now worrying if she should go through with this dangerous, but exciting, reunion. Her head was racing. She hoped she would recognize Geoff right away, and that he would be as wonderfully nice, funny, and yes, good looking, as she had remembered from that blissful night. She stopped ten paces from the front door, and put her bag down next to a small garden, took a deep breath, steadying herself.

Just then, the front door opened, and an African-American man walked towards her. "Ms. Meredith?" he inquired. He was smart looking, preppy almost, like she had been used to seeing years ago in New York. He was dressed in khaki pants with a pressed blue shirt with a logo on it and wore a brown leather jacket. The logo was on the jacket, too. The way he carried himself exuded confidence.

"Possibly," Meredith said slowly. "Who's asking?"

"Let me take your bag," the man said. "My name is Booker."

Before she let him have her bag, she inquired, "Do you work here?"

"No. I am working on a special assignment for Mr. Geoff." She let out a little breath. "He has asked me to bring you to him. Do you need to use the restroom before we go?"

"I think I can hold it until we get to my room. But, thanks for asking, uh, Booker."

He laughed easily, and picking up her bag, said, "Well, all right. Please come with me."

Instead of heading back to the lobby, he headed back to the parking lot. Meredith was still a bit unsettled, but walked with him out to a shiny black Escalade parked on the other side of the lot from her own vehicle. He unlocked the doors and loaded Meredith's bag into the rear luggage compartment. Before he opened her door, he reached into his pocket, and pulled out a heavy, thick, envelope, and handed it to her. "I've been instructed to give this to you, and for you to read it before we depart. You can sit in the car while you read it, but I can't leave without your permission, understand?" Meredith looked at him inquisitively, but nodded.

Booker walked away from the vehicle, and sat on a bench nestled in a near-by garden. She opened the envelope. Inside, was a older style cell phone, and a typed note. It read:

M,

Welcome to Gateway Canyons Resort. If you are reading this, then you have made it safely, and have met Booker. He is a highly professional service provider with whom I have contracted to bring you safely to me. Booker is to make sure you are completely comfortable, and to make sure that nothing you might want, or need, is overlooked. Unfortunately, he has been instructed to tell you nothing about where you are going. It may be obvious to you by now that we are not staying at Gateway Canyons. Maybe someday…

Before you leave with Booker, I need you to leave your cell phone in your car. I have provided you with a prepaid phone that, while not very sexy, works well, and will allow you to call anywhere, anytime, without being traced. The number is 404-281-3264.

Finally, this day has arrived. I can't actually believe it—it has been the longest week for me. I can't wait to see you! I hope you are hungry. I am. Very.

G

Meredith finally relaxed. No wonder Booker asked if she needed a bathroom. "Booker!" she called out. He stood and came straight over to her. She was smiling now. "I'm ready to go. Can you stop by my car so that I can leave something there? And, how long is our drive? I think I would like to use the restroom."

"Yes, Ms. Meredith," Booker said as he headed for the Escalade. He joined Meredith in the front of the vehicle, and closed his door. "How's the temperature for you?" he asked.

"A little warm," she replied. Then added pointing to her left, "My car is the white Explorer over there by the tree."

"Got it." Booker drove over to her car, and Meredith jumped out, unlocked her car and placed her switched-off cell phone in the center console. The car chirped when she re-locked it.

Now back in the car, she asked, "So, where are we off to, Booker?" Meredith wanted to remember his name so she used it in her question committing it to memory.

"The bathroom first. There's one at our first stop—about ten minutes away. Will you be OK with that? I can always stop at the lobby, and you can use the facilities there."

Meredith still was not completely relaxed, but she felt in her gut that she could trust Booker. The fact that Geoff had signed his note with his usual "G" also made her feel more comfortable. But seeing Geoff in ten minutes, she didn't want her having to pee be the first thing they discussed when she arrived. "Can we stop briefly at the lobby?" she asked.

"Sure, no problem." And with that, Booker went straight to the front door, and Meredith hopped out and hurried inside.

She was back in just a couple of minutes, and said, "thanks," as she climbed back in, and Booker closed her door for her. "So, where is our first stop?" she asked again.

Booker replied, "Ms. Meredith, I have been instructed, specifically, to disclose nothing to you about where you are headed. I was told this was for your personal safety. Geoff has taken every precaution to insure your trip is one in which you can feel completely at ease—and that starts with your safety."

Meredith pondered that for a minute, then replied, "OK, Booker. Let's go." She was looking out the passenger window and marveling at the pristine grounds amidst the rock formations when Booker pulled away. Her mind was not on nature.

* * *

They pulled out on Colorado State Highway 141 and turned back to the northeast—the direction Meredith had just come from. About ten minutes later, they pulled onto a very narrow, but paved, road, and there was a sign pointing straight ahead that read, "Airport—Gateway Canyons." It didn't register with Meredith. Her mind was completely overwhelmed with seeing Geoff again, and she was worried about how she looked—even though she had checked, and re-checked, her make-up back at the resort.

The Escalade pulled into a small parking lot, and came to a stop next to a one-room building that had the words "Gateway Canyons International Airport" etched into a large sandstone monument by the entrance. Meredith started to focus. "Where are we?" she asked.

"Gateway Canyons Airport," Booker replied. "I'll grab your bag and meet you inside."

They both climbed out, and Meredith took stock of where she was standing. There was a long runway stretched out down a valley bordered on both sides by mesas and buttes. The sky was blue, and she could feel the weather warming.

There were no planes present, but on the other side of the "terminal" stood a gleaming, dark blue, helicopter. What?

"I'm meeting Geoff, HERE?" she inquired.

"No. Not exactly. I am taking you to him. I'm sorry if there was any confusion," he said sincerely. "There is a restroom inside; our flight will be about forty-five minutes, and there is no bathroom on board. I have to file our flight plan and inspect the aircraft before we depart. We should be ready to board in 20 minutes."

●　●　●

Meredith walked out to the helicopter with Booker. It looked brand new, but she was petrified. She had never been on one; never wanted to. "You sure this is safe?" she asked.

Booker laughed. "Very. I've been flying helicopters my entire adult life. I flew a very similar model to this beauty when serving in the U.S. Army. This here is what's called a LongRanger. It's made by Bell Helicopters out of Quebec. It seats seven, but today, you and I will be the only ones aboard. It can fly 430 miles on a tank of fuel at a maximum speed of 138 miles per hour. It is powered by twin turbo jet engines, and can fly as high as 13,500 feet—high enough for us to fly over and around any mountains anywhere in North America. On board, it is fitted out with the finest of avionics and electronics. And, I must say, I have never seen such a luxurious craft—ever. I know the base price for one of these babies is around $1.2 million, but the owner has spent a fortune on customizing the cabin. You can, of course, have the choice of flying up front with me, or back in the cabin. What do you say?"

She was impressed with Booker's experience and knowledge. It calmed her to know she was in such good hands. "I see that the logo on your shirt matches the one on the door here," Meredith pointed out.

"Yeah, I noticed that, too. Classy. Anyway, this is my first assignment with this company so I didn't ask a lot of questions except for copies of the service records of the chopper and its flight logs. This bird has been pampered. But, we need to get going. It's 3:25 PM, and Mr. Geoff was expecting us at 4:00, so we will be a little late as it is. I will radio him once airborne. So, Ms. Meredith, what will it be? Front or back?"

"It's Meredith. You can drop the Ms."

"Sorry, Ms. Meredith. I would really like a full-time job flying for this company. They have a portfolio of aircraft, and jobs like this are rare. Mr. Geoff has asked me to address you as "Ms. Meredith," and in fact, until I land a job with his firm, I will be addressing him as Mr. Geoff."

"A portfolio of aircraft?" Meredith said more to herself, nodding. "I think I will ride up front with you, Booker."

The two of them walked around to the passenger door, and Booker held the door open while Meredith climbed aboard. She settled into her seat, and Booker got up on the outside step and reached over Meredith's head and brought down two seat belts that fell over her shoulders—one on either side of her head. "Can you fasten your lap belt and hand me the attached buckle," he said. She did as she was told.

Booker took the loose belt and buckle, and snapped the two shoulder belts into it merging them above her breasts. He pulled firmly on the lap belt and then the chest belt making sure she was securely restrained. Meredith experienced a very strange sensation. In addition to feeling safe, and excited, she had to admit to herself that the restraints had an erotic thrill to them.

Booker was back in his seat in no time, and easily fastened all his belts in the same way as he had for Meredith. He put on a headset. He then reached up to the ceiling and flipped a couple of switches and the engines started to spool up, and the massive blade above their heads began to rotate. He handed a headset to Meredith and helped her put it on. The ear-pieces were soft, and cupped her ears comfortably. Booker adjusted the mouthpiece to be right in front of her lips. He switched on a small dial attached to her right ear pod, and she heard him say, "Can you hear me?" Meredith nodded "You can adjust your volume by turning this knob in either direction. I do need you to be quiet for a few minutes as I need to communicate with the resort alerting them to our departure, OK?"

"OK, Captain!" she laughed. But, she was still weak with anxiety. What in the hell was she doing?

The engines where whining, and the rotor was spinning fast enough that Meredith could now see through it. The earphones muffled the outside noise, but she could hear Booker clearly. "Gateway Control, this is Bravo-Zero-Six-Tango requesting immediate departure from Gateway Airfield. Over."

"Roger, Bravo-Zero-Six-Tango; Gateway Control clears you for departure. Radar and communications show no additional aircraft in our airspace. Please come again and visit."

"Roger. Bravo-Zero-Six-Tango, out." And with that, Booker increased the engines—the rotor now spinning at full velocity, and he pulled back on the stick between his legs. The aircraft started to lift. Meredith was mesmerized trying to take it all in. She couldn't help but look out the windows around her as the helicopter lifted to the sky. She was literally strangling he arm rests. Swiveling left, the helicopter flew low and fast down the valley above the runway, then climbed suddenly up. The sensation was thrilling. Booker banked the bird to the right heading north back towards Grand Junction.

"You OK?" he inquired through his headpiece. Meredith turned, and with a big grin nodded vigorously at him. "You can talk now!" This time it was his turn to smile.

"Yes!" she said excitedly. "This is great! It's so…" Her voice trailed off as she gawked at the scenery unfolding before her. She literally had a bird's eye view.

In a few minutes, the helicopter banked right, again, and headed northeast. Booker reached down to the instrument cluster and flicked a switch. Turning to Meredith, he held his index finger to his lips. She nodded. "Mr. Geoff, this is Booker. Do you read me?" Meredith could hear every word, and she held her breath. She had not heard Geoff's voice since she left him at the penthouse of the Grand Hotel many weeks ago. Or was it months? There was static, then there was him…

"Roger, Booker. Do you have my precious cargo?"

"10-4, Sir. She's a little scared of flying—this being her virginal flight on a whirlybird, and all—but I will have her safely on the ground at approximately sixteen-twenty (he was using military time for 4:20 PM). Unless, of course, she wants to do a little sight-seeing."

Geoff laughed easily. "No, Booker, bring her straight in. The welcoming committee is anxious to inspect your cargo in daylight, and I need you to get back in the air before the sun goes down."

"Roger that, Mr. Geoff. I'm heading straight to the landing field."

"God speed. Over and out." Geoff clicked off the air.

Booker deftly played with the control panel, and then spoke, "Aspen Air Traffic Control, this is Bravo-Zero-Six-Tango requesting city flyover and private dispatch two point three miles northwest of airfield."

Meredith's eyes widened, but she looked straight ahead. The city approaching below them must be Aspen. She had never been there. Not even close. Now, she was being whisked there on a helicopter. She sat in silence, her body safely restrained, transfixed, trying to take it all in—visually and mentally.

"Roger, Bravo-Zero-Six-Tango. Police bird at nine-five hundred feet; forty degrees to port. Visual flight rules. Only traffic reported. You are cleared for private dispatch."

"10-4, Aspen Air Traffic Control. Have visual on police bird. Bravo-Zero-Six-Tango, out." And with that Booker lowered the nose of the helicopter and banked to the right so that Meredith was looking straight down at Aspen and the surrounding snow fields. "Beautiful day for flying, isn't it?"

Without taking her eyes off the city below her, she uttered, "Very."

43

NICK

O N THAT FRIDAY MORNING, GEOFF AND NICK ARRIVED TO INSPECT
the house that Nick had arranged for Geoff's rendezvous with Meredith. The
night before in Grand Junction, at approximately 10:45 PM, CBC's big deal had
finally closed. Nick would normally attend all the closings of the firm, but had,
on this trip, headed to Aspen to prepare for Geoff's weekend.

The house was a large, 5,400 square foot, mountain home on twenty acres. It
was overkill, Nick knew, but he had been given specific instructions for the house.
It needed to be special—a modern log home if possible, fireplaces, great views
and an adjacent space to land a helicopter. Nick would make sure the home was
stocked with the best food and wine, and that the bar was a cornucopia of choices.
Geoff couldn't remember what she drank, or liked to eat, but he wanted to make
sure that whatever she wanted, he could make for her.

Booker had flown Nick out on Thursday morning, and Geoff Friday. It was
too early Friday morning to land the 'copter on site, so they had landed at the
Aspen Airport, and Nick had met the LongRanger in a rented white Range Rover.
Nick and Geoff talked all the way to the house—mostly about the deal that had
just closed. But as they approached the house, Geoff said, "What do you think?"

"I think you're crazy."

"I know you think that. But, is the house safe?"

"Yes. I've checked on every detail that is controllable. The house has an alarm
system, and you have all the codes. It is out of earshot from any other house in the
area. Most of the homes here are on larger plots of land, and I took some time to
make sure that the neighbors wouldn't be able to spy. I've left some high-powered

binoculars in case you want to keep an eye out, yourself. You know, when that helicopter lands, every Tom, Dick and Harry is going to be curious. Their wives? Even more so. Just be extra careful is all I am saying."

They walked into the front entry and into the great room. There was an enormous fireplace and mantle, and a fire had already been laid, just waiting for a match and two lovers to enjoy it. There were large, overstuffed, chairs and sofas strewn around—some oriented to the fireplace, other pieces facing the floor-to-ceiling windows. The towering beamed ceiling rose impossibly high with a cathedral of freshly washed glass exposing a spectacular north-facing view.

"Beautiful. Thank you, Nick," Geoff expressed with a warmth of a knowing friendship.

"You haven't seen the master suite, yet. Hold your compliments."

"Fair enough," Geoff replied. Smiling, he added, "Take me to your master, then."

They could have taken the elevator, but they chose the grand staircase instead. Once upstairs, they went down the hall, and Nick led them through the double doors that opened into a sanctuary of beauty. The room itself was nearly 1,000 square feet, vaulted ceilings, and like the great room, it had an oversized fireplace (prepared; waiting for a match), cathedral glass, overstuffed furniture oriented to the view and a massive balcony. But, unlike the great room, it had a voluptuous king-sized poster bed with a richly upholstered headboard, and a doorway that led to the master bathroom.

The entire west side of the master suite was dedicated solely to the bathroom. What struck Geoff was the design: lots of glass that, in summer, would slide into the wall bringing the outside in. Even in winter, the shower was a wall of clear glass fronting a very private and serene grove of pines and aspens. The oversized tub could also be exposed to the woods with the touch of a button. There were "his and her" vanities with large walls of mirrors to reflect the snow-capped mountains and adjacent fields. The floors were heated. No detail was overlooked.

"Can I thank you now?" Geoff pleaded.

"Nope. Last stop: the kitchen."

They made their way downstairs and into the sprawling kitchen—fitted out with every conceivable professional appliance. This was a chef's dream. But what struck Geoff was that the kitchen was fully stocked. Produce, meats, cheeses, fruit, sweets, spices, sauces, beverages of every sort. "You've thought of everything, haven't you, Nicolas George?" Geoff said, impressed.

"I've certainly given it my best. I'm sure there are things that I have forgotten. If you find you're missing anything, text or call me. I've got a concierge here in town that can deliver you anything you need. As a matter of fact, keep in contact with me. And have that Meredith of yours call and check in with her friend, Jessica. You know, the one that tried to have me arrested? I like that girl. Wouldn't hurt for your partner to have a safety contact, too." Nick headed for the front door. "Will you drive me back to the Aspen Airport? That way you will have wheels."

"Sure," Geoff replied.

• • •

Geoff pulled up to the curb, and kept the engine running. "Thanks, Nick. I mean it. This is completely stupid, I know. You're a great friend."

"No worries. I know you would do the same for me."

"Would? I think you mean, will." They both laughed. Geoff added, "And, can you arrange a closing dinner for all our team that worked on the Grand Junction deal for next Thursday, the 27th? Spouses invited. I want it to be special."

"Sure. Consider it done," Nick replied. "The usual place?"

"No, let's do something different. Private room. On the water. Your choice."

"Got it. Let me know if I can do anything else," Nick added.

"Travel well, my friend. I think Mike is waiting for you with his toy jet."

"Oh, and Geoff?" Nick stopped before closing his door. Geoff turned and looked back at Nick. "The condoms are in the bedside table."

44

GEOFF

GEOFF HAD BEEN IN THE KITCHEN FOR THE PAST TWO HOURS. HE was preparing a special dinner, and he had started early to make sure that when Meredith arrived, the preparation would be largely complete. He could hardly concentrate. He was like a kid on his first date. Why so nervous?

Susie had called a little over an hour ago. He had kept his room at The Grand allowing him to have plausible deniability, as Nick called it, in case she got suspicious. But, Geoff was sure she wouldn't. Keeping the room also had the advantage of being able to hide behind his room's voice mail—an expensive insurance policy that had already paid off. He had checked his voice mail, and was surprised to hear Susie's voice.

"Hi Honey, it's me," it had recorded. "Just wanted to see if your deal closed. Good luck. There is no one on this planet more capable than you. If it closes early, any chance of a swing home to coach CJ's game? He misses you. They all do. Call me later. Bye." She sounded to be in a pretty good mood.

Geoff did call immediately and said that his deal was on "life support," and that he was doing everything to get it closed, but he did not expect to be home this particular weekend. Susie took it in stride. She didn't really expect him anyway.

"What are you going to do this weekend?" she asked.

"Oh, I don't know exactly," he said. And added, "I'll probably just hang here and enjoy some down time. Take a hike, maybe. It's supposed to be warm here this weekend. I haven't had time to myself for as long as I can remember."

Susie then launched into all the things that she was doing that were exhausting her: shuttling the kids, going to yoga and spin class, racing to the beauty parlor, getting her "mani" and "pedi," heading back to her meetings with the National Charity League, instructing Rosanne what to prepare for dinner tonight. Then she added, "And, I haven't had TWO SECONDS to find a gardener. This house is getting to be an embarrassment, Geoff. Maybe you can do some research, and find someone, with your free time this weekend."

There was a bit of truth to that comment. He was sure that their 7,000 square foot house, on the water in Tiburon, was NOT an embarrassment, but he was sure the lawn and yard needed care. But, he really didn't want to get into it with her now. He assured her that he would look into it when he returned.

"Give all the kids a hug from me, OK?"

"Sure," she said a little too curtly. "I wish you were here to do it yourself. It's not the same."

"You're right, Honey," he answered trying to keep his voice even and understanding. "I'll send them each a text over the weekend. I didn't mean it to be an imposition. I'm sorry."

"No, I'm sorry. It's just that all this crap that I have to deal with every day is getting to me. That's all."

"Well hang in there. I'll see you on Tuesday." Geoff then quickly added, "Oh, I forgot to tell you, there is a closing dinner for the entire team and their spouses next Thursday. Should be fun."

Susie then said, "I thought you said your deal was on 'life support' and it wasn't closed yet. Why are you scheduling a closing party?"

Shit. He needed to be very careful. Think.

"Nick is planning the event in anticipation that we can get this over the line. You know how hard it is to get reservations in The City for a party of that size, right? And, as you said yourself, I'm a pretty good closer."

"OK. Have a great time to yourself this weekend." The sarcasm evident.

"Oh, I will. Speak soon." And with that Geoff had hung up, and headed back to that gourmet kitchen in the mountains.

. . .

He barely heard it at first. He was busy chopping chives on the built-in cutting board on the kitchen island. An hour ago, he had turned on some beautiful background music that combined American Indian flutes with the sounds of the wind, rain, birds and the cascading water of a spring creek. He had an apron on, and was concentrating. A glass of chilled Chardonnay at his side.

He stopped what he was doing and listened more intently. He found the remote to the music system and muted the flutes. There was no doubt; there was a helicopter overhead. He went to the sink, and washed his hands. He hung his apron on a hook by the two ovens, and quickly ran to the near-by powder room. Looking in the mirror, he swept his hair back with his hands, and checked his teeth. All good. But, he felt very shaky. He had to remind himself that he was the head of one of the most powerful venture capital firms in the world. Wasn't his picture just on the front page of the New York Times? "Get a grip!" he said to no one.

Geoff found his leather coat draped over one of the over-stuffed chairs in the great room. But, before he put it on, he walked over to the fireplace, checked the flue, and then struck a blue-tip match on the stone hearth. The match-head sparked to life in a fluorescent flash—then settled to a joyous flicker. He leaned down, and touched the flame to the crumpled newspaper below the kindling that sat below the two dry sections of pine. One piece was clearly larger than the other - with the smaller one on top. The fire hungrily devoured the flammable foundation, and quickly worked its way up to encircled the two logs holding each other tightly together.

PART II
THE HUNGER & THE HUNTED

45

BOBBIE

HIGH IN THE UINTA MOUNTAINS OF NORTH-CENTRAL UTAH, BOBBIE sat calmly as the wind-driven snow whipped his face like sand. He felt nothing. His yellow goggles kept the shards from blinding him as he peered intently in the direction of a stand of Aspen trees several hundred yards in the distance. It had taken him over two hours, but he had tracked this wounded buck by expertly identifying its hoof marks, and staying downwind of his prey. Oh yes; the blood had left a trail, too.

Bobbie was after four things: First, he wanted his razor-tipped arrow back. He would clean the torn flesh from it, but the blood would remain, undisturbed, until it wore off with time and use. His arrows were trophies of kills and hits, and this buck was a beauty. Second, he wanted the deer's head—holding a huge rack of antlers atop its soon-to-be glass eyes. He had no interest in hauling this animal back out of the forest four miles to his camouflaged truck. He didn't eat venison, either. He wanted the head proudly mounted for display in his living room— which, until three days ago, he was planning for his new house. That would now have to wait. Fuck them. Third, he didn't want to get caught. And, although it was a Friday morning, the 21st of November to be exact, and it was unlikely any authorities would be out snooping deep in the woods where Bobbie stalked, it still was not hunting season. He could be arrested here in Utah for illegally bagging a deer—particularly a buck—and that was the last thing he needed right now.

Finally, and most importantly, he craved the thrill of the kill. Finding the buck always took patience and skill, but tracking the beast was the real fun. As the animal bled and ran, it lost strength and speed. Bobbie's tracking skills were keen—honed from years in the woods alone. He had sharp eyes and a polished instinct for following a trail even in the harshest of conditions. Snow, leaves, gravel, sand, dirt; it didn't matter. Sometimes it would take hours to find the wounded animal, but Bobbie always found his victim. He could be more careless about approaching his prey in those waning moments of its life. And, oddly, he always spoke to his prey before his signature coup 'd tau: an arrow speared through the exhausted creature's eye straight into its brain. The death was quick, but the fear and panic in the bulging eyes, as he stood over his prey and pulled back his death arrow, was worth everything. He was getting excited just thinking about it.

At first, the buck was with another deer—a doe - in a clearing quite a ways down a wooded valley when Bobbie spotted him. It had taken him almost an hour to approach the duo while they contentedly meandered together. His camouflaged clothing kept him hidden as he quietly moved into a position where he could take a shot. He quietly clipped his scope onto his bow, and adjusted the optic sight bringing the buck into focus.

Bow hunting took strength, endurance, experience and patience. It was one thing to stand casually at an archery range and fire arrows at a target attached to a hay bale. It was quite another to carry your bow and quiver of arrows on your back while you crouched and crawled—often for hours—getting in position to make that first shot. And, once in position, the hunter was often kneeling, leaning or awkwardly standing while he placed the slotted butt of the arrow onto the tensioned string and pulled back on the weapon. Holding the arrow with his fingers—his thumbtight under his chin and cheek while he scoped the almost always-moving animal, Bobbie would have to then smoothly position the crosshairs of his scope over the victim's midsection as close as possible to the heart before releasing his projectile.

Bobbie pulled an arrow out of his quiver, and loaded it with his index and middle finger (his "fucker finger" as he liked to call it) with his thumb providing helpful stability. He pulled back on his bow drawing the arrow into firing position under his chin as well as bringing the scope to his left eye. Holding the bow and arrow with maximum tension, he sighted the buck. He exhaled slowly to calm himself and steady his hand. The arrow released with a barely audible throng of the string, and the hiss of exhaust, from the departing arrow. He didn't hear the thud of impact, but the doe, standing along side of the buck, did, and she darted, panic-stricken, into the woods. The buck squealed, and he, too, slashed into the woods in a different direction.

Bobbie didn't hurry; the damage had been done, and the fun was just beginning. He unclipped the sight from his bow and placed it back into his pack. He
made sure his quiver of seven remaining arrows was secure, and that the bow, itself
was repacked. It might be several hours before he would need it again to finalize
the death ritual.

● ● ●

As he slowly, and carefully, tracked his prey, Bobbie's mind was razor-focused.
He frequently crouched and studied the direction of the hoof-prints while dabbing his fingers into the splotches of blood staining the virgin-white snow before
sucking those fingers testing for freshness. He sensed the wind temperature and
direction always calculating time, temperature and weather conditions. He cared
little about being detected by the wind at this stage, for the wounded animal was
hemorrhaging precious blood. And, the faster the buck bolted, the faster it would
be forced to lie down, expended, and await its fate.

Far away were the obscene events of Monday. Bow hunting was therapeutic
and meditative. It allowed Bobbie to free his mind of everything. He had fled the
school, and his house, intent on getting drunk with his friends. He had quickly
packed all his camping and hunting gear into the bed of his truck, and had roared
out of town before he had to be confronted by his wife—or anyone else who
would, for sure, have heard the free-flowing gossip of that one-horse town. Did
they really have to email everyone and anyone involved at Granite High? He had
left with no plans, and the note he left Meredith was vague: he was hunting and
would likely be home Sunday. But, fuck that; he might stay out for a week or
more; maybe not come back at all.

Bobbie rubbed his thumb and index fingers together bringing them to his
nose. The smell of fresh blood excited him. The tracks were fresh also. He knew
he was getting close, but he was also running out of time. There was plenty
of daylight; that was not the problem. The wind had picked up and whipped
stinging snow across his face, but importantly, the snow would soon cover the
buck's tracks—filling hoof marks and erasing blood evidence. He had to pick up
the pace.

Finally, he saw the buck moving slowly, alone, now towards an aspen grove—
its once proud head bowed forward under the weight of its large antlers. Hidden
in a large stand of bushes, Bobbie pulled out his bow, and clipped on the sight.
He raised it to his eye. Once focused, he could see the buck breathing heavily,

his legs unstable, his first arrow sticking out of the creature, just behind its front leg—like a misplaced antennae. He could see the animal call out before he heard it. Then, this majestic creature fell to its front knees as though praying, gasping for precious oxygen and struggling to stand. Bobbie seated his next arrow onto the bow, and calmly pulled the gut-string back under his chin. He sighted his next target: the buck's rear thigh. The arrow hissed its exit. It tore through precious flesh and muscle. The buck's eyes bulged, and he remained in that position for only a moment, then toppled over onto his side.

Bobbie stood slowly, and loosened his quiver drawing out another arrow—careful not to cut himself on the dangerous tip. He walked slowly, but evenly, across the field of blowing snow until he had reached the aspen grove. The buck wasn't far from the perimeter of the grove, and lay panting heavily. Bobbie approached it from the rear, and when he was within a few yards of the dear, it heard the crunching snow behind it. The buck tried to stand, but failed—its one good back leg kicking wildly, but its front legs failing him. This magnificent specimen had all but given up—its forced breathing clearly audible now with white puffs firing from its bleeding nose.

Bobbie walked around so that its head was directly below him. The eyes were bulging, pleading. He fitted the death-arrow onto the tensioned gut, but did not pull it back immediately. Bobbie had a vision of Don DeLatore, the Granite District Supervisor, in his mind—that hateful man who had disrespected, and talked down to, him a few days ago.

Bobbie's eyes glazed over, and he spoke to the buck, "Listen here, you limp-dicked little faggot, maggot of a life-form. You and I will meet again—this time on my terms. And this time, you will be begging me for your life, Donny ol' boy."

The buck jerked quickly which got Bobbie's attention. He took his boot and stomped on the animal's neck temporarily stilling it. "So, you want to escape do you? A little late for that, Don-Don you moron." Its eyes were wide with unrelenting fear. Bobbie drew the arrow back to its full tautness, and lowered it towards the creature's head. He took a deep breath and exhaled slowly—his full, unaltered, attention now on sighting his shot. He released his weapon, and within a split second, the arrow entered the buck's eye socket and burrowed into its brain. Bobbie heard nothing at all. As he lowered his bow, the animal was jerking spasmodically.

Bobbie waited a few seconds until the convulsions of death ceased. He then removed his pack, and knelt on the ground beside his kill. He grabbed the first arrow, the one the buck had carried around with him for hours, and yanked it free from the carcass—flesh clinging and dandling in tiny globs and ribbons. The second arrow had torn through the animal's thigh and had exited through to be a painful scalpel for the buck's remaining good rear leg. This arrow was slippery with warm blood, and Bobbie had to use a rag for purchase. He pulled this arrow easily in the direction of initial flight—the feathers fed last through the leg. Then, he took ahold of the arrow imbedded in the dear's head, and pushing against its antlers, carefully removed it—making sure not to damage the circumference of the socket where the glass eye would soon be fitted. Without making any attempt to clean them, he re-seated his arrows back into the quiver.

He then reached into his backpack and drew out a large, sheathed, ten-inch, serrated hunting knife. He carefully unsnapped the cover flap and removed it. Bobbie leaned down so that his mouth was literally in the buck's ear. He could smell the creature, and feel the still-hot temperature of life. "Fuck you," he whispered. Then, he started laughing—hysterically. He couldn't stop. Tears were coming to his eyes, and the laughter continued until his macabre humor shaded into anger. Bobbie sat back on his heels, and looked up into the sky - screaming at the top of his lungs. His eyes, now themselves bulging, were still red and wet. His lungs emptied into a soundless, thick, forested, abyss.

Bobbie grasped his knife more firmly, and holding it against the animal's windpipe, began to saw. The sounds of tearing flesh, ripping muscles and grinding bone were a symphony to his ears. He didn't stop until the head was freed from the torso.

46

ASPEN

BOOKER BANKED THE HELICOPTER STEEPLY TO THE RIGHT, AND then leveled it above an empty lot adjacent to a magnificent contemporary log home. Meredith could clearly see smoke emanating from one of the chimneys. A man was standing at the railing of the balcony - watching, intently, their descent. She suddenly found it hard to breathe. Her heart was racing.

The rotors whipped the snow beneath them, and temporarily obscured the view, as they delicately settled out of the late-afternoon sky. The runners of the helicopter softly touched the ground beneath them, and immediately, Booker flicked a few switches and the engines spooled down as the large rotor above them slowed.

"Ms. Meredith, please stay where you are until the rotors have completely stopped," Booker requested.

"OK," she said looking back towards the house. She could see now, but the man on the balcony was gone.

The massive blade stopped, and Booker said it was now safe to unbuckle her seat belts. She reached below her breasts and pressed the quick-release button. The shoulder harnesses uncoupled from her lap belt, and she slithered out of them. Just as she was pulling the tab on her lap belt, the door on her side of the helicopter unlatched and swung open. She was startled, and a gust of cold air rushed in. Instinctively, she leaned away from the door, but looked back towards it. There, holding his hand out to her was Geoff.

Meredith took a few seconds to take stock of her greeter. My God, he was even better than she remembered. Today, he was wearing a brown leather bomber jacket lined with lamb's wool, and a turtle neck sweater underneath. His salt-and-pepper hair was swept back and he had on round horn-rimmed dark glasses. But it was his smile that unnerved her—the easy warmth emanating a welcome of safety.

"Hey," he said.

"Hey," she smiled and took his hand.

He pulled her to the door opening, then, reaching down around her waist, he lifted her out of the cockpit into his arms. He held her tight for quite some time—her head buried into his shoulder and neck; her feet still not on the ground. He finally put her down, but immediately moved his warm hands to her face where he tilted her face upwards so that their eyes could meet. With both his thumbs, he wiped away her delicate tears. It was Booker that broke the silence.

"Mr. Geoff, I've unloaded Ms. Meredith's bag and placed it over there out of the way," he said pointing to a large suitcase at the edge of the lot.

Geoff looked over his shoulder, and then turned his gaze right back to Meredith. "Maybe there was a typo," he laughed—his smile widening. "I meant to say two NIGHTS, not two WEEKS! Let's just say that my hands were a little shaky."

That seemed to break the ice. Meredith almost choked when she, too, started to laugh. "I didn't know what to bring! I was nervous! I didn't know where we were going, or what we were going to do. I tried to think of everything, and tried my hardest to think of what you would be wearing. I thought…"

Booker cleared his throat. When neither of them responded, he said firmly, "I'm sorry to interrupt, but mission complete, sir. I need to head back to base."

"Oh, of course!" Geoff said coming back to reality. Thank you, Booker. Do you need to use the bathroom or get a snack before you head back?" Geoff inquired.

"No sir. I'll be on my way. It's a five-minute flight from here. I'm staying downtown if you need anything at all. Here's my card with my phone number on it. Call me if you need anything. If I…"

"My phone!" Meredith exclaimed. "It's in the envelope by my seat in the helicopter. I almost forgot."

Booker stepped over and unlatched the passenger door and retrieved the package.

"Thank you, Booker. " Meredith looked him in the eyes with sincerity, and added, "For everything."

"Don't mention it, Ms. Meredith, it was a pleasure. And Mr. Geoff, if I don't hear from you, I will be here at 11 AM Sunday to pick up Ms. Meredith for her return flight to Gateway Canyons. I'll not start the engines until you both are safely inside. No need for snow burns or blindness," he added.

"Thank you, Booker. Well done. See you Sunday," he replied.

And, with that, he returned his gaze to Meredith, and held out his hand. She took it, and they walked silently to her suitcase. Geoff picked it up never letting go of her hand - hers feeling so small and soft in his. They reached the house and both stomped off the loose snow on their feet. As they entered, the warmth of the home, and the smell of cooking, overtook them.

"Can I help you off with your coat," he said as stood behind her and reached around to unzip the front.

"Please," she said softly.

As he pulled the coat from her shoulders, he leaned down and softly kissed the back of her neck. She unperceptively shivered. He inhaled deeply, and he whispered, "I love the smell of you." Her back still against his chest, she leaned her head back and closed her eyes. This had to be a dream.

They could hear the engines alight and gain strength. It took no time at all for the Bell Long Ranger aircraft to lift to the clouds. Once clear of the treetops, it spun and tilted towards Aspen airport—leaving Geoff and Meredith to their long-awaited weekend together.

● ● ●

"Come on in," Geoff offered. "I've got dinner underway, and I need to check on a few things. Can I pour you a glass of wine?"

Meredith didn't reply right away. She was looking around the great room astounded at the scale and beauty of this amazing house: the floor-to-ceiling windows affording an incredible view down the canyon, the fireplace ablaze and crackling, and the kitchen alive with what appeared to be quite a preparation. The sun had already disappeared behind the western mountains, and dusk was turning to night.

"Please. Chardonnay?"

"Coming right up," Geoff said as he opened one of the two refrigerators on the far wall. He had already opened a bottle of ZD Black Label—a wine rumored to be served frequently at the White House—and pulling a delicate crystal goblet from the leaded glass cabinet, he poured her a nice portion of the lightly golden wine.

He gave her the glass, and lifting his towards her, he said, "Welcome to Aspen. Here's to a special person, sharing with me a special weekend, exploring answers to our questions, but asking of ourselves nothing but to be open to every, and all, possibilities."

She bowed her head and closed her eyes for just a second, nodded her head, and looked up into Geoff's gaze. "To answers and possibilities," she replied. Meredith held her glass out towards him, and never taking their eyes off one another, touched glasses. Then, each sipped, and enjoyed, the silky smooth, earthy, oak-touched, wine.

Meredith, holding her glass, came to Geoff's side, and wrapped her other arm around his waist snuggling against his side. "Thanks for this dream. I still cannot believe I am actually here doing this with you—a man I hardly know, but strangely, trust. A man I want to get to know, desperately." She pulled away and shook her head, astounded, as she looked around again.

"Why don't I help you upstairs with your shipping container, and you can freshen up before dinner?" Geoff smiled. Meredith pursed her lips and gave him a mock-frown. He continued, "I have loads more prep work on dinner here before I can feel settled enough to sit with you, and relax."

"That would be great. Do you have a crane? Or should we call Booker back with his helicopter to hoist this beast upstairs?" Meredith teased.

"Oh, I think I can handle it—so long as I am accompanied for moral support."

Geoff checked the kitchen one last time before heading towards her bag and the grand staircase. When they got to her suitcase, she pointed at the over-sized door by the stairs. "That's an odd-looking coat closet."

"It's the elevator. In case you're too tired, or too drunk, to navigate the stairs." Geoff winked.

"Or…to relive a recent rendezvous at the Grand Hotel," she deadpanned, smiling.

"Or that," he said as he put a hand behind her neck, pinching her softly before removing it.

He grabbed her suitcase, and together they mounted the stairs. Once at the top, Geoff pointed left down the hall to the double doors and said, "That's my room. Yours is down to our right."

Meredith never hesitated, nor spoke a word. She walked straight down to those double doors, and opened them. Then she froze. She had never seen such a bedroom before. The whole house, actually. But, the bedroom before her was so grand, so warm, so inviting. There was an unlit fire in the fireplace just waiting for a match. Picture windows framed the same, spectacular, northerly view. She could see the lights of homes far off in the distance, but she was struck by the privacy they enjoyed here.

"You can put my freight container on the bed, please, sir," she said. "Any other surprises for me today?"

"Is that your first question?" he asked sincerely.

"Yes. That's my first question. You must be 100% honest with your answer."

Geoff looked deep in thought, then replied, "Many."

"Oh?"

"Dinner for starters. Which reminds me, I need to get back downstairs and put my apron on," he said. "Hope you like veal."

Meredith was already heading for the bathroom when Geoff swung her suitcase onto the bed.

"Holy shit!" he heard her exclaim from the bathroom.

"Your towel is the one hanging over the tub," he directed.

She turned and raised her eyebrows. "I thought my room was in the South Wing."

"It is, if you want it to be."

"No, this room will be just fine. YOU can have the South Wing!" They both laughed.

Meredith turned and walked straight into Geoff's waiting arms. The embrace was passionate and immediate. She pulled his shirt out of his pants and slid both her arms up his bare back pulling him into her. He could feel her fingernails. He wrapped his arms around her lower back and urged her body against his. He moved his hands up her sides, brushing the sides of her breasts, before lifting, and cradling, her face. He leaned down, eyes open, lips parting and his heart racing wildly. She leaned back, eyes closed, and welcomed him. Their kiss was greedy and urgent. The strength and confidence of his embrace was matched by her total abandonment. Their tongues explored each other's—interrupted only by passion-laden nibbles and bites to their mouths, ears and necks. It was when Meredith grabbed Geoff's hand and gently placed it on her left breast, that Geoff stopped the furious fumbling, and slowly caressed her—feeling her hardened nipple through her sweater and bra.

Panting hard, he gasped, "Dinner. I've got to…I've got to get back to our dinner. I'll burn it."

She pulled him closer, and more urgently saying, "Burn, baby, burn," this time covering his mouth with hers so that he could feel the words as well as hear them. They both felt the excitement between their legs, and knew, for certain, that they would not be in separate rooms tonight. Joking or not.

He delicately eased her face away from his, and looked deep into her beckoning eyes. "I will be right downstairs. You'll find me easily. I'll be the guy with the apron on and an erection. I'll be hard to miss—if you know what I mean."

She responded quickly, saying, "I hope this suitcase is not the only thing you throw on this bed tonight. See you shortly."

And with that, they broke their embrace. Meredith was already pulling her sweater up and over her head as she was entering the master bathroom - the doors closing behind her. Geoff just stood there; so many thoughts racing through his mind. Then, he heard the water in the shower turn on, and he focused. He left the room closing the double doors behind him. At the top of the stairs, he stopped to tuck in his shirt and brush back his hair. He was still swollen with desire. He took a deep breath, listened once more to the water in the shower—trying to imagine the sight of Meredith's naked, wet, light cocoa-brown, body. Shaking his head, he quickly headed down the stairs, anxious for a fresh glass of cool white wine, and to let the evening unfold.

47

SUSIE

"THAT GODDAMNED RHONDA," SUSIE THOUGHT AS SHE WAS unpacking her gym bag. "She sure thinks she knows everything. Amazing what a little unexpected wealth does to a person from HER side of the tracks. Why, out of all forty-odd people in my spin class, did I have to ride next to her?"

Susie had a very busy Friday ahead, and she wasn't at all happy about it. Rosanne had called in sick today meaning she would have to run several unexpected errands. She had over-scheduled herself, once again, and Rosanne obviously wouldn't be there to make dinner for them. "I'll take the kids out for some steak tonight." The thought calmed her somewhat.

After her shower, Susie went to her closet to gather the dry-cleaning. This was Rosanne's job, but she needed that new skirt pressed for her luncheon next week, so she just decided to add another errand to her unraveling day. She had a large basket under her arm with her clothes, and she stopped at Geoff's closet to see if he had anything to take in. His closet was also a large walk-in with floor to ceiling racks, organizers, shoes and hung clothes—all surrounding an island of drawers for his socks, t-shirts, sporting gear and undergarments. She had to admit, she hadn't been in here for months. It was all very tidy, and she immediately spotted his dry-cleaning and laundry hampers back in the corner. The laundry could wait for Rosanne, but she grabbed his dry-cleaning and started sorting his clothes.

Something stopped her mid-sort. One of Geoff's shirts was smudged with a tan smear. Make-up? She drew the shirt out of the hamper for a closer look. She knew what base she wore, and had seen it on his shirts from time-to-time, but this was not her color. Instinctively, she brought the garment to her nose and inhaled softly. What was that smell? She sniffed at his shirt once more. Perfume. No doubt about it. What? Not hers. The odor was sweet, but unrecognizable. It certainly didn't come from her array of perfumes. She looked more closely at the shirt, and sure enough, there was more make-up, or lipstick, smudged on the collar in two places. Couldn't be. Geoff? No way. "I know that man inside and out. He would NEVER," she thought. There must be a very logical explanation, she concluded. He has many maddening habits and idiosyncrasies, but infidelity was certainly not one of them—completely out of the question.

Susie piled all of his clothes—including the tell-tale shirt—on top of hers, and gripping the basket in both hands, made her way down the hall, down the stairs, across the large family room to the attached garage. She loaded the basket into the back of her Range Rover, and as she was pulling out, she started to panic. What time was her hair appointment? She slammed on the breaks—tires screeching in her driveway. Susie pulled out her iPhone and checked her calendar. "Crap. 10 AM. I'm going to be late," she said to no one.

As she raced up the street, she swerved, and braked, to avoid a cat. Then, she floored it, roaring much too fast through the deserted streets of Tiburon. She had already forgotten about the shirt.

48

ASPEN

THE LARGE SAUCEPAN WAS TEEMING WITH BUTTER AND SPICES— the garlic, in particular, filling the whole downstairs with an inviting, and rich, aroma. He had tenderized the veal chops, mashed the potatoes and trimmed the broccoli. He had set a table by the fireplace. Geoff was impressed with his effort. The table was elegant, and inviting: white linens, sterling silver, bone china and crystal water and wine glasses.

He was stirring the French onion soup when he sensed someone behind him. He could then feel Meredith's arms wrap around him and then move up so that each hand caressed his chest. "Nice apron. But, I thought you would have an erection," she deadpanned.

Geoff laughed. "Oh, right. Sorry. I didn't find the veal as appealing as your breasts." He immediately turned around and stepped back to appraise this beautiful woman sharing this kitchen with him.

She was fresh out of the shower. Her hair was still damp, and pulled back into a short ponytail tied with a black velvet bow—exposing her bare neck. She wore black stirrup pants and red pumps. The sweater she wore was impossibly soft—and tight. She had omitted one very important detail: her bra.

He held out both arms, and they embraced again. This time, the holds were tender, the kisses soft. He loved her smell.

"I like your perfume. What do you call it?" Geoff asked.

Meredith thought about making a joke and being funny, but thought better of it. She was having a hard time believing where she was, and what she was doing. As she thought about just the last twelve hours, she could only summon the thought that this was all not really happening.

"Allure. It's called, Allure. I'm glad you like it. I bought it just for this occasion. It's the one thing I splurged on. I don't make that much money, and I had to take a bit from my savings, but it, for me, represented this whole weekend: doing something just for myself that was special."

"Well, I like your perfume, so you are doing something special for me," Geoff said sincerely. "Say, can you get the veal out of the refrigerator?"

"Sure. Which fridge?" she inquired.

"The one by the bar."

Geoff turned the heat on under the steamer. The broccoli would only take a few minutes. The potatoes were ready, and warming in one of the ovens. He ladled the onion soup into two small tureens, and shredded a generous amount of mild mozzarella cheese on top of each. He put them on a tray and slid them into a different pre-heated oven. She handed him the veal, and stood next to him—their arms touching—and watched intently while he grabbed the chops with some tongs and lowered them one-by-one into the saucepan. They sizzled and steamed. It was like a jailbreak of effervescence and aroma.

"Would you mind pouring our wine at the table?" Geoff asked.

"Sure," Meredith replied. "Red or white? And, where do I get it?"

"Red. I've already opened a beautiful bottle of Nicholas-Jay Pinot Noir. It is decanted on the table. All you have to do is pour it," Geoff said.

Geoff turned the heat down under the veal, and checked the soup. He turned off the broccoli, and fetched some plates, and put them on the counter next to the stove. He flipped the veal chops, and enjoyed the culinary show once again. The chops were golden brown on the bottom when he flipped them. He added lemon and capers, a little extra spiced pepper and a pinch of salt. He left the kitchen to check on the fireplace.

Meredith was standing at the table with her back to him. He walked up behind her as she was straightening some silverware, and put his arms around her. She sighed and laid her head back against his shoulder. He said quietly, "I have been beyond excited, and a little anxious, about tonight. You are so beautiful. I don't deserve this. Or you."

"Me?!" she answered, incredulous—tilting her head back and up so that she could get a glimpse of his face. "Me? You don't deserve ME?"

He turned her around, and still holding her waist, looked directly into her eyes and said, "Yes. You. I can't wait to spend the evening with you, tonight,

Meredith. And, all day tomorrow. And, tomorrow night. I want to get to know you. All of you." Geoff gave her a light squeeze of assurance, then moved to the fireplace where he grabbed two fresh logs from a large copper bin and placed them together on top of the low flames. They quickly ignited, and their crackling and popping added to the growing ambiance of the room.

As he was poking at the fire, she said, "Can I ask you a question?"

"Sure," he said smiling, "but, don't you want to wait until our third glass of wine at dinner?"

"Well, my question is, do you smell something burning in the kitchen?"

Geoff looked up, panicked. "Oh no!" He ran to kitchen and turned off the heat under the veal. He inspected them carefully, and it sure looked to him as though he got to them in time. They may not be as pink as he liked them, but hopefully, he hadn't ruined them. "The soup!" he cried. Running to the oven, he turned that off, too. He opened the door, and the cheese had turned into a dark gooey miasma that had oozed down onto the oven floor. That's probably what Meredith had smelled.

Meredith watched, with great amusement, at her chef at work. He was pretty cool under pressure, she had to admit. Her smile turned to laughter as Geoff gained control. She followed him into the kitchen, and helped plate the dinners. Soon they were seated at the table, and each took a moment to look at the other. Geoff raised his glass, and said, "To answers and possibilities."

"Geoff, this is amazing," Meredith said without losing eye contact. She continued in a soft voice, "It is really so good to see you, again. I tried to prepare myself for the feelings not to be the same, but they're better somehow. This is truly a fantasy of epic proportion. Can I ask you a serious question?"

"Sure. But, can we start in on our dinner while it is still burned—I mean, hot?" he said, smiling. "Sorry if I over-cooked the veal and scorched the cheese on our soup."

"First of all, NO man has ever cooked me dinner. Don't get me wrong. I'm not counting hot dogs and hamburgers on a barbeque. But, a proper dinner...I don't care if you incinerated the meal, and we were eating charcoal. The fact that you went to so much effort to arrange and prepare this meal for me is so incredibly thoughtful—and sexy." Meredith cut a small piece of her veal, swirled it in the sauce, and urging it with her tongue, slid it off the fork and into her mouth. Closing her eyes, she chewed slowly—savoring the flavors. "My God, this is good."

Geoff sat across from her, astonished. He didn't feel like eating. He hadn't felt this way for longer than he could remember. Here sat a woman who really wanted to be here with him, appreciated what he had done for her—not just the wild adventure and the accommodations, but the smallest things like the dinner he had prepared. It was intoxicating. He forced himself to eat.

"Not bad!" he exclaimed. "The veal is a bit too well-done for me. Would you like me to cook you another?"

"What? No way. Mine's delicious." Meredith sipped a spoonful of her French onion soup. "Mmmmm."

From the kitchen, Geoff's cell phone started ringing. He jumped up, and hurried to the counter where his phone sat. He muted the ringtone looking briefly to see who was calling. Susie. He let it go to voice mail.

"I'm so sorry. My cell phone is my lifeline to work, and even on weekends, I am frequently called. That, however, was my wife. I'm so sorry for the interruption. I'll call her back later." Geoff was clearly uncomfortable.

"Don't worry about it," Meredith replied. "Of all the people in the world, you have chosen me to spend this priceless time with. Life, for all of us, is very complex. And, I can't begin to imagine your life at home. No one should judge anyone else on their personal lives. I am so happy to be here with you, full stop."

Meredith sipped her wine; the glass getting low. Geoff refilled it from the decanter.

"Why me?" Meredith inquired. "Of all the people in the world, why me?"

Geoff refilled his glass, too, and took a sip. "I don't know, exactly. I certainly wasn't looking to get involved with anyone. I'm not a 'player'—if you know what I mean. I've never cheated on my wife; never, ever, intended to."

Meredith interrupted, "You haven't cheated yet, Geoff. We could call it quits right now. I could sleep in a different bedroom, and Booker could take me back to Grand Junction in the morning. We could simply part as great friends. This has already been such a thrill for me. I will never forget it."

"No, Meredith. I have already cheated. With you. You are here, and I desperately want to be with you. I made that decision a while ago—when I arranged for this weekend."

Meredith let that soak in. Then she said, "OK. Why me?"

Geoff thought for a few seconds before replying. He put down his wine glass and took a deep breath. "Chemistry is a very powerful force between humans. Usually, it is one-way. One person is attracted to another. But, when there is two-way chemistry? Whew. There are few things in life, I imagine, more addicting than knowing someone desires you. I connected with you the other night when we were together. I just felt it. I sensed that you felt it, too. And, I wanted it. I wanted that feeling. I wanted you. Physically? For sure. But, I wanted *you*: the joy; the smiles; the warmth, the carefree personal connection. You made me feel important, Meredith: wanted, desired, and appreciated. You were like a great drug. I had a taste of you, and I was hooked. I had to see you again. It was chemistry. I just had to see where this thing would lead. How about you?" Geoff picked up his glass and held it. "Why did you risk everything to meet me here?"

"Like you, I felt it; the chemistry. No getting around my attraction to you. I suppose I'm lonely. I wasn't looking for anything outside my world when I met you. Steve, the bartender at the restaurant where we met, is a friend, and I was just stopping by to get a bite to eat - and avoid going home, I guess. I should never have gotten married to begin with. Still, it amazes me how I ended up in Grand Junction of all places. The girl from New York..."

"Well, if you hadn't lived in Grand Junction, I never would have met you, would I?" Geoff asked.

"You have a point. But still..." she laughed. "You have rocked my world, Geoff. Your kindness is comforting. You have a wicked sense of humor. You are successful. You are great looking. Don't get me wrong, I'm not that shallow, but you are captivating. And, you are actually interested in me. You. Of all people. You could have anyone. This is crazy."

The conversation continued, unabated for two-plus hours. They didn't move except to open a new bottle of wine and to stoke the fire. They shared everything about their lives, their loves, their interests, their fears, their dreams. Each listened intently to the other—alternately laughing, questioning, agreeing, comforting, probing, understanding. Meredith learned how important Geoff's kids were to him, and how passionate he was about giving back to those less fortunate. He steered clear of talking too much about his increasingly stagnant marriage or his business successes and international reputation. One of the attractions he had for Meredith was that she didn't know, or care, about what he was; she cared deeply about who he was. He, on the other hand, learned about her love of dance, and what brought her to Colorado (couldn't get a job in New York or LA—wrong body type), her friendship with Jessica, life in a small town and her emotionally painful relationship with her football coach husband. She withheld much of the details of what she suffered at home. But, she felt that eventually she could tell him everything. Being in the presence of a man who treated her with so much kindness, tenderness and compassion overwhelmed her. This felt so right.

Finally, after they had opened their third bottle of wine, Geoff said, "Question Game! You game?"

"Absolutely!" Meredith exclaimed. "I'm more than ready. But first, I need to shed some of these clothes, I'm burning up." And, before Geoff could reply, she stood and came over to him, leaned down and softly kissed him on the lips. The kiss lingered and both their eyes were closed—each soaking in the moment. She put her hand on his chest, and pushed slowly back uncoupling their lips. She grabbed an armload of dishes, dropped them at the sink, and ran down the hall to the stairs, calling over her shoulder, "Be right down!"

. . .

Geoff took the opportunity to call Susie.

"Hey there, I see you called. What's up?" Geoff asked.

It was late, and Susie was obviously tired, and very likely in bed. "Oh, hey," she said. "I was just checking in. Did you get your deal done, with Hudson-what's-its-name?"

"We did," Geoff said with real satisfaction. Closed it today. Nick was there with me to get everything signed, and the money transferred. He's great. I'm not sure what I would do without him."

"Did you have dinner with him, tonight?" she asked.

"Nope. Room service for me. Simple meal after all the dinners this week." He felt more than a little guilty lying to her, and he hoped it didn't show in his voice. "Nick headed back several hours ago; he had a few things he had to tie up at the office over the weekend."

"Why didn't you come back with him?" Susie asked, almost pleadingly.

"Well, he's not going with me to New York on Sunday, and like I said, I have desperately needed some down time. How are the kids?"

She replied, "Same old; same old. I'm just a bit worried about CJ. He really misses you, and he has a big game tomorrow. Will you call him in the morning? I know it would mean a lot to him."

"Sure, Honey," Geoff replied. "His game's at ten, right? "I will call him an hour before, OK?"

"That would be great. And, Geoff?"

"Yes, Babe"

"Hurry home would you? I'm really feeling the weight of carrying this entire family all by myself. I need some help around here. The garden's a mess, and I haven't had two minutes to myself to find that gardener. Rhonda, that girl at spin class, was blabbing on about their garden team, and how immaculate their yard was all the time. I was…"

"OK, all right," Geoff interrupted. I promised you I would get on it as soon as I got home. You can count on me."

Susie continued on about her rough day, but Geoff wasn't paying any attention. She was in midsentence about her National Charity League meeting when something caught his eye. He looked up, and there stood Meredith in the family room. She was wearing his red and gold San Francisco 49er t-shirt. It came down mid-thigh on her bare legs. Her hair was loose, and once she caught his eye, she sauntered over to the oversized sofa by the fireplace and stretched out, full length, putting her arms behind her head. That action raised her shirt enough for Geoff to see her lacy red thong that ironically matched the shirt—and her red toe nails.

"Geoff? You still there?" Susie was now aware that she had lost Geoff, and was trying to regain his attention.

"Sorry, Honey," he said without taking his eyes off Meredith, "I just need to go to bed."

Susie replied, "All right. Call in the morning. We can get caught up then. Sleep tight."

"Oh, I plan to. Thanks, Babe." And with that, and without taking his eyes off of Meredith, Geoff disconnected, and turned his attention to the couch.

* * *

Meredith stretched and sat up, cozying herself in the corner. "So, do you have another question for me?" She slyly asked.

Without uttering a word, Geoff walked over to the far wall and switched off the lights—the flickering firelight dancing around the room adding both heat and a landscape of color. He approached the couch, and without saying a word, came to Meredith, and offered his two hands. She obliged by placing her hands snuggly in his. He raised her to her feet, and they stood together facing each other. "So," she said looking up, "do you have a ques…"

He leaned down, and softly kissed her mouth. As he kissed her, he mouthed and exhaled these words, "Sorry, I don't right now."

His breathing was heavy; his eyes heavy and hooded. He reached down, and with both hands, grabbed the bottom of her t-shirt. Meredith knew exactly what was now beginning to unfold: the moment she had been dreaming about, and craving, since she and Geoff had extended their first encounter six weeks earlier.

She raised her arms above her head as he slowly slid his red, 49er t-shirt from her exquisite, impossibly beautiful, body. She was shaking. The heat of the fire warmed, and ignited, her. Meredith felt that an intense orgasm was floating near the surface within her - on a delicate trip-wire.

Geoff pulled her into him, and she allowed herself to be held, virtually naked, to his fully-clothed body. His scent was a mixture of garlic and spices laden with cologne or deodorant—she couldn't tell which. She couldn't care less. Whatever it was, it was intoxicating. Meredith tried to absorb every texture, every sensation, every emotion.

He slowly sat her back on the couch, and before he could lay her against the over-sized throw pillows, she leaned forward, spread her legs and pulled him nearer. With him now between her legs, and inches from her French-cut thong, she untied his apron, throwing it aside. Then, she pulled out his shirt, and one by one, starting at the top, carefully unbuttoned his shirt—exposing a well-conditioned bare chest. She pulled the shirt back and off his shoulders. Never hesitating, she reached up behind his head and slowly drew him into her—her hardened nipples delicately brushing his chest. Their now-naked upper bodies were moving erotically against each other as they kissed. The erotic sensations of a mutually virginal caress were met with labored breathing from both. Meredith reached forward and carefully undid his belt buckle; then, the top button of his pants. Unzipping him, she reached inside and grasped his engorged and aching manhood. "Now THIS is more like it. Sorry, I had to get rid of your prized apron."

Geoff couldn't muster an immediate response. He had lost himself in the moment. He responded by caressing both her breasts and drawing them to his mouth. Using the tip of his tongue, he circled one nipple and then the other, softly kissing, sucking and lightly nibbling. Meredith could feel her hips starting to involuntarily, but rhythmically, thrust towards him, and that unmistakable tidal wave was beginning to grow in her lower abdomen.

Sensing the growing urgency, Geoff gently laid Meredith back on the couch. He was paralyzed with the sight of her: a face of knowing, wanting, passion; golden brown skin, perfect breasts with up-turned hardened nipples, impossibly soft stomach, and smooth, well-shaped legs. He didn't want to remove her thong, because they, too, were part of this perfect picture. But, it was nearing that point of no return for both of them.

He started back with her neck, and slowly kissed and licked his way down her body, stopping judiciously at her breasts, her stomach, her belly button. When he reached her panties, Meredith raised her hips so that Geoff could slide them off. But, before he removed them, he moved his face to her inner thighs resting his cheeks between them. He inhaled deeply imbedding the scent of her to his memory. He softly kissed and licked the length of the thong that protected her. She moaned loudly. "Oh God, Geoff, please," she begged. "Please."

Using his thumbs and forefingers, he slowly slid her thong from her hips revealing a perfectly smooth, and hypnotically enticing, erotic entrance. He lowered his head back to her, and as he slowly explored her, she wrapped her legs around his head, crossing her ankles. The tidal wave was surging now; unstoppable. She choked out a scream—her hips violently shivering, then bucking. Her eyes rolled back as wave after wave washed over her—her fingers grabbing handfuls of Geoff's hair pulling him tightly to her pleasure.

As she regained consciousness, Meredith's senses were electrified. The passion that had flooded her was still whispering between her legs; the desire to have this beautiful man fill her completely was overwhelming. As she slowly opened her eyes, she was dimly aware that Geoff was now sitting astride of her, stroking and caressing her face.

Meredith didn't hesitate. She sat up, and told Geoff to stand. At first, she was surprised to see his shirt off and his pants undone, but she quickly remembered. She slid his pants from his hips down to the floor, and he easily stepped out of them. She stood, too, and led him to the large leather chair on the other side of the fireplace. There, she sat him down at the edge of the chair, facing her. She slowly knelt on top of him—her knees on either side of his muscular legs. Meredith's hands were shaking, but she managed to guide him to her entrance. Lowering herself slowly, she felt the slow and erotic sensation of being filled. She could feel him deep inside her abdomen, and as he moaned, she pushed herself up using the soft leather armrests, and lowered herself again—this time more quickly. Her hips were now thrusting at the same time in rhythm with him.

"I'm coming," he said softly at first. "Oh, Meredith, I'm coming. I'm COMING!"

Meredith could feel the unmistakable waves quickly building within her loins. It was as if the prior waterfall, that had rushed over her cliff, had quickly returned with its own urgent flood. As her body felt the powerful, and uncontrollable, release of Geoff's passion, the flood within her raged throughout her valley once more—shaking her to the core. They both involuntarily, and deliriously, cried out—the raging fire and the massive log home in the woods protecting their secret.

• • •

Meredith climbed up into the large, welcoming chair. Both completely naked now, they melted into each other. They said not a word—deep in their own thoughts. She sat on his lap and laid her head on his shoulder. As she lightly stroked his chest, he could feel all of her. Her soft hair brushing over his shoulders. Her breasts pressing against him. Her legs on his. Her feet and toes slowly rubbing his calves. Her ass in his lap—the wetness between them a delirious reminder of their passion.

Her heart, too. He felt that. Not the beating, but the emotion. It was all too hard to explain. He could hold her here forever. With the fire reducing to warm embers, and the audible flickering and hissing of the flames softly ebbing—dimming the remaining light in the room, Meredith and Geoff fell deeply asleep in each other's arms.

49

BOBBIE

THE TEMPERATURE WAS DROPPING RAPIDLY AS THE SUN SET IN THE Western sky, but Bobbie pressed on. He had his trophy head strapped to his pack adding about twenty pounds of weight. As he walked confidently back towards his make-shift camp, he could feel the blood, leeching from the severed arteries, warming his lower back by soaking his shirt and draining onto the backs of his calves. The thought of drinking blood from his shoe crossed his mind, and made him chuckle.

Once at his camp, he would have to quickly break down his tent, and re-pack his belongings. There was no way he could spend the night out in the wilds with the smell of fresh blood permeating the air. One of the few things Bobbie feared the most was a hungry bear exploring his campsite looking for fresh meat. There were also mountain lions, coyotes and birds of prey to worry about. The wind had died, and that would help by not accelerating the allure of recent death.

Soon, he was at his camp. It had been undisturbed while he was away. Not that he expected it to be. He had a keen instinct for setting camps in undetected locations taking into consideration sight lines and wind direction. He had bear pouches for his food that he dangled high in the adjacent trees far out of their reach. He detected no sign of bears, but he knew enough that he was pressing his luck with his newly acquired cargo. Fortunately, his truck was just a mile away, but he would have to hurry, nevertheless.

Within minutes, Bobbie had the camp broken, and it was now on his back. He had a tarp draped between his kill and his packed belongings as he started the arduous, but victorious short march back to his truck. The stag had stopped bleeding; however, Bobbie took no chances. Slung over his left shoulder was his loaded Remington hunting rifle—just in case trouble (human or otherwise) surprised them. He was an excellent bow hunter, but his marksmanship with bullets was as good, if not stronger, than his success with arrows.

Bobbie was sweating profusely when he arrived at the spot where he had parked his truck. He stilled himself to listen intently to his surroundings. Hearing nothing unusual, he allowed his load to slide from his back to the ground. Looking around in the darkness with his headlamp, he spotted the thicket of branches that camouflaged his truck. Slowly, quietly and carefully he removed the branches. Placing the stag trophy in the bed of the pick-up, he covered it with his tarp. He cinched the tarp tightly to make it look like he had only cargo. The last thing he needed was for a Park Ranger, or police, to spy antlers hitching a ride with him. He placed his considerable pack, now stained deep red with dry, crusty blood, and his personal belongings, in the back seat. Removing his headlamp, and his overcoat, he jumped in the front seat with his guns and closed the door.

Before Bobbie started the engine, he fumbled into the center console and found a beer. The truck was a natural refrigerator in this weather, so while not ice-cold, the beer was refreshingly cool and quenched his immediate thirst. The entire twelve ounces was drained before the can left his lips. He crumpled the can in his right hand, and rolling down his window, he pitched it into the night. He felt around in the compartment once again - this time for the pot brownies he had stowed. He was starving. His hand found the round pill bottle that held his various pellets of recreation, but he kept them intact. No need for drugs or Viagra tonight; he would save them for tomorrow when he would get home to Meredith.

After wolfing down two brownies, he wiped his hands on his pants, and started the engine. The masculine V-8 powerplant roared to life. He let it warm for a minute, then slowly backed the truck from its man-made hiding place. As he shifted the truck into Drive, he looked intently for his previous tire tracks that would lead him back to the Utah interstate. His eyes were now blurring—the pot and the beer mixing to make a debilitating cocktail of night blindness.

He pressed forward, impaired, for the next twenty minutes until he struck something hard. "Damn it to hell," he growled. He tried to put his truck in reverse, but he had high-sided onto something. "Goddamn it," he yelled as he pounded his fist on the steering wheel. Leaving the motor running, he got out of the truck and then stumbled; his balance deteriorating. Using his headlamp, he checked under the vehicle. Sure enough, he had parked his truck atop a hidden rock. He would need his wench, daylight and a clear head to extricate himself from this mess.

He thought about pitching his tent, but he wasn't exactly sure where he was. And the truth be known, he was still hungry, thirsty and high. He climbed back into the cab of his truck, and before switching off the engine, he grabbed another beer, two more brownies, and a couple of pills that would help him sleep. Thirty-five minutes later, with his loaded 357 Magnum hand gun in his lap, Bobbie put his head back on his headrest and reclined his seat as far back as it would go. It didn't go back far because of his pack, but it went back far enough. Bobbie passed out without remembering to lock the doors and crack the windows.

50

ASPEN

MEREDITH WOKE WITH A START. WHERE WAS SHE? PUZZLED, SHE looked around the room, and then she started piecing it all together. Aspen. But, she was in bed, alone, in that beautiful master bedroom, cozied by deep, goose-down, comforters. The last she remembered—and, oh what a memory—she was in Geoff's arms, naked, snuggling in front of a waning fire. How did she get up here?

The doors to the master bedroom were closed, but she could smell the inviting aroma of bacon and coffee. A fire was crackling in the fireplace, but it had been aflame for quite some time. What time was it? She looked around the room for a clock. Spying her new cell phone on the bedside table, she activated it, and saw to her surprise, that it was already 10:14 AM. And, no messages. Of course. She jumped out of bed, and realized to her horror, that she was wearing her flannel two-piece pajamas. Oh God.

When she entered the bathroom, it was the first she time had been able to inspect it closely in daylight. At the far side was a wall of clear glass that bordered the shower and massive tub that sumptuously brought the outside forest into the decadent ambiance of the entire room. Meredith started the shower and climbed out of her nightwear. It didn't surprise her to learn that she wasn't wearing panties; she just noticed is all. Climbing into the shower was like climbing, fully naked, into a hidden forest waterfall. The privacy was exquisite. The water poured generously over her sensitive body—massaging away the cobwebs, but not the memories, of the day and night before. She could have stayed there forever—feeling the water slipping over and caressing her body, but she was acutely aware of what awaited her downstairs.

• • •

When Meredith came downstairs, she could hear Geoff on the phone. He was in the kitchen, but it sounded like he was talking business. He was emphatically outlining the details of a new transaction to someone. As she entered the room, Geoff had his back to her. She was barefoot and silent. What startled him was when she pushed the button activating the Italian espresso machine. He turned around quickly—still holding a spatula. What he saw took his breath away, and he stopped mid-speech, and said, "Look, Nick, I've got to go. Something just came up. Can I call you later today?"

Meredith was in a sumptuously soft robe, tied at the waist—and nothing more. She hoisted herself up so that she was seated on the counter next to him and the espresso machine. The robe gapped generously revealing the insides of her round and firm breasts. She winked.

"Hey Nick, one more thing. Are we all set for today's adventure?" he said without taking his eyes off her. She raised her eyebrows inquisitively. "Great. 1:30 PM? Sure. We'll look for him. Yep. Thanks, again. You're the best."

Geoff hung up and removed his earpiece. He smiled warmly, and walked over to her. She spread her legs exposing her sex, and held out her arms welcoming him. "I was looking for the man in the apron with an erection," she teased.

"You found him," he replied. "A little harder this time, right?"

She laughed easily. "Come here. I missed you this morning."

Geoff moved to her, and reaching up, pulled the tie loose from her robe. He placed both hands on her shoulders by her neck, and sliding them outward, pushed the robe from her shoulders. He hadn't planned on this. He slid his hands down and over her freshly-bathed body stopping at her breasts, and cupped both in his hands—lightly fingering her nipples. As he did so, Meredith unclasped his belt and unbuttoned his jeans. With her bare feet, she reached up and pulled his pants and underwear to the floor. He worked his hands down and around her small waist, and drew her closer. She raised her arms, and running her hands through his hair behind his head, she embraced him—their mouths hungry and probing. They had both lost their grip on their lust. "Take me," She choked. Now."

He picked her up slightly from the counter, and standing with his feet spread apart, lowered her slowly. Her wet, fleshy, warm, tightness enveloped him completely. When he was at their deepest intercourse, he lifted her slowly but not completely, and then lowered her again fully. Meredith gasped. Her body responded rhythmically, and she used Geoff's shoulders to pull herself up, and to lower herself, over and over again—feeling all of him in her. Finally, Meredith leaned back on the counter, and her moaning quickened. Her body stiffened, and started into the uncontrollable spasms that were the signature of her passion. Geoff let out a cry, too, as he climaxed deep within her. He grabbed her waist and continued to thrust. Meredith allowed her second orgasm to reappear and crash unabated between them.

● ● ●

It was a bright, sunny, clear and unseasonably warm day for a late November Saturday in Aspen. The early season snow was melting quickly. Geoff couldn't have ordered a more perfect afternoon for what he had planned. Meredith had begged him to tell her what was in store for them, but he insisted on keeping the surprise a secret.

They were seated at the table by the dancing fire enjoying crepes, fruit and granola—and each other. Meredith was still in her robe, and she clearly wasn't worried about its gaping front. Geoff could only shake his head and smile when the view across the table became too much for him.

They had been talking, non-stop. It was just past noon. Meredith inquired again, "So, where exactly are we going this afternoon? What should I wear? All you have said so far is to ask me if I get motion sickness. I'm dying of curiosity!"

Geoff seemed really excited. "Wear warm casual clothes and your walking shoes. It will be cold."

Meredith couldn't imagine. "Are we going sledding? Snow shoeing? Hiking?"

"I'm not saying," Geoff laughed.

Meredith pulled her robe open tantalizing him. "So, what do I need to do to get you to spill the beans?"

"Well, actually, you know EXACTLY what to do to get me to spill my beans. You did a noteworthy job of that this morning on the counter." Geoff got up from his seat and came around behind her. Massaging her neck, Geoff worked his hands slowly over her shoulders and into her gaping robe lightly stroking her aroused breasts. She leaned her head back, and Geoff kissed her upside down. He separated from her leaving her breathless.

"I've never done what we are doing today," he said. "I've always wanted to do this. And, today seemed the perfect opportunity to try out something new and exciting with someone I find so refreshingly new and exciting."

"But, Geoff, what…"

He cut her off, saying, "Why don't you go get ready while I do the dishes and clean up? We need to leave at 1:30, and I still need to pack our lunch."

"What?" She shook her head; then nodded. "This all too much. You do dishes? You clean up? You cook? You pack lunches? And, did I say that you are an incredible lover? Is there anything you can't do?"

Geoff replied, "I just can't tell you what we are doing this afternoon. It's a secret. And, one thing I can keep, is a secret."

"OK. Have it your way." Meredith stood, and looking right at Geoff, slowly removed her robe. Completely naked, now, she threw it over her shoulder. "I guess I'll just have to go get dressed." And, with that, Meredith headed out of the kitchen, laughing, towards the grand staircase leaving Geoff with his mouth open and speechless. She had "the walk." And, the ass.

51

JESSICA

JESSICA'S PHONE STARTED RINGING AT 12:30. SHE DIDN'T ANSWER, because she didn't recognize the number. 303 area code, OK, but she didn't have a caller ID confirmation on her screen. She let it go to voice mail.

"Jess! Oh, my God! Pick up next time!" It was Meredith's voice on the voice mail. "You absolutely wouldn't believe any of this. I'm having an impossible time believing it myself. I need to talk to you. I have a different phone with me, so don't share this with anyone, OK? Especially, not Bobbie. Have you heard from him? He's supposed to be hunting. 'Til Sunday. Call me!"

Jessica dialed back immediately. "What's up, girlfriend? Where ARE you?"

Meredith replied, "I've got to be quick. I'm in Aspen. Long story. Don't worry, I'll share with you all the gory details when I get back."

"Meredith," Jessica interrupted. "Have you heard about Bobbie?"

"Heard ABOUT him? Or, heard FROM him? Either way, the answer's no. He's hunting. What ABOUT him?"

"It's all over town. He's been accused of a shit load of bad stuff: rape, harassment, assault, dealing drugs—the works. According to the press, he's skipped out of town. The school suspended him for 90 days—with pay you would be happy to know—while they investigate all the allegations."

Meredith closed her eyes. "Shit. That's it," she thought. "No more."

Then she said, "Jess, listen. I should be back in Grand Junction tomorrow afternoon. I'll come straight to your place. I should be there by 2:00 at the latest. Can I stay with you while all this gets sorted out? I know it's a big ask, but..."

Jessica cut in, "You are family. Jazzy will love having her Auntie Meredith here. Don't say another word."

"I owe you, big time, Jess."

"Don't mention it again. You would do the same for me."

Before she hung up, Meredith asked, "Hey, will you let me know if you hear anything—or if he calls?"

"Of course. Be careful," Jessica said.

"Not to worry. He'll never find me here. Love you loads, girlfriend." And, with that she hung up.

52

BOBBIE

BOBBIE AWOKE SATURDAY MORNING IN A FOG—LITERALLY. HE HAD passed out in his truck without cracking the windows, and his brain was as clear as mud. Eating three pot brownies was bad enough, but beer and sleeping pills on top of that? Hell, he could have died on that cocktail. "Who the fuck cares?" he thought.

It didn't take him an hour to free his truck. Once he could see, he used the wench on his front bumper, and a sturdy tree branch, to raise the front of his Ford enough where he could pack more timber under his wheels. That enabled him to clear the rock and back out of his predicament. Once back on the interstate, he figured it would take him seven hours to cross Utah and Colorado to get back home to Grand Junction.

He thought about the day ahead. He would drop off the trophy at Dave's. He would be the only taxidermist he trusted with his secret, illegal, prize. And hell, he was good at his trade. Then, he would go meet some of his friends at Pistol Whipped Willy's (Pussy Whipped Willy's as they all liked to call it) to have some drinks, shoot some pool and relax. Then, he would go home, fuck his wife, explain what really went on at school (yeah, right), pack some things and head out of town to some secret place where he could think things through.

He pushed his foot to the floor, and watched as the speedometer edged past 100 MPH. Hell, maybe he would be in Grand Junction sooner that he thought.

53

ASPEN

MEREDITH CAME DOWNSTAIRS AT 1:15 IN JEANS AND A MATCHING plaid Pendleton shirt. She was wearing her hiking shoes and was carrying a parka, and a few personal items: lip gloss, tissues, dark glasses and her wallet.

She looked darling, but Geoff could tell that something wasn't quite right. "You OK?" he inquired.

"Yeah. Fine, I guess," she replied. "Will you do me a big favor?" she asked.

"Sure. Anything," he said concerned.

Meredith put her things on the entry table, and walked to him. Without looking up, she wrapped her arms around him tightly and said, "I just need to be held."

"What's up, M?" he said using her code name.

She didn't reply right away, and didn't move either. He could feel her taking slow deep breaths. He stroked her hair and the side of her face as she seemed to just need a moment to gather herself.

"Thanks," she smiled still holding him. "You do not know how simple and meaningful it is to just be held. And, to feel safe."

Geoff didn't know why he said the following, but it flowed freely from his lips, "You never have to worry about being safe with me. I will always protect you, Meredith." He could feel her nodding slightly. He put his head down against the top of hers, and inhaled deeply. He could smell her shampoo. "Always."

• • •

It was approaching 1:30 PM, and Meredith had just volunteered to start taking their things down to the car. Overhead, the unmistakable sound of a helicopter emerged. "Don't tell me," she laughed. "Really?"

She and Geoff ran out on the sun-soaked balcony and watched as the same navy-blue Long Ranger helicopter hovered and pivoted to land in the lot next to them. The snow whipped furiously around the aircraft as it landed obscuring their view. But in no time, the engines relaxed, and the blades slowed until they were still.

"Let's go!" Geoff called out. He was as excited as a little boy, and his enthusiasm was contagious. They grabbed their day-packs filled with meats, cheeses, crackers, fruit and wine—and their essential sundries—and hurried downstairs to meet Booker as he came to greet them. He had a broad smile on his face.

Mr. Geoff! Ms. Meredith! Very nice to see you both." he said. "Please, let me grab your packs, and I'll help you load them once you are on board." Booker opened the rear door to the passenger compartment, and Meredith accepted Booker's hand to climb aboard. "Watch you head." Geoff followed right behind her.

They walked over and sat in facing leather seats next to the large window. Booker handed them their back-packs. "We'll be airborne in just a minute or two for our short flight. Be sure to buckle your lap belts. No shoulder harnesses required back here, Ms. Meredith."

"Yes sir," she smiled and saluted. "Thanks, Booker."

When he had left and latched the door, she looked up at Geoff and said, "Thanks. This is so amazing and beyond my wildest dreams."

"Don't thank me yet. You have no idea of what I have in store for us this afternoon."

"No, thanks for somehow bringing me into your life. Into all this," she said sweeping her arm in a wide circle. "For opening your heart to me. For listening to me. For being so understanding and thoughtful." Meredith noticed she was raising her voice; the engines were winding up, and she could see and feel the rotor sweeping its accelerating arc above them.

Geoff reached down to the side of his chair, and picked up a set of headphones with attached microphone. Before placing them on his head, he pointed to the side of Meredith's chair, and motioned for her to do the same as he did. They both put their headsets on at the same time. Meredith now knew how to adjust her microphone and volume.

"Well, hello there handsome!" she said.

"Good afternoon to you both," came Booker's voice through the earphones. Meredith immediately bulged her eyes and put her hand over her mouth in surprised embarrassment. "Who were you referring to Ms. Meredith? But, before you answer that, let me say that I need to request departure instructions so I need you both to be silent for the next few minutes. Thanks."

Meredith mouthed exaggeratedly, "I'M SORRY!"

Geoff smiled broadly, nodded his head and gave her the thumbs-up.

Then over the headsets they heard, "Aspen Air Traffic Control, this is chopper Bravo-Zero-Six-Tango requesting departure from private residence 1.62 miles northwest of Aspen City Center."

"Roger that, Bravo-Zero-Six Tango. No aircraft in the immediate area. VFR applies."

"10-4 and thanks Aspen Air Traffic Control." And, with that, the engines spooled up, and soon they could feel the aircraft ever-so-slightly lighten itself before climbing effortlessly to the sky.

Once well above the trees and surrounding hills, Booker cut back in and said, "OK to talk now. We will be at your destination in about 17 minutes. Now Ms. Meredith, I won't make you answer my previous question, because we all know the answer. But, welcome aboard, and enjoy your short flight."

She smiled, and Geoff could see that the pain or stress that she felt earlier was abating. "Thanks, Booker," she said.

"Don't mention it. Thought I would point out to you, if Mr. Geoff hasn't already, that there is a toggle switch on the side of your seat by the headphone jack. It's a privacy option. Once you switch it, I can't hear you both conversing, but you will always be able to hear me. Just remember to switch it back if you need me for anything."

They simultaneously said, "Thank you, Booker." And laughed. They both reached down and switched their communication system to "Private."

"Can you tell me NOW where we are going, Man of Mystery and Surprises?" Meredith asked.

He nodded and replied, "Out of the mountains to get a better perspective."

"That was certainly helpful. Should we play Twenty Questions to see if I can guess?"

"No need. We will be there in a flash," Geoff teased.

They both looked out the window as the helicopter banked to the left leaving them a breathless straight-down view of the valley below.

Their earphones crackled, and Booker's voice spoke, "Bravo-Zero-Six-Tango to Whitehaven Airport. Requesting landing permission at Heliport, over."

"Roger, Bravo-Zero-Six-Tango. Permission granted. Private aircraft at 8 o'clock; ascending through 8,500 ft."

"Roger, Whitehaven. Have visual. On the ground, shortly. Over and out."

As Meredith peered out the window below her, she saw a small airfield with two runways and a small building to the side of a large paved square. On one of the runways, she could see two small planes attached by some kind of rope or chain. "What's that?" she said pointing.

"Oh, we're both about to find out," Geoff said, again giving the thumbs-up sign.

"What?" Meredith looked a little nervous.

Booker banked the Long Ranger and positioned it above the concrete square. They slowly lowered until they felt the runners below them touch ground. The engines immediately seemed to sigh as they were switched off, and the rotors slowly wound to a stop. Soon the door opened, and there was Booker, smiling as usual, "Welcome to Whitehaven International Airport!"

He helped them out—first grabbing their day-packs, then lending a hand to each as they disembarked.

A woman approached them as they walked towards the small building. She extended her hand, and said, "Welcome to Aspen Soaring Experience. My name is Vanessa. You are Geoff and Meredith, I suppose?"

Both Meredith and Geoff answered simultaneously in the affirmative.

"Well great, then," Vanessa said without skipping a beat. "We are ready to go if you are. I would suggest using the bathroom as there isn't a toilet on board."

Meredith looked out at the two planes with astonishment. "What are we doing?" she said hesitantly.

"We're going to see the mountains as the birds do: soaring on the wind," Geoff replied.

"What?" she exclaimed. "In THAT?" she pointed to the glider which was attached to the plane in front by a cable.

Vanessa broke in, "You'll love it. It's the best way to see the Rockies, and today is perfect for soaring: plenty of wind and thermals for lift. We could literally stay up all afternoon; although, I have you scheduled for an hour and a half."

Nick had booked Aspen Soaring for the entire day—not because they were going to be up in the air that long, but to be overly cautious to not inadvertently run into any other people.

Meredith then deadpanned, "To heck with the bathroom, I think I just peed my pants!" Everyone broke into laughter, including Booker who was walking with them across the landing pad to the building.

"Ms. Meredith, you will absolutely love the experience," he said. "Once they release you from the tow-plane, you will fly like the eagles. It's really unique."

"Well, thanks, Booker. I think I will still use the bathroom, though," she said a little nervously. Everyone again chuckled.

● ● ●

They all gathered on the tarmac. Booker joined the group because of his innate interest in all things that flew. Also, the pilot of the private plane was there for the briefing. Vanessa counseled, "The glider holds three adults. You two will sit in front of me in the bubble—that's what we call the small enclosed cockpit, there," she said pointing. "Geoff, when instructed, you will get in first, and fasten your seat belt. Meredith, you will sit in front of him between his legs. I will need you, too, to fasten your seat belt. I'll climb in behind you both. Once seated, I'll close and latch the roof pod. The Cessna will pull us down the runway up into the air until we are at a high enough elevation, and near the mountains and updrafts, where I will pull the lever that releases us from the tow-plane. Then we will be on our own. Any Questions?"

Meredith said with more than a little bit of anxiety, "How long can we stay flying until we need to find a place to land?"

"Good question," Vanessa responded. "We actually, on a day like today, could stay up indefinitely. The wind blows up against the mountainsides and creates a thermal, or updraft. As we fly closer to the mountains the wind picks us up by our wings and lifts us skyward. As we pull away from the thermals, we glide ourselves pretty much anywhere we want to go. We can explore the various valleys, hamlets and mountain passes that make up this beautiful part of the world. Or, we can chase clouds. It's a bit bumpier than other modes of flying, but I think you will find it infinitely more thrilling. It's quieter, too; although, you will be very cognoscente of the sound of the wind. Any other questions?"

Geoff asked, "What is your safety record?"

"The man who called to book the afternoon wasn't you, I am guessing," their pilot replied.

"No, that wasn't me," Geoff said.

"Well, whoever he was, he asked for an endless amount of documentation - starting with me and where I got my flight training, my hours logged in a glider and my age and experience," Vanessa said. "Then, he requested copies of all our State of Colorado inspection reports from the FAA. Frankly, we've never, in our seventeen years of operations, ever had a customer demand of us such background material. And, we've never had an accident, injury or negative report from the FAA. You're in good hands, Geoff."

"Thank you, Captain!" Geoff replied with enthusiasm. "I think we're ready for take-off."

The pilot of the Cessna, who had been quiet the entire time of the briefing, headed to his plane to commence his last-minute inspections, and Vanessa had Geoff and Meredith put on their coats. "It can get quite cold up there," she said. "We don't have a heater. You have each other, but I have to go it alone. But, I'll be just fine."

Booker chimed in, "See you all when you return. I'll wait for you here at the international terminal," he said with a wink.

They all said their goodbyes, and Vanessa helped Geoff into his seat in the glider. After he put on his lap belt, Vanessa helped Meredith get seated comfortably in front of Geoff between his legs. He reached around her waist and pulled her snuggly back against his pelvis. As he helped her with her seatbelt, he whispered in her ear, "I think I'm going to like this."

Once they were both situated, Vanessa handed both of them earphones attached to microphones that they immediately placed on their heads. Meredith was getting good at this. Vanessa climbed in, and after getting herself situated and comfortable, she tested all of the flaps and gauges. The radio fired up, and Vanessa said, "OK, you two, are you ready?"

Both responded with a mixture of "Yes!" and "All good!"

Vanessa lowered the clear plexiglass canopy and sealed it above them. Then she said, "Joe, ready when you are. Take me to my favorite spot where I will release when we confirm 11,000 feet."

"Roger that, Vanessa." They had an easy, but professional, communication between them. They had covered this routine hundreds, if not thousands, of times before. They usually had five flights a day—two in the morning and three in the afternoon, six days a week, when the weather allowed. But this was the first that either of them could remember that their company had been paid for the entire day when they were only going to be in the air about ninety minutes. The forty percent, pre-paid, tip was unusual, too.

Meredith could hear the Cessna as its engine came to life. She had to admit that this all made her incredibly nervous, but Geoff's arms wrapped reassuringly tight around her. He patted her on her shoulder and gave her the thumbs-up. She grasped his hand and drew it together with hers in her lap.

The two aircraft were already positioned on one of the two runways, and were joined by a cable that became taught as the Cessna slowly accelerated pulling the glider behind it. The glider was actually airborne before the powered airplane, but soon they both were away from the earth climbing swiftly into a strong and helpful headwind. The planes seemed to being flying in a straight line—each pilot reciting and confirming altitude until they reached the agreed-upon 11,000 feet.

Vanessa said, "Geoff and Meredith, are you ready to uncouple and soar free?"

The irony was not lost on either of them. But, they both smiled to themselves—not aware of the other—and with great excitement, yelled "Yes!" into their microphones.

Vanessa then spoke, "Joe, releasing in five, four, three, two, one…and at that very moment, Vanessa pulled the lever that uncoupled them, and she banked the glider hard to the right while Joe turned his Cessna west—away from the now-freed bird.

Meredith was speechless with awe. As she felt the wind beneath her, and Geoff behind her, and as the world opened up before her, she didn't want to blink. Or, wake up.

"Now," Vanessa said through the headsets interrupting Meredith's thoughts—and Geoff's, too, for that matter, "Let's go explore this magnificent landscape, shall we?" And, without waiting for a reply, she tipped the glider slightly towards a nearby hillside catching a thermal that pushed them up aggressively skyward allowing them to pass soundlessly, and effortlessly, the snow-capped peaks around them. And just as suddenly, she banked and swooped down into a long and unexplored valley—opening before them a new, snow-splashed, Eden.

54

SUSIE

SUSIE WAS CONCERNED. GEOFF HAD NOT CALLED CJ BEFORE HIS GAME as he had promised he would, and it was almost noon, and she hadn't heard from him either. It was most unlike him. She had called him several times, but she had been sent directly to his voice mail. "Thank you for your important call. You have reached Geoff Cameron's voice mail. Please leave a message, and I'll get back to you as soon as possible."

Didn't he say last night that he was exhausted and was headed to bed? And, that he would call CJ before his game? And, that he would call me to finish our conversation about our house maintenance? He did sound a bit distracted last night; not himself. "I sure hope he is not sick," she thought. "I don't need him coming home and giving everyone the flu."

She put the whole matter quickly behind her—along with the winding road into town—as she sped to make her Saturday spin class. Arriving as everyone was already on a cycle warming up, she quickly slipped out of her sweats and mounted a stationary bike at the rear of the room, and started warming up.

Goodness, it was hard work toiling her body into shape. Keeping up with her girlfriends' athletic physiques, so that she could avoid feeling self-conscious when they were out together, took a lot of her time. And, all this labor had a downside. The better shape she got in, the more Geoff wanted sex. Maybe she should just blow off her girlfriends, and get fat. Then, she wouldn't have to worry about this stupid spin class, what to wear, and Geoff would stop with all of his advances. The thought amused her.

"What are you smiling at, Hon?" Susie was surprised and looked up. Rhonda was already breaking a sweat in warm-up. Looking back over her shoulder, Rhonda said, "Saw the news that Cameron, Boone and Covington just bought another company - in Colorado of all places. No picture this time, damn it. He's a hottie, Mrs. Cameron."

"So you've already told me," Susie replied coldly as she started to pedal.

"So, what's this that I am reading that CBC has closed a $500 million fund to buy businesses in the energy sector? Colorado has coughed up the first big prize, a company called Hudson Environmental?"

Rhonda couldn't see the annoyed look on Susie's face. "Oh, I don't follow exactly what Geoff and his company are up to. But, I do know that he is very busy and has been traveling a lot. He's going straight from Colorado to New York tomorrow to chase another deal."

"As long as he is not chasing skirt, if you know what I mean," Rhonda said between huffs. "Actually, I don't think he has to chase anything." She left the comment hanging as the music started up, and the spin instructor got everyone to focus. Ricky Martin's "She Bangs" was now pumping through the gym pushing everyone's adrenalin—except Susie's. Her legs were feeling heavy and tired—and she was still warming up.

After a few minutes, as the pace slowed for a brief interlude, Rhonda continued on with her diatribe saying, "If he were my man, I would hire a private eye just to make sure."

"Make sure of WHAT, exactly, Rhonda?" Susie was now visibly annoyed. Looking around and sensing a lot of ears and cross-glances coming their way, she continued, "He has a lot MORE than he can handle in his own bed at home as it is." There were many swoons and hoots coming from around them.

Rhonda laughed along with the crowd. "Just sayin'. Don't think your great-looking, globe-trotting CEO husband is ever short of female companionship—that is, if he ever wanted to be."

"Thanks, again, for the compliment, Rhonda," Susie said a little too loud. "I'll let you know if I ever need a private investigator. Actually, maybe I will hire your guy so that he can chase down my husband, tie him up and make him return his calls to his wife and kids." Susie was instantly regretful that this comment had slipped from her lips. She said nothing more.

Rhonda, on the other hand, put her head down, but raised her eyebrows in astonished surprise—and kept on peddling.

55

BOBBIE

BOBBIE PULLED HIS OVERSIZED TRUCK INTO HIS DRIVEWAY AT PRE-cisely 9:47 PM Saturday. Not only had he raced across Utah and up through Colorado at break-neck speed, but he hadn't stopped at Dave's like he planned. The taxidermist could wait until tomorrow. After calling Meredith at least 10 times during his drive home, getting only her voice mail, he decided to stop for dinner and a few drinks, at a dive bar just across the border into Colorado off Interstate 70.

Bobbie sat at the crowded bar and pounded down beer after beer—quenching his thirst and fertilizing his testosterone. There was nothing to hit on except what he called, "cheap skanky chicks." The bartender made him order dinner before granting his demand for another double bourbon. Bobbie ordered what appeared to be a house specialty, "Wing-Rings" - chicken wings with beer-battered fried onion rings. While he waited for his order, he strolled outside to his truck, and from the center console pulled out his pill bag. Removing two pink Viagra's, Bobbie opened a warm can of Coors, popped the pills into his mouth and shot-gunned the beer without taking a breath.

When he returned, his food was on the bar. "We thought you had pitched and ditched," the burly bartender said without much expression.

"Naw, I may not be from around here, but I ain't that kind of guy," Bobbie said smiling.

Two women that night had asked Bobbie to dance as their favorite song seemed to magically appear on the jukebox. He just shook his head at each of them and shoo'ed them away with an expressionless back of his hand. He had better things on his mind…Meredith. And, besides, he had his gourmet Wing-Rings to eat.

He excused himself and told the older woman next to him to save his place; he needed to pee. He swerved unsteadily towards the bathroom—almost falling when the door opened precisely when he was going to push it. Fortunately, the guy exiting was large himself, and caught Bobbie before he fell, but their momentum took them straight back into the men's room. Propping up Bobbie next to a urinal, the stranger looked him over, then said, "Hey, aren't you the coach at Granite who punched out the opposing coach at Silverton a couple of weeks ago?"

Bobbie, peeing now and breathing hard, didn't answer. "Hey, buddy, I asked you a question," the man was saying. "Were you, or weren't you, the guy that sucker-punched that coach? You sure look like the guy in all the papers."

Bobbie was finishing his business, and tucking his equipment back in his pants. He looked straight at the stranger narrowing his eyes and said, "What if I was?"

The stranger hesitated for a second, sizing up the situation. But, the assault came too quickly and ferociously. In a quick motion, Bobbie smashed his knee into the guy's balls, doubling him over. And, without thinking or hesitating, Bobbie followed with an almost instantaneous upper cut under his victim's rib cage. The man fell to the ground, and began to vomit beer and blood. Bobbie calmly placed the trash can under the door knob so that no one could easily get in from the bar, and wading casually through the downed man's vile mess, he opened the window, and while not easy, climbed out.

Once on the ground outside, Bobbie turned and stuck his head back in the window. "I would be much obliged if you would pick up my tab at the bar." He started laughing. "You didn't answer MY question: What if I was?"

And with that, Bobbie headed for his truck. As he pulled out onto the highway, a Colorado State Trooper, with lights flashing and siren blaring, sped past him in the opposite direction. It neither stopped for him, nor at the bar. Some other poor fuck was going to get a shit-full from The Man tonight.

56

ASPEN

T HE NINETY MINUTES FLEW BY—LITERALLY. IT HAD SEEMED LIKE they had been in the air for just a short period when Vanessa announced that she would be catching one last thermal that would get them the altitude they needed to get back to the airstrip. "So, THIS is what it's like to be a bird!" Meredith thought.

Because Meredith was in front, she could only hear Vanessa, but she could hear and feel Geoff. He frequently nuzzled her neck in between pointing out interesting lakes, peaks, valleys and landmarks. The whole sailing adventure, particularly when tucked into this weekend fantasy, was surreal to her. Helicopters and sailplanes. "What next?" she wondered.

Soon the glider circled out of the sky, and lined up with the runway. They could see the tow-plane and the midnight blue Long Ranger. They could see Booker, too, waving as they touched down and slid to a stop about a hundred yards from the lone building. Vanessa released the canopy and pushed it open. Booker was there in no time to lend a hand to each of them as they deplaned. Once everyone was out, Vanessa had them each take a spot along the wings, and together they maneuvered the feather-light aircraft back to its resting place where it would be secured for the night.

They were all talking and laughing at the same time. Geoff, too. This was also his virginal soaring experience, and he couldn't have been more impressed. He asked Vanessa about licensing requirements and just how much one of these gliders cost.

Soon they were back in the building taking turns using the restroom. Geoff wanted to make sure that Aspen Soaring Experience had received payment—including the generous gratuity. Vanessa assured him that they had, indeed, been paid, and thanked him profusely for the money—and for the rest of the afternoon off. And, the strategy worked: they had run into no one, and had the entire airfield to themselves.

While Meredith was using the facilities, Geoff fetched his phone from his day-pack. He hadn't thought to check it all morning or afternoon. He hoped there wouldn't be any crisis at home or at work. He saw instantly that there were eleven voicemails, and nearly as many texts. Emails were expected. He received hundreds a day it seemed, but the voicemails and texts were unusual. He sat down in one of the comfortable chairs by the window and started listening to his messages.

"Hi Honey. Don't forget to call CJ before his game. He misses you. Call me afterwards when you get a chance." Shit.

Beep

"Did you call CJ? He didn't say anything. What are you up to today? Call me."

Beep

"Where are you? Why are you not answering you phone? Did you forget your charger?"

Beep

"Hey, Boss." Nick's voice. "How's it all going? Smoothly, I hope. If you need anything, call me. Hope your soaring experience was fun."

Beep

"It's the fourth inning. CJ just got a hit and drove in two runs. Score is tied. The girls are at school working on different projects. Lots of people asking about you. You must have a dead battery. Call me."

Beep

"Confirming that I'm sending the large Gulfstream to pick you up Tuesday in Grand Junction." It was Nick again adding, "The small bird is transporting our due-diligence team on a short-notice assignment. I'll fill you in Tuesday afternoon. How's Booker working out? Later."

Beep

"Home now. We won our game, and everyone is so excited. Text or call CJ, okay? Can I ask you something? I know I am being completely paranoid and silly, and I am sure there is a perfectly good explanation for this, but in taking the laundry to the cleaners, one of your white shirts had, what looked to me, to have make-up on it, and it smelled with someone else's perfume. I'm getting a little jealous—I'm sure for no good reason. Think your travelling so much is finally getting to me, and I am cracking up. Seriously. Call me and tell me you love me!"

Beep

"Forget my last message. I'm just getting silly. I trust you completely. Enjoy your time off. Get home safe. I love you. And call CJ."

Beep

Geoff looked up and saw Meredith and Booker talking across the room by the entrance, and he yelled over, "I've got to make one call. I'll be there in a minute." Both waved back at him. He dialed his Chief Operating Officer.

Nick picked up on the second ring. "What's up, boss?"

Geoff exhaled quietly and said, "Everything is going great here. But, at home…? I need to be quick, but I need two things."

"Shoot."

"Not a good choice of words, by the way," Geoff chuckled nervously. Nick could sense it. "First, can you call Susie, and let her know that I didn't charge my cell phone battery last night. Took it on my hike today, and it died. I'll call her later this evening."

"No worries. What else?" Nick urged professionally.

"For the Hudson Environmental due-diligence team, will you get them each a gift from the Company? I don't care what for Charles, Brody and Glen. I'll leave that to you. But, for Mary, can you get her a bottle of perfume called Allure? I'll explain later. Let them all know how much we appreciate them, and I am looking forward to celebrating, big-time, Thursday night with them and their spouses/ significant others."

"Consider it done. I'll see you Tuesday for a de-brief lunch, OK? Don't worry if you are running a little late."

"Thanks, Nick. You're the best. Got to go. Booker, and my friend, are waiting."

"OK, Chief. Safe travels." And, with that, both hung up, and Geoff jumped to his feet.

. . .

The ride home was peaceful and uneventful. Meredith, in fact, sat on Geoff's lap, and laying her head against his chest, fell fast asleep. Geoff couldn't help but wonder at her angelic expression. She clearly was carrying unimaginable burdens from her home life, but kept it all to herself—except for the questions he asked. He didn't want to pry, but then again, he did. For instance, on that first night (answering one of his questions), Geoff learned that Meredith was medically unable to have children. He could tell the disappointment was deep, and it also explained the significant interest and questioning about his own kids. But, tonight was going to be special, and he would do everything in his power to bring this magical weekend to a very memorable, and personal, climax.

As the short trip unfolded, Geoff sat very still making sure to not disturb his sleeping guest. But, in a few minutes time, Booker's voice filled the cabin asking his passengers to prepare for their arrival. Meredith stirred, but Geoff held her tight.

"Shhhh," he whispered. "I love holding you while you sleep. Let me help you." She just nodded drowsily. Geoff slipped an arm under her legs, and one behind her back; she wrapped her arms around his neck. He lifted her easily, and softly laid her in her seat. He fastened her seat belt for her, too. Saying nothing, Geoff kissed her softly on her forehead, and returned to his seat facing her. They just stared at one another. And, smiled. It had been a very adventurous and exhilarating afternoon, and both knew, with certainty, that the coming evening would be even more so.

57

BOBBIE

IT WAS APPROACHING MIDNIGHT SATURDAY WHEN BOBBIE'S TRUCK came to a sliding stop in front of their house. He was hammered and horny. Where was her car? He jumped out of his cab and headed straight for the back door. It was locked, and the lights were off. How many times had he reminded Meredith to leave the side-yard light on? A thousand? At least. But, then again, she wasn't expecting him tonight. SURPRISE!

Bobbie unlocked the door, and made his way directly to the bedroom—the ardor in his loins building. Flinging open the door, he said loudly, "I'm home!" And, once again, Meredith had disappeared. He simmered.

He went to the kitchen and pulled out a cold, long-neck, Coors, and then headed for the front porch where the cellular reception would be better. When he opened the door, a bunch of papers, rubber-banded to the door knob, tussled against the door frame.

"What the fuck?" Bobbie growled as he wrestled one of the papers from its perch. It was an Arrest Warrant—and a Summons to Appear—for one Robert James Edmonson. Granite County Sheriff. He sat on the plastic chair and stared forward a few feet into the dirt processing nothing. Even as impaired as he was, he could feel his throat constricting—almost as though a noose was being tightened. Where was she? Why was she gone when he needed her the most? Then, at 12:09 AM, he dialed Jessica.

There was no answer, of course. But he let fly a drunken tirade of obscenities before demanding to know where Meredith was. "I am sure you know exactly where my little Meredith is," he said, panting. "Have her call me. It's urgent." And with that, he hung up and headed back to the bedroom.

Once there, he pulled a large duffle bag from under the bed, and started to pack his clothes. He didn't have much in the way of a wardrobe, but he loaded what he owned. Before he departed, he took one more look around the room. His eyes settled on Meredith's picture by his side of the bed. He went and retrieved it. He stood and looked at it for some time—breathing heavily. He went to throw it into his duffle, but stopped himself. Still holding the framed photo, he walked around to Meredith's side of the bed, and pulled the bedspread back—exposing her pillow. Unbuckling his pants with his other hand, Bobbie let them slip to his knees. Grasping his Viagra-fueled member, he stroked himself vigorously, staring at her picture, until he could feel his eminent explosion. It didn't take long. He growled as his powerful ejaculate erupted from his body in uncontrolled jerks - and splashed onto where her head would have been laying. After wiping himself on her blanket, he threw her photo into his duffle, and pulled up his jeans.

"Later, Babe," he said to no one.

58

SUSIE

SUSIE THOUGHT A LOT ABOUT HER COMMENTS AT THE GYM THIS afternoon. They were completely unwarranted. The more she pondered the reasons for her uncharacteristic outburst, the more she questioned herself. She was lucky indeed. She didn't have to look around her very far to see the lifestyle that she was fortunate enough to lead. She had three great kids, a fabulous home, and a husband that adored her. When she would check in with her sorority sisters, they had all married middle managers at best. Nice guys; well, most of them. But, they were all working to make ends meet with little or no help at home.

She felt terrible and guilty when she thought about how she had been treating Geoff these past few weeks. He was pretty simple after all. Yeah, he didn't get around to all his chores as he promised. Yeah, he was a terrible chef. Yeah, he wanted sex all the time. And yeah, he had missed a few practices and games of CJ's as well as events with his daughters. But, he loved them. He loved us. He was a good provider. And, speaking of providers, he was just in a very busy cycle—and his business was flourishing. She knew what she was going to do…

• • •

It was now 4:00 PM Saturday, and Susie had just parallel-parked her Range Rover in front of a small French boutique that specialized in lingerie. She was petrified. In fact, she kept walking. She tried to act nonchalant as she passed by the storefront with her large Dior sunglasses. She caught a glimpse of the displayed merchandise on those perfect little mannequins with those perfect little perky tits. "Really? Who wears red lingerie? Maybe I could do white," she thought. "Better stick to basic black." Then she tried to convince herself it wasn't worth the time and money. "It won't stay on me for more than a few moments," she rationalized.

Susie walked three blocks debating with herself, and in the process, building up her nerve. Then, thinking of Geoff returning Tuesday night, and her important mission, she turned around and headed back. Before crossing the street to the block with "the" store on it, she carefully looked around to see if she could possibly know someone or be recognized. It appeared to be safe. She turned quickly in at the door. She could feel her damp palms, but with resolution, she reached out, grasped the doorknob and entered.

● ● ●

"Oh…my…God," was all she could think to say. Over and over.

"What's THAT?"

"What do you DO with THAT?"

Brandy, the sales girl, was laughing at every comment. She was relaxed, fun, free-spirited—and obviously had zero inhibitions. Susie was relieved when this happy and energetic salesperson approached her. Brandy knew instantly that she was dealing with a virtual virgin.

"Can I help you?" she had asked. When Susie blushed, she smiled.

Yes. Well, I guess so. I…I've…" Susie stammered.

"…never done this before, right?" Brandy said, lighting up. "A little excitement for your man?"

Susie seemed to calm a bit, and said, "Yes, actually. I'm a pretty conservative girl. Just want to surprise my husband when he gets home from his trip."

"Atta girl!" Brandy encouraged. "My name is Brandy, by the way." Then, she added, "Sex is a beautiful and raw expression of two persons being in lust. It can also be a heartfelt expression of the complex intimacy that two people have built together over time. Sex is physical, emotional—and highly visual and tactile. And, that's where I come in! What are you thinking?"

"What am I thinking? I am thinking is that you moonlight as a sex therapist!" Susie was relaxing. She really liked Brandy. At least liked the way she made her feel about being in this sinful place. Susie kept checking the storefront and window, however. "Maybe some nice underwear and a top?"

Brandy then walked over to the full-length, three-panel, mirror. "Come over here a sec," she said. When Susie arrived, and situated herself inside the panels,

Brandy moved behind her, and grabbed her blouse at the sides and pulled it tight backwards. Susie jerked away and wheeled around.

"What in Heaven's name are you doing?" Susie blurted.

Brandy laughed. "What's your name?"

"Susan."

Well, Susan, I'm trying to get an idea of your figure so that I can recommend the best thing for you to wear. I'm sorry. I should have asked you first. May I?"

Susie hesitated, then said, "OK. Just no hanky-panky."

"You really have never done this before, have you?" Brandy asked easily as she guided Susie back in front of the mirror.

* * *

Susie just couldn't go for the stockings and garter belt. One step at a time. She selected black lace panties and a black-edged grey camisole with a plunging neckline. She was exhausted, and just wanted to quickly purchase her things and get out of there before someone she knew saw her.

As Brandy was wrapping her purchase in chiffon, she casually asked, "So, how are you for vibrators?"

"What?" Susie was incredulous. What did she say?

"We carry every conceivable make and brand with any features that tickle you here, throb you there, pulsate you to wonderful orgasms. We even have some that specialize in reaching your…"

"No, no, no, no, no," Susie interrupted holding her hands up in front of her—talking over the top of her very enthusiastic sales girl.

"Listen, Susan, you DO masturbate, right?"

Susie was losing it. She had had enough. She was nice, but firm, when she said, "No thanks. Just wrap up what I bought."

Brandy kept talking, "You know, men LOVE it when you masturbate in front of them. Really gets them off." Susie was trying now to ignore her. "Listen, get the vibrator for him for a little extra excitement. You know, for a little voyeuristic show. I promise you, you will thank me. And," she hesitated for effect and looked up from her wrapping, "It will be a secret treat for yourself. Believe me."

Susie gathered her purse and put her sunglasses back on. "I believe you, Brandy. Thanks. But, no thanks."

Brandy handed Susie her package, and handed her a business card. "Call me any time. You can make an appointment. And ENJOY yourself!"

"Oh, I know my husband will. Thanks, Brandy."

Susie accepted her package from Brandy, and looked out the front window before opening the door. Once outside, she stood in the door well and looked both ways carefully. When she was sure no one could see her, she bolted for her car. She sat in the front seat before starting her engine, and just shook her head. It was over. The worst was over. Lord. She turned the key, and the engine roared to life.

In the café across the street, Rhonda couldn't believe what she just saw.

59

ASPEN

GEOFF HAD LAID A NEW FIRE AND HAD SHAKEN THEM EACH A GEN-erous martini before they had headed upstairs to prepare for another fireside dinner. Meredith helped by putting away the breakfast dishes. The day had been so full of surprises and emotions that both were wonderfully mellow. Each was ready to lounge and linger over another home-made meal.

They had showered together—in the waning light of the forest. The intimacy was expected, but even given their fresh infatuation, they were both surprised by their passion. Their bodies felt wonderful against the other's, and the liquid soap added a slippery aphrodisiac to the encounter. The water was steamy hot, and loosened their muscles and inhibitions. What happened after they stepped into the shower—occurred without a spoken word. There would be plenty of time for dialog at dinner.

● ● ●

The only light in the room came from the flickering candles on their table and the roaring fire in the fireplace. They were on their second bottle of Pinot Noir—their plates and bowls were empty. Their chairs pushed back. Their appetites, but not their curiosities, sated for now. They had been talking, laughing easily and probing all evening.

Geoff was speaking. "If I could make a fantasy of yours come true tonight, what would it be?" It would be the first time that Meredith had hesitated in her answers all night. Geoff took a sip of his wine, waited and never took his eyes off of her.

After a long pause, she said, "You know, it's trust. Trust for me is a fantasy that I have never allowed myself the luxury of experiencing. That trust would lead to other freedoms, I suppose, that would be both satisfying and enlightening. I have felt that trust with you, Geoff. Trust *and* safety. And while I am still just getting to know you, I feel that you would never do anything to harm me or to hurt me—physically or emotionally. I would like to deepen that trust tonight and see where this all leads us. You? Same question."

He nodded quietly taking it all in. He then said, "I want for you to fall deeply asleep on my shoulder tonight. I want you to feel safe—and trusting—in my arms. And I want to feel the rise and fall of your chest on mine; your soft breath whispering peacefully across my body. I want to hold someone who wants to be held—knowing that she trusts me utterly." They both sat there and listened to the fire.

Then Geoff continued, "Those were probably not the answers we would have given yesterday." They both smiled and started laughing. "Hey, let's clear these dishes. I have a surprise dessert for you. That is…if you trust me."

60

DON

GRANITE DISTRICT SCHOOL SUPERINTENDENT, DON DELATORE, lived alone in a small, well-kept, single-story, ranch house on the outskirts of Grand Junction. The house sat on an oversized, and overgrown, lot. In the early years, he had kept up the large, and secluded, property, and his son had helped with the yard work. But these days, he only worked on the lawn and gardens immediately adjacent to his house, and let the perimeter shrubs and trees grow unfettered providing a natural ring of privacy around his three-acre property.

He was with kids and adults all day, five to six days a week—if you counted sporting events and special school activities on Saturdays. He was very popular with everyone in the District, including the parents. He showed up to most of the sporting events, plays, and community projects that his "kids" were involved with, enthusiastically cheering and rooting them on. But, that amount of activity had to be counterbalanced by a cherished peace. He had, therefore, grown to love his quiet, and peaceful, sanctuary of a home.

He had lived in the house for twenty-three years where he and his late wife, Harriet, had raised their two kids. When his wife passed away from a long battle with cancer, he had contemplated moving, but remembering his wife, and the raising of their kids, were too rich, and too raw, for him to move away from this treasure trove of good memories - at least for now. Much of Harriet's belongings were still where she left them before leaving, for her final trip, to the hospital.

• • •

It was early Sunday morning, the 23rd, and Don awoke to a strange smell. Bacon? What? He sat up and swiveled his feet to the floor. He listened intently, and could hear movement towards the kitchen. He then smiled. Since his wife's death, his kids visited often to make sure he was OK and had some company. They usually called first before coming over, but there had been times when they just popped in. But, at 7:40 AM on a Sunday? The thought quickly evaporated. He was so excited to see one of his kids that he decided to not change out of his plaid flannel pajamas. Instead, he slipped on his loafers and hurried down the hall.

Don got to the kitchen door, and turned the corner with a big smile. But, then he froze. The blood drained from his face. He started to hyperventilate.

"Sit down, Don. Can I pour you some coffee?" Coach Edmonson never turned around for these initial pleasantries. He was hard at work at the stove toying with some familiar tongs flipping the Oscar Meyer bacon Don had bought yesterday. "How do you want your eggs?"

Don took a quick look around the kitchen, and nothing seemed out of place or different—except this unannounced visitor. The drip coffee maker was on, and sat in the corner, three-fourths filled. Harriet's favorite coffee mug sat next to the stove. Bobbie reached down and picked it up. He first licked the rim, then slurped his coffee loudly. "Nice mug. I particularly loved it because of the pink flowers."

Bobbie started to whistle softly. Don didn't recognize the tune. "You haven't answered me, Donny boy. How do you want your eggs?" Don slowly started to retreat back out the door.

"Don-Don? Can I call you that? I think that fits you. Don-Don." Bobbie seemed deep in thought. "Two faced." Bobbie started laughing. Then he got serious. "Don-Don? I asked you a question. You don't want to piss off the cook, do you?"

At last, Bobbie looked back over his shoulder. Don was gone. A smile slowly made its way to his face. Bobbie yelled, "Black? Or cream and sugar?" He could hear the unmistakable sound of feet running down the hall. Bobbie kept whistling and turned back to the stove. He twisted up the heat under the already-burning bacon, and took another swig of his coffee. Still yelling with his head tilted back, he fired off, "Whipped, beaten or scrambled? How do you want it, Donny old boy? You sure weren't this polite to me in the principal's office last week, now were you, Don-Don?"

Bobbie went to the sink and rinsed off his hands - the smoke from the burning grease filling the kitchen. He then walked slowly over to the kitchen door that led outside. Before exiting, he reached into his pocket and pulled out his fingerless leather gloves, and slowly put them on. He stepped out into the crisp Colorado morning air. He took a deep breath and exhaled slowly—calming himself. Resting against the side of the house was his hunting bow and quiver.

* * *

Don slowly, and quietly, slid open his bedroom window. He listened intently. He could hear the whistling all the way back here. He slid one leg over the window sill and then the other. He slowly slithered to the ground. What were his options? He could try to get to his car, but it was in the detached garage by the kitchen. His only other real choice was to get to one of his neighbors. He could do so by quickly slipping into the woods behind his house. His breathing was erratic, and his heart was pounding. He took stock of his surroundings. It was time. He needed to get away. Now.

Don looked both ways. Even though he was outside, he could still hear whistling coming from the kitchen area. He moved in the opposite direction, took a deep breath, and bolted for the overgrowth across the short clearing. He didn't look back, but rather kept focused on a gap in the trees ahead of him as he sprinted towards safety.

Bobbie calmly pulled an arrow from his quiver and set it onto the string using his pointer and fucker fingers. He pulled the taught gut string and arrow back locking his thumb under his chin. He sighted his prey through his scope. He didn't want to kill it. The thrill was in the chase.

Don heard nothing. The searing pain slammed into him just under his rib cage, and his legs gave way. Reaching instinctively for his side, he was unable to arrest his fall. He stumbled awkwardly forward—his upper torso and face taking the full impact. He was conscious, but panic and shock were unhappy and unwanted passengers along within him. He rolled over; the pain exploding through his side. He looked down, and to his horror, saw a jagged razor tip of an arrow sticking forward out of his body. His eyes were bulging in fear as his bladder immediately released mixing urine with his blood.

Adrenaline was now coursing through his veins. He couldn't stand; the pain was so severe—his whole right side now on fire. He crawled into the bushes; every movement excruciating. His breathing was labored, but he tried to focus on the next shrub that would help him advance while giving him cover. But, he found it difficult to focus on his far-away neighbors. His life was the only thing that mattered now, and he scoured his surroundings for a hiding place where he couldn't be found.

The second arrow arrived silently and sliced cleanly through his pajamas entering his upper thigh just below his buttocks. Both arrows were now grotesquely protruding from Superintendent Don DeLatore's body. But, he didn't notice. The force of the pain splayed him forward, arms back and face-first once again onto the cold and hard dirt. Darkness engulfed him as he slipped quickly, and mercifully, into another realm.

● ● ●

Don was moving cruelly between consciousness and delirium. He was distantly aware of some talking, and when he was finally able to focus through the slits of his eyelids, he blanched.

"I've asked you, now, what? A hundred times? How do you want your eggs?" Bobbie smiled as though he and Don were best friends. "Coffee?"

When he fully came to, Don was seated in his kitchen, back against a wall, facing Bobbie. Actually, he was tied securely to a chair, arms fastened behind him, and his legs spread and affixed to a separate chair leg. The two arrows were still sickeningly protruding from his body, and with every movement Don made, the arrows twitched and swayed—pulling damaged flesh and muscle with them. He was mumbling incoherently and his head was swaying from side to side. He was drooling on himself.

"What do you mean, 'no'? I've worked really hard here to fix us some breakfast so that we can talk. You know…man-to-man? I'm sure we can work out our little misunderstanding from the other day. You just need to explain to your asshole principal, Charlie 'Freakin" Freddricks the real facts."

"Please, Coach," Don was able to choke out of his bloodied lips.

"Oh, great!" Bobbie exclaimed. "You want breakfast, finally? Let me start you off with some coffee." Bobbie poured a large mug of scalding hot coffee, and came over and stood before Don. "Oh, that's right. You can't use your arms. Here. Let me help you."

Don was shaking his head aggressively—his eyes staring at the mug approaching his lips. His voice was now a hoarse whisper, "No, please…no."

"No? What do you mean, 'no'? Your little slutty head of Human Resources— what's her name? Janet 'Giant Jugs' Jacobs? You have to get her to say 'no,' OK? She is one tight-assed little bitch. And that fuckin' scum lawyer of yours? I'll teach him a thing or two about the law of the jungle."

Don was now broken; his head lolling back and forth and he was whimpering like a child; the tears unabated. He just kept shaking his head mumbling, "No. No. No…"

The scalding liquid hit him full in the face. He could feel his flesh cooking. The blackness returned, and Don, once again, passed into the unknown.

* * *

The second time the fog started to clear for Don, his face was badly blistered and bubbling. But, he was choking. He couldn't get a breath. His mouth had been stuffed with something, and he was sucking hard to catch just a hint of oxygen. His nose was filled with dried blood, too, blocking that airway. He leaned his head forward and opened his mouth, and tried, in vain, to choke out the sloppy mass. Panic seized him again as he started to gag. He could only lean over as he was still securely strapped to his kitchen chair as his body convulsed.

Bobbie came over and asked quietly, "Can I help you?" Don's eyes were now bulging and imploring. "That's what friends do, right? We help each other." And with that, Bobbie put his right finger inside Don's mouth, and reaching back to the back of his throat pulled out the mess that blocked his windpipe. It fell into Bobbie's left hand—cupped under Don's chin.

"What?" Bobbie said. "You didn't like your breakfast? I worked so hard preparing it for you."

By now, Don was delirious. He just wanted his eyes to close for one final time.

"Hey! I'm talking to you!" Bobbie screamed. But, Don's head was now resting motionless chin-on-chest. Bobbie fetched a glass of water from the sink, still holding Don's breakfast in his left hand. He tossed the water into his face. Don stirred. His head rolled slowly from side to side, and his eyes tried to focus. He looked up at Bobbie, and then back down at his outstretched hand. He tried to make out what Bobbie held. Then his eyes seemed to come to life and clear for a brief horrified moment. Bobbie was holding a penis.

* * *

The news spread through the city as fast as the fire raced through the Superintendent's house. A lone body—burned beyond recognition—was found in the master bedroom. The intense heat of the fire consumed both structure and flesh.

The inferno erased the arrow that had penetrated Don DeLatore's left eye, and had ended his life by angrily imbedding itself in his brain. The other two arrows had been pulled free and carefully placed, unwashed, back into their quiver. Foul play was not suspected. At least not on this day.

61

ASPEN

THEY CLIMBED THE GRAND STAIRCASE, HAND-IN-HAND. WHEN THEY entered the master suite, Geoff turned around and faced Meredith. He put his arms around her waist, and she rested her arms comfortably on top of his. He leaned down, and closing his eyes, kissed her on her forehead.

"I've made a very special dessert for you, M," he said. "But, you are going to have to trust me. I know I am asking a lot. You said feeling trust was a fantasy I could possibly unlock for you. But, I also know that trust takes time. So, can you trust me a little right now?"

Meredith, with her big brown eyes never departing from his gaze, said simply, "I trust you."

Geoff said, "Stay right here; I'll be right back." He let go of her, and walked into the closet. Meredith was anxious with curiosity. The fire was low, but still radiating heat. When he returned, he was carrying the sash from one of the robes. She raised her eyebrows and tilted her head slightly. Putting his index finger softly across her lips, he said, "Shhh. Trust me." She nodded.

Geoff turned her around so that her back was to him. He softly pulled the wide sash across her eyes, and tied it snuggly. "Can you see anything?" he asked.

"Nothing."

"Good." Geoff, never taking his hands off her, circled around so that he was facing her. Kneeling on the ground, he asked her to steady herself on his shoulder and raise one of her feet. He then slowly removed her pump. And then the other. He stood and placed a hand behind her head, leaned down and kissed the side of her neck. She shivered. He then moved his hands down and slowly and deliberately unbuttoned her blouse. When it was open, he slipped it off her shoulders.

● ● ●

Meredith awoke peacefully sometime in the middle of the night. Her head rested comfortably on Geoff's shoulder. They were both naked and cocooned under the sheets and the plush down comforter. She must not have been asleep for very long as Geoff still had his arm around her. She could hear the soft hissing of the waning fire as she turned the events of last night around deliciously in her mind. It was not at all what she had expected.

Geoff had led her to the large over-stuffed chair that sat in front of the fire. Her blindfold was secure, and as he carefully guided her across the large room, she could feel her other senses heightening. She felt the changing textures of hardwood floor giving way to the oriental carpets from the bottoms of her feet. Her ears picked up the crackling of the fire—and Geoff's breathing. She could smell him, too. His cologne—a musky natural scent—mixed with the soap from the shower. This brought a smile to her face. She had washed him. All of him.

Once seated on the chair, she could feel the radiating heat on her nearly naked body. The snapping and crackling of the pine logs tickled her ears. She exhaled deeply when Geoff massaged her neck and shoulders. "I'll be right back," he had said. "Trust me, OK? Please, enjoy this short respite between main course and dessert," he had teased. "No peeking."

Meredith could only nod and smile. "Please hurry," she replied.

Once Geoff had left the room, Meredith focused on herself and her surroundings. He had slowly removed most of her clothes—leaving her in her red lacey thong and a robe sash around her eyes. Her skin was sensitive and alive. She gently rubbed the upper swelling of her breasts, and this made her shudder. She could feel the goose-bumps emerging on her skin like foam on the ocean. As she concentrated, she could almost feel a transformation from the mountains to the sea, and for a moment, she pictured herself up on a warm, windy, bluff overlooking the Atlantic—her skin tantalizingly absorbing all the elements.

It wasn't too long before she could hear footsteps approaching, and she could make out the tinkling of glassware and china. She listened as Geoff entered the room and carefully placed whatever he was carrying on the side table. The unmistakable aroma of bittersweet chocolate entered her nostrils and lingered there. Her lips parted exposing her radiating smile. "How did you know?"

"How did I know what?" Geoff asked. "That you liked chocolate fondue?"

She nodded, "Are you a mind-reader?"

"Nope, I remembered that you had had a craving for chocolate the night we met. So, I decided to surprise you with something special for our last night together."

"I hope not," Meredith whispered.

Geoff let the comment pass, and rather than replying, he placed his finger softly across her lips. "Shhhhhhhhhh." He quietly continued, "Are you ready for dessert?"

Meredith smiled and softly kissed his finger, replying, "Yes. I can hardly wait."

Just then, she felt something cold brush her belly button. Meredith flinched. Once again, she felt his finger touch her lips. "Trust me," he said.

She immediately relaxed and reclined in the chair spreading her legs slightly and bringing her arms to her side. Meredith exhaled. And, even under the blinding sash, she closed her eyes. The cool sensation that started in her belly button slowly made its way up her stomach, slid between her breasts, traced north up her neck, traveled below her ear and across her cheek—and settled softly on her upper lip just under her nose. Strawberry. "Mmmmmmmmmmmm," she murmured tilting her head back slightly parting her lips. She took a bite. The fruit was crisp on the outside, but in no time, the sweet, fleshy, succulent middle was in her mouth—her tongue and teeth playing with it for a prolonged period while she savored its flavor.

Soon, something else was resting on her lip. This time, it was gooey and warm; the rich smell of chocolate begging. She again tilted her head back and parted her lips, but this time Geoff said playfully, "Please don't bite this time." He delicately spread the chocolate across her lips—one by one—and then inserted his finger into her mouth. She reached up and took hold of his wrist making sure he couldn't withdraw, and with a slow, erotic, flourish, fellatio'ed his finger—licking, sucking and nibbling until every spec of chocolate was consumed.

The next piece of fruit was a chocolate- dipped banana, and this made its way on a similar expedition across the smooth hills and succulent valleys of Meredith's body. Geoff carefully kissed away any and all accidental journey markers. Her blind experience sent unusual sensations rippling through her brain.

"You're turn," she said holding out her hand. "Guide me to the chocolate, will you?"

He took her hand in both of his, and placed it on the fondue pot saying, "Be very careful, there is a flame underneath keeping the chocolate very warm and liquid."

"I think I can handle it," she said as she sat up in the chair. She placed two fingers of her right hand into the cauldron, and with her left searched the air until she found Geoff. Her hand found his bare chest. He couldn't see her eyes widen under the cloth. She continued to search his body. No shirt, no shoes, no apron, no pants. She ran her hand down until she found his erection. Wrapping her fingers around him, she said, "Now THIS is the next banana to get dipped." And in one motion, leaned over and took him deeply into her mouth. As she withdrew from him slowly, she flicked her tongue along the main vein until she reached his tip. She stopped, and ever so lightly, kissed him at his opening.

Geoff stroked her hair, then grabbed her sinful, wandering hand and brought it to his mouth. "This is what I think you were looking for young lady."

Meredith laughed, and brought her right hand, covered in chocolate, slowly to Geoff's face. He opened his mouth to receive her, but when she got close, she smooshed the warm chocolate all over his face. For the next ten minutes, she cleaned him. With her mouth.

* * *

Meredith rolled to her side and nestled back against him in a spontaneous spoon. She brought his arm up and over her, and drew it to her chest. What a day. What a night. They had, in the end, not made love, but Geoff had said that he wanted to fulfill her fantasy.

He had picked her up and carried her to the large bed at the far end of the room, and laid her gently onto the sheets, that just moments before, he had turned down. He reached down, and slipped off her panties. Now, she was as naked as he was. As he walked over to the fireplace to stoke it with three new pine logs, she couldn't help but admire this man.

He turned out the dim lamp at the desk and returned to their bed. He climbed in, and rolling onto his back, physically invited her to join him. Once he had her comfortably against him, with her head on his shoulder, he said, "I had a wonderful day, M. I could not have asked for a better companion. It's beyond description to be with someone who is just as excited to be with you as you are with them. I don't want this weekend to end."

Meredith threw her arm across his chest and pulled him snuggly saying, "Thank you, Geoff. Thank you for everything. I'm living a fantasy that I do not deserve, and I am incredulous as to how our paths crossed and brought us here. I've never felt so alive; so free; so…so…safe to be me. How will I ever repay you?"

Geoff took a deep breath, and absorbed the moment. He could feel her naked body directly against his—the full length of it—and it felt so right. Her head rested softly on his chest. "I have heard you say several times today that you feel safe, protected, trusted. When I asked you about a fantasy to be fulfilled tonight, you said you wanted to be safe, free of worry—essentially. I may not have gotten that precisely right, but I think I am close." Meredith nodded her head. "So, that's why tonight, I want to assure you that your safe. Safe here. Safe here in my arms. Safe and free to have a peaceful night's sleep." Geoff's strong arms now wrapped tightly around her. "And as for repayment? I have a ways to go to repay YOU. You have given me the most priceless of gifts…you. Your beauty, your laughter, your body, your warmth, your acceptance. I don't want this to end." Meredith didn't hear him. The last bit anyway. She had fallen into a deep and delirious sleep.

And now, as she lay against Geoff, deep in his arms, in a house so far removed from her own life, she felt ecstatically safe and at peace. She closed her eyes once more. Tomorrow they would go for a walk and get some fresh air before returning to the lives they had left so far behind, but not so long ago.

62

SUSIE

IT WAS SUNDAY MORNING, AND SUSIE AWOKE FEELING UNUSUALLY light-hearted. She made the bed, and threw on a robe over her flannel pajamas. Rosanne was back from her brief "sick leave" and was already at work fixing eggs and bacon with blueberry muffins when Susie came into the kitchen. "Can I help with anything?" Susie inquired.

"No, that's OK, Mrs. Cameron," Rosanne replied. "You have church today, and will have your hands full with the kids." She had been working for the Cameron's for seventeen years dating back to when Susie was pregnant with Lucy. Unmarried, Rosanne cherished Lucy, Brooke and CJ as if they were her own. She loved Mr. Cameron, too. He was always so nice and pleasant to her. Treated her just like one of the family. Mrs. Cameron, on the other hand, had always been a bit cold to her with unpredictable mood swings. She had overheard her one day telling someone on the phone regarding an errand she needed to make that she would just get "the help" to do it. But today, Mrs. Cameron seemed in a particularly good mood.

"All right. Thanks, Rosie. I'll go wake the kids, and then jump in the shower." Susie grabbed a hot blueberry muffin off the baking tray and took a bite. "Ummmmmm. No one makes muffins like you do, Rose." She started out of the kitchen and then returned. "Say, Rosanne, can you go to the store today and get fixings for Mr. Cameron's favorite meatloaf. He's coming home Tuesday, and I want to have a special dinner prepared for him. If you can get it all prepared Tuesday morning—a salad, the meatloaf and maybe some mashed potatoes, all

I'll have to do is put the meatloaf in the oven, and warm the potatoes and toss the salad. Oh, and Rosie? Can you make one of those yummy apple pies, too?"

Susie didn't see the controlled look on Rosanne's face. She looked up from scrambling the eggs and said, "Sure, no problem Mrs. Cameron. Can you tell the children to come straight down? I don't want them to have to eat cold eggs."

Susie said, "Just put them in the warming drawer with the bacon, will ya? You know those kids: sometimes waking them up requires a three-alarm fire under their tushes." Then she continued, "And one more thing? Once you have the kids to school on Tuesday, and everything is ready for Mr. Cameron's and my dinner, you can go home early. In fact, I am farming out the kids to friends' houses so that Mr. Cameron and I can have a long-overdue date night."

"Yes, Mrs. Cameron. Thank you."

Susie rushed up stairs and stopped at each of the three children's doors and knocked. With a mixed reaction from each—all mostly groans and "I don't want to get up's," Susie added that "breakfast was served," and to hurry down to eat before getting ready for church. She didn't wait around for replies.

Once in her room, she closed the door. She went to her closet, and walked to the back where one of her dressers was located. She opened the top drawer, and pulled out the little pink bag from "the" boutique. She removed the impossibly small black lace panties and the gray camisole. "Dear sweet Jesus," Susie shook her head as she held up the camisole in front of her. She then went back, and closed the door to her closet. She slipped out of her pajamas and underwear, and tried on her new outfit. She could hardly get herself to the full-length mirror, and she arrived there backing up to it with her eyes closed. She turned around, and slowly opened her eyes. What she saw surprised her, to say the least. She looked kind of…uh…hot? No, not HOT; maybe a little sexy. That Brandy girl was maybe right. She would soon find out. Two more nights until Geoff got home. "Boy, will he EVER be surprised!" she almost choked laughing. That's if she didn't chicken out at the last moment.

Well, it was time for her to slide out of her slut-wear and get ready for church. Susie was singing in the choir today.

63

BOBBIE

BOBBIE'S TRUCK WAS PARKED INSIDE OF AN OUT-BUILDING AT THE far end of Jay's property. Years ago, he and Jay escaped to the "barn," as they called it, to smoke weed and escape their troubles. Jay worked as an electrician and handy-man, and existed in a never-ending cycle of odd jobs and sub-contractor work. To say he was often hand-to-mouth was an understatement. His wife had left him two years ago with their two kids. She was sick of him, their lifestyle and his low-life friends—especially the one friend with a legitimate job: Bobbie Edmonson. But luck had smiled down on Jay for once. He had recently been hired to upgrade the wiring at Grand Junction's airport; a massive job that would keep him busy, and employed, for the next six months, at least.

"Where is he?" Bobbie wondered. He had already drunk all the cold beer in the fridge, and was scavenging through all the cupboards in the kitchen looking for something to eat. Breaking in to Jay's house was the easy part. Feeding himself was proving more difficult. Then he heard the unmistakable sound of tires on gravel. Bobbie knelt by the window, and peered out carefully. His gun was loaded and on the floor next to him.

Bobbie could hear howling laughter, and knew at once that Jay had company with him. It was getting dark, so Bobbie had a hard time making out just who was with his friend. But, then he recognized the voices: Tommy and Mal. He would have fun with this—scare the living shit out of all of them. Mal had his own security firm and was currently employed by the Grand Hotel in town. And, Tommy worked construction. They were all hunting and drinking buddies—not necessarily in that order.

The living room was dark, and Bobbie could hear the key in the door; the fumbling; the laughter. Finally, the door swung open and all three men stumbled in. The lights came on and temporarily blinded Bobbie, but he held his position behind the couch against the window. The guys headed for the kitchen, never closing the door. Jay pulled open the fridge. "What?" Jay questioned. "Where's all my beer? I had two six-packs of Bud in here."

Then, without warning, Bobbie let out a huge, guttural belch from his hiding place. The men froze. Bobbie then jumped to his feet with his gun drawn and pointed directly at them. "On your knees, you mother fuckers!"

All three literally fell over themselves to the floor. And all three instinctively raised their hands in the air in surrender and ducked their heads. They all seemed to be blurting "Don't shoot!" over the top of each other—and over the top of Bobbie's peeling laughter. They each carefully glanced up and saw, with enormous surprise and relief, their friend now hunched over laughing hysterically. It took them several seconds to put it all together, but there was Coach Edmonson, their fearless fourth, smiling broadly, gun still drawn.

"Now get to your feet, you chicken-shits!" As they struggled to stand, Bobbie turned his loaded 357 Magnum towards the open front door, and pulled the trigger. The boom was deafening, and the three friends all hit the floor once again. Bobbie was laughing again, and all three leapt to their feet—shouting and swearing—and came straight over and bear-hugged their buddy. "Together again!" Mal shouted.

After the high-fives and fist-pumps, Bobbie exclaimed, "I'm starving. Let's get a couple of pizzas delivered. Two of you can go get some more cold beer and bourbon. My treat."

"No. No. No," Jay said. "We will split the bill like always."

"Not today," Bobbie retorted. "I have a little extra vacation pay burning a hole in my pocket. Literally. I'm dying to feed you blokes. Must be my day for charity. I made breakfast for an old friend this morning."

64

ASPEN

THE UNSEASONABLY WARM WEATHER OF THE PAST TWO DAYS HAD given way to a grey overcast, and a cold Sunday morning. Geoff had prepared an egg scramble of French cheese, shallots, mushrooms and bell pepper, whole-grain toast, fresh squeezed orange juice and hand-pressed coffee. He delivered this to Meredith in bed on a lap tray. She couldn't believe it. He joined her in bed and sat, legs crossed under him, across from her, and they ate off the same plate.

Now, they were walking along a meandering path that paralleled the stream behind many of the impressive Aspen mansions. They were in their hiking gear, and bundled up against the approaching storm. It was fresh and windy, and the air carried the aroma of rich soil, fallen leaves and smoke from the ample near-by fireplaces. It was 9:30 AM, and Booker was due with his helicopter in a couple of hours.

"I don't want to go home, Geoff," Meredith said in almost a whisper. Geoff was deep in his own thoughts, and her almost pleading voice, broke his meditative thoughts. Truth be known, he was thinking the very same thing, but mixed in his thoughts was the week ahead: arriving home, papering the deal they had just closed, more due-diligence on three more deals they were in the middle of and the special morale-building closing dinner on Thursday.

"Me, either," Geoff said turning his head towards her as they walked. "This weekend has been memorable on so many fronts." He took her hand. They walked slowly and silently—drinking in the environment and their emotions. Her hand felt so soft in his. After a few minutes, he said, "You're beautiful, M, inside and out." He hesitated then added, "I don't want this to end. You?"

"Sounds like a rhetorical question to me," she replied as they strolled still hand-in-hand. She then pulled him to a stop. She took both of his hands in hers, and looked up into his eyes. "Geoff, I just…" She choked, and tried without much luck to gather her emotions. Tears came freely, and slipped down her cheeks. When Geoff tried to remove his hands to wipe her sadness, she held tight, and never broke eye contact. The smile returned to her face, and she said, "Thank you. Thank you for everything. Not just all this, but restoring in me a smidgeon of hope. Restoring in me happiness. You have no idea. You couldn't. But thank you." She pulled him to her and they held each other in a warm, knowing, embrace.

Geoff then became aware of a commotion up in a tree above them. When they broke their hold on each other he looked up, and exclaimed, "Look. It's a red-tailed hawk. One of the most efficient birds of prey in nature. Pretty, isn't he?"

Meredith didn't see the predator right away. Geoff put his right arm around her shoulder, and leaned in so that their heads were together looking along Geoff's other arm—now out stretched pointing towards the hawk. Then she saw it. "He IS beautiful, isn't he?' she said pulling away and looking at him. "Where does he…"

The sound of a strong voice interrupted them. "Geoff! Geoff Cameron! What are you doing here?" Walking up the trail from the opposite direction was one of Geoff and Susie's neighbors, Bill Thomas. Bill had his own successful recruitment agency, William Thomas & Associates. Geoff had used Bill's firm to source some key positions over the years, but their relationship was mostly personal.

Geoff looked up in such surprise that he was sure his guilt emanated from every pore, and every muscle, in his face. "Bill! What are YOU doing in Aspen?" Geoff asked—a little too loudly.

"Here on a little 'vaca' away from the kids. We rented a house just upstream; a beautiful place Emily picked out. You? And who is your friend here?" he said as he took in all of Meredith—if, a little too slowly.

"Oh, I'm sorry," Geoff blushed. He turned to Meredith and said, "I didn't catch your name."

Meredith's eyes imperceptibly narrowed a bit, but she caught on and recovered quickly saying, "Andrea. Andrea McAllister."

"Bill, meet Andrea. Uh, Andrea, and I just happened to meet on the trail, and we were looking at a red-tailed hawk." Geoff motioned up in the tree, but when they all looked, the hawk was nowhere to be seen. "Well, it was just here."

Without skipping a beat, Bill said, "Say, you and Susie want to come over tonight for some cocktails and dinner?"

"Can't. Thank you for the invitation, though. Susie's back home, and I am taking a little fresh-air hiking break between my meetings in Grand Junction and New York. I fly out this afternoon."

"Some hiking break," Bill chided. "In case you didn't know, this is a path—not a hiking trail!"

"Yes, but if I had been up in the high country, I might have been trapped by this incoming storm. And hey, I wouldn't have met Allison here, or run in to your good self."

"Andrea," Meredith corrected.

"I'm so sorry! Yes, I meant Andrea. I'm so bad with names!" Geoff played the role well. "In fact, I need to get going to catch that plane."

"You mean catch YOUR plane, don't you?" Bill kidded.

"Yes, that would be the one," Geoff said.

"Well, I could ask you WHICH one," Bill joked, "but, I'll leave you two to your bird watching."

"I guess I'll see you back in Nor Cal, Bill. Great running into you. Well, walking into you, anyway." Geoff said. Turning to Meredith, he added, "Nice to meet you, Andrea. I hope our paths cross again." And with that, Geoff headed downstream; hands in his pockets, whistling.

"Hey!" Meredith yelled. Geoff turned around. "I'm headed that way, too," she said. "I'll keep you company until my turn-off. Is that OK?"

"Sure. You're a lot better company than Bill, here. And, much easier on the eyes." She ran to join up with him.

Bill didn't move a muscle as he stared pensively after them as they walked together and disappeared around the bend.

* * *

When Meredith led Geoff back into their house, Geoff stopped in the entry, and put his head back and closed his eyes. "Shit, that was close." He grabbed her hand and placed it on his chest. "Can you feel my heart?"

"How well do you know that guy?"

"Very. We are neighbors and friends, as I mentioned. His wife Emily and my wife, Susie, are close."

"Will he say anything?"

"No doubt. And, I am supposed to be in Grand Junction—not Aspen—this weekend. But, I am pretty sure I can work that one out."

Meredith took Geoff in her arms. Putting her head against his chest she said, "I'm sorry if my being here has caused, or will cause, any problems."

"Geoff hugged her tighter, and replied quietly, "You most certainly have caused me problems. Problems with my heart. I am scared, overjoyed, fearful and jubilant—all at the same time. Oh, M. I don't want this journey to end here."

"It won't. It can't."

Geoff reached down, and grabbed Meredith - caressing her face. He pulled her to him, and their soft kisses turned immediately urgent - their hunger almost desperate. Each felt the pull of the other, and fully clothed, their hands explored the now-familiar territory of their bodies' most erogenous zones. Only the sound of a helicopter overhead broke the spell.

"Shit!" Meredith panted.

Geoff could only stand there and shake his head. He placed his hand under her chin and pulled her face up. He smiled. "That Booker. He's very punctual. I love him for that. But, God, I wish he could have been late for once!"

Both now knowing that their time together was waning, softly and slowly broke their hold of the other. "I haven't even packed yet!" Meredith exclaimed as she raced up the curved and majestic staircase.

Geoff called after her, "Remember, your room is down the hall to the right!" She stopped mid-ascent, and whirled around. She was smiling broadly. Meredith brought her hand to her lips, and tilting it forward blew him a magnificent kiss. She then turned, and raced to the summit—never stopping to contemplate a change in course.

● ● ●

The Long Ranger helicopter lifted carefully skyward. The weather front was nearly upon them, and even Geoff felt a pang of worry, as he watched Meredith pull away from him, and twist back to the southwest disappearing into clouds. He knew his worry was irrational as Booker was an expert pilot, and was instrument trained to navigate in precisely the weather, and the territory, that was surrounding them. He waited motionless staring at precisely the spot where the helicopter had been swallowed by the approaching storm until he could hear nothing but the wind whistling through the needles of the towering pines.

He then turned and headed indoors to straighten up, and to get himself packed. He had about ninety minutes before he expected Booker back to pick him up. It would be a short shuttle to Denver where he would be flown to New York on his more spacious Gulfstream 550.

Once in his bedroom, Geoff quickly threw his dirty laundry and shoes, along with his toiletries, in his suitcase before carefully packing his clean folded clothes on top. He checked and rechecked the closet and all drawers, under the bed, everywhere. He was sure he hadn't left anything behind. Zipping his bag closed, he took one last look around this beautiful room that now held so many memories. And, as he headed for the door, he had no idea that his prized 49er t-shirt was now packed away in a different suitcase. A suitcase that was now high above the Rockies—in fact, safely above the clouds of the storm that was now boiling below it.

65

MEREDITH

HIGH ABOVE THE BOILING CLOUDS, THE LONG RANGER WELCOMED the sunshine as it settled onto its course back to west-central Colorado. The flight out, two short days ago, had been so full of mystery, excitement and intrigue. Now, she was grappling with the torrent of emotions that suspended her between her two, now very real, worlds.

Never, in her wildest imagination, could she have conjured up such a fantasy weekend like the one she had just experienced. She had a hard time believing it all had happened. But, here she was, in a helicopter, sitting in the front seat, cross-chest restraints tightly on, a headset over her ears, and nothing but Heaven in front of her. She shook her head almost imperceptivity as she pondered the enormity of the weekend—and the man whose arms had comforted her, whose smile had captured her, and whose enormity had filled her.

"Ms. Meredith? Can you hear me? Is your headset working?" Booker looked over at his deep-in-thought passenger, and could only make out the back of her head as she stared, virtually motionless, out the window at the scene below her. He could tell she wasn't sleeping, but was personally absorbed.

He decided not to interrupt her any further. It was a short flight back. But, soon Booker was back on the airwaves announcing his arrival to the airport office at Gateway Canyons International Airport. This brought Meredith immediately back to reality—and the life that was waiting for her below. A dark foreboding began to seep into her conscience as she was nervously alone in her thoughts— piecing together her re-entry into her real life in Grand Junction.

"We lucked out on the weather here," Booker said as he banked the Long Ranger steeply to the right. Meredith could see straight down now to the helipad below. "We'll be on the ground shortly."

"Thank you so much, Booker," Meredith exclaimed. "You have made me feel very safe, and maybe even more importantly, very welcome. I couldn't be more appreciative."

"You are most welcome. You can fly with me any time," he replied.

In moments, the aircraft nestled softly on the tarmac, and Booker reached above his head and flipped several switches and twisted a couple of small knobs. The motor immediately exhaled as the rotors slowly came to a halt. Booker turned to open his door, but felt a hand on his arm. He stopped and turned to look back at Meredith. She sat there and their eyes met—their headsets still on.

"I meant what I said, Booker. Thank you. I was so nervous when I met you. And you made me feel so comfortable—not just flying with you, but GOING with you. Do you understand?"

"Yes, Ms. Meredith. I think I do."

"Now that I am back home, or at least near to my home, I need to make sure that this little trip never happened, understand?" Her voice caught on her last word, but she never broke eye contact. "I am mar…"

Booker interrupted her. "Ms. Meredith. I am employed by Mr. Geoff as an exceptional pilot, and a trusted confidant. My loyalty, and trustworthiness are unassailable. This will be the last conversation you and I will ever have to have on the subject, OK?"

She nodded her head. Her eyes expressive and knowing. "Thank you."

● ● ●

When Booker and Meredith arrived at her car, it was as she had left it: in the far corner of the resort parking lot under a tree. She hopped out of the Escalade while Booker fetched her bag. He loaded it into the trunk as Meredith fished out her phone from the glove box and turned it on. The chimes of the backlogged phone messages began their cacophony of reality.

Meredith opened her purse and pulled out the new cell phone that had been wrapped in a brown envelope, along with Geoff's welcome note. She handed the phone to Booker, and without a word, he slipped it into his jacket pocket. He held out his hand, and Meredith took it in both of hers. "I hope I see you again, Booker," she said.

"Oh, I have the feeling that we will be seeing each other together again, soon," he replied.

They both nodded and smiled. Each turned away and climbed into their respective vehicles. Booker's car was already running, and he quickly backed up, and headed for the exit back towards the tiny private airport that would initiate his return trip to Aspen to pick up Mr. Geoff and shuttle him to Denver.

• • •

Meredith closed her door, and the silence was overwhelming. She just sat there and tried to make sense of all that had just happened to her. She placed her forehead on the steering wheel and closed her eyes. She slowly rolled her head back and forth several times as she tried to process the enormity of what had just happened to her. At long last, she sat up, took a deep breath and turned the key. To her relief, her car started up without drama. She let it idle there for a minute before she turned on the heater.

Should she wait until she got home before checking her voice, and email, messages? It was Sunday, and Bobbie was not due home until the evening. And while it was just past 12:30 PM, she was still full from breakfast in Aspen. She didn't need, or want, to stop for a meal. She felt she should head home and get her things, and the house, in order. There, she could relax and take her time in responding. But, something made her decide to sit in her car and listen to her voice mails.

The first message startled her. Her voice mailbox was full. Then she noticed that there was the number 29 in a bubble above her text-message icon. And even more emails.

Life had indeed gone on while she was away. Little did Meredith know just how much life had gone on in her absence.

And, so too, had death.

66

GEOFF

GEOFF WAITED PATIENTLY, AND ANXIOUSLY, FOR WORD FROM BOOKER that his delivery to Gateway Canyons had been accomplished without incident. He was as worried about the storm as he was about the secrecy of the weekend, and he wanted to make sure Meredith was safe. He actually heard from Meredith first.

> From: mquest99@aol.com
> Subject: Back to Reality
> Date: November 23, 2014 at 12:34 PM MST
> To: gquest100@hotmail.com
> Deep breath. I'm back at Gateway. Booker great pilot. He has my temp phone. You have my heart. Shit. Now what are we going to do? I'm scared. Thx for breathing life into my heart & soul. I'll never forget our time together.
> M

He stared at his screen and smiled an exhale. He shook his head. Then he shook it again more slowly thinking back to some of the more memorable moments they had shared. His heart ached—literally. He longed to have her back in his arms, to relive their conversations, their easy laughter, their uncomplicated acceptance of one another. Letting time go lightly.

> From: gquest100@hotmail.com
> Subject: Breathing

Date: November 23, 2014 at 12:38 PM MST
To: mquest99@aol.com
Hardly breathing. So glad you are safe. Storm raging now. Great afternoon for a fire and a bear (did I spell that right?) rug. Wish you were still here. Heading soon to Denver by 4WD for my flight to NYC. Sending Booker back to SF. Glad you felt safe with him. Already thinking of our next rendezvous. That is, if you want to come…
G

There was no immediate reply. That worried him. She was so quick to respond to his texts, and he expected that he would hear right back. The "silence" would grip him for hours.

67

NICK

THE GLEAMING GULFSTREAM 550 TURNED SLOWLY AWAY FROM THE Private Aviation Terminal at New York's La Guardia International Airport. It was Wednesday at 2 PM EST, and Nick watched out the window as the powerful aircraft taxied into position, and swiftly lifted to the sky towards the sunshine of a beautiful fall Wednesday afternoon in Northern California—four and a half hours away. He observed carefully the entire pre-flight procedure by the two pilots. He missed nothing, and took nothing for granted—even though CBC's two best, and most trusted, pilots were in charge on this trip. Mike Parrish was in the right seat, and John Bartlett was Number Two today. And Geoff had taken the opportunity to squeeze in a cat-nap—seat-belted into his soft leather chair across from Nick.

Once the plane had leveled off, and Mike had announced it was OK to roam about the cabin, Stephanie emerged from the galley with a tray of canapes and bottled water. She looked beautiful, and very professional, as always. She wore the CBC uniform of khaki pants and light blue shirt, with logo, that all staff wore on assignments. She wore it proudly. There was, however, no doubt that underneath that formal uniform, Stephanie sported an enviably fit, but quite feminine, body. Nick could testify. He had carnal knowledge.

Stephanie had unclasped an additional button on her shirt, and came directly to Nick first with her tray. Geoff was still napping. She leaned particularly low as she silently offered her treats to him. He couldn't help but look straight into her revealing cleavage at her baby-soft flesh and lace. They made eye contact, and Nick winked but said nothing. He removed two pieces of sushi, a small baked crab roll, and his favorite: caviar on toast points with onion and egg. Stephanie made sure to have that on board every time they flew together. He lightly traced his finger along one of hers holding the tray, and blew her a kiss. She responded by touching the tip of her tongue to her upper lip—and returned the wink.

Nick had to admit, and it disturbed him quite a bit, that he had a weakness for this woman. And, weakness, as he knew all too well, led to mistakes and consequences. If it was predictable, Nick always espoused, it was preventable - whatever "it" was—and, he made every effort to take chance out of every conceivable risk. But, both he and Stephanie were single, and they seemed to be innocently in love. There was a big risk, however, that Nick was intimately aware of: he was Stephanie's supervisor. Rarely did that turn out well at any place of employment. More times than not, it turned into a quid pro quo sexual harassment, and/or hostile work environment, lawsuit. He had represented CBC in numerous situations over the years where his supervisors had gotten sloppy. This, for him, was a monumental risk, but it made their relationship that much more electric.

Geoff was stirring as Stephanie re-emerged with her small drink cart. She had fastened her loose button, and was nothing but professional. "You gentlemen interested in a libation?" she asked.

"I see I've already missed the first course," Geoff said smiling. "A Diet Coke would be great. Thanks, Stephanie."

"Water for me, Steph. Thanks," Nick added.

"No worries, guys," she said. "Mr. Cameron, I'll bring the hors d'oeuvres back with me shortly."

"That would be great. Then, can you check on our pilots? It's most important that they are fed and watered," Geoff chuckled.

"Of course," she replied, then turned back to the galley.

Turning to Nick, Geoff said smiling, "Be careful with that one, Sir Nicolas! She's really into you."

"You think?" Nick let out a rare chuckle. He continued, "I'm seriously worried that she works for me directly, Geoff. Is there any way to get her transferred to your staff?"

Both Nick and Geoff knew that was futile as all employees, except Geoff's direct reports, reported in one way or another up to Nick. Geoff replied sarcastically, "No, but we could fire her."

Nick winced painfully. If it was predictable, it was preventable… All he could do was nod his head.

Geoff held out a clenched fist across the aisle, and Nick bumped fists in a knowing and warm symbol of their lifelong, enduring, knowing, friendship. No more talk on this subject was necessary between the two of them.

When Stephanie returned from the cockpit, and checked in on her VIP passengers, Nick said, "Steph, can Geoff and I have some quiet time to discuss this New York deal?"

"Of course," she replied smiling warmly to them both. "I'll check on you in about an hour to see if I can fetch you anything." And with that, she retired to the aft cabin, which was the luxurious executive stateroom, and closed the door behind her.

● ● ●

"Well,' Nick said smiling just after the stateroom door closed, "can we get down to business?" He reached into his briefcase and brought out a thick, rubber-banded, file with "Empire Energy" scribbled across the front.

"I think you sent me all that material as an email attachment Sunday, and it was enormously important, and helpful, in my meetings with Empire." Geoff reached into his own briefcase and brought out his own files along with his computer. "Empire is willing to consider a sale of their upstate hydroelectric facility, but is hedging on selling us the entire company. I had very productive, and encouraging, meetings with their CEO and their Board. Think we need to pull back and wait. Let them make the next move."

"Agreed," Nick replied. "Speaking of closing deals, you did remember the closing dinner tomorrow night at the Yacht Club?"

"Oh, that's right. Did you remember the gifts for the team?"

"Yep. They were all delivered to their offices today. Monogrammed leather portfolio's for the guys, and for Mary, I got her a bottle of that Allure perfume that you requested. It wasn't very expensive, so I took the liberty of also getting her a gift certificate to Barney's. Hope that was OK."

"Perfect. What time should we be there?"

"Reservation is at 7 PM. Why don't you and Susie show up fifteen minutes early, at 6:45, so that we can work out the logistics of seating, and the order of the toasts."

Geoff laughed. "Let's let everyone sit where they want, and I am sure the toasts will be free flowing—just like the booze. Are all the drivers scheduled?"

"Of course! Who are you dealing with, here? I leave nothing to chance. And, yes, I think who sits where is important. As in, I will sit next to Susie. Let's put

Brody and his wife next to you. He worked especially hard on this Hudson Environmental deal, and it would be an honor for him."

Geoff held up both his hands as he acquiesced to his Chief Operating Officer.

"And now that we have all the important stuff out of the way, how did your weekend go?" Nick, as he was speaking, pulled from the middle of his Empire Energy file a file marked, "AC." He looked over at Geoff, and the mood in the room transitioned easily from business into friendship.

"AC, huh? Aspen, Colorado?"

"No, but that certainly could work. I was thinking Aspen CONFIDENTIAL." Nick tilted his head and raised his eyelids and said, " Talk to me."

Geoff seemed lost in his thoughts for a moment, but then swiveled his chair towards Nick, and the two of them engaged in a conversation that lasted for more than an hour. Geoff left out the most intimate details, but certainly shared his thoughts on the weekend, and the house that had been set up for their meeting. He also shared, unsparingly, his feelings for this special woman that he was now profoundly, and happily, entangled with - emotionally and physically. They spent a great deal of their time reviewing logistics and risk factors, and the conversation quickly turned to Geoff's shock in running into Bill Thomas on the walking trail along Aspen Creek.

"Meredith was awesome. She was cool, and played along perfectly as I concocted a story of meeting her that very day on the trail. She could be an improv actress. Really. But, Nick, I cannot let something like that have a chance of happening again, right?" He wasn't chastising in any way, just exclaiming the obvious. "Also, I now have to come up with a reason why I was in Aspen because, sure as hell, Bill and his wife, Emily, will mention to Susie that we ran into one another. Which leads me to my next question: 'WHAT AM I DOING?'"

"Got it, Boss," Nick replied impassively. "I'll put in place extensive precautions on the next trip—IF there is a next trip."

"You didn't answer my question. What in the hell am I doing getting involved with another woman?"

"I don't know, and I don't care. I am your friend, and I don't judge you. I presume you are following your heart. And, that makes me very happy. Look, I like Susie; she's fine. And, if she makes you happy and fulfilled, then that's great. But, I have seen you frustrated, and enormously unhappy, recently. To see you this happy and carefree makes me want to help you."

Geoff took it all in, and nodded, as he put his head back on his headrest and closed his eyes—this time not to sleep, but to think. Nick let him have his space.

. . .

Captain Mike Parrish came on the intercom and announced their initial decent in to San Francisco. Stephanie emerged from the rear cabin to ask if there was anything else the two executives wanted from the kitchen. Both greeted her warmly, but turned down any further service. She picked up the now-empty tray that had the assortment of seafood delights, and the empty glasses, and disappeared into the galley.

She checked on the aviators in the cockpit, then returning to her seat, brushed past Nick making sure her leg rubbed lightly against his arm. He would be staying at her place tonight.

As Geoff buckled his seatbelt for landing, he felt his phone vibrate. He had mail.

68

SUSIE

ROSANNE HAD BEEN GIVEN THE NIGHT OFF. THE KIDS WERE ALL farmed out: Lucy was at Natalie's, and Brook was at her best friend, Elaine's. Young Scott was at a sleepover with some of his friends. The school was having a "Science Adventure Day" at the local museum tomorrow, and Scott's class took the opportunity to turn it into a holiday of sorts. Susie was alone in her home for the first time since…when? She couldn't remember.

Her heart was racing. This was not just any reunion dinner for she and Geoff—there had been hundreds of those. Geoff was on the road constantly keeping up an unbelievably energetic schedule, and Susie had welcomed him home on almost all of them. But, tonight was going to be different.

Susie was unusually self-aware tonight, and not just because of her daring plans for the evening ahead. She felt surprisingly insecure. She wasn't sure exactly why, but she had to admit that she had been especially testy with Geoff lately about many insignificant things. He took it well, but still…Then there was Rhonda—that little nosy bitch at spin class who certainly had the hots for her husband. And, how about Geoff's laundry? Was she allowing her imagination to run away with itself? The make-up and the perfume…undeniable. But his explanation was completely believable.

Susie took a deep breath and closed her eyes for a moment to reassure herself. There was something important about tonight; her intuition acute. And, Susie was going to make sure this evening was going to be special. Yes, it would be memorable.

• • •

Susie's cell phone rang, and she dashed to pull it out of her purse, but she didn't get it in time. There was a message. It was Geoff.

"Hey, Honey. Just landed. Great meetings in New York. Nick flew back with me, and we had a great opportunity to catch up on things. Frank has me in the back of his BMW, and we are headed your way. Should be home by around 6:30. What's up for dinner? Can't wait to see you and the kids. Remember we have the Closing Dinner at the Yacht Club tomorrow. See you soon."

6:30? That should be fine. Susie thought to herself, "I'll put the meatloaf and potatoes, that Rosanne prepared, into the oven at 6:15, and have the salad tossed by the time Geoff arrives." Susie ran upstairs to shower and dress for the evening.

With the kids gone, she decided to take a bath—a luxury she rarely afforded herself. She slipped into the hot water, and let the temperture, the steam, the pressure and the vitamin-enriched bubbles envelop her. She exhaled slowly as she closed her eyes. She thought of Geoff, and her mind wandered back to their early marriage days. "My God, I am lucky," she pondered. That, she knew, but had somehow forgotten.

Susie rubbed her neck, and massaged her temples. Silence welcomed her, and the calming sounds of the bath water relaxed her. Susie slid a little lower into the tepid water and allowed her fingers to brush over her smooth skin. Moving her hands from her neck downward, she was surprised at the sensitivity of her breasts. She explored herself softly, and felt a welcome tightening between her legs. Her soft touch felt wonderful.

"What time is it?" she thought with a start. One thing she was petrified of was having Geoff walk in on her while she was in her bath and so exposed. "Shoot!" she said aloud looking at the Cartier clock she kept by the tub, "I need to get going!" And with those thoughts, Susie stood up, stepped out of her bubble bath, grabbed her thick, soft, monogrammed towel, and darted for her dressing room.

● ● ●

Once she had her make-up applied, and her hair dried and brushed, she went to her closet to decide what outfit she was going to put on for Geoff tonight. As she entered her spacious walk-in, she looked around and said loudly, "I have absolutely NOTHING to wear!" Frustrated, she dragged dress after dress, blouse after blouse and pant after pant across the hanger rods—pulling out something ever-so-often and holding it up to her body. She finally decided on a scooped-front, casual, black, silk dress that she had bought years ago; yet, had never worn.

She reached up and lifted the hanger free from the rod, and hung her chosen dress on a hook near her vanity where her little package from "the" store sat. Susie saw that the price tag was still on the dress, so she cut it off, and not once looking to see what she had paid for the dress, tossed the tag into the garbage bin—price side up. $2,199. On sale.

There was a commotion downstairs, and Susie could hear the unmistakable barking of their Labrador Retriever as he raced across their hardwood floor and bounded down the stairs to greet this newcomer. The excited whimpering left no doubt that the intruder was indeed his best friend. Geoff was home.

● ● ●

Susie came downstairs, very self-consciously, in her beautiful chosen dress. Geoff was at the bar making himself a tall gin and tonic. It had been a long day.

"Hi."

Geoff turned around, and stopped; gaping. Susie looked sensational. There was something different about her, too, but he couldn't quite make out what. She certainly had dressed up for the evening, and then Geoff panicked.

"Do we have dinner plans tonight?" he gasped.

"Nope. Nice to see you, too, big boy. Come here," Susie cooed.

Geoff put his drink down, and came immediately over to her. He placed his arms around her, and they kissed softly. "So, to what do I owe this special greeting?"

"Kiss me again, and I'll tell you," she whispered.

He kissed her again, but this time with his eyes open and questioning.

"So…?" he probed again.

"No reason. Just very happy to have my husband home after he has been out there slaying those dragons."

Geoff stood back, and appraised his wife. Beautiful. "Nice dress. Did you buy the outfit just for tonight?" Geoff could feel his phone buzzing in his pocket.

"Oh, you could say that," she teased.

"Well, you look sensational. And, I…feel like a grunge. I'm going to head upstairs to shower and freshen up."

OK. I'll put dinner in the over, and it will be ready in forty-five minutes. Does that work?" Susie asked.

"Yes, Honey, that works perfectly. I'm still on New York time, so I'm very hungry. And tired. Can't wait for dinner and to go to bed."

And, with that, Geoff grabbed his suitcase and headed up the stairs. About halfway up, Geoff stopped and turned back towards Susie, and said, "Where are the kids?"

Susie smiled and said matter-of-factly, "I sent them all away so that you and I can have a special night together. Go take your shower."

Geoff laughed and nodded. "Thanks, Hon," he said as he picked up his bag again, and returned to his ascension of their long twisting staircase.

● ● ●

Susie put the dinner in the oven and set the special round table in the study. She then waited until the water was running in the shower before she went upstairs to help him unpack his bag. Geoff's bag was open on a table in his closet, and she started to sort through his clothes separating his laundry from his dry cleaning. She pulled out lots of casual clothes, and found a few dressier shirts. But one in particular caught her attention. She hadn't seen it before, and as she held it up to look at it, she smelled a familiar and distinctive scent.

69

MEREDITH

MEREDITH SAT STILL IN HER CAR—THE ENGINE RUNNING AND THE heater on—as she sifted through her endless voice mails, texts and regular emails. She didn't bother to check the times and dates of her voice mail messages. There were just too many of them.

Beep…"It's me. Where are you? I need to talk to you. Call me." (Bobbie)

Beep…"Hey Babe. Call me ASAP." (Bobbie)

Beep…"Mer, the school's fucking with me. I need to talk to you." (Bobbie)

Beep…"CALL ME. Where the fuck ARE you?" (Bobbie)

Beep…"Fuck it (Slurred speech). I'm going hunting. The school's accusing me of some shit. Fuck them. Fuck everyone." (Bobbie)

Beep…"I'm outa here. Thanks for being there for me." (Bobbie)

Beep…"Meredith, call me as soon as you get this." (Jessica)

Beep…"Oops, forgot. You have a new number. Calling it now." (Jessica)

Beep…"Mrs. Edmonson? This is the Lieutenant Vendaland of the Granite County Sheriff's Department. Can you please give us a call back at 303-248-1200 ext 145?" (Unknown)

Beep…"Meredith, it's Jake Edwards, your principal at Grand Junction High. Can you call as soon as you get this? (Jake Edwards)

Beep…"I'm (unintelligible); fucking gonna kill someone. Going away. No fucks 'll find me. Gone. Bye." (Bobbie)

Beep…"Mrs. Edmonson? This is Lieutenant Vendaland calling again from the Granite Sheriff's office. Can you call us please at 303-248-1200 extension 145. (Unknown)

Beep…Long Silence followed by rustling in the background. (Butt dial?)

Beep…(Heavy breathing; drudging footsteps in brush)

Interspersed with the numerous calls were an astounding number of hang-ups. Meredith dialed Jessica, and got no answer. She put her car in gear, backed up, and then headed for the exit of Gateway Canyons Resort.

Three days earlier, she was excited and anxious—her senses absorbing everything around her. Today, she was making a very hasty exit, and scared to death. She was numb and felt nothing. She turned left and headed north on the breathtaking Highway 141. She didn't notice the rising thunderheads boiling up as an anvil above her head.

70

JESSICA

MEREDITH WORE AN EASY SMILE AND POSSESSED AN AURA OF HAPPI-ness and calmness that Jessica had never seen in her friend before. But she also had a strange look of consternation.

The first thing Meredith wanted to know was about Bobbie. "I received numerous messages on my voice mail from him that scared me. Do you know what's going on?"

"No. Not exactly," Jessica replied. "As I told you Saturday, he has been given a leave of absence from his coaching job while the school completes an investigation into what they are calling 'inappropriate behavior.' This was all in yesterday's newspapers. As you can imagine, it is the talk of the town. I saved some of the articles for you."

"Did they say what exactly he is accused of doing?" Meredith asked.

"No," she repeated herself, "not exactly. There is gossip and speculation around town—mostly having to do with potential drug use on the team, and Bobbie's erratic behavior. He got into a mid-field fight with one of the opposing coaches at Granite High's last game," Jessica said. Then she added, "There was a memo circulated by a group of District personnel to all the parents and faculty that they were investigating 'allegations of misconduct within the football program,' and that Bobbie was taking a paid leave of absence to help them with the investigation."

"Oh, dear God," Meredith exhaled. She was silent for a few seconds. Then, almost as though she were talking to herself, she said, "THAT'S why he went hunting. I didn't understand. He was so drunk."

"What?" Jessica asked.

"He left me several voice mail messages that I just picked up about an hour ago. Some, he appeared angry and hurt. The later the messages, the more obvious he had been drinking. He said he was leaving town and wouldn't be back for a while. Hunting. It's what he loves to do in the off-season. This is all starting to make some sense to me." Then switching her thoughts back to her local reality, she asked, "Who is going to coach the game on Saturday?"

Jessica replied, "Coach Bossick, apparently."

Meredith just shook her head and mumbled, "What a mess." Then she looked up and said, "Jess, what am I going to do?"

"Well, first of all, you're going to stay with Jazzy and me for the time being. I don't want to see you harassed by the local press, and all the snoopy gossipers around town. You'll be safe with me. Second, we're going to go over to your house together to get your things. You should plan on staying with me until this whole thing blows over—or until Bobbie shows up and you can get to the bottom of everything."

"Thanks, Jess. I always knew I could count on you. Hey, one other thing: the local Sheriff 's office is trying to get in touch with me. Any guesses why?"

"None," Jessica responded. "Except, there is talk of a restraining order being placed on Bobbie restricting his access to certain people and the school."

Meredith sighed trying her best to comprehend all this that had greeted her upon her re-entry into reality. "Let's just hope that this is all a big misunderstanding, and blows over quickly."

"I hope so, too, for yours and Bobbie's sake," Jessica said.

Meredith could only shake her head so as to clear sticky cobwebs. "Can you take me to the house so I can get my things?"

"Sure. But when were you going to share with me the details of your little weekend getaway?" Jessica smiled for the first time.

"Oh. Right. THAT weekend. There will be plenty of time tonight. You will not believe it. Let's just get my things and head back to your place. I could use a glass of wine or two."

* * *

The quick visit to Meredith's house was as shocking as it was depressing. It was dark and cold, and her house had, again, looked as though it had been ransacked—minus the vomit. Only Bobbie's drawers and closets, though, had been violated. The kitchen was strewn with empty booze bottles and beer cans, and the counter was an ant infestation that emerged from under the sink and had set up camp throughout a greasy pizza box. Jessica gagged when she saw the mess and smelled the stench. She didn't see the hypodermic needle in the trash bin.

While Meredith was in the bedroom, Jessica took a paper towel and started to clean up when she heard, "Leave it." Turning around she saw Meredith with a suitcase in hand; her expression resolute. "We're outa here. Bobbie's taken most of his stuff. Don't think, by the looks of things, that he plans to return any time soon. All his hunting and camping gear is gone, too. What in the hell have I gotten myself into here, Jess?"

Jessica took the suitcase from Meredith and headed for her car. Turning over her shoulder she added, "Grab whatever else you want to take, and leave the rest. We can come back later, if necessary."

Meredith sensed that she wouldn't be back any time soon. She had packed her essentials; all that she needed or wanted. It wasn't much. But, it would do.

She joined Jessica as they walked purposely, but silently, towards her car.

71

MEREDITH

EREDITH LET THE HOT WATER WASH OVER HER, AND EASE THE tension from her neck and shoulders. Jessica's shower had become an oasis of escape for her, and she cherished her friend, and her generosity, more than ever. As she scrubbed her body with her washcloth, she could literally feel her past being scrubbed away. She watched as her private history circled her feet, then ran down the drain.

When she emerged from her shower, wearing an oversized San Francisco 49er's t-shirt, Meredith was relieved to see Jessica and Jasmine were there to greet her with smiles on their faces. "Jazzy just wanted to say hi," Jessica said. And, Jasmine ran over to Meredith and gave her a big hug.

"Mom says that I can have dinner with you, but I have to go upstairs and do my homework afterward."

"I'll take whatever time I can get with you, Jazz," Meredith replied. "If I could ever have a little girl of my own, I would hope that she is exactly like you." Jasmine, with her head on Meredith's shoulder, broke into an undetected affectionate grin.

Jessica cut in, "Jazzy, can you set the table?" She reached over and handed Meredith a generous glass of Chardonnay as daughter and friend slowly pulled apart.

Meredith took the wine and went over to the couch as Jasmine headed for the dinner table. Meredith sat down deep into the folds of its elbow, and let the everyday sounds of dinner prep, and chatter between mother and daughter, lift her spirits. Was she *really* in Aspen this morning? It seemed like months ago.

• • •

When the dinner dishes were done, and Jasmine had disappeared upstairs, Jessica and Meredith settled into the comforts of the couch—which would be Meredith's bed for the foreseeable future. A new bottle of wine was open in an ice bucket on the table in front of them. Meredith leaned forward fetched the bottle, and poured them each another generous portion. They both sat back and looked at each other saying nothing right away. But then, Jessica launched right in, "So. Since when did you become a 49er's fan?"

72

GEOFF

THE DINNER TABLE WAS BEAUTIFULLY SET, AND HE WAS SURPRISED that they were seated in the den at the little round table by the fireplace.

"Meatloaf. You know this is my favorite," Geoff said as he cut off his first bite and slid it into his mouth savoring its moistness and flavor. "It's so nice to have a home-cooked meal after you have been on the road for so long. We haven't had this in such a long time, I can't remember. To what do I owe this special treat?"

Geoff took a sip of Pinot Noir, and looked at his wife. The warmth of the fire felt good, and the shadows of the flames danced across them both. The lights in the room had been dimmed. Susie looked unusually beautiful. He couldn't quite put his finger on it, but there was a sexiness to her tonight. Perhaps it was because she was wearing a plunging neckline that revealed a little lace and a generous cleavage. Or was it that she wore a new dress that he had never seen before? Geoff thought hard about where might an appropriate occasion be where Susie could wear such a revealing dress? Maybe it was her voice—the softer tone she took when she spoke?

"You have been working so hard, and I have been more than a little bitchy, lately. So, I decided to farm off the kids, give Rosie the night off and put together a memorable night for the two of us." Susie smiled coyly. "Wait 'til you see what I have up my sleeve for dessert."

Geoff's eyes grew wide, and he cocked his head animatedly. But, Susie could sense something. She wasn't at all sure what exactly she was picking up on. But, there was a very imperceptible distance to their reunion tonight. But, then again, maybe she was just imagining things.

• • •

They talked throughout dinner. Susie asked an unusually detailed array of questions regarding the deals Geoff was working on, and Geoff deflected most of her inquiries with detailed financial jargon or by simply stating that he was done for work for the night, and could they talk about anything else—like the gardener? He did mention that he had taken a side trip to Aspen on his way to New York, and that he had run into their friend, Bill Thomas, on the creek-side trail on his departure day.

As he was speaking, his phone buzzed silently in his pocket. Likely, the email was from someone from the office, but he couldn't help but smile.

"That much fun running into Bill, huh?" Susie intoned as she noticed Geoff's smile.

"Not so much fun. He's actually quite a boor, but the coincidence was amazing, you have to admit," Geoff replied. "He invited us to dinner with Emily, but I was thankfully flying out that afternoon."

"Us?"

Geoff hesitated for a split second. "Yes, he thought you were up with me, and thought it would be fun for the four of us to have a little rendezvous."

The rest of the dinner proceeded happily and lightly enough. When they were done, Susie got up and gathered their dinner plates. When Geoff started to get up, Susie stopped him. "No, this one is on me," she winked and smiled at her pun. "I'll just be a few minutes." She poured him a fresh glass of the light burgundy wine. "You just relax." And with that, she disappeared into their cavernous kitchen with the dishes.

• • •

Geoff reached into his pocket and pulled out his cell phone, and fingered over to his secret account. He almost choked.

> From: mquest99@aol.com
> Subject: I'm Coming
> Date: November 26, 2014 at 7:32 PM MST
> To: gquest100@hotmail.com
> Do you realize that your last email asked me if I wanted to come? Oh God. You just say when…
> M

Geoff blushed and let out an audible cough/laugh. His eyes bulged, too. They were connected again—at least he hoped they were. He responded immediately.

> From: gquest100@hotmail.com
> Subject: Come Again?
> Date November 26, 2014 at 7:27 PM PST
> To: mquest99@aol.com
> You MUST come again. Please. With me. I'm obsessing over your smile; no, actually, all of you.
> G

Geoff sat back in his chair and let his mind wander back to Aspen. He couldn't help but relive the warmth and ease of his all-too-brief time with Meredith. It seemed like a long-ago dream. But, he was holding her in his arms just this morning.

Taking his large wine glass, he pushed his chair back so that he was facing the fire away from the kitchen. He crossed his legs, and swirled the wine in his glass looking straight ahead into the flames—but saw nothing but the fireplace in Aspen and Meredith's warm smile, her inviting eyes and her intoxicating buttery brown body. He brought his wine goblet to his nose and inhaled the perfume of his wine and took a sip. He laid his head back and let his mind wander. Soon, he drifted off into a deep slumber—his cell phone, face-up, on the table next to him.

73

SUSIE

"**Y**OU LOOK RELAXED," SUSIE SAID FROM BEHIND HIM. GEOFF jumped—clearly startled. He hadn't heard her approach from behind him. "Maybe not," she continued as she started massaging his shoulders and neck. She worked her fingers and thumbs into his tense flesh. The house was quiet except for the background music and the crackling of the fire. Geoff tried to look, without turning his head or being obvious, for his phone sitting on the table beside them.

Susie continued with her massage for a couple of minutes, but tired easily. She leaned down, and softly kissed his neck and whispered in his ear, "Give me five minutes, will you? Then let's *us* rendezvous in our…"

Susie's mouth was pressed against Geoff's ear breathily speaking when Geoff's phone lit up, and buzzed with the unmistakable sound of an incoming message. Geoff reached for his phone, quickly grabbed it with deliberate ease, flipped it over face-down and put it in his lap. He fumbled for the button that would close his private email and send it back into the secret corner of his phone where he would access it later.

"I'm so sorry, Honey. Everyone wants a piece of me tonight, it seems," Geoff said in as believing a tone as he could muster.

Susie replied, "Go ahead, see who is trying to get ahold of you."

"No…it, or he, or she, or they, can wait until tomorrow. I'm not even going to look to see who called."

"OK. But, I need a few minutes upstairs by myself. So, if you need to check on a few emails, go ahead. It doesn't matter to me who in the world wants to get a hold of you tonight, because tonight…you are mine." And, with that, Susie retreated away from the fireside table, and headed upstairs.

. . .

When Geoff thought he heard his bedroom door close upstairs, he turned his phone over and activated his screen. He thumbed over to his private email and entered his password.

74

MEREDITH

MEREDITH COULDN'T HELP HERSELF. SHE HAD SPENT THE LAST two hours with Jessica sharing almost everything about her exotic time in Aspen. Jasmine was up in her room with the door closed and the music blaring. Jess had just sat there, and with a look of amazement, took it all in—asking few questions and letting Meredith reveal this fantasy in her own way and in her own time.

When the second wine bottle was empty, they decided it was time to get some shut-eye. It had been a very long day. Jessica headed up to her room—stopping to tell Jasmine to turn down her music.

Meredith was stretched out on the living room couch. She picked up her iPhone, and couldn't wait to connect with the man with whom she had shared so much over the past three days. Bobbie, for the time being, was a muddled memory.

With a mischievous smile, Meredith wrote,

> From: mquest99@aol.com
> Subject: Coming Tonight
> Date: November 14, 2014 at 10:46 PM MST
> To: gquest100@hotmail.com
> I am obsessing: thinking about coming tonight. Is that OK? I may have some more time to come together with you in the coming weeks.
> M

Geoff's heart raced as he smiled. His mind wandered again back to Aspen. He knew he didn't have much time before he was expected back upstairs in his bedroom, but he couldn't just let that message sit unanswered.

> From: gquest100@hotmail.com
> Subject: OK
> Date: November 14, 2014 at 9:51 PM PST
> To: mquest99@aol.com
> Anything you want to do is OK with me. Already strategizing on our next adventure where we can come together. Is THAT ok? Maybe mid-week next. Can you get off from work?
> G

Within seconds, Geoff's phone buzzed.

> From: mquest@aol.com
> Subject: Getting Off
> Date: November 14, 2014 at 10:53 PM MST
> To: gquest100@hotmail.com
> I will make it happen. Will ask for leave from work. Aspen? The "bare" rug needs more attention.
> M

Meredith lay back on her pillow, and pulled Geoff's 49er's jersey up to her nose and inhaled deeply. With her eyes closed, she pulled the first memory from her mind: surprisingly, it was their soaring adventure with her sitting between Geoff's legs—his strong chest against her back, and his strong, reassuring arms wrapped around her waist—as they explored the clouds around them and the mountain hamlets below them. That was just yesterday!

And today, she was cleaning out her important belongings from what could be best described as a shack that served as her and Bobbie's home. Meredith shook those thoughts clear from her head as best she could, and concentrated on her most improbable weekend in Aspen.

There was no immediate reply on her email. Meredith put her phone on the coffee table, and pulled the soft comforter up to her chin. She pulled something else up to her chin, too. The 49er's jersey. After all, she had promised Geoff that she would be coming tonight.

75

SUSIE

GEOFF WAS DEEP IN THOUGHT, CONSTRUCTING A TEXT OR EMAIL ON his phone. Susie quietly watched him from the den door. He had no idea she was there in her bathrobe—and little else.

"Poor guy," she thought. "He never is able to walk away from his work. Always at it. 24-7."

She cleared her throat, and even that didn't catch his attention. Then she said, "Oh, Geoffrey Cameron?"

Geoff quickly turned his phone over after fumbling with it. That struck Susie as particularly odd—as though she had caught him doing something he shouldn't be doing.

"Secret admirer?" she teased.

Geoff laughed. "Busted!" He continued, "I promised you I would be right upstairs, and instead, I couldn't keep my damn cell phone off. I feel really bad. Sorry, Honey."

He stood, and came over to Susie where she was holding out her hand. When he got closer, he could see that her robe was generously open at the front, and that underneath she had on a beautiful silk camisole. His eyes explored for more details, but she pulled him into an embrace before he could discover anything further. Their kiss felt oddly stilted and strange to both of them. It had been months. But, Susie was determined.

She took his hand and led him up the broad staircase to their bedroom suite. The lights were dimmed, and their master window framed a view of San Francisco Bay reflecting the bejeweled city skyline. Their bed was turned down, and their pillows were perfectly plumped.

Geoff kissed her softly on the cheek, and dropped her hand.

He didn't bother to check for any more emails, but turned off his phone leaving it on the bedside table. He couldn't help but think of the irony of this… seduction? This hadn't happened in how many years? And, for this to be occurring right after his secret weekend? Coincidence? It felt awkward, if he were being completely honest with himself. But at least she was trying. Unfortunately, he was unmoved.

Geoff slipped into bed, and snuggled up behind Susie who lay on her side. In past encounters, Geoff would have tried to arouse Susie for some long-overdue lovemaking. But, that usually led to an unhappy exchange and a rebuke that he was sure would be her epitaph: "Don't touch me. I'm too tired. Let's do it tomorrow."

Tonight it was his turn. He was simply too tired, and unmoved, to be touched.

76

NICK

IT WAS NOW THURSDAY MORNING, AND GEOFF'S PHONE WAS IN HIS back pocket and was ringing without him even realizing it. Nick was desperately trying to get ahold of his boss to go over the remaining details of this evening's Closing Dinner at the Yacht Club. He had wanted to make sure his seating assignments were appropriate, and he wanted to know when to expect Geoff and Susie at the celebration tonight. But, as was usually the case, Nick had to go it alone relying on his experience and instinct. He was rarely wrong.

Geoff was busy hitting ground balls to his son's teammates before their game this afternoon. He was full of encouraging and enthusiastic banter—even when one of the boys made an error. The kids loved him, and they played better when Geoff was there leading them. The parents loved seeing him there, too. The game was soon to start, and would be over by 5 PM. He and CJ would race home as soon as the last pitch was thrown, and with any luck, he would be showered and dressed, and ready to leave their home with Susie at 6:15 PM with their driver, Frank, at the wheel.

As luck would conveniently be on their side for once, the game moved quickly. CJ's team won in a low-scoring game, 3-1, and Geoff and CJ left arm-in-arm for their car laughing and reliving the various plays that led to their victory.

• • •

Nick sent Geoff an email outlining all the final decisions that he had made: the food, the wine, the seating arrangements. There would be two tables of ten. Nick sent the seating chart along with pictures of the spouses so that Geoff could welcome, and thank, them personally. At Geoff and Susie's table would be the "traveling team" that went to Grand Junction to finalize the due diligence and close the Hudson Environmental deal. Brody, who handled Operations, and his wife, Darlene; Glenn, who oversaw Human Resources and his wife, Jane; Charles, who handled Information Technology, and an unnamed date; and Mary, their Finance Manager, and her live-in boyfriend, David. At Nick's table would be four other key employees and their spouses/dates who managed the acquisition from the home office in San Francisco. Stephanie played an important role, too, but it surprised no one that she would be sitting to Nick's right co-hosting their table.

Susie was not at the game today. She was home primping for the big company dinner tonight. She had bought a new outfit for the event, but needed to stop by the dry bar to get her hair washed and styled. That left little time for her manicure and pedicure. She was rushing.

What had actually happened last night? It all seemed to be going so well. Everything was perfect, and she actually had gotten the nerve to put on those trashy little undies and the slippery top. Did she pass out? Probably. "It must have been the wine. I drank too much trying to get the courage to be a seductress," she reasoned. After all, Geoff was the aggressor ninety-nine percent of the time. Anyway, she would be a good wife tonight and put out. That she promised Geoff this morning when they woke up.

●　●　●

Nick was there to greet Geoff and Susie when they pulled up to the Yacht Club at 7:30 PM. He had hard copies of the seating chart, the attendees and their guests (with photos), and a list of names and roles he wanted to make sure Geoff mentioned in his toast. Geoff took the papers, already folded for his breast pocket, and nodded a warm communication of understanding and appreciation to the man he couldn't live without. They all walked in together.

The room erupted into a wild crescendo when they entered, but they weren't cheering for Geoff per se. They were acknowledging themselves, as a team, for completing another strategic deal for CBC. They had worked together successfully on many deals, and having Geoff walk in just completed the team. That's how Geoff built his company.

The liquor had been flowing freely for over an hour, and many of the attendees had arrived early to "pre-game" as the Millennials like to call it. Geoff loved the youth and vigor of the professionals he surrounded himself with. He and Nick were clearly the senior statesmen.

Nick whispered to Geoff, "Your gin and tonic is waiting for you at the bar, and Susie's Fume Blanc is there, too. Why don't you grab your drinks and circulate for a few minutes to socialize before we seat everyone. Dinner needs to be served in about thirty minutes—max."

"Will do, Sir Nicolas. Thanks as always. Susie and I will divide and conquer as we usually do." And with that, Geoff offered Susie his arm and they headed to the bar—stopping frequently for a high-five or an introduction. Once at the bar, they retrieved their drinks.

"Let's go say hi to the A Team, shall we?" Geoff said to Susie. And with that, they flowed easily into the small crowd.

• • •

There was a tingling of a wine glass, and everyone quieted after a few additional whistles. Nick was holding court, and he said, "Welcome, again, and congratulations to our indispensable team in the Hudson deal!" A robust cheer erupted. "Please find your place at your table. Tonight, we have assigned seating, but we didn't split you from your significant other. There is a bottle of Cabernet and a bottle of Chardonnay on each table, so please pour yourselves a glass. The company has assigned each of you a driver for the night, and a paid day off tomorrow, so please have a great time! Dinner will be served shortly."

Everyone started moving to their places; the conversation resumed its excitement. When they were all seated, Susie saw a young woman across the table from her that was clearly a part of the CBC team, but she hadn't met her before. She leaned over and asked Geoff, "Who's the cute brunette across the table?"

77

SUSIE

GEOFF LOOKED UP ACROSS THE TABLE, AND WITHOUT TURNING directly to his wife, but tilting his head her way, said quietly, "Oh, that's Mary Sullivan. She is relatively new. Joined us six months ago, and is a whiz at accounting. She handled the forensic audits for this deal."

"Not bad looking either," Susie let slip without intending to.

Geoff seemed a bit surprised and sat back in his chair, but added, "Yes, she is quite attractive, but her mind and reasoning are far more beautiful."

A few minutes of small talk ensued, but soon Susie got up and went directly over to the new employee and sat in the empty adjacent seat. "Hi Mary. I'm Susie Cameron, Geoff's wife. I understand 'Welcome' is in order." Susie extended her hand and smiled broadly and warmly.

Mary was dressed in a nice casual blouse that was unbuttoned one button too low, in Susie's opinion. She had on an expensive pair of fitted slacks that crowned her new and expensive pumps. Mary seemed surprised, but responded in kind, and in fact, leaned over and gave Susie a hug. She was one of the earlier evening arrivals and was clearly feeling relaxed. "It is so nice to meet you, too. It has been an absolute pleasure working with Geoff. I just love him," she gushed.

Susie immediately smelled a familiar aroma. It took her a few seconds to identify its source. "I am so glad, Mary. I know my husband works hard to make this a very inclusive and exciting place to work for everyone." Mary was wide-eyed, and nodding quickly. "He says you are very smart and did a great job on this latest transaction."

Mary loved the compliment, and was absorbing the moment when Susie spoke again, "Say, I just LOVE your perfume. May I ask what it is?"

Mary blushed, and said, "Sure. It's called, 'Allure.'"

"And where did you buy it? I've never heard of it before," Susie probed.

"I don't know." Mary hesitated, then glanced over Susie's shoulder quickly then back. One would have had to be very perceptive to notice the break in eye contact, but Susie picked up on the subtlety.

"Actually, I didn't buy it," she said turning bright red. "Geoff bought it for me."

• • •

Susie, this time, had no problems squirming into her thong and camisole. Geoff was in his bathroom brushing his teeth and washing his face as he loved to do every night. He said it made him feel fresh, and it made his pillowcase feel especially luxurious. Maybe he was a little OCD like other successful CEO's. On another night, this would have made Susie smile. But not tonight. She was on a mission to seduce her husband. She was not going to pass out like last night, and in fact, had consumed only Perrier after her first glass of wine.

Geoff came to bed wearing only his briefs and a t-shirt. He really was in great shape, she had to admit, and it certainly crossed her mind, especially tonight, that other women found him sexy, too. And while she always felt that sex was her wifely duty, she was actually looking forward to being the aggressor tonight.

Geoff turned off the lights in the room and crawled into bed. He fluffed his pillow, and settled his head and closed his eyes. He hadn't noticed that Susie was lying on her side facing him with her head propped by her elbow. She rolled over, and put a leg over his waist, and said, "Not so fast my sleeping giant."

Geoff seemed genuinely shocked. He rolled himself over facing her and said, "Hon, I am so appreciative of the advance here, but I am absolutely exhausted. And, the kids are home tonight, and they might hear us."

"Since when did that EVER make a difference to you?" she retorted—a little louder than she had planned.

"Yeah, you're right," he said sleepily. "Sorry, Baby, I'm just too tired tonight." And, with that, he rolled over and was asleep within seconds.

He dreamed that night that he was on a picnic on a remote crystal white beach with an azure sea. And while the scenery was vivid, he couldn't immediately place who he was with. But he did awake knowing that he hadn't been with Susie.

78

BOBBIE

IT WAS BITTER COLD OUTSIDE THE SMALL TENT, AND THE WIND whipped furiously through the trees. Small ice shards of corn snow pelted the nylon cocoon in unceasing waves. The temperature had to be near zero. It had been another very quiet day—just as Bobbie had expected. He cherished his "alone" time deep in the mountains, and today of all days, he felt a particular satisfaction at his ability to literally disappear. He would ride out this storm, feasting on nuts, beef jerky and water—and the odd narcotic—and plan his next hunt.

Food and water were abundant all around him, and he could survive out here as long as he chose. Maybe not all winter, but his survivalist instincts were keen. He had both his bow and his rifle, and knew in his heart that no creature could harm him—possibly an avalanche, or an act of God, but hell, he could get struck by lightning on a football field just as easily.

That thought pushed his mind back to feeding Don Don the Moron his own genitals. He chuckled out loud at the memory. "Oh, there will be more laughs ahead, for sure," he surmised. He reached for his wallet and drew out a small piece of paper. On it, he had written five names. One of the names had a line through it: Don DeLatore. The other names were Charlie Fredericks, the school principal, Hugh Preston, the school district lawyer, and Janet Jacobs, the district's human resources manager. He had an asterisk behind her name. The last name on the list was in pencil.

• • •

A few nights earlier, the Wrecking Crew, as Bobbie and his friends liked to call themselves, consumed mass quantities of bourbon, beer, pizza and pot. They were loud, rowdy and out of control. Jay's secluded house on the outskirts of Grand Junction was the perfect place for a party. At around 1:30 AM, as they all sat around a table playing poker, Mal slurred in the direction of Bobbie, "Hey, shit-face, did you know your wife is fucking another guy?"

Bobbie howled with laughter. "Yeah, right, dick-brain!" he retorted. "She can't even handle me let alone another guy." Bobbie threw three cards in the middle, and asked for fresh cards. Most of the money gambled that night, sat in front of him, and he was on a hot streak.

"No, seriously," Mal continued, "I have proof."

"Fuck you, Mal," Bobbie laughed, "and your girlfriend is sucking my cock!" He threw down his cards and exclaimed, "Two pairs; Aces and fours." The rest of the guys groaned, and with that weak hand, Bobbie had won another round.

"No seriously," Mal said as he shuffled the deck. "I think I have video evidence."

Jay jumped in, "Fuckin' A, boys! Mal has nude videos of Meredith fucking another guy? Didn't think you security guys at the Grand Hotel were allowed to set up cameras in the rooms!"

"Not in the rooms, cock-sucker," Mal replied. "But, we do have security cameras in the elevators. What I've got is a bit grainy, but if the chick isn't Bobbie's loving, devoted, wife, she sure is a dead-ringer for her." And with that, Mal threw the cards on the table. "I need to take a pee break."

When he returned a few minutes later, he had his laptop.

79

MEREDITH

IT WAS NOW FRIDAY NEARING 10 AM. MEREDITH WAITED PATIENTLY in the lobby of the Granite County Sheriff's station. She was incredibly nervous. Lieutenant Vendaland had been vague about the meeting, but had said it was important that they meet. That was yesterday, and here she was, sitting in a pair of jeans, and a pull-over turtleneck sweater—probably not a good idea as the temperature in the station had been increased to ward of the bitter cold of the snow storm outside.

She was thumbing through a Field & Stream magazine, not paying attention to the text or the pictures, when the door to the waiting room opened, and a middle-aged man in uniform with a ruddy complexion walked over to her and said, "Mrs. Edmonson?"

Meredith nodded.

"I'm detective Guy Vendaland." He extended his hand. As they shook, he said, "Thank you for coming in on such short notice. We've been trying to get ahold of you for the past week to ask you some questions." She nodded.

He led her down the hall and into a small room that held a large desk covered in piles of paper files. There were three chairs, two facing his across the desk. In the room along the side-wall was a credenza with framed citations, pictures and diplomas above it. On the other wall by the lone window was a water cooler. "Can I get you some water? A coffee?" he asked.

"Coffee would be great," she answered looking around the room without making eye contact.

Lieutenant Vendaland picked up his old-fashioned desk phone and punched a number. "Hey, can you bring in two cups of coffee? My usual. And…?" he hesitated and looked up at Meredith.

"Oh, sorry," she said. "Black is fine."

"The other, black." He said before he hung up.

Sitting back in his chair, the Lieutenant asked, "Mrs. Edmonson, do you know why you are here?"

"I don't have a clue," she said quietly shaking her head. "And, you can call me Meredith, if you like."

"OK, fine, it's Meredith then. Let me first congratulate you on your team's big win last week at Silverton." The lieutenant smiled. "Very impressive, indeed. The offense was on fire, but a shut-out? The defense has never looked better."

"Thanks," was all Meredith could think to say.

He went on, "I think we won a total of five games in all four years I played for the team. What a change your husband has brought to the program."

"Thanks."

"He's quite a coach. What's his secret, Meredith?"

"Please excuse me Lieutenant, but did you ask me to come in here today to talk football?"

"No. No. Sorry. I didn't mean to get side-tracked. But, I did want to talk about Coach Edmonson—your husband. He is your husband, correct?"

"Very much so," she replied. "What would you like to know?"

"A lot of things, actually. Let's start with the altercation he had after last weekend's game with the opposing coach. What, in your opinion, was that all about?"

"I don't know. You'll have to ask him."

"We'd love to, but we can't locate him. That's why we wanted to talk to you. Are you able to contact him, and let him know we need to see him?"

"Well, yes and no," she replied. "I can leave him a message on his phone, but he is not here, and is likely not getting his voice mail."

"Look Mrs. Edmon…Meredith. Your husband has been accused of assault. We are handling the initial investigation. He is a very popular guy around here as you must know, and we want to make sure we hear his side of the story. The folks in Silverton are furious, and the school district there has hired an attorney. We are only looking into whether we think a crime has been committed or not. It was a big enough deal that the local police were called after the game. But, by the time they arrived, your husband was gone. They called us hoping we could apprehend him here for questioning. But, he seems to have disappeared. Do you know where he is?"

"He went hunting."

"What? Hunting? Now? It's a blizzard out there, and well, I frankly find that hard to believe."

"All I can tell you is that my husband is an expert hunter. He enjoys, and actually thrives, in the solidarity of the backcountry in the harshest of conditions. It is not at all unusual for him to set out, by himself, for a week or two in the wilderness. He always comes back. We eat what he kills, by the way; our freezer is always full of fresh meat."

"Where is he hunting?"

"I have no idea."

"Didn't he tell you?"

"He never tells me where he goes, and frankly, I don't really care. He could be local, or he could be in Wyoming for all I know. But, what I do know, is that he always comes home."

"So, you'll let us know when he comes home?"

"Yes. Of course. Better than that, I will have him call you himself."

"That would be appreciated, Mrs.—sorry…Meredith. So, Meredith, before you leave, can I ask you…? Do you mind if we station a car down the street from your house. You know, to keep an eye out for Mr. Edmonson's return?"

"Sure. But, I won't be there."

"No?"

"No. I'm staying with a friend here locally."

"Does your husband know where you are staying?"

"No, but he will be able to figure it out easily enough."

"And, why, may I ask, are you not staying at your own home?"

"To be honest," Meredith continued, "he and I had a bit of an argument before he left, and I am catching a break at my friend's place."

"Has your husband ever lost his temper with you or threatened you in any way?"

"I don't think he is any better or any worse than anyone else," she said matter-of-factly.

Lieutenant Vendaland continued, "Does he drink?"

"Of course. Doesn't everyone?"

"Drugs?"

"What?" Meredith replied hesitantly. "Not that I'm aware of."

"I'm not talking here about pot or recreational drugs. I'm curious about performance enhancing drugs—Human Growth Hormone; Testosterone—stuff that might alter his behavior?"

Meredith seemed surprised as the Lieutenant flipped through his yellow note tablet without looking up. "No. Nothing that I have ever noticed. Why? What does that have to do with anything?"

He raised his head, "Just curious is all. Just trying to figure out the unexpected outbursts. By the way, do you need any type of restraining order?"

"What?"

"There have been several restraining orders filed, and secured, against your husband. The judge deemed your husband a risk in all the filed cases."

"How many were filed? And, by who?" she inquired.

"Don't know exactly, but it involves his school—including his team, the parents, the faculty and staff, and senior administration and contractors of the district. Well, less one. As you know, the district Superintendent died in a tragic house fire Saturday morning."

"What? Superintendent DeLatore? *Died?*"

"Yes. You seem surprised. It's been the number one news story around here. How could you not know? It's another reason we want to talk to your husband. While the fire appears accidental, Mr. Edmonson has been listed as a 'person of interest.'"

Meredith was silent, and dropped her head. After a moment she said, "I don't know. I hadn't heard. I wasn't here, Lieutenant."

"You weren't here? Where were you last Saturday?"

80

GEOFF

IT WAS TUESDAY, DECEMBER 2ND, AND GEOFF WAS ON HIS WAY TO work. He had a full day of meetings ahead, and Nick had asked for some time as well. The only way to make that happen, given the back-to-back schedule, was to meet him in the office for a coffee at 6:30 AM. It was still dark as Geoff navigated the refreshingly light freeway towards the Golden Gate Bridge and his office in San Francisco.

When Geoff arrived at his corner office, Nick was already sitting at the small conference table. "Good morning, boss," Nick said.

"Well, aren't we the early riser!" Geoff joked.

While Geoff shed his overcoat and fiddled with some things at his desk—including numerous notes from his secretary, Cindy, Nick poured Geoff a mug of steaming coffee. Soon, they were seated together next to the large picture window, and Nick had Geoff's undivided attention. The sun was just rising above the City and painting the morning sky in soft hues of pink and blue.

Geoff started in. "Everything all set for Thursday?"

"Yes. Completely. I was there yesterday, and met with the caterers for your Saturday night dinner." Geoff sat back, crossed his legs and sipped his coffee—never losing eye contact with Nick. "I also arranged for the consultant you requested for Thursday afternoon. Her resume is stunning—as is her reputation."

"Good," Geoff said. "And transportation? It could get a little complicated."

Nick purposely smirked at his friend and CEO. "Nothing is that complicated. I was able to get Booker again, and both Mike and John have been given their instructions—particularly, to not engage with their passenger."

"Great. And the credit facility? Have all the arrangements been made with the consultant vis-à-vis a private credit card?"

"Yes. All taken care of. The card has already been delivered, and we can track all activity real-time. Any concerns and we can turn it off with the click of a mouse."

"Mighty Mouse?"

"You could say that." They both laughed.

Geoff continued, "Not to change the subject, but are our meetings all confirmed for Thursday with the co-CEO's of Wonderland Energy?"

Nick replied, "Yes, all set. They want us to meet with their entire executive team, and have each member present an overview of their line of business, and/or their responsibility in their company. The meeting should run all afternoon, and there is a dinner they are hosting directly afterwards. All the due-diligence material has been sent to your email in an encrypted file code named, "Project Wonder Bread" to assure secrecy."

"Sounds like every detail has been looked after, Nick. I can't thank you enough," Geoff expressed. "I better take a bite of that Wonder Bread, and start to digest it before my day really begins." Geoff stood and headed back to his desk.

"Geoff." Nick lightly grabbed his arm. "There's one more thing we need to discuss."

"Oh. OK. Shoot." Geoff sat back down, and took another sip of his coffee.

"Susie called me."

Geoff's eyes lifted noticeably. Nick had Geoff's full attention. "When?"

"Yesterday afternoon. Late. Around 5."

"And why, pray tell, did she call you?"

"Well, originally, she called to thank me for setting up all the arrangements for the Closing Dinner last week. But, the conversation shifted quickly to other things. She was pleasant enough, but wanted to know about our new employee, Mary. And, wanted to know a little bit about you, my friend."

"What do you mean, 'wanted to know about our new employee, Mary'?"

"I'm not sure, Geoff, but she asked a lot of things about her like…when she was hired, where she came from, how old she was, how long had she been married, what her husband does for a living. You get the drift."

Geoff nodded. "I wouldn't worry about it, Nick. Mary was wearing a low-cut top, and was a little drunk and flirty. She was obviously having a good time. Susie's probably getting the low-down on the new employee who was sitting at our table."

"No, Geoff. I think she is on to something. She asked about you, personally. Asked if I had sensed, or seen, any changes in you. Everything at peace at home?"

"Yep. As a matter of fact, Susie was the nicest she has been to me in recent history."

"Well, don't get overconfident and sloppy. Her radar is up on something. I know how excited you are for this weekend. The house is very secure, private and secluded, and I have arranged for a different phone for your friend's use. Just be extra careful, OK? Forewarned is forearmed, right?"

"Thanks, Nick. As always, you are on top of everything. I will be especially careful. I won't lie to you either. I feel really guilty about what I am doing. Maybe that is showing. Women have a sixth sense when it comes to stuff like that. But, I just have to see her again." He paused. "Maybe things will be different. Maybe this will be it. But I have to see. I can't keep her out of my mind."

They both stood. Nick put his arm around Geoff's shoulder, and pulled him into a tight bear hug. Whispering into his friend's ear, Nick said, "I think YOU are out of your mind."

Nick broke his hold as they approached Geoff's closed door. They both laughed as Geoff was opening it. What greeted them was a beehive of activity—even at 7:30 in the morning. The energy was infectious. Nick walked straight out of Geoff's office into the energy that was Cameron, Boone & Covington, but was immediately stopped by Geoff's loud voice. He stopped and turned in time to see a broad smile and a finger being pointed at him. And, then this: "I think you are right, Mr. George."

81

MEREDITH

THE PRIVATE EMAIL HAD BEEN PROVOCATIVELY MYSTERIOUS, BUT clear. She had read it over and over again. Each time, Meredith got more excited, but maybe just as importantly, she was grasping emotionally at her desperate escape from the small-town gossip and news that choked every headline, every email and every conversation: the League Champion Granite High Grizzlies; her husband's leave of absence and the investigation into wrong-doing at the high school; and the tragic death of Superintendent Don DeLatore.

She had asked, and had been compassionately granted, some vacation time from her school duties, and had notified the families of her dance studio, that she would be taking some time off. Everyone understood, because everyone just KNEW. Meredith had become a bit of a celebrity herself—for all the wrong reasons. Her now-deserted house was under surveillance not just by the County Sheriff, but by the press as well. It was a miracle that the press hadn't yet discovered her new temporary residence at Jessica Stevens' place. Meredith was grateful for her friend beyond words.

Meredith had not heard a word from Bobbie. This both surprised her and it didn't. From his voice-mail rants, she knew he was off somewhere, and felt ninety-nine percent sure he was hunting. He always went hunting after the football season in the dead of winter; he called it "ice fishing." And, the fact that his season had come to an abrupt end, and he seemed to be in a bit of trouble, made her believe, even more securely, he was up in the high country thinking things over—if not hiding. And, all his hunting gear was missing.

• • •

Meredith stood in the cold garage of a small office building on the northeast side of town. It was 7:35 AM, Thursday morning, December 4, and according to Geoff's note, someone would pick her up there.

Jessica had been working late on Tuesday, when a FedEx envelope was delivered to her office. The delivery required the recipient to present positive ID as well as a signature. When she opened the envelope, Jessica found another sealed envelope inside. On the front was typed, "Meredith—To be opened by addressee only. Thank you, Jessica." She smiled. Meredith deserved this. Her friend had been through so much. As she looked again at the envelope, she reread what could very well be taken as a salutation: "Thank you, Jessica." Very smart.

That evening when Jessica came home, she found Meredith at the kitchen table checking her email. She was smiling. "Hey girlfriend," Jess said as she came in the door with grocery bags dangling from her arms. Meredith jumped up to help her. They hugged. "Nice to see you with a smile for once!"

"Well? Do you have something for me?" Meredith asked.

"Maybe. What are you looking for?" Jessica gave a look to her friend that told her everything she needed to know. She went over to the fridge and grabbed a bottle of Chardonnay and fetched two glasses. "If you are a very good girl, and open the wine and pour us a glass, I will search through my things to see if I have something for you."

"Ok. Ok. Give that to me." And, with that, Meredith snatched the bottle from her friend's grasp, and opening a drawer, she pulled out the corkscrew. Within seconds, the wine was poured, and Meredith stood at the counter, staring at Jessica, with her hands playfully on her hips. "Well?"

Just then, Jasmine came bounding down the stairs. "Hi Mom! Hi Auntie Meredith! I'm starving. What's for dinner?" She gave each a quick hug and went straight to the refrigerator door, pulled it open and started exploring.

Jessica said, "Say, Jazzy, can you help me make the salad? Meredith has a little more business to finish before dinner, and I said she could use my room."

Jazzy pulled out a piece of cheese and popped it into her mouth. Then replied still chewing, "Sure, Mom."

Jessica said to Meredith, "So Mer, can you come with me to the garage? I've got that package for you."

• • •

Meredith sat at Jessica's desk, the unopened envelope at her fingertips. She sat back in the chair, closed her eyes and took a deep breath. She then took a sip of her wine, and it felt good sliding down her throat. She wanted to first review the exchange of emails that she and Geoff had sent each other over the past few days. Her favorite was the last one she received.

> From: gquest100@hotmail.com
> Subject: Busting
> Date: December 1, 2014 at 9:55 PM PST
> To: mquest99@aol.com
> Details firming. So am I. Can hardly believe we will be together again—and so soon! It has felt like a year. Glad we are following the "no pictures" rule—but, not for security reasons. If I had your picture, I wouldn't be able to get any work done. God, I've missed you, M—and it's only been days. I miss your smile. I miss your warmth. I miss your touch. I miss your soul. I miss my 49ers jersey. With you in it. Or you without it. Instructions and details forthcoming. Hint: warm weather!
> G

That was the last she had heard from Geoff. Until now. In rereading this last email, she started to panic once again. Warm weather? Shit! What was she going to bring? And, the clothes she had brought to Jessica's were for only winter and work. She'd have to go back to her house to pick up what else she needed. Maybe she could send Jessica. Would that be too much to ask?

She had sent Geoff a reply.

> From: mquest99@aol.com
> Subject: Don't Know What To Come In
> Date: December 1, 2014 at 11:15 PM MST
> To: gquest100@hotmail.com
> Now you have really thrown me. I can't think of anything else but you! Just thinking of you has been my refuge. And oh yes, WHAT TO WEAR?!!
> I know…I know…Not much! But you forget I live in the mountains. Don't want to bring another shipping container like last time. Hope you don't mind my wearing my pasty white skin. There will be a lot of it. I promise.
> M

The envelope was plain white and had no return address. And, she could tell that it had only a sheet or two of paper in it. It was thrilling to hold this little mystery in her hand unopened, and she took another sip of wine and hesitated. But, slowly she turned it over, and slid her finger inside the flap imagining the pleasure she would get in unlocking this next adventure. It opened easily, and she pulled out a single piece of paper. It read...

> M,
> Let's rendezvous Thursday morning, December 4, at 7:45 AM in the subterranean parking lot of the Stanton Building on Commerce Street. Park in the "Visitor" parking area. Your car will be safe, hidden and untouched—by snow or anything else (the building management has been notified that your car will be there through the weekend).
> You will be gone three nights, and will be returned to your car late Sunday afternoon. Hope that is OK.
> Don't stress too much about clothes; you will have the opportunity to do some shopping where we are going.
> Sorry, I can't tell you our destination, but as we have discussed, this is for your safety.
> Trust me.
> See you VERY soon. —G

● ● ●

At 7:45 AM, on the dot, a dark Mercedes S Class, with blacked-out windows, rounded the corner in the underground garage, and pulled up behind Meredith's Ford Explorer. The engine stopped, and the driver's door opened, and a 60-ish man got out. He was wearing a now-familiar uniform of khaki pants and a pressed blue shirt with the distinctive CBC logo on it. He said, "Are you Meredith?"

"Yes, I am. Who are you?"

He replied, "I have been told not to reveal my identity until after you read this..." And, with that, he handed Meredith a sealed legal envelope. She took it, and at once felt the weight and shape of a portable phone. And while she expected this package, she felt immediately better. Meredith asked if she could have a minute to herself. The driver nodded. She excused herself, and went back, and sat in her car, closed the door, and opened the envelope.

Sure enough, inside was her "temporary" cell phone—same one as the last trip, and along with it, was this note that she read:

> M,
>
> I can't believe we are doing this again!
>
> Your driver is Mark. He will be driving you to me. He has been completely vetted and background-checked by my COO (you remember Nick, right?), and can be 100% trusted.
>
> All folks you have, and will, encounter have years of experience shuttling top-secret, VIP clients, and friends of the Firm, around to very unusual locales. Therefore, no one will question you, ask your identity or do anything other than what they have been instructed. Mark is no different. We have changed the number of your temporary cell phone to 412-944-7159. Don't give that number out to anyone except your trusted friend, Jessica. The phone has been pre-loaded with Nick George's cell and office numbers in case of an emergency, or if you need anything at all. Be sure to leave your own phone in your car.
>
> Now hurry up. Come for me.
>
> G

Now, Meredith hurried. She placed her cell phone in the glove box of her vehicle, and jumped out. She opened the back door, and pulled out a well-worn suitcase. She called, "Mark? I'm ready."

Mark hurried over, and before picking up her bag, extended his hand and said, "Hi Meredith. I'm Mark."

"It's nice to meet you, Mark. Sorry the bag is so heavy." She smiled sheepishly.

He replied moving swiftly to her bag, "Please jump in the back, Meredith. I'll load your bag."

He was soon in the driver's seat, and asking about her comfort. There was bottled water and juice in the spacious cabin where she sat. She stretched her feet out, and still couldn't reach the seat in front of her. The engine roared to life, and soon they were pulling out onto Commerce Street.

"We will be at our destination soon," Mark said over his shoulder. "Ask me if you need anything."

Meredith took that as a comment and not a question. She pulled out the letter she had just read, and perused it again. She closed her eyes and smiled. But, then she thought of her wardrobe and felt instantly apprehensive. How could anyone look twice at her? And Geoff? Shit. I haven't bought any new clothes in years. Her insecurity started to overwhelm her. Funny her clothes did that to her. She started to panic. Sure, I'll get to go shopping when I get there. Jessica loaned me $400. That would help.

Just then, the car slowed and turned off the expressway. Meredith looked out the windows, and could see they were approaching the Grand Junction Regional Airport. She had been there numerous times—mostly picking up and dropping of visitors. But, this time, when they reached the main entry they turned right and on to a narrow paved one-lane road that wrapped around the far end of the runway to the other side of the airport. Once across the property, they turned into a small parking lot that had a few cars in it, and pulled right in front of a small modern building. Mark stopped the car and jumped out. He came around and opened Meredith's door.

Please head right on in; I'll grab your bag. Meredith grabbed her purse, and stuffed the note and her new cell phone inside it, and draped it over her shoulder. Mark grabbed the front door underneath a sign that read, "Private Aviation," and let Meredith inside before going back to fetch her bag. Once inside, she was met by another man in khaki's and the distinctive blue shirt.

"Booker said to call you, Ms. Meredith." He extended his hand. She took his hand and instantly smiled.

"Say 'hi' to Booker for me. He's special."

"Will do, Ms. Meredith. My name is Mike, and I, along with my co-pilot John, will be transporting you this morning. We are ready to go if you are."

"Wow. This is all happening so fast." She turned around and said, "I just wanted to thank Mark for his…" She looked left and right, but Mark was nowhere to be seen. "He was going to bring my bag in for me," she said—a little anxiously.

"It's been loaded already by my co-pilot. There is coffee on board along with some refreshments. There are restrooms on board too, but if you would like to use the Ladies Room while we are on the ground, please feel free."

"No, I think I am all ready to go."

And with that, the two of them walked out the door and into the sunshine onto the tarmac. And there before her, stood the most beautifully sleek aircraft she had ever laid her eyes on. It was a slippery missile of an airplane with oval windows, and glistened in the brisk winter sun. It looked as though it had just been polished. Meredith looked around to see if there was a helicopter nearby, but it was the only aircraft there this morning. There was a small staircase at the front of the plane, and they headed right for it. But as she neared the stairs, she stopped just to take it all in. That's when she noticed the CBC logo on the tail.

The next several minutes were a blur. She was lead up the stairway and into the main cabin of the Gulfstream 550. What she saw when she looked around amazed her. There were a few seats up front facing forward, but behind those, was what she could best describe as a small but comfortable sitting room with leather chairs and casual tables. There were a couple of sideboards with drawers. Of course, they were all affixed to the floor, but the allusion was complete—and quite real.

"Ms. Meredith, please have a seat in one of these front seats and fasten your lap belt until we are in the air; then we will notify you when it is safe to roam about the cabin," Captain Mike said. She did as she was told, and sat in the front by the window in a plush leather seat. It smelled new. She fastened her seatbelt. He then turned and ducked into the open door where Meredith could see a thousand gauges, dials, needles, electronic numbers and blinking lights. There was also another pilot sitting in the seat to the right.

Before the door closed and latched, she heard from inside the cockpit, "Hey, Mike. Pre-flight complete. Visual inspection perfect. Is our passenger on board and secured?"

Mike replied, "Thanks, John. Yes. All good. Let's roll."

82

JAY

UP ON THE ROOF OF THE MAIN TERMINAL, JAY FIDDLED WITH A FUSE box. All the new electronics for the regional airport were a blessing. Not only did the facility badly need the upgraded capabilities, but Jay needed the work. His life was measured job-to-job, and this gig was a jackpot for this small market. And, his buddy, Tommy, was one of the air traffic controllers, so he got to see him regularly. But, today it was very cold, and his hands needed to be warmed constantly so that he could take advantage of his normally dexterous fingers.

Jay paused from his tedious work to take a break. He lit a cigarette and pushed his hands deep into his pockets to warm them. He took another drag on his Marlborough, and surveyed the view atop the airport. It was a beautifully clear day. A flash caught his eye, and he looked across the field and saw a very large private jet coming to a stop at the Private Aviation Terminal across the way. He had never seen such a stunning airplane before—certainly not here in Grand Junction. No one ever flew into Grand Junction in such a sweet ride.

After his break was over, and his cigarette consumed, he pulled his iPhone out of his pocket, and turned on the camera feature and pointed it across the airport. He zoomed in on the plane until it fit the entire frame. He snapped several pictures. He planned on asking Tommy if he knew anything about it. Maybe movie stars were here for a shoot and needed a good electrician? He was always looking for an angle on work.

He snapped a few more. And, unbeknownst to him, one of those snapshots had captured the pilot and a passenger heading out to the plane.

83

MEREDITH

MEREDITH SAT LOOKING OUT THE WINDOW AS THE ENGINES ROARED to life. She had never been on a helicopter before her last trip to Aspen a couple of weeks ago. And now? A private plane? And, this certainly didn't strike her as any ordinary private plane. She looked down at what she was wearing, and again felt very self-conscious.

She was wearing gray jeans and a complimentary top—that matched both her pants and her figure. She had stewed for what seemed like hours last night trying to decide on what to wear. What would take Geoff's breath away when he first laid eyes on her? She decided on a casual, comfortable, outfit in lighter colors as they were headed to warmer weather, but she also had a charcoal sweater and a warm scarf for the journey. They still had to travel out of Grand Junction. But, to...? And, she wore comfortable shoes with treaded soles. She would change those later, too.

The Gulfstream started to roll, and within minutes, it was lined up on a north-leading runway. The intercom interrupted her thoughts. It was Mike's voice. "We have been cleared for take-off. Please recheck your seatbelt and make sure it is tight across your hips. Once airborne, we will let you know when it is safe to roam about the cabin."

She could barely hear the powerful engines spool up, but when the brakes released, the plane jetted down the runway with such force that it pushed her back into the deep leather folds of her seat. In no time, the G550 lifted easily, and headed towards the heavens. Almost immediately, the plane banked left, and she could see straight down onto the cityscape below. Her breath caught as she recognized the grounds of Granite High School. She inhaled quickly, held her breath and looked to the horizon. The stab of anxiety passed quickly.

In what seemed like seconds, the door to the cockpit opened, and Mike emerged. Closing the door behind him, he said, "Ms. Meredith, it is now safe to get more comfortable. Please feel free to relax in our sitting room. There is a cappuccino maker in the galley as well as a tray of pastries and light fare in the refrigerator if you are hungry."

"Galley?" she asked.

"Oh, sorry. Galley is transportation-speak for kitchen."

Meredith was aghast. "This plane has its own kitchen?"

"Yes, it does. The plane was custom designed for long flights and maximum comfort. It is WiFi-enabled , and the entertainment system and surround-sound is remarkable. I've been flying for so many years that it is hard to impress me, but I love flying this beauty. However, it is quite simple in its layout. Our front seats are for take-offs and landings, and behind the sitting room is our kitchen, or 'galley' in official jargon. There is a restroom just to the side," he said pointing aft and to the right, "And, sealed off at the rear of the plane for privacy is a formal stateroom and small office which is unlocked today. You are free to check it out if you like."

"Well, I guess I will head back to the kitch…I mean, the galley, to get a cup of coffee. Can I make you one?" she offered.

"Oh, no thanks. We have our coffee up front with us already." Mike turned to head back to the front of the plane, but stopped. "We will be in the air about two hours. If there is anything at all that you might need, there is a little red button on this small hand-held device." He handed her what looked like a walkie-talkie. When you push it, you will connect straight up to me in the cockpit. Please call if you need anything."

"Thanks, Mike. I doubt I'll call for anything, but I appreciate the kindness."

Mike nodded easily, and said, "Enjoy the flight." He slipped back inside the cockpit door and closed it.

Meredith headed back for her cappuccino—and her self-guided tour of this magnificent aircraft. Her curiosity was killing her.

84

SUSIE

"WHAT MAKES YOU THINK YOUR HUSBAND MAY BE HAVING AN affair?" Trevor inquired of the tall, sophisticated, blonde across the table from him. He was scribbling notes as they spoke.

Trevor, a former Navy Seal, was the managing partner, and majority owner, of a very exclusive private investigation firm that was based in an obscure freestanding building on the outskirts of San Francisco. The non-descript building was in a rather rough neighborhood, and stood unmarked except for the numbers 928 above the front door. Susie had to circle the block three times before she could locate it. She had been lucky to find a parking spot three blocks away.

"A hunch mainly. Call it a wife's intuition. When you are married to someone for as long as I have, you definitely notice when your husband's behavior is oddly different," Susie explained.

"Go on," Trevor prodded.

"Well, add to that some things that I have seen and experienced that didn't add up to me."

"Like what?"

"Some of this gets rather personal," Susie hesitated.

"If I am going to help you, Mrs. Cameron, I need to know everything. Please don't be withholding important information. I wouldn't have this successful business if I didn't honor confidentiality and my clients' identities. I do this for a living."

Susie took a deep breath and closed her eyes briefly. Then she pulled a little white-papered notebook from her Louis Vuitton purse, and spoke from several pages of notes. When she was outlining her husband's recent lack of interest in their bedroom, she felt as though she was speaking to a marriage counselor. But, she pressed on.

When Susie had finished, she turned the questioning towards Trevor, asking, "So, what do you think?"

Trevor finished writing before he looked up at her. "First of all, it sounds as though you have enough evidence to be concerned. But, everything is not always what it seems, and I would urge you not to rush to judgement. Let us do some deep investigative work, and we will get to the very bottom of this, I assure you."

"How are you compensated?"

"We're not cheap, Mrs. Cameron," Trevor started. "But, we will be successful. If your husband is cheating, we will find out. And with who. And, if he isn't, we'll find that out, too. We will provide you with all the evidence—photographic and otherwise. We charge an up-front engagement fee of $40,000 which also serves as our minimum fee; then $950 per hour is credited against that fee plus travel and actual expenses. Because of the import of your husband, and his company, I will handle this case, personally, along with some hand-picked colleagues. My personal travel time I bill out at fifty percent, so $475 per hour. My associates bill out at a far more reasonable rate of $350 per hour—half of that for their travel. I estimate that this case will be more complex than usual assignments as I am guessing your husband travels extensively, is very smart, and will - if he is cheating—cover his tracks." Trevor continued, "Clients always feel that they have been cheated (no pun intended) if we find the suspect innocent. But, Mrs. Cameron, what is your peace of mind worth? My estimate of the cost of this case to be around $180,000 if he is guilty, and approximately $90,000 - $100,000 if he is innocent."

Susie nodded without showing as much emotion as resolve.

Trevor asked, "Do you have any other questions for me?"

"No, sir, other than when can you start?"

85

GEOFF

NICK CAME INTO GEOFF'S OFFICE AND CLOSED THE DOOR BEHIND him. Geoff was finishing a heated conversation with the president of one of his company investments. "I want a thorough, all-hands-on-deck, review of how we got into this mess. Be sure to have your company lawyer on the call, and I will be joined by my Chief Operating Office, Nick George, and our lawyers as well. The call will be recorded, so please come prepared." There was a pause. Geoff turned around and saw Nick standing by the door. Geoff rolled his eyes, nodded and motioned for Nick to take a seat.

Geoff started in again abruptly, "I know. I know." There was another pause, then he broke in, "Believe me, Richard, I want you to fix it—and, I trust you have the ability to do just that. But if you can't, I will. I want this conference call arranged through Nick and my assistant, Cindy, ASAP. In the next twenty-four to forty-eight hours. Got it? Thanks." Geoff hung up and shook his head thinking.

Nick cleared his voice, and Geoff turned around. Nick said, "So is this THE Richard of the green construction company we purchased four years ago?"

"That's the man. Nothing but problems and excuses since day one. Frankly, I am getting real tired of his schtick. This time we are being sued by a client claiming we are falsifying our billable hours by unverified employees on a work site and padding overtime. Sounds like a fucking lawyer's involved, doesn't it?"

"Don't worry, Geoff," Nick said calmly. "I'll get the call set up, and lead the discussion."

Just then, Geoff's cell phone pinged. By reflex, he picked it up, and his face softened. A smile came to his lips.

From: mquest99@aol.com
Subject: Jet-Setting
Date: December 4, 2014 at 10:24 AM MST
To: gquest100@hotmail.com
OMG! You really know how to spoil a girl! This is a serious ride! Where are you taking me? The smoked salmon and caviar are delicious. OK, and so is the Dom. I'm excited and scared. Counting every second until I am safely in your arms! Is this what they call The Mile High Club?
M

"She must be in the air by now," Nick deadpanned.

Geoff looked up and smiled. "It appears so. Think she likes the Gulfstream. Hang on, let me write her a quick reply." He kept smiling as he thumb-typed…

From: gquest100@hotmail.com
Subject: The Mile High Club
Date: December 4, 2014 at 9:28 AM PDT
To: mquest99@aol.com
No, you are not in the Mile High Club…Yet. You have to come with me to join that club. We'll make sure you are a full-fledged member in due course. Glad you are enjoying the light snacks on board. Trust John and Mike are taking good care of you. Did they weigh your bag? ;-)
G

Nick stood. Geoff remained seated and he kept his cell phone in his left hand as he listened to Nick give his final rundown of the days ahead. "The house is ready. It is truly a special and unique place. I know you and Meredith will thoroughly enjoy yourselves. The staff at the hotel has been briefed, and all the appointments have been made. She will be surprised, and I am guessing, a bit overwhelmed. But, if she is half of who you say she is, she will adapt to this unexpected adventure. I have personally looked after every detail. You fly out tomorrow morning early. Frank will pick you up at the house at 7, and John and Mike will want to depart no later than 8:30 AM so that you can arrive before she does—as you have requested. They will be in contact with Booker to coordinate. Any questions?"

"No. Not at all. Nick, you are truly one of a kind. Thank you. I told Susie I was going to be in LA over the weekend meeting with some investors and clients."

Geoff arose from his chair and extended his hand. Nick took it shook firmly. "Be careful, Geoff. You are my friend - first and foremost. I'll get that call set up with the almighty Richard and his gang of thieves, and let you know the timing. Let me know if you need anything."

Geoff's one-word reply of "Thanks"—spoken slowly with deliberate eye contact—expressed a sincere love of, and trust in, his consigliere.

Geoff's phone pinged again.

86

BOBBIE

BOBBIE SAT BY HIMSELF AT THE FAR END OF THE BAR AT PISTOL Whipped Willy's, and fumbled with a brown paper bag in his lap. No one saw him come in with it—at least he didn't think anyone saw him. Maybe it wasn't as dark in here as he thought. The drinking had started early for Bobbie and his friends, the Wrecking Crew. Mal and Tommy were both working night shifts, and Jay was done at 2:30 that afternoon, so they had congregated at Jay's for some adult beverages.

It was now well past 9 PM, and Bobbie had driven alone to the "Pussy Whip" for his rendezvous with The Dispenser. In addition to the usual Human Growth Hormone, Spencer Miller had been asked for another illegal substance. Fentanyl was easy enough to get these days on the street, but the quantity requested would be enough to sedate an elephant for a week. The watchful eyes were dangerous, and to avoid suspicion, Dr. Miller wrote small prescriptions, and collected the drugs over the course of a couple of weeks from various small pharmacies he knew well in the area.

Spence was on time, and strolled casually to the back of the bar where he sat in the empty barstool next to Bobby. Neither spoke nor acknowledged each other. They ordered their drinks separately. When the bartender was distracted having a conversation with an obviously inebriated prostitute, the doctor pushed a small briefcase under Bobbie's feet. Within ten seconds, the brown paper bag was in Spence's lap. Neither needed to check the contents of their gifts. They now knew each other well, and had made too many transactions together.

Bobbie left first, paying his bill with cash and tipping the bartender heavily. "Got to run along and get some work done," Bobbie said to no one as he pushed back his stool. The music was loud, and the bar was crowded. As he strolled out to his truck, Bobbie didn't look back. He climbed into the front seat, and started the engine. Idling in the parking lot, he pulled a folded piece of paper from his breast pocket. It was his list. The first, Don DeLatore, had a line through it. Charlie Fredericks and Hugh Preston, the Granite High Principal and the District lawyer respectively, were the next two names. The forth name, Janet Jacobs, the District HR manager, had an asterisk next to it. He couldn't wait to put a line through it. In ink.

87

MEREDITH

MEREDITH SAT COMFORTABLY IN HER PLUSH LEATHER CHAIR, mid-cabin, as she sipped her champagne and tried to soak in her surroundings. The jet was whisper-quiet. She was all alone with herself and her thoughts. She couldn't help looking out the large windows as the Rockies, and then the Sierras, passed beneath her—wondering where she was headed. Soon they were over the Pacific, and the G-550 took a large lazy turn to the left. They were headed south.

The cockpit door opened, and Mike emerged. After stretching, he came over to Meredith and knelt beside her. "How's the flight been? The flight attendants treating you well?" he laughed.

Susie smiled broadly. "Well, you asked…The service sucks, the plane is shabby, and the pilot keeps pestering me while I am raiding the fridge. Other than that, I think it will do."

Now, they both were laughing.

"We will be starting our decent into Santa Monica shortly. We must cross the coastline and land towards the west. If you need to use the restroom, or grab an additional refreshment, please do so now, but I will need you seated in one of the forward seats in about ten minutes."

"Thank you, Captain," Meredith said. "This has been a special treat." It was all she could think to say.

Mike nodded, and headed back to the cockpit. Meredith didn't move, but pulled out her phone.

From: mquest99@aol.com
Subject: California Dreaming!
Date: December 4, 2014 at 10:15 AM PST
To: gquest100@hotmail.com
Santa Monica?!! I am shaking with excitement. I don't know what I'm
going to do when I see you again! Landing soon. Be there for me, OK? I
want to fall off this plane into your arms…
M

The seat belt light came on, and Mike asked all passengers to take their seats, and buckle their belts, in preparation for landing. It was hard extricating herself from that overstuffed leather seat, but Meredith did as she was told—sitting by the window. It was a very clear morning in Los Angeles, and the urban sprawl seemed to go on forever. The jet banked left, and then took a sharp right as it settled into position to land.

The Gulfstream glided easily over the runway and touched down smoothly—the engines reversing, and the strong brakes, slowed the aircraft. As it pulled up to the small terminal, Meredith's phone pinged.

From: gquest100@hotmail.com
Subject: Keep Dreaming
Date: December 4, 2014 at 10:30 AM PST
To: mquest99@aol.com
Not so fast! I have plans for you this afternoon. Go with the flow. See
you soon!
G

As Meredith started to respond, the plane came to a stop. She put her phone in her purse and unbuckled her seatbelt. The engines spooled down, and soon Mike and John entered the cabin. John unlocked the door and the staircase unfolded into the crisp Southern California sea air. They waited a few minutes and then John invited Meredith to deplane. Mike said simply as Meredith passed him, "Nice to have you on board." Meredith stopped, looked up at him and shook his hand. "Thank you, again, Captain."

John was already outside, and lent Meredith a hand as she stepped down the stairs onto the tarmac. There, at the bottom, waiting for her was her bag. And Booker. "Ms. Meredith, so great to see you again." He smiled.

She shook her head. "This can't be happening," she mused. She hadn't seen the helicopter as it was on the other side of her plane when they pulled in. "Don't tell me…We're not staying in Santa Monica?"

"Not today," Booker replied. "Do you need to use a bathroom before we depart?"

"Yes, thank you," she laughed. "Too much champagne."

88

SUSIE

SUSIE COULD HEAR THE GARAGE DOOR OPEN AND GEOFF'S CAR PULL in. When he came into the house, he was wearing his suit with his tie loosened and his sleeves rolled up just below his elbows. Their Labrador Retriever made a bee-line for his master, and the thumping of his tail as he rolled over on his back always made him laugh.

"Where are the kids?" Geoff said looking up from the belly scratching.

"Nice to see you, too!" Susie replied. "Come here and give me a kiss."

"Oh, sorry, Honey," he said sincerely. "Crazy day. How are you?" Geoff came over, gave Susie a hug and a kiss on her cheek. "How was your day?"

Turning to the counter where she was unwrapping a meal Rosanne had made earlier in the day, she said, "Busy. Spin class at 9, then had my mani-pedi. Raced into the City to run a couple of errands. Can I fix you a drink? Dinner will be ready in about forty-five minutes."

"Sure. A gin and tonic. That would be great. I need to attend to a few emails before we eat, but before I do, I'll run up and change," Geoff said as he picked up his briefcase and coat and turned towards the staircase.

"The girls are in their rooms studying, and CJ is having dinner with the Smith's tonight. They picked him up from practice."

Geoff hesitated ever so slightly. He had told CJ, and then the team, that he was in a very busy period at work. He would get to practice when he could, but the assistant coach would be taking over for a while. He loved working with the boys—and especially CJ. Geoff would break the news to him when he got home that he wouldn't be there for his game this weekend. He bounded up the stairs and headed straight for the girls' rooms.

. . .

Geoff was already in his jeans and Polo shirt when Susie came upstairs with his drink. His briefcase was on the bed, and he was texting someone when she walked into the bedroom, but he quickly stopped and put his phone in his pocket.

"Here Sweetie," she said as she placed the drink on the dresser. "Can you barbeque the chicken tonight?"

"Sure. Happy to. What were you unwrapping downstairs? I thought that was dinner."

"Rosie made us a green bean casserole to go with the chicken she bought. The kids won't like that much, but I wrapped up some corn that you throw on the grille while you are cooking."

"No worries. I'll go light the barbeque." Geoff turned and went downstairs leaving Susie alone in their bedroom.

She walked directly over to the bed, and when she heard the back door open and close, she opened Geoff's leather briefcase that she had bought for him last year, and quickly thumbed through the contents - scanning the files that were neatly stacked against each other. Nothing seemed out of the ordinary. The tabs on the files all had hand-written names on them. Some names she recognized, others she did not. The one marked PS/LQ certainly would have been quite interesting to her had she pulled it out and leafed through it. But, she didn't have much time.

Susie reached into her purse and pulled out a wafer-thin disc the size of a dime. She removed the paper from the adhesive backing, and slipped it down onto the back rear corner of an unused pocket of the briefcase. She smiled when she thought, "So, this is what $180,000 buys me."

89

MEREDITH

BOOKER HELPED STRAP MEREDITH INTO HER SEAT IN THE BELL LONG Ranger helicopter. She couldn't help but feel an eerie sense of déjà vu. She had done this before. And just like before, the cross-chest restraints had lit a small fire deep in her. She put on her headset, and quietly watched as Booker went through his pre-flight check. Once convinced all was in order, he flipped a switch that started the large rotor in motion.

"Bravo-Zero-Six-Tango requesting departure from Santa Monica Heliport. Departure west then north along the coast at required altitude. Then east to the Peninsula."

Meredith could hear the reply immediately in her headphones. "Roger Bravo-Zero-Six-Tango. You are cleared for immediate departure following outbound Gulfstream."

The rotor gained speed, and soon Booker pulled back on the stick between his legs, and the helicopter slowly lifted off the ground. It rotated slowly to the west, and the nose of the aircraft, and its occupants, dipped forward and the helicopter raced forward and skyward towards the deep blue of the Pacific Ocean. Once they reached the beach, Booker banked north and pointed out the Santa Monica Pier with its iconic Ferris Wheel and roller coaster. The day couldn't have been clearer or more spectacular. The Hollywood sign could be easily seen standing as a sentinel over the Rich and Famous of La La Land.

Booker maneuvered the helicopter to circle the pier a second time so that it felt like Meredith was staring straight down on it. Leveling off, he headed back south. Pointing straight ahead, Meredith said, "Is that the peninsula where we are headed?"

He replied, "I'm afraid not. You are looking at the Palos Verdes Peninsula. Mr. Geoff has arranged for us to land on a different peninsula." And, with that, they turned east and headed inland over the city.

It took them only four minutes. Booker eased back on the throttle and the helicopter started to gently lower itself. The buildings were getting closer and closer to them. "Where are we going?" Meredith inquired.

"It will become crystal clear when we have landed," he said allowing himself a quick sideways glace and a smile.

The Long Ranger seemed to have picked out a roof-top that had a large, elevated, square on it with a painted circle further defining a landing pad. Meredith's heart was racing. She looked out the windows scanning the whole area for Geoff, but there was no one around. Booker lowered the helicopter ever so slowly until it alighted in the middle of the painted circle. The engine immediately began spooling down, and the rotors slowed.

As Meredith unhooked her shoulder harness and seat belt, she asked, "So… where ARE we?"

As Booker pushed open his door to de-plane, he spoke over his shoulder half laughing, "You're about to find out."

Just then, a door opened on the roof, and a very handsome, older, man sporting a deep tan, and wearing an impeccable suit and silk tie, walked purposely up to Meredith and offered her a hand as she stepped from the aircraft. "Ms. Meredith, I presume?"

Meredith nodded, and more than a little enthralled, said, "Yes, that's me. Seems everyone is calling me that lately."

"Well then, welcome to the Peninsula Beverly Hills."

90

BOBBIE

SHE WAS BARELY CONSCIOUS. JANET JACOBS, AGE 48, HUMAN Resources Manager for the Granite School District, lay on her bed remotely aware that she was naked and tied up face down and spread eagle. She was breathing very slowly now.

A strange man was in her bathroom. Or was he? She concentrated as best she could on what was happening. She wanted to remember everything, but her mind was fuzzy. She heard a rattling sound. The toilet flushed. Laughter.

Then the man was back in her room. The gag in her mouth prevented her from saying anything. Her dull and dilated eyes were following him. She could only grunt.

"There, there, Janet. Can I call you Janet? You can call me Coach." He kept talking as he seemed to be working on something on top of the dresser across the room. "You give good head, by the way. But, your love-making leaves a bit to be desired. Like fucking a dead fish. I actually thought I might want to fuck you again, but then, you weren't all that good. Maybe I should have held the gun to your head like I did when you were blowing me. Ah, was that your favorite cocktail? COCK-tail?! Get it?!" Bobbie started laughing.

Janet grunted again. Images raced in and out of her head. She was on her knees in her living room. She had a loaded gun stabbing at her forehead, and an erect penis in her mouth. Dear God. She tried to clear the fog about the rest of the night, but couldn't quite get there. The man began speaking again.

"You will feel a little prick in your ass." Bobbie started laughing uncontrollably. "Unlike earlier tonight." He started coughing as he was laughing. He gained control of himself. Then he belched—long and deep. This started him laughing again. He was like a kid in church. "You probably want a big prick like earlier, but I am not going to give you that pleasure. Maybe three little pricks in your ass will equal the big one."

Bobbie drove the hypodermic needle into Janet's left rear buttocks, and pushed the plunger until the contents were completely injected. It didn't take long. Her fuzziness turned to darkness. She didn't feel the final two shots.

• • •

Bobbie untied her, ungagged her and clothed her. It was like trying to put clothes on a loose, heavy, sack of sand. Getting her bra back on was tricky. It didn't help that he kept breaking into laughter, and had to stop to calm himself several times. He repositioned her on her side and threw a comforter over her. He brushed her hair. Before he stood, he leaned down and whispered into her ear. "Guess who fucked who? Thanks for the paid vacation, bitch."

He picked up the four syringes, the ropes, the gag and his gun, and placed them in his gym bag. He then went to the bathroom and fetched the empty prescription bottles for Fentanyl, expertly forged with Janet Jacob's name on them. He wiped them carefully with a towel, and tossed them on her bedside table.

91

MEREDITH

BOOKER CAME AROUND AND JOINED THEM BRIEFLY AFTER HE HAD unloaded Meredith's suitcase. The nicely dressed gentleman extended a hand and introduced himself. "Nice landing. My name is Bradford Willoughby. I am the Executive General Manager of the Beverly Hills Peninsula Hotel. I have been honored to have been asked to look after our special guest, personally, while she is here for her short stay."

Booker replied, "Very nice to meet you. Thank you for looking after Ms. Meredith. I will be returning tomorrow morning at 11 AM sharp to pick her up right here." He turned and winked at Meredith. She just looked at him and shook her head in disbelief.

Bradford unhooked his two-way radio and called for assistance with a bag on the roof. He put a tag on it, and turned to Meredith saying, "Please. Come with me. I will show you to your suite where you can freshen up before your 1:30 PM appointment." Turning to Booker he said, "Be safe. Travel well. See you tomorrow." Offering a welcoming gesture towards the rooftop door, he said to Meredith, "Please. After you."

Meredith led the way through that portal that opened into a whole new and opulent world. The heavy drapes, the deep plush carpeting, the artwork on the walls, and the gilded gold vases with fresh flowers in spectacular arrangements. Bradford now led her to the private elevator that led down to the penthouse suites. Actually, there were only two on the top floor, and when the elevator opened, Bradford led the way to a double door entrance, and unlocked the door with a swipe of a card key. The doors swung open.

She fully expected Geoff to be there with open arms and his open heart, but the suite was vacant—except for the salt water aquarium that made up the dividing wall between the kitchen and the living room. The suite was 3,000 square feet housing two master bedrooms with their own master baths, a guest bedroom and bath, a powder room, fully stocked kitchen, a dining room, and a living room with a 108" flat-screen HDTV and a massive balcony overlooking the hotel's lush gardens and some of the most expensive real estate in the world.

Bradford gave her a tour of the place, but she hardly paid attention. She couldn't wait for him to leave so that she could fling herself on the California king bed and text Geoff. As he was concluding the tour by the front doors, Bradford said, "If there is anything you need, Ms. Meredith, please call me on my personal extension. I am here until 10 PM, and will be back on property at 6 AM." He handed her his business card. "Oh, one more thing. There is a fresh lobster and bay shrimp Cobb salad in the fridge should you wish to indulge yourself before your 1:30 PM appointment. The chef delivered it just as you were landing."

She smiled and looked up at him and said, "What appointment?"

"I don't know exactly. I was just told to tell you to be ready at 1:30 PM to do a little shopping."

92

GEOFF

HIS PHONE pinged.

He was just explaining to Susie and the kids that he would be leaving early in the morning for Los Angeles. Unlike his other recent trips, this was not a trip to put another deal together, but rather to visit some of his successful ventures and schmooze with the managers of some of the larger pension funds that had co-invested with Cameron Capital—a division of CBC. Much of this flew well over their heads, but Susie was registering "Los Angeles" and that it was unusual in another way: this was the second trip in a short time span where he would be away from the family for a weekend. Something, up to this point in their marriage, he almost never did. He was missing another of CJ's games, too.

He glanced down at his phone knowing how annoyed Susie got when he interrupted their time together. It was just a quick glance, but Geoff saw that it was from Nick. He had last minute "details" to discuss. He wanted a quick call before Geoff turned in. Geoff punched "K," then looked up and apologized. "It was Nick. He has some last minute trip details he wants to go over with me. I'll call him back after dinner." Susie's glare could peel paint. Geoff held up his phone so that everyone could see it, and he turned it off.

• • •

Nick was resolute. "We think someone tried to hack into our server today. They tried to get into your email account, too. Our head of security is all over this, and will do their best to uncover who might be after our, and your, shit. They are constructing new firewalls, too. We all will need to reset our passwords."

Geoff sat there in his home office stunned. "What do you think they were after? Our bank accounts? Our client's confidential information?"

Nick said, "I have no idea at this stage, but because it appears the only email accounts they were trying to hack here were yours and mine. Listen, Geoff. I may be way out of bounds here, but I am getting a little nervous, no…a lot nervous, about your rendezvous with this mysterious Meredith. I think you should call it off."

"You think someone is trying some grand espionage on Cameron Boone Covington because of my special project? I think you are way over-reacting."

"OK. OK. Maybe I am," Nick confessed. "But, you WILL follow these instructions, boss, PLEASE."

"Go on."

"Frank is picking you up at your place tomorrow morning at 7 and driving you to private aviation. You will leave your locked phone in his car when you depart. Pilot Mike will have a new pre-paid, untraceable iPhone for you with a new phone number. I will have all your cell phone calls, texts and emails forwarded to that new phone." Nick continued, "I will update you all day tomorrow on our progress, and our hopeful big fix."

"Nick, once again, you are a total pro. Thank you. I'll do exactly what you say."

Nick responded, "Well, that's it for now. I'm here at the office with our emergency tech professionals and programmers. It'll be a long night ahead."

"Thanks, Nick. Thanks for everything."

"Geoff? One more thing. Don't use your phone again. If I need you, I will call you on your house phone."

"Got it." And with that, Geoff hung up. As he stood to go back downstairs to help with the dishes, he didn't hear Susie pull her attention away from his closed door, and walk barefoot down the hall to the stairs.

93

MEREDITH

THE SOFT KNOCK ON THE DOOR CAME AT EXACTLY 1:30 PM. MEREdith was just finishing brushing her hair and applying a little make-up. She couldn't imagine what was in store for her. She rushed to the door and looked through the security peep hole, half expecting it to be Geoff. She took a deep breath and opened the door. There, standing in front of her with her hand extended, was this most beautifully put together exotic woman. She was tall. Meredith was guessing 5'10". And she had a body that neared perfection—at least proportionately—that was largely hidden beneath very expensive clothing.

"Hi, Meredith?" This woman spoke in a strong foreign accent. French? Without waiting for a reply, she continued, "My name is Dominique. I am your personal fashion consultant. May I come in?"

Meredith stammered, "Uh…of course. Please." And, she stood aside while Dominique came into the entry of the grand penthouse. "Would you like a refreshment?" she thought to ask.

"Bottled water would be great if you have it," she replied as they moved to the living room. As Meredith fetched a bottle of cold Evian for each of them, Dominique continued, "We only have a little bit of time before we need to be at our first appointment." Meredith came in and sat across form her.

Meredith launched in, "Humor me. What are we going to be doing this afternoon?"

"Well, Mr. Cameron has hired me to help you pick out some special things to make your weekend a bit more comfortable—and memorable. He didn't give me any details other than you are going to have a very fancy meal on Saturday and he wanted to treat you to a new cocktail dress or two, shoes, a swim suit, some casual wear, etc., as he knew you were from a cold climate and weren't expecting spending the weekend in the heat of Southern California."

"That is so very kind of Mr. Cameron. I brought some money, and a credit card, so I am ready to go. Not sure I will be able to buy more than one outfit, but it will be fun looking," Meredith smiled.

"Great. But before we go, I need to get your measurements. And, I hope it's OK for me to get a good look at you. We will be finding the most suitable apparel that shows off your best assets. That's always our plan, no?" Her French accent was totally disarming.

Meredith didn't know what to say, exactly. Go with the flow. Isn't that what Geoff said? "OK. I'm in your hands," Meredith demurred.

"Great!" Dominique exclaimed as she stood. "Our first appointment is at Valentino on Rodeo Drive at 2:30. We need to leave by 2:10 at the latest. Is there a full length mirror in the master bedroom?"

"Yes. There is actually a triple floor-length mirror in there." Meredith rose. "Follow me."

The two entered the bedroom, and Meredith was embarrassed because she hadn't unpacked and had thrown her travel clothes on the bed. If she cared at all, Dominique didn't show it. In fact, her fun, positive attitude was rubbing off. Meredith was relaxing.

"Stand in front of the mirrors," Dominique requested. Meredith did as she was told. This exotic foreigner started to slowly walk around her eyeing her every square inch. Meredith found herself strangely loving this attention.

"Do you mind if I pour myself a glass of wine? I think we have time," Meredith asked.

"Sure. Go ahead. But hurry. When you get back, slip out of your dress, would you?"

Meredith raised her eyes a bit as she rushed to the kitchen, but had to giggle to herself. This was crazy. When she returned, Dominique was having a swallow of her Evian, and had her measuring tape ready. "Get your gear off so I can look at you and measure you."

"My gear?"

"Your clothes. Off. All except your panties."

Meredith blushed. She took a deep swallow of her wine, and started undressing. Dominique was watching her every move. She stepped out of her shoes; then her skirt. She unbuttoned her blouse, and let it fall from her shoulders. She stood in front of the mirror feeling exposed and embarrassed in her thong and bra. Dominique paid no attention except to start measuring her in every way. Girl, you are one of the most naturally beautiful women I have ever had the pleasure of working with. This is going to be fun!" She grabbed her bra strap from the back, and looking at Meredith in the mirror, she said, "May I?"

Meredith shrugged and nodded. Snap. "My God. You have the most beautiful breasts," she said in a completely authentic and adoring tone. This time she didn't ask, but as she circled in front of her, Dominique slowly reached out with both hands and cupped Meredith's breasts. As she did so she fingered her nipples to purposely harden them. Meredith flinched, and could hardly breath. Her eyes were closed. Dominique then stood back and admired Meredith's body. "Exquisite. You are blessed. They are real. And firm. And perky."

A strange emotion unexpectantly bloomed deep inside her. Dominique's soft touch was a totally new sensation. She had never allowed any woman that kind of intimate access to her body. It was equal parts erotic and forbidden. She pushed this emotion back to some deep recess in her mind, and focused back on the modeling.

Dominique approached her again, this time taking her hands in hers. "Here. Feel." She placed Meredith's hands over her clothed breasts and continued with a laugh, "These are not real. Man made. I love my surgeon, and I paid a fortune for these, but there is nothing like the real things." Meredith self-consciously removed her hands from this other woman's chest.

"Lucky Mr. Cameron. We will dress you up so that he will never be able to concentrate on anything but his image of you for the rest of his life!" she said with natural enthusiasm. "Now, get your gear on. We're going shopping. We can't be late. Valentino is just our first stop."

Meredith took a deep breath and nodded silently. Dominique turned away and headed for the kitchen. And, as Meredith fetched her "gear" and redressed herself, her mind was spinning.

94

GEOFF

S USIE'S ALARM WENT OFF AT 6 AM FRIDAY MORNING. SHE FUMBLED for it, and turned it off. She vaguely remembered Geoff had asked to use it last night as they climbed into bed. She could hear Geoff already up and in his shower. When he emerged, she sleepily said, "Tell me again why you used my phone for your wake-up call?"

"Dead battery. I was so concentrating on packing that I forgot to charge my phone. I'm fully charged up now."

"Nice to see the CEO of CBC struggling with third-world problems," she said as she rolled over and pulled the covers tight up to her chin. "Don't forget to throw your charger into your briefcase." Within seconds, she was asleep again, breathing easily. At least that was what Geoff thought.

● ● ●

Frank was waiting in the black company BMW in the circular driveway when Geoff walked outside with his suitcase and briefcase right at 7:30. Frank immediately jumped out and took Geoff's luggage from him, and loaded the trunk. "Good morning, Mr. C," Frank said cheerfully. "Beautiful day for your flight. Where are you off to today?"

"Los Angeles area for several meetings. Will be coming back Sunday in the afternoon."

"Yep. I'll be picking you up around 4 PM. There's a bit of traffic this morning, so it will take us about an hour to get to Oakland for your departure. I have a venti Starbuck's in the back for you, along with the <u>Wall Street Journal.</u> There is also a package from Mr. George for you in the back seat. He said I am to collect your cell phone and bring it back to the office."

Geoff said, "Yep. Thanks, Frank. Here you go." He handed his phone to him before slipping into the back seat. Frank climbed in, started the engine and pulled away.

Once Geoff was settled, and had had some of that glorious coffee, he picked up the brown package on the back seat, and tore it open. In it was a new iPhone and a note from Nick. It read: "Remember to leave your personal phone with Frank. Here is your new pre-paid phone with your new number. 415-765-7888. Your password is the same as your old phone, except I changed the last digit to a 5. YOUR CONFERENCE CALL TODAY IS AT 2 PM. I will send dial-in instructions. Hopefully, you did remember to turn off your old phone last night after we spoke. Once you turn your new phone on, it should start downloading your email and messages form your old phone. I took care of the forwarding. You will be untraceable unless you give your number out to someone. I suggest you only give it to M. Busy day for us here with the cyber-security forensics folks. Have a great time. Call/text if you need anything. Be safe. Be careful."

Geoff turned on the new phone and waited a few seconds for it to load. His new password worked perfectly. Soon, it was pinging away as both emails and texts came pouring in. He pushed through to his email, and was not surprised to see several from Meredith. He decided to read them first, and in order.

> To: gquest100@hotmail.com
> Subject: Going With the Flow
> Date: December 4, 2014 at 1:03 PM PST
> From: mquest99@aol.com
> Well, if I couldn't fall out of a plane into your arms, Booker was a huge consolation prize! The "shuttle" to the Peninsula was spectacular, and it has been surprise after surprise…I am speechless! You should SEE my room—I mean, villa! Holy crap, it's huge!! Sorry for all the exclamation marks, but geez!!! Who is my 1:30 appointment? My curiosity is overwhelming me at the moment. Is it YOU???
> Breathless in Beverly Hills.
> M

To: gquest100@hotmail.com
Subject: So It Wasn't YOU
Date: December 4, 2014 at 8:56 PM PST
From: mquest99@aol.com
Pinch me…Valentino, Saint Laurent, Dolce & Gabbana, Dior, Louis
Vuitton, Versace. My $400 for new clothes didn't even buy me a
g-string! I'm not sure how much I owe you, or how long it will take me
to pay you back, but THAT was an experience I will NEVER forget!
Dominique was exquisite, beautiful and oh so fun to be with. She's
very well known around here, and all of my store visits were by private
appointments. Can't wait to model for you—particularly the lingerie. ;-)
Drawing a bath. Come join me…
M

To: gquest100@hotmail.com
Subject: Where ARE you???????
Date: December 4, 2014 at 10:08 PM PST
From mquest99@aol.com
[photo of Meredith, nude, straddling a huge roman tub; bubbles
covering her nipples and her love triangle; she was holding a champagne
glass]
Caption: Appreciative, horny and wanting. Come for me.

Geoff spit his coffee, and was choking. Tears came to his eyes. Frank immediately slowed and looked in his rearview mirror with obvious concern. "You all
right, Mr. Cameron?"

It took a few seconds for Geoff to gather himself. His coughing turned to laughter, and while he couldn't yet speak, he made eye contact, smiled and nodded. The
BMW accelerated. Frank said, "Glad to hear it, Mr. C."

•   •   •

The BMW sped into Oakland Alameda International Airport, and took an immediate, and now routine, detour towards Private Aviation. Jeff could see the Gulfstream glistening in the morning sunshine. Mike and John were both there as the
larger G-550 required two pilots. Geoff made a direct dash for the bathroom as he

had coffee that he could hopefully remove from his clothes. "Won't be a minute, boys. Had a little accident on the way over here," he said as he jogged away.

When he returned, he had wet splotches all over his shirt, pants and coat. The pilots pretended not to notice. His bags were already loaded, and he walked out to the jet and jumped aboard. They were airborne in no time, and Mike announced they would be on the ground in Palm Springs in an hour and ten minutes. Geoff pulled out his laptop to get some work done.

> To: gquest100@hotmail.com
> Subject: Taking Matters Into My Own Hands
> Date: December 5, 2014 at 8:37 AM PST
> From mquest99@aol.com
> Topped off yesterday with a screaming orgasm. Hope I didn't wake the neighbors. I was clearly overwhelmed by your generosity and the fantasy of this weekend already gripping me. You really should have been here.
> I even tried to entice you with a very personal selfie. Oh well, guess you were tied up (oh don't I wish!). Hahaha!!
> Booker picking me up at 11. I guess we are not staying here. WHERE ARE YOU TAKING ME?
> Wait 'til you see my red dress Saturday night. And, what's under it. Or, what's not.
> M

Any work Geoff had envisioned for the day was now simply hopeless. Instead, he flipped to the photo gallery of the amazing house that was awaiting them in La Quinta. As he clicked through the pictures that Nick had provided, his heart raced. He turned to his email.

> To: mquest99@aol.com
> Subject: Re-Entering
> Date: December 5, 2014 at 10:15 AM PST
> From: gquest100@hotmail.com
> I can hardly type—emphasis on hard. What great notes (and PICTURE!) from you!
> Sorry to be OTG (off the grid), but security issues at my office forced me to shut down my phone. While I left it in SF, it does forward to my

new phone. But, please use this new number: 415-765-7888. I'll fill you in when I see you.

Glad you had a fun day shopping. Dominique came highly recommended. She is known to navigate Rodeo Drive and get appointments like no one else. I felt bad bringing you out to warm weather when you are still fighting the elements in Colorado. Hopefully, the little shopping excursion made up for it.

As for this weekend, I am way ahead of you! Sorry about all the surprises, but its for our safety. I'm cooking dinner tonight, so hope you are hungry.

I simply can...not...wait...to see you, M.

G

Geoff hit the send button, and folded up his laptop. He closed his eyes and tried to imagine Meredith in his plane, then being greeted by Booker, then being greeting by the Peninsula, then finally, Dominique. He smiled.

Then he tried to imagine Meredith in that bathtub. Screaming.

95

JESSICA

HER PHONE BUZZED. JESSICA'S ASSISTANT SAID ON THE INTERCOM, "Meredith. Line 1." She jumped for the phone.

"Where are you? Everything OK?"

"Jess, you absolutely wouldn't believe this. I was flown in a private jet—a SERIOUS private jet—to Santa Monica."

"What?"

"Yes, Santa Monica—as in beach; Pacific Ocean, WARM WEATHER! But hold for this…It's not where I am, and not where I am going."

"Come on; spill it, girl!"

"OK, I'm actually in Beverly Hills."

"WHAT?!"

"Peninsula Hotel. Rodeo Drive. Shopping. Now I am awaiting my departure to another secret location where I am supposed to meet up with Geoff. I can't believe this is all happening!"

"I am so jealous!"

"Well don't be. You have that beautiful Jazzy Girl. Money can't buy that, and besides, Jasmine's my baby, too—don't you forget it!"

"You're right. But I can still be envious!"

The conversation quickly grew more serious. Meredith asked, "Any word from, or about, Bobbie?"

"Nope. It's been deathly quiet around here. Rumor mill churning, though. Most folks believe he skipped town. He could be hunting, right?"

"Yeah, very likely. I think that is more likely than him skipping out of town. Where would he go? He's lived in Grand Junction all his life, and his buddies are all locals, too. Frankly, I really don't care. I am totally, and completely, done with him."

"Does he know that?"

"Probably not. We've certainly had our share of rough patches, but this time is different. Way different. Anyway, enough of him. I don't want Coach Bobbie Edmonson to get in the way of this weekend. I don't want to talk about—or think about—him again."

"OK, Mer. Thanks for checking in. Have a great time, and I can't wait to her all about it when you get home. The Chardonnay is already chillin'!"

"Thanks, Jess. I love you. Give Jazzy a big squeeze for me."

"Will do. Call if you need anything."

"OK. Bye."

In about seven hours, Jessica would know exactly where Bobbie was.

96

LA QUINTA

WARM, AND SUN-CARESSED, LA QUINTA LIES AT THE BASE OF THE San Jacinto Mountains in the magnificently scenic desert landscape known as the greater Palm Springs area east of Los Angeles. Here, the rock formations, and the desert sunlight, intertwine together to form an ever-changing panorama of light and shadows. Deep canyons fingering off the desert floor provide beauty and serenity—and for a very lucky few—their own sanctuary of tranquility.

High above La Quinta proper, and nestled deep within it's own private canyon, lies the Johnson Estate. Built in 2012, the main residence, and the grounds surrounding it, are an architectural wonder. How the house was actually constructed takes quite an imagination. It was literally built amongst the existing giant boulders and granite walls high in a massive cleft, and made to fit perfectly into this otherwise inhospitable environment. Starkly modern, the Estate was constructed of concrete and steel—with the main feature being the ample glass walls that afford view corridors throughout the house as well as stretching across the desert valley floor below. Much of the natural rock serves as a design feature within the home as well as accents the vanishing-edge pools between the home and the view beyond. There are no window coverings as the Estate is entirely private. Certain glass walls are electronically darkened, as if by magic, to assist with sleeping or watching movies or TV.

The Estate is accessed by a long, twisty, private driveway that is nearly a half-mile in length. The snaking driveway, itself is a construction wonder - and access to it is by an unmarked private gate at the end of a small cul-de-sac in an upscale neighborhood far below. Security cameras and sensors abound. Only a very small number of people have ever seen the Estate, because it is literally invisible until you are cresting the driveway and entering the motor court at house level.

Nick did well to find this place.

. . .

Geoff punched in the code at the innocuous key pad at the gate. The code was custom programmed; only he, and Nick, possessed the code. The gate slowly swung open, and Geoff moved his rented grey Mercedes GL500 SUV through to a second gate below a camera, that held him until the gate behind him was closed and electronically locked. Then, the second gate slid open granting him access to this breathtaking, and often scary (if you were afraid of heights), ribbon of concrete that led to the aerie.

When he arrived, he was the only one there, but the house was stocked with all the food they would ever need for their planned meals—including the picnic he planned for tomorrow. The caterers for the Saturday night formal dinner would bring their own food and wine in small vans so that they, too, could navigate the driveway.

Geoff got right to work. After arriving, he found the master bedroom and adjoining office overlooking the pool and all of La Quinta. He unpacked his clothes and sat at the desk getting his notes and files in order for his call at 2 PM. Then he went to the granite and stainless steel kitchen where he started preparing a simple cheese platter complimented with rustic whole grain crackers and fruit—strawberries and seedless grapes. He went to the wine refrigerator and pulled out a bottle of Cloudy Bay New Zealand Sauvignon Blanc from the famous Marlborough region and placed it in an ice bucket. It was already 84 degrees out, and the cool wine would go down easily.

Today, there would be no helicopter landing on an adjacent pad. Given the locale, it was impossible. But, Geoff had schemed with Nick as to how to get Meredith to the estate and to him. It was a lot of fun to plan. If only it would work.

97

MEREDITH

A T 10:50 AM, MEREDITH HAD HER SUITCASE, AND ALL HER SHOPPING boxes and bags, stored together just inside the roof-access door. Bradford, the Peninsula manager, had made sure that Meredith had all the assistance she needed to transport these items to the roof.

At 10:58 AM, she could hear a helicopter. As she peered out the double-paned window of the door, she watched as Booker landed his aircraft skillfully and gently on the top of the Peninsula. She was so close she could see his face as he concentrated on the touchdown. In no time, the engines were switched off, and the rotors slowed to a stop before Booker exited the craft and headed to the door.

The look on his face when he saw all the packages was one of concern, but when he felt how light they were, he relaxed. "Ms. Meredith," he laughed, "I WAS going to give you an award for how much less you packed for this trip, but now I have to reconsider."

"I'm truly sorry, Booker. I had a little retail therapy yesterday."

"A *little*?"

They laughed together as they, and two bellmen, all grabbed items and headed out to the helicopter. Booker, personally, would only allow himself to load the aircraft to assure proper weight distribution, but it didn't take long—and the packages were light. Meredith tipped the bellmen a few dollars each, and climbed into her seat next to her pilot. By now she knew how to fasten her harnesses and tighten them for her flight. She had her headphones on already when Booker climbed into his seat. After his pre-flight check, he ignited the engines and in no time they were lifting off, yet again, for some untold adventure.

Once airborne, Meredith asked, "So, Booker, where to now?"

He smiled, and replied, "Palm Springs. Have you heard of it?"

"Really?" she seemed very excited. "I've never been there. How long until we arrive?"

"We should be there in 35 minutes. We're using the helipad of a resort there. Just sit back and enjoy one of the clearest and prettiest days for flying above LA."

That she did. And, before long, they were descending to a small asphalt pad behind a sprawling resort with numerous pools teaming with children, attendant adults and teens on lounges.

Once on the ground, Booker and Meredith unfastened themselves and hopped out of the helicopter. Next to the helipad was a white Range Rover. Booker fished around in his pocket. "Here. This is for you." Booker had a key fob that he used to unlock the car. He handed her the key and an envelope. "You have a read while I unload and repack your things."

Meredith hands were shaking when she opened the envelope.

> M,
>
> Welcome to Palm Springs! I cannot wait to see you! This is your vehicle for the weekend. It has been preloaded with the GPS coordinates that will take you to me. Once you turn the vehicle on, push the button for the navigation system, and there is a GPS option. Once you push that button, you will be told exactly how to get to the security gate to our private escape. The code for the gate is *7657880# (same as my new phone number). The gate will open, and you will pull up to a second gate. Nothing else to do, except let the gate close behind you, and the second gate will open automatically. That's about it. Be very careful driving. You are precious cargo indeed…
>
> G

Booker had pulled all the luggage out of the helicopter and was putting the last few packages into the Range Rover. "Thank you, Booker. Once again, you have made me feel so safe and welcome. Will I see you Sunday?"

"You're very welcome Ms. Meredith. It has been my sincere pleasure. Sunday? Likely not. I believe you are flying directly out of Palm Springs by jet. Have a great time here."

She blew him a kiss, and this time didn't wait for the helicopter to lift off. She climbed into the Range Rover, and took a few seconds to acquaint herself with the SUV—including the new-car smell of the leather seats. She then started the engine.

It was a balmy 86 degrees. She did exactly as she was told—but carefully as she had never driver a vehicle so exquisite. Sure enough, once the GPS was enabled, a woman, sounding strangely like Dominique, directed her out of the little heliport.

98

LA QUINTA

MEREDITH TURNED ONTO A DEAD-END STREET LINED ON BOTH sides by beautiful desert homes adorned in stunning rock gardens sprinkled with drought tolerant foliage. As she approached the end of the street abutting the dramatic craggy rise of the San Juaquin Mountains, Meredith searched for the entrance the friendly GPS voice told her was there. "You have reached your destination," it said. Then she saw the camouflaged iron gate tucked between two huge boulders. "That must be it," she reasoned.

There was nothing there other than the gate, and a keypad. No address. No names. There were, however, a few hidden cameras that even if you knew they were there, and you were looking for them, you would never spot them. She pulled up next to the gate and rolled her window down. She punched in the code Geoff had left for her, and the gate reacted by sliding quietly behind one of the boulders. She pulled forward to the second gate, and sure enough, the original one slid back into place behind her temporarily trapping her vehicle.

"My God you are beautiful," Geoff's voice sounded from somewhere nearby from the desert.

"You can see me?" Meredith exclaimed.

"Oh yes, and I can't wait to…"

"Well then," she interrupted, "hurry and let me in—so that I can hurry and let *you* in!" she laughed until her throat caught.

Geoff said seriously, "Please be extra careful driving up here. The driveway can be quite scary the first time you navigate it. I'm glad it's day and not nighttime. I know you are a mountain girl, but last I checked, you were not a mountain goat.

The drive is one-way, and only allows one vehicle on it at a time, so you will not have to worry about on-coming traffic." And with that, the second gate pulled away exposing a smooth ribbon of concrete that immediately twisted left and crossed a bridge with flowing water beneath, and disappeared into a cleft. "Now, come for me," Geoff's voice said.

● ● ●

Meredith pulled into the motor court. When she had crested that last rise, and discovered what so few had had the privilege of experiencing, the words "holy shit" escaped her lips. Her eyes didn't blink as she drank in her first impressions of the Johnson Estate. Starkly modern, and with so much glass, the house seemed to disappear into the mountain behind it. And then, all that slipped from her consciousness.

Geoff stepped out of the front door, barefoot, in blue jeans with a crisp white linen shirt. He came straight to the driver's door as Meredith opened it. She had hardly uttered "Hey," when he reached in and pulled her easily from her seat and into his arms. She wrapped her bare legs around his waist, and ran her hands greedily through his wavy hair, and pulled his face to hers. Her mouth opened to welcome his. They could scarcely breath; their passionate tongues exploring each other's and the warm soft environs of their mouths. She could feel him harden between her legs as her breath shortened and her heart raced.

He put her down briefly, then picked her up in his arms and carried her into this architectural masterpiece. The car door was left open—as was the front door. She didn't even look around as she was carried to the bedroom. Her face was now nuzzling his neck, and she was delivering soft bites to his throat. Geoff placed her softly on her back on top of the bed, and then knelt on top of her. He caressed her face with both hands before moving to her soft and inviting cleavage. "Please," she begged as she struggled to unbuckle his belt. He grasped her dress at the collar, and without warning, tore it open down to her waist. Her breasts were unrestrained, and her hard nipples invited his large hands—and then his mouth. Their passion consumed them.

Geoff lifted Meredith to a sitting position and pulled her dress back away from her shoulders. He laid her back down on the bed, and unbuttoned his shirt. He then slowly removed her thong—never loosing eye contact. She, her eyes also locked on his, urgently used her feet to push down his unfastened jeans and underwear. He leaned down until their mouths were again locked—both were speaking through gasps unintelligently as she spread her legs. Meredith could feel his rock-hard erection at her entrance, and lifted her hips to welcome him. He did not hesitate, moving in slowly but strongly. She was very wet making for a delicious reunion. He pushed in to her all the way to the back of her passage. Meredith uncontrollably screamed as her emotion and gut-clenching pleasure overcame her. Geoff continued his deep and rhythmic thrusting until he could feel the two of them getting close to their climaxes. Meredith's eyes rolled back as her body gave in to the deliriously uncontrollable passion that took hold of her and shook her in violent ecstasy. As she convulsed, Geoff felt his control totally letting go, too. His throbbing gave way to a massive eruption that Meredith could feel deep within her belly that only heightened, and prolonged, her own pleasure.

Geoff collapsed on top of her softly kissing her face. He rolled over and drew her into a warm snuggle on his shoulder. Her bare chest felt so natural on his. Meredith whispered softly, "I missed you."

And Geoff replied quietly, "You are all I have thought and dreamed about since we were together in Aspen." He was softly stroking her face and neck with his fingertips. "As your helicopter disappeared into the clouds on that stormy afternoon, I actually had a small panic attack wondering what I would do if I lost you. It was an agonizing several minutes before I heard from Booker that all was fine. Of course it was; you were in Booker's excellent care. But, that experience enlightened me to the depth of my feelings for you."

He didn't see her smile. She just wrapped herself tighter to him. "Oh, Geoff, what are we going to do?"

He laughed. "First of all, I'll grab your things from the car while you freshen up. Seems we forgot them. Then, I've prepared a light lunch. I have a call I have to make at 2 PM, and it shouldn't last ninety minutes. While I am on my call, you can relax, explore, and just chill. The fridge is stocked, the wine is cold, the swimming pools refreshing and the jacuzzi hot. Please feel free to have the run of the place. I will get off as soon as I can."

This time it was Meredith's time to laugh. "You already did. Hope you left more for later." Meredith took Geoff's face into her hands, and kissed him softly on the mouth. "Thank you. I mean it. I am back in this dream. And, I love it."

And with that, Geoff helped Meredith to her feet and removed what remained of her dress. "I know where we can get you more of these."

"And, that reminds me. I'll never be able to pay you back, but my 'thank you' starts right now." She took Geoff in her arms and wrapped her fully naked body around his. She pushed herself up onto her tiptoes, and they again consumed each other in a hungry embrace.

"You are so welcome," Geoff replied. "I can't wait to see what you and Dominique picked out."

"You won't have long to wait. But, I need to get to that shower." She started giggling. "I am feeling the best of both of us escaping."

99

JESSICA

FRIDAYS WERE ALWAYS FUN AT THE OFFICE. THERE WAS A LIGHTNESS to everyone, and everything, as the minutes clicked down on the afternoon. Jessica's office mates, who had all enjoyed an impromptu TGIF party in the conference room, packed up and headed home for their weekends. Jessica was the last to leave—finishing up a few things including her weekly operations assessment of the business. She thought of Meredith as she locked the doors to her office and to the general office suite before heading downstairs to get her car. She needed to pick up a few things at the market for dinner.

Once home, and struggling with her weekend groceries, Jessica fumbled for her keys—finally getting her house key to work its magic on the lock. She pushed the door open with her foot and entered her townhome—closing the door with her same foot. She walked into the kitchen and put the groceries on the counter while she called over her shoulder, "Jazz? You home?"

"No, she isn't," came a male voice that made Jessica instinctively shriek. She spun around. There, sitting on her couch with a drink in his hand, was Bobbie. He lifted his glass towards her and tipped it slightly. "Cheers," he said.

"How did you get in here?" Jessica stammered.

"Jasmine. That daughter of yours sure is a sweet, pretty, young woman," Bobbie replied. "We had a real nice talk—her and me. I think she digs me."

Jessica could hardly speak. She had to force out her words—choosing them carefully. "Where is she?"

"Don't know. She left right after telling me that her Auntie Meredith has been staying here. I asked if she had seen her today, and she said no. I thanked her, and asked her to give her Uncle Bobbie a tour of the estate. Seems Meredith left some laundry lying around. Sorry she is such a mess. I picked them up for you, and will take them home to wash them.

As I was leaving, I asked Jasmine for a big hug for her Uncle Bob. And, boy did she ever! Pressed those little fawn-like titties right up against me. Now, if I weren't a married man, I would have…" Bobbie hesitated. "Well, let's just leave it at that. For now."

Jessica turned her back on Bobbie and started to unpack her groceries. Without looking at him, she said, "I'm going to have to ask you to leave. I wish I could be more hospitable and ask you to stay, but I am exhausted and need to prepare dinner."

"Where is she?" Bobbie said quietly.

"I don't know. I just asked you."

"Don't humor me with your stupidity. You know goddamn well who I am asking about! Where is she?" Bobbie's voice went from even and calculating to barely-controlled anger.

"I don't know, Bobbie. That's the truth. She is staying here, that's true. But, I am not her mother or her supervisor. She's a big girl. I don't keep track of her comings and goings. I have my own life."

"Where is she?" Bobbie stood and took a couple of steps in her direction.

Jessica quickly grabbed a large carving knife from the block on the sink, and held it straight in front of her, and Bobbie stopped. "Get out," she said coldly.

"Not until you tell me where your girlfriend is."

"I told you, I do not know. And that is the truth, Bobbie. Please leave now."

"Where is she?" he said, not moving a muscle.

Jessica paused, then said, "I think she may be visiting her mother. She packed a few things and left yesterday, but I was at work."

"Packed a few things, did she? Did she pack her cell phone? If she did, she isn't answering my calls."

"I imagine she did, but I promised to not call her unless there is an emergency," she explained.

"Why don't we give her a call on your line." It was a statement—not a question. "You and me. Right now. Wouldn't you say this is an emergency?"

Jess thought quickly, and said, "Sure. OK. I'll call her." She slowly backed away from Bobbie and grabbed her purse. She pulled her cell phone out, tapped in her security code, and for the briefest of moments, took her eyes off her guest. Bobbie lunged and snatched the phone away from her. Jessica screamed and dropped the knife. Bobbie could have cared less. But, he did kick it across the room.

"Let's see who you have been calling recently," he said as he scrolled her phone. "And, who has called you." He went through the list going back a few weeks. Fortunately, Meredith's regular cell number did not appear.

"Back to our little phone call," he smirked. "I think I know her number," he smiled as he dialed his wife. When the call went to voice mail, Bobbie calmly handed the phone back to Jessica. "Leave her a message, and find out where she is."

Jessica looked straight at him as she said into her phone, "Hi Meredith. Hope you are having fun wherever you are this weekend. I think you are visiting your mother. If so, I hope she is doing better. Call me and let me know, OK?" And with that, she ended the call.

Bobbie didn't move. He put his glass up to his lips and tipped his head back emptying the contents down his throat. "Thanks for the scotch. I'm leaving now. When you hear back from my wife, ask her where she is. And, oh-by-the-way, who was she kissing in the Grand Hotel elevator? And who's big private jet was she climbing onto yesterday? Seeing her mother. *BULLshit.*"

Bobbie put his glass down on the table, and calmly walked to the door. When he got there, he opened it and turned and faced Jessica. "And, tell your sexy little daughter, Jazzy, that I want to fuck her."

100

SUSIE

TREVOR LEAFED THROUGH HIS MANILA FOLDER TURNING OVER SEVeral sheets before finding what he was looking for. "We have been able to hack into CBC's computer network and did some pretty deep dives into your husband's email account. He is clearly very close to a Nicholas George. His Chief Operating Officer?"

"Yes, that's his right-hand guy," Susie responded. "They are very close, personally. Geoff doesn't do much without him—or at least without his help."

"Well, he is quite capable. Within twelve hours of our successful hack, he had discovered the breach, and put up a new seemingly impenetrable firewall. My experts will get back in, for sure, but it may take another week or two. They are very good. But here's what we found out that may be of interest to you. If your husband is having an affair, he is covering his tracks well. Most men don't. Likely, he has help. All communication leads me to this Mr. George. We have put a tail on him along with his boss—your husband."

Susie took a deep breath and looked down at her shoes for moment, then lifted her head and exclaimed, "I'm not interested in what you didn't find. While my husband's elusive nature is interesting, it's not what I am paying you—how much? $180,000? What have you found?"

Trevor pulled out several more pages, and said, "We've checked both his corporate and personal credit card accounts, and found nothing unusual." Susie exhaled deeply, but kept her eyes on Trevor. "However, Mr. George's accounts are far more telling. Seems he arranged for a house rental in Aspen at the time you say your husband was there."

"He told me that he stopped over in Aspen on his way to meetings in New York, to relax and prepare for these meetings. Nothing new there. Go on," Susie encouraged.

"Did he tell you that he rented a sail plane for the day?"

Susie was silent. "Go on," she said.

"And there was enough booze and food purchased for quite a lavish party. Did he tell you he was entertaining anyone?" he asked smiling smugly.

"Nope."

"Well, that little button you placed in your husband's briefcase is now in Palm Springs. Our tail followed him to the airport where he boarded a private jet. We obviously couldn't follow him once he was airborne, and we, as yet, haven't infiltrated the FAA to get copies of his flight plans. And, we will. But, as long as he takes his briefcase with him, that may not be necessary."

Trevor walked around the desk while turning his computer. He sat next to Susie so they were both facing the screen. "Google Earth is an amazing app," he said as he clicked through several screens. We can zoom in and get a very clear picture of exactly where his briefcase is. And, if it is sitting outdoors and there is a coin next to it, we will be able to tell if it is heads up or down." Trevor was concentrating as he stared at the screen. "Let's see where you husband is staying, shall we?"

101

LA QUINTA

"I DO NOT UNDERSTAND THE EXCESS OF YOUR AGED RECEIVABLES," Geoff said into the phone. "Can you explain this to us, and how Wonderland Energy plans to significantly collect on these receivables before they turn into write-offs?" He stood, ran his fingers through his hair and walked around to the large plate-glass window that silently opened his office to the shimmering pools and magnificent hardscape that defined this masterpiece of a property. "You're taking notes on this, right, Nick?"

As he was listening to the responses from Wonderland's Chief Financial Officer, and their executive team, he was suddenly distracted. Meredith emerged outdoors wearing a robe and carrying a handbag. She was maybe sixty feet away from him but seemed unaware that he was watching her. She settled next to a chaise lounge and kicked off her flip-flops. From her handbag, she pulled out a towel, some magazines and some baby oil. She then untied her robe, and pulled it off her shoulders—letting it fall to the ground. Meredith was completely nude. She rose to her tiptoes and stretched—exposing herself to the warmth of the caressing sunshine and cloudless sky. Her smooth skin, and beautifully proportioned figure, took Geoff's breath away—as well as his concentration.

Nick was now saying something, but Geoff didn't hear.

Meredith leaned over and picked up her robe - draping it over the adjacent chair. She laid her towel out on the chaise lounge and sat. She picked up the baby oil and unsnapping the lid, generously drizzled the oil over her shoulders and breasts. Putting the bottle down, she then proceeded to knead the oil into her skin. She started with her shoulders, but her hands quickly moved to her breasts and stomach where she took her time enjoying the application of this deliciously slippery liquid, and continued until her entire body was glistening.

Geoff's total attention was now on Meredith as she lay down on her back—a pair of sunglasses the only thing that covered her. Geoff's view was from the side, and he watched as she plumped a towel behind her head and plugged into her earbuds. She parted her legs slightly and stretched her arms at her side allowing the sun to erase those embarrassing tan lines. Dominique had been insistent. "As soon as you can, get your gear off, and get that beautiful body of yours in the sun. You got it, girl?" she had said as they were parting. "That red dress from Valentino demands it."

As she drifted off into a deliciously exposed slumber, Meredith smiled to herself. She couldn't get her mind off this latest fantasy, her shopping adventure with her personal, and stunning and mysterious, fashion consultant—and the beautiful man that made it all possible.

102

BOBBIE

BOBBIE SIPPED FROM A BEER AS HE OPENED THE <u>GRAND JUNCTION</u> <u>Sentinel</u>. It was Wednesday's edition that someone had left on Jay's kitchen table, but today was Friday morning, December 5th. He couldn't remember the last time he woke up without a hangover or still high from booze, drugs, pot or all three. Today was no different, but the beer was helping. Hair of the dog. After visiting Jessica, he had returned to the Pussy Whip for a night of pool and tequila shots. He didn't remember driving home, but his truck was parked safely inside Jay's barn.

The lead article was titled, "Suicide Claims Life of Second District Executive." Bobbie smiled. The article read in part, "Highly admired and universally adored HR Director for the Granite School District, Janet Jacobs was found unresponsive in her home by colleagues late Tuesday when she failed to show up for important meetings and couldn't be reached by phone. It had appeared that she had taken her own life. Her colleagues were stunned, and all who were interviewed insisted that Ms. Jacobs had everything to live for, and had led a very full and seemingly satisfying life. Her passing was the second among the leadership of the Granite School District. Ten days ago, District Superintendent, Don DeLatore, tragically died in a house fire that completely consumed his home. Both had worked together for years, and were recently looking into the circumstances behind the suspension of Granite High football coach, Bobby Edmonson. The Sentinel tried to reach Coach Edmonson for comment but calls to him went unreturned."

"Bull fucking shit," Bobbie said to no one. "Called me for comment. Right. Wouldn't you just love getting a fucking comment from me." He belched loudly, and instantly felt better.

His thoughts darkened as he suddenly got an overwhelming urge to hunt down his wife and find out what the hell was going on with her—and who she was fucking. Bobbie's rage boiled up to the back of his throat. He would kill that cheating bastard first—very slowly and very painfully - with her tied up and watching. Then, he would kill her—but only after releasing the cunt into the woods.

Immediately, his mind started planning his next visit to Jessica's. He was absolutely certain that she was his ticket to finding his Meredith. He would just need to punch that ticket.

But first, he had two other places to go - and people to see. It was 10 AM. Time was a-wastin'.

103

LA QUINTA

THE RICH AROMA OF GARLIC FILTERED PLEASANTLY THROUGHOUT the house, and Meredith was hungry. She and Geoff had largely skipped lunch although the meat and cheese platter coupled with the Sauvignon Blanc, after their reunion, had been divine. Dominique had been insistent that this first entrance in her new casual outfit would set the tone for the entire trip.

She had said, "You want to take his breath away. Show him enough skin to be hypnotically inviting. The rest of your beautiful body you want covered in an enticingly loose, light-weight fabric that is as erotically accessible to him as it is stimulatingly delicious to your naked body beneath. You need to enjoy being in it, as much as he will be fantasizing about getting you out of it. All night."

Meredith shook her head and smiled as she thought back to yesterday afternoon and evening with Dominique dipping into and out of such famous stores as she had only seen and heard of in the movies. Some of the small, unknown, boutiques also held items for her that she knew no other woman would be wearing. They had been on a schedule, but the whole affair had felt unrushed. Meredith loved the attention Dominique paid to her. Particularly when she adjusted each fitting with the seamstress in front of the mirror—pulling here and tightening there—to make sure the final product would be a perfect fit for her "sumptuous ass and perfect tits" as she called them.

It was soon time for that grand entrance. She walked to the bed to where her Dolce & Gabbana floral print cotton dress lay. She picked it up and slipped it on. It felt exquisite and cool against her sunburned skin. Then, she stepped into

a pair of what she guessed were impossibly expensive Christian Louboutin high
-heeled shoes.

There were no price tags on anything they looked at or purchased. Dominique never discussed prices with her or the store employees. She had just said,
"Mr. Geoff wanted to make sure you had a few special things for your trip, and
for you to not fret about the cost." The purchases were made by Dominique out
of sight of her client.

* * *

Tonight, Geoff was preparing skewered salmon interspersed with sourdough toast
squares and prosciutto. He had been soaking the Kale for the last hour in anticipation of tossing it together with some arugula and avocado in a home-made lemon
vinaigrette—he was hoping would be the perfect accompaniment to a simple
light meal on a warm, breezy evening.

Geoff poured himself another glass of Chardonnay, and adjusted his apron.
He was being careful not to spill on his linen slacks and collarless cotton shirt.
When he heard footsteps come up behind him, he turned and stopped dead in his
tracks. There before him, Meredith stood in the most beautifully simple and airy
outfit. Her enticing figure was perfectly wrapped and presented. The dress was
mid-thigh and cut daringly low. He audibly exhaled, and reached behind himself
and untied his black apron. He then held out his hands inviting her. She came
to him, and they embraced gently—neither saying a thing. Geoff softly stroked
Meredith's back with his finger tips.

There was something different about their embrace that Geoff couldn't immediately figure out. Then, he got it. She was four inches taller. He had never been
with her when she was wearing heels, and the sensation of their chests and their
faces aligning was a new and wonderful experience. Why did he get such joy out
of something so simple?

He broke the embrace and with both hands on her shoulders, he lightly
pushed her away so that he could have another look at her. Her eyes were wet; her
make-up running. He brushed away her tears with both thumbs, and said, "Hey.
What's up, M?"

"Oh, Geoff." She looked down, then lifted her head so that their eyes locked.
"I am a princess in your presence. And, I feel so unworthy; yet, so incredibly
happy and lucky. Why me? Why did fate find me? Of all people." She shook her
head slowly.

Geoff waited until Meredith was quiet, and he said, "Why ME, Meredith? Of all people. I am a prince tonight—intoxicated by your beauty that radiates from your heart. You are literally sunshine to my soul. I want to do nice things for you. I want to buy you nice things. Why? Because, you are so unabashedly appreciative in such an innocent sort of way. I love that you are interested enough in me to spend time with me. Please accept all this with the intent with which it was planned: for us to explore and enjoy each other—in a place that allows us to do just that - unfettered, and uninterrupted - by the worries and pressures of our lives."

Meredith nodded again, this time with understanding. A smile came to her face as she slipped free, and snatched a tissue from the counter. She started laughing as she turned away and blew her nose. "Sorry!" she exclaimed. "Can I help with dinner?" she said, still laughing.

* * *

They ate outdoors. Meredith had come back from freshening her make-up, and sat at a very casual, but beautiful, table poolside. A carpet of diamonds—the city lights—lay far below them. They had plated their meals and grabbed a fresh bottle of white wine to ice in the bucket next to Geoff's chair. Dinner prep had been spontaneous and fun. They had laughed and joked and told stories, and each had shared just a little bit more about themselves. Now they sat across from each other.

Meredith raised her glass and asked, "You ready to continue our game?"

Geoff picked up his own glass and responded, "And, what game would that be?"

And she said, "The Question Game, of course. Only this time, I get to go first."

He looked at her and nodded, "Shoot."

She smiled coyly and started in, "Remember: 100% honesty here. OK. Let's start with 'What is missing in your sex life at home that you would like to experience this weekend?'"

Geoff sputtered, but gathered himself. "Skinny dipping."

Meredith laughed and said, "That can be arranged!"

But, Geoff continued on. "Metaphorically. My wife, Susie, is sweet and a great mother. Don't get me wrong here. But, sex with her redefines 'vanilla.' The lights are always off. We are always in a bed. It's almost always the missionary position. No foreplay. Rarely, an orgasm. On her part. So, I guess I would say, I would love some adventurous sex with a partner seeking the same gratification. How about you?"

Meredith felt very comfortable with Geoff, and said, "It's all about him. When he wants it. How he wants it. His way or the highway, so to speak. I want the freedom to explore my body and its pleasures, and be the aggressor from time to time. He thinks if I am being the aggressor, that it is somehow a hit to his masculinity. I want to share my fantasies with someone who would be excited to help me fulfill those—without judgement. I want to feel safe and loved, unconditionally."

"You haven't really answered the question. What would you like to experience this weekend that is missing at home?"

The answers came quickly, "Sex outdoors, sex toys, sixty-nine, a G-spot orgasm…"

"That can be arranged!" Geoff interrupted, laughing.

She got an impish smile on her face. "Would you?"

"It would be my pleasure," he retorted.

They picked up their wine glasses and clinked them softly.

"You know what else?" she asked. "How would you feel if I told you that I had never been with another woman, but had just recently been awakened with those feelings?"

"Go on," he said with interest.

"Dominique. There was something about her. Her confidence. Her physicality. Her beauty. She possessed the confidence I would like to have someday. So free with her inhibitions and her body. I admired her. Not the same way I admire you, but in a purely erotic sexual way."

Geoff thought about that for a minute, then replied, "They say that all women have some lesbian tendencies imbedded in their DNA, but most are too afraid, or morally bound, to do anything about it. Not much I can do about that here this weekend, but your honesty is refreshing."

"Refreshing?"

"Confirmation of trust. I love that we can talk openly about anything. I am sitting across from a treasure. 'A lover who won't blow my cover.' But more."

Meredith arose and picked up the now near-empty wine bottle from the ice bucket and held it to her chest allowing the ice water and ice chips to soak her dress top and stimulate her nipples. "God, it's hot out here."

She then poured what was remaining into Geoff's glass. She took a step back away from the table, and never losing Geoff's gaze, she started at her top button, and slowly, one-by-one, released the restrictions that held her in. And, when she had finally unbuttoned her dress down to her waist she pulled it back off her shoulders, and let it fall to her feet. There was nothing underneath. Stepping out from her dress in her Louboutin's, she boldly walked over to Geoff and pulled his head between her breasts. She nuzzled her face in his long, wavy, hair and said, "Care to join me for a refreshing dip before dessert?"

The question was rhetorical. Meredith backed away, stepped out of her heels, walked over to the edge of the beautifully lit and glassy pool, stopped for a second and looked back. She winked; then turned quickly - presenting her beautifully sculpted rear end, newly sunburned—and dove in head first.

104

GEOFF

IT WAS 5:42 AM, AND GEOFF SLIPPED OUT OF BED TO GO MAKE SOME coffee. Meredith was sound asleep, and he darkened the glass walls of the bedroom so that the lights from the kitchen and the workout room wouldn't awaken her. He grabbed his iPhone.

Once in the kitchen, he prepped the espresso machine with freshly ground beans, and started to work on last night's wonderful mess. He plugged in his earbuds and touched Pandora bringing up one of his favorites: 80's Rock. Prince started playing "Erotic City":

"Every time I comb my hair

Thoughts of you get in my eyes.

I'm a sinner, I don't care

I just want your creamy thighs."

An hour later, the kitchen was spotless, and he had prepared all the fixings for their breakfast: vegetarian omelets, crisp bacon and hash browns. He would throw it all together as soon as Meredith arose. He then went to work preparing lunch, and their backpack, for their late morning hike. The day promised to be warm, but not hot, with freshening breezes kicking up in the afternoon. The caterers would arrive around 4 PM.

• • •

Jeff walked outdoors and made his way all the way to the leading edge of the lower pool that overlooked the city. As he had promised himself, he wouldn't let email, texts and voice mail get in the way of this weekend. But, he thought he should check in nonetheless - as well as give Nick a call. He activated his phone, and the pinging started in earnest. He started with his texts. There were a few from his executive assistant, Cindy, which could wait until Monday. Most of his texts were personal - not like his email. He then saw a text from Susie. "What are you doing in Palm Springs? Thought you were going to LA. Call me."

Shit. Think. Geoff dialed Nick. He picked up on the second ring, "Hey Boss." Obviously, he had been up for a while and had had his Saturday morning coffee. "I hope you are not calling about what I think you are calling about."

"What would that be?" he responded.

"Well, for starters, someone has their nose up my ass. And, if whoever-they-are are that interested in a full cavity search of my rectum, I can only imagine the great lengths they are going through to explore yours." He sounded a bit more agitated than normal.

Nick continued, "Our new firewall is holding, but our email servers are under assault again. Whomever wants to snoop around at CBC is determined—and good. And, I have shaken two tails off my ass in the last twenty-four hours. No doubt I was being followed. I think whoever-it-is wants us to know that they are amongst us. Keep your eyes open."

"Geoff said, "Now that you mention it, Susie sent me a text today asking what I was doing in Palm Springs. What do you make of that?"

"Your darling sweet wife may be the instigator of all this. Remember, I told you she called and was asking some very pointed and personal questions about you last week. Hey, listen, Geoff. Be careful. I know the house is highly secluded and secure, but…"

Geoff cut him off. "OK. OK. Got it. Say Nick, I need a personal favor from you ASAP. Did I remember reading in Dominique's bio that she was also a licensed masseuse?"

Nick was a little put off by the quick change of subject. "Yep. At least now I know you read what I send you. Even though you don't listen to me," Nick then laughed. "What about it?"

"Can you have her cancel her appointments for this afternoon and hitch a ride, along with her massage table, with Booker out here to La Quinta? We'll have her back in Beverly Hills for a late supper. We'll leave the Range Rover at the small resort helipad along with the same instructions for access and entry in the Rover. Anytime after 3 PM would be great." There was silence. "Nick? You there?"

"Yes. Sorry. Just writing a few things down. Done. You can count on me. And Geoff?"

"Yep."

"Be very, VERY, careful, OK. We don't want a stupidly expensive weekend tryst turning into an insanely expensive divorce."

"Ten-four, good buddy."

Just as he hung up, Geoff heard a big splash behind him. It startled him. He looked around quickly. There, gliding under the water quietly, was the most beautiful, raven-haired, brunette: her naked body ascending up to the pool's edge at Geoff's feet. She had a big smile on her face. Geoff looked down on her beauty. Her face radiant, her breasts soft and wet.

"Care to join me for another dip before breakfast?" she teased.

She didn't have to ask twice. As Geoff was peeling off his workout shorts, shoes and sleeveless t-shirt she asked, "So what was your phone call about this morning?"

"Absolutely nothing at all. Just making sure all our 'i's' are dotted and our 't's' crossed for our day ahead. It should be memorable."

And with that, Geoff jumped into the pool for his second skinny dip in ten hours.

105

BOBBIE

"**H**IS NAME IS GEOFF CAMERON. SAYS HERE THAT HE IS THE CHIEF Executive of a firm he founded some seventeen years ago in San Francisco. Cameron, Boone & Covington, L.L.C.—whatever LLC means."

Mal was very proud of himself for triangulating all of this with the information gathered by the Wrecking Crew. Jay had taken a rooftop picture of the private jet he saw in Grand Junction in which he thought he saw Meredith get on board. The tail had a distinctive logo on it: CBC, and through the wonder of the Internet, Tommy was able to track down what company owned it. Tommy, the Grand Junction air traffic controller, confirmed all arrival and departure times for the aircraft, and illegally through his contacts with the Denver FAA, got the destination off the flight plan filed by the pilot. Santa Monica. Then, Mal went on the CBC company website and downloaded pictures and names of all key executives. And while the elevator kissing video was grainy, it didn't take long to make a match. The Crew all agreed.

Bobbie was already on his third scotch. "I'm going to kill that mother fucker. Right in front of my *fucking* whore. All I have done for that ungrateful cunt is provide for her and work my ass off to give us a life. A great life. And, this is the thanks I get?"

"This. Will. Be. Fun."

106

LA QUINTA

GEOFF HAD INSISTED THAT THEY TAKE BOTH THEIR VEHICLES ON the hike. He wanted to leave one of them, the Range Rover, at the heliport where Meredith had been dropped off. He wouldn't say why. He just smiled and said, "It's a surprise. Trust me."

They were now on their way up Highway 74 to an unmarked trailhead exactly 14.8 miles west from the intersection of Highway 111. When the highway shrunk into two lanes and started snaking its way high up in the foothills, Meredith asked, "Where are you taking me?"

"There is supposedly a rarely-used, and secluded, hiking trail that winds its way amongst desert boulders and vegetation, has exceptional views and terminates at a waterfall. My research says that the round trip is 7.2 miles, and is 'moderately strenuous.' But, apparently the seclusion and the beauty are worth it. And, my beautifully sculpted, M, you appear to be in excellent shape. We should be at the waterfall around noon where we hopefully can enjoy a little picnic I prepared for us this morning."

"Nothing you share with me is little," she laughed.

"Let's just say that my backpack will be a lot lighter on our return."

As they headed out up the small road towards the trailhead, Meredith engaged Geoff in a conversation about his job and his company. She was so curious, and he relished speaking with someone who seemed so interested in his work life. Before he knew it, Geoff had passed mile marker 17, and realized that he had driven straight by their destination. He pulled over, and carefully made a U-turn. In a few minutes they were parking at a small dirt turn-out. There were no other cars.

Geoff and Meredith jumped out of their vehicle and reunited at the tailgate. Geoff grabbed the backpack, flung it up on his shoulders. They found the small trail, unmarked, but leading them away from the road towards the deserted foothills beyond. He let her lead.

It was a much more physically demanding hike than what Geoff had envisaged. They had seen no other hikers—surprising for a Saturday. But, this was an unmarked trail that only the locals knew about. By the time they reached the waterfall and its pristine pool, they were both sweating and hot. Geoff put the backpack down and pulled our two large bottles of cool water. They drank deeply sating their thirst.

Meredith said, "I need to pee. I'll be right back."

Geoff replied, "Wait a sec." He rummaged around in the front pocket of the backpack and pulled out a Baggie with tissue paper inside. "Here," he said handing it to her.

"You think of everything. Is there anything you can't do?" she smiled.

"I'm not good with blood and guts, so don't fall and hurt yourself," he chided.

When she returned a few minutes later, she found a large blanket spread out across a large flat rock that had been heating in the sun now for hours. On it were deli sandwiches, salads, and plastic wine glasses.

"So, when you asked me last night what was my favorite sandwich, I am guessing I will find something similar here?"

"Exactly," he deadpanned.

She sat by his side as he reached into the pack and drew out an ice pack wrapped around a bottle of his favorite ZD Chardonnay. He popped the cork, and poured each of them a generous serving.

"Shall we enjoy a glass before the main course?" Geoff said.

Meredith lifted her glass to his and they toasted. She said, "To new adventures."

And he replied, "To being adventurous."

* * *

It was now 3 PM, and Geoff and Meredith made their way down hill towards their transportation and their relatively quick drive back to the Johnson Estate. They had met up with no other hikers, and enjoyed the tranquility that this deserted trail gave to them. They had stopped several times on their hike to kiss and cuddle but had chickened out when it came to skinny-dipping in the pool below the waterfall. The dry wind had picked up, and they were physically tired and sore when they reached their Mercedes SUV. It didn't take long for them to mount up and head back to their home base.

Meredith inquired about the Range Rover they had left at the heliport, but Geoff had insisted, "All would be taken care of; not to worry."

As they wound their way back down Highway 74, they were unaware of the activity at the Estate. In the motor court, there were two catering vans, a white Range Rover and a small wrapped box sitting by the front door. As Geoff punched in the gate code, and safely entered onto the serpentine driveway, he was unaware of the drone that was hovering high above them departing the airspace of the Estate—having already completed its mission.

107

BOOKER

BOOKER SAT IN THE SMALL AIRPORT CAFÉ ENJOYING A DOUBLE espresso and reading the morning paper. He had just returned to Santa Monica after his latest delivery to Palm Springs. He had been told to stay there through the weekend in case there were any other missions to be flown. And, he was being put up at the world-famous Shutters on the Beach Hotel—yep, on the beach by the Santa Monica Pier. He was getting to really enjoy this temporary work—which he hoped would turn permanent, soon.

Booker's thoughts were interrupted by a male voice that said, "Excuse me, sir, but can I grab this chair and sit at your table? All other spots are taken."

"Sure. Help yourself, " Booker replied. "Must be a busy morning." He went back to reading his paper.

"Sir, I don't mean to pester you, but that logo on your shirt. I've seen it before. And, it's on your helicopter. What does it stand for?"

Booker replied, "Oh, it's the company logo of a firm that I pilot some aircraft for."

"I see. Fun job?"

"The best."

Sorry to be so nosey, but I am an air traffic controller from a smaller city, and I always see these guys coming and going on these beautiful private planes. Some are pretty spectacular—and expensive, I am guessing. How much does a job like that pay?"

"Not as much as you might think. And, anyway, I am currently working as a contract pilot who is looking to get hired on permanently so I can get some benefits and a consistent paycheck."

What did you say is the name of the company that you are working for?

"Right now, CBC. Cameron Boone and Covington out of San Francisco. Great folks. Why you ask?"

"No reason. Just curious." The younger man was silent for a while sipping his own coffee. Then he asked, "Say, you want to make a few extra bucks in your spare time? Umm…?" he questioned clearly searching for a name.

"The name's Booker, and sure, I could always use some extra cash. What do you have in mind?"

The younger man said, "Look, I am developing an app that tracks private aviation traffic patterns across America. The commercial flights are all logged, and that data is being mined by some pretty inventive retailers and service providers. But, no one, to my knowledge, is tracking the privates. I am travelling around to all the private aviation hubs and soliciting help from pilots like yourself. I give them $35 for every flight plan they can confirm. I then make a record and plot them on this cool app. So, if you flew three flights today and had one still to fly, and you can let me know where you have been, and also importantly where you are going, I drop $140—tax free—into your bank account using a secure process over your cell phone. Completely confidential. What do you think?"

Booker, finding this young man very nice and approachable, said, "So, if I let you know where I have been flying yesterday, today and the rest of the weekend, you can pay me?"

"That's right."

"Do I need to sign a contract?" Booker inquired.

"Oh no, that isn't necessary. We're just a small start-up who is trying to keep this under wraps until we can make a little something out of it. You give us your flight plans and we deliver cash. So, if we ever don't put cash in your account, you can just stop providing us the information. Sound fair?"

"Yeah, sounds harmless enough. So, let me test this out. The jet outside is also ours; you can tell by the logo. I fly the Long Ranger beside it. I know the plane in the last few days has flown from SF to Grand Junction, Colorado, made a pick-up and flew here to Santa Monica. Then it flew back to San Francisco for a pick-up then flew on to Palm Springs then it returned here. And, I flew from San Francisco to here yesterday for a pick-up and delivery to Beverly Hills. Then returned to Santa Monica for an overnight; then, flew a round trip yesterday to La Quinta and another one today. So twelve legs in total."

The young man was writing all this down. When he finished he said, "Let's see…that's twelve legs at $35 per leg." He did some quick math on his paper.

"$420. What's your cell phone number?" Booker told him. The young man typed a few entries on his phone, and in no time, Booker's phone pinged, and he could see that a deposit receipt had be funneled to his account in the amount of $420. "Does that work for you?"

Booker was impressed. Leave it to this younger generation to develop all these apps—and, transfer money effortlessly through your cell phone. "Sure does," he said. "How do I interact with you? And, what did you say your name was?"

The young man pulled a card from his pocket and handed it to Booker. Booker read it. Thomas Burnes. Air Traffic Controller, Grand Junction, Colorado. A P.O. Box address. And, a cell phone number. "Small world," Booker said. "As I mentioned, one of our pilots was just in Grand Junction."

Thomas responded, "I know, right? Small world. Anyway, all you have to do is text the flight plans or trips to me. It's more helpful if I can get them in advance. Then, I will transfer funds. Deal?" Thomas held out his hand. Booker took it and shook it.

"It'll be a pleasure doing business with you," Booker replied confidently.

Young Thomas got up and walked out of the café. He had a spring in his step. He had just hit the rare inside-the-park home run. Their hunch had been right. Go to Santa Monica and wait. They would show up. They did. Tommy couldn't wait to share all this with the Wrecking Crew.

108

LA QUINTA

GEOFF AND MEREDITH PULLED INTO THE CARPORT AT A LITTLE PAST 4 PM, tired and dirty. Meredith was surprised with the activity at the house. There were people walking about; two of them unloading items from one of the vans.

"What's all this?" Meredith said turning to Geoff.

"Just another little surprise. Our formal dinner tonight is right here. Wolfgang Puck is catering. And, I don't think we could find a better view."

Once again, Meredith was rendered speechless. "Wolfgang Puck?" She just shook her head. "I didn't think I could eat again for a week after those yummy sandwiches and accompaniments on the trail today. I guess I'm just going to have to suffer through another meal with you!"

Geoff chuckled as he jumped out of the vehicle to fetch the backpack. Meredith groaned as she slid out of her seat. "God, I'm sore. You really put me through quite a workout."

"You haven't seen anything yet. Just wait for your post-dinner workout. Hope you can handle it." He winked.

"Don't you worry, young man, I will be fully recovered by then. But, I need a hot shower—both to wash this delicious grit off my body, and to sooth these tired, aching, muscles."

Something caught Meredith's attention, and she turned towards the front entry. There, standing barefoot in a white smock with a towel over her shoulder, was Dominique. Stunningly beautiful. Meredith jaw came open, she turned quickly to Geoff with questioning, raised, eyes.

"Dominique is a licensed masseuse. So, in addition to helping you get ready for our dinner tonight, she is here to help you relax and work out some of those tight, sore, muscles."

"Hi Meredith!" Dominique waved. "Didn't think I would be seeing you again so soon."

Meredith smiled warmly and responded, "Great to see you, too." As she stood there taking this all in, she couldn't help but think back to her admission to Geoff last night. Meredith felt a little short of breath and flush. "So, you're a masseuse? If your hands are as good as your taste in clothing, this will be memorable."

Dominique responded, "Why don't you jump in the shower, and I'll meet you in the back room in fifteen minutes. My table is all set up."

"Sure. Sounds terrific, Dominique." Meredith turned to Geoff and smiled broadly. She said softly so that only he could hear, "Thank you. The fantasy weekend continues, apparently. Pay back is tonight." She lifted up to her tiptoes and kissed him softly on the mouth. Holding his face in her hands she said, "See you at dinner."

As soon as Meredith had disappeared, Geoff walked over to Dominique and handed her a small envelope with the letter M on the front. He then spoke quietly to her. Dominique listened attentively, nodding her head. Finally, she said, "I completely understand. The massage will be special—and memorable. I promise."

109

SUSIE

GEOFF THOUGHT THIS WOULD BE A GOOD TIME TO CALL HOME. HE dialed Susie on her cell, and she picked up on the first ring. "So, how's Palm Springs?"

"It's really nice," Geoff said without skipping a beat or acting in the least bit nervous.

"I thought you were going to LA," she pressed.

"I am. Palm Springs is LA."

"No, it isn't," she said. "Palm Springs is Palm Springs."

"It's a two hour drive from the airport," he exaggerated. "Anyway, everywhere around here is a two-hour drive from the airport. You have never questioned me about entertaining clients before. Heck, I was just in Aspen, which is a lot farther from Grand Junction than Palm Springs is from LA Downtown. You didn't question me then. This is a much better place to say 'thank you' to important financial backers of the Firm than smoggy LA. Why do I feel like I am being interrogated?"

"I'm sorry. But, you haven't been acting lately like the Geoff Cameron I have known intimately for so many years. Maybe I am being overly sensitive. But, the kids are feeling it, too. You have been missing in their lives—and seem unattached in mine."

"You know how busy I have been putting all these deals together. It has been the busiest I have ever been. For sure, coming to Palm Springs has been good for me to blow off a little steam with a few clients. Just like my taking a couple of days in Aspen before my New York trip. How did you know that I was in Palm Springs?"

"One of my girlfriends saw you in town."

"I wasn't in town. In fact, I am in La Quinta at a private home. Who saw me? Why didn't she come up and say 'hi'?"

"It was Rhonda from my spin class. She doesn't know you well enough to intrude."

"I see. OK. Anyway, I'll be home tomorrow, late afternoon. Let's barbeque at the house with all the kids," Geoff suggested.

"I am sick and tired of cooking meals in this house—I'm getting claustrophobic," Susie blurted. "I want to go out to dinner for once."

"That's fine. Let's go out to that local Mexican restaurant that the kids love so much."

"No. Let's go to a restaurant that I love, and leave the kids at home. We need to talk."

Geoff didn't want to engage any more as the conversation was laboring.

"Listen, Susie, I've got to go. We'll catch-up tomorrow. You pick the place. You are welcome to meet the plane and we can have dinner in the city, or we can leave after I get home. Just let me know so I can arrange for Frank to pick me up, OK?"

She had already hung up.

110

GEOFF

"**S**AY, DID YOU GET THE LITTLE PACKAGE I HAD DELIVERED TO THE house this afternoon?" It was Nick. Was Geoff ever happy to hear his friend, and confidante, calling.

"No, sorry. I must have been distracted. What did you have delivered?"

"That necklace you wanted for Meredith. Shit, Geoff, you better go find it. It was crazy expensive."

"How do you know it was actually delivered?" Geoff asked.

"Get this…It was delivered by drone by a company called PinPoint. Talk about a company we should buy in our tech fund. I received a confirming email with a link to a video showing the actual drop off at your front door. Here's the cool part: It uses a technology called 'what3words'—an app developed that has covered the globe in a grid of one-meter squares, and each of those squares is uniquely named with three different English words. All I had to do was find you on their satellite imagery, find a square meter on the front entry, type in the three words associated with that square, and just like that, your delivery was executed with pinpoint accuracy."

"That is very cool. And, very scary, too. How's the security breach at CBC unfolding?"

"Good so far. We haven't seen any other unwanted assaults today, but it is Saturday. We are actually working on backing into the hacker. Hopefully, we will find out who it is before they can hack us again."

Geoff changed the subject. "I think you are right about Susie. I just got a call from her, and she was clearly suspicious. She knew I was in Palm Springs. I asked her how she knew, and she said a friend saw me. Impossible."

Nick waited a few moments then slowly imparted, "Geoff. Please listen to me. I think you have had your fun. Enjoy tonight, and tomorrow morning, then cut this thing off. You are risking too much.

"Nick, you just don't understand. If I asked you to stop seeing Stephanie for the good of the firm, would you do it?"

"Yes." He hesitated for effect. Then added, "But, I'm not married, and neither is she. You, my friend, are. You have three great kids, you're a little league coach and you are the pillar of the Bay Area community. And, you are the 'lead from the front,' 'lead-by-example,' heart and soul of Cameron, Boone & Covington. As your Chief Operating Officer, I will continue to do anything you ask of me, but as your friend, I think you need to walk from this little affair."

Geoff closed his eyes. "I can't."

111

LA QUINTA

MEREDITH WAS STILL IN WITH DOMINIQUE, SO GEOFF HAD THE master suite to himself. He showered and shaved, and tried to put out of his mind the two phone conversations, with a probing wife and an imploring friend. Tonight was going to be special, and he wanted to be present for it all.

He hadn't told Meredith about the tuxedo he was putting on; he wanted to surprise her. He loved surprising her—even in the smallest of ways. The shear delight always oozed from her, and her reactions were like a drug. He couldn't wait for her to come in to the great room and to see him in a tux. What would be her reaction? And, what would be her reaction to the necklace?

• • •

Jeff fixed himself a Grey Goose martini—the same drink he was enjoying six months ago when he met Meredith. He walked into the kitchen. It was buzzing with activity. He spoke warmly with the staff, and inspected the hors d'oeuvres. How could anyone create such beautiful little pieces of art, and then watch them being eaten? It must give them the same type of joy he got by giving to others.

As Geoff was chatting with the cooks, Dominique stuck her head in the door. "Mr. Geoff? I'm leaving now. Everything went as planned." Geoff grabbed her massage table and followed her to the front door. They stepped outside.

Geoff said, "So, did Meredith enjoy her special treatment?"

"She was a little stiff at first, but I just let my fingers work their magic." She winked. "I hope I can be of service again in the future."

Geoff reached into his breast pocket and pulled out an envelope that had ten $1,000 notes in it. "I'm certainly guessing our paths will cross again. Should that be the case, my associate, Nick, will be in touch." He extended his hand, and they shook. He walked her out to the Range Rover, and loaded the table into the back. He opened her car door and said, "Drive carefully. The helicopter is waiting for you at the resort. Thank you, again, for changing your plans for us."

She smiled broadly and said, "The pleasure was all mine."

● ● ●

Geoff was outdoors by the pool. It was a warm, breezy night, and he was enjoying his second ice-cold martini. The stars above seemed closer than the lights far below, and he took a deep, deliberate, breath to calm his anticipatory nerves.

"Hey."

He turned around. He knew to expect something special, but he was unprepared for this. Meredith stood before him, and said nothing more. She was in a full-length red dress that fit her perfectly. The halter-top exposed her back to the warm, breezy, evening and presented her plunging neckline between her tightly wrapped and ample breasts. A slit up the side of the dress exposed beautiful, muscular legs, calves and thighs. She wore a different pair of heals—Jimmy Choo's that were black with red accents. He circled her slowly, shaking his head, drinking in all of her; he didn't want to miss a thing. He didn't think he did.

"Are you going to offer me a drink?" she said breaking into her heart-warming smile. "Nice tux, by the way. When I have my drink, I am going to circle you - leering at *your* goods." They both laughed.

"Of course, you can have the drink - and the leering session." Geoff smirked. "What'll you have?"

"I'll have what you're having."

"Coming right up." Geoff lifted his hand slightly and a bartender appeared instantly. Without taking his eyes off Meredith he said, "Please prepare this beautiful woman an ice-cold Grey Goose martini, extra dry, with a twist of lemon."

"Yes sir!"

Geoff put his drink down and the two fell into each other. Geoff reached down and tipped up Meredith's chin so that he could look directly into her. "You are absolutely stunning," he said. "Seeing you all dressed up excites me in a way you wouldn't understand."

Meredith's martini arrived, and they had to pull themselves apart. She held her glass in one hand while picking up Geoff's drink and gently handing it to him. "To us," she toasted.

"To us," he replied.

They touched glasses and each had a generous sip. He took her by the hand, and they walked together to the edge of the property overlooking the city. Her gown flowed effortlessly behind her. As they walked, he was obsessed with the beauty of her. When they got to a place where they could be by themselves, Meredith stopped, but never let go of his hand. She turned and said, "Thank you. Thank you for all of this." She hesitated. Geoff wanted to say something, but she held up her finger to his lips. "I'm overwhelmed and I'm scared," she continued. "I'm falling for you, Geoff. There is no other way to say it."

Geoff finished his martini, and took Meredith's half-consumed drink, and put their glasses on a table. He took her into his arms, and wrapped her up as tightly as he could. "I want everything for you. I want everything *with* you. I don't know what I would do without you in my life."

He then reached into his jacket pocket and pulled out a long jewelry box. Handing it to her, he said, "This is a little something for you that hopefully expresses how much you mean to me. It will go particularly well with your gown." She was speechless. "Actually," he said, "let me open it for you."

He took the box from her hands and opened it. He reached in and pulled out a platinum and diamond necklace. He moved behind her, and clasped the necklace around her neck. Then he moved back to have a frontal look at her. It was even better on than in the showcase at Barney's. It literally tumbled diamonds in strands down her neck and into her cleavage.

"Let's just say that I am falling for you, too."

• • •

They sat under the clear desert sky—the stars a canopy of diamonds over them. The pool was beautifully lit, and the Jacuzzi above it was steaming and ready. The white linen tablecloth accentuated the utensils of the evening: crystal water and wine glasses, sterling silver flatware and napkin holders. There were more forks and spoons than Meredith had ever seen. She picked up one of the forks in the middle of the set to the left of her plate and twirled it in front of her face. It was surprisingly heavy.

"What are we dong with these? Operating on the wounded?" she laughed.

"No, actually, Wolfgang Puck has prepared a tasting menu for tonight. There will be nine courses, paired with appropriate wine. The caterers have arranged the silverware to match the courses. All we have to do is start from the outside, and work our way in," Geoff explained.

"Sounds like my plans for you later tonight," she winked. "Does that also explain all the wine glasses?"

"Yes. As a matter of fact, our first course is here, and we can try this all out."

From behind Meredith, the waiter, wearing white tie and tails, appeared and gently placed a small tureen in the middle of the table. From it, he deftly ladled a deliciously small amount of chilled vichyssoise into both their bowls starting with Meredith. He then sprinkled finely chopped fresh chives on the surface of each. When finished, he pulled a bottle from an adjacent ice bucket and started the uncorking process, saying, "Tonight we are starting you off with a chilled potato soup with organic baby chives. We will be pairing this course with a crisp, dry, wine with some intensity and persistence. I have selected, for your enjoyment, an Albarino from Spain."

He poured the wine into a small, stemmed, glass on the table, picked it up, swirled it in front of the flickering flame of the table lantern, and then lifted it to his nose. He inhaled deeply, and as Geoff and Meredith watched, he smiled and nodded his head. He brought the glass to his lips and transferred a small amount into his mouth. He seemed to chew it, then let it settle in the back of his throat. After swallowing it, he declared, "Sensational." He then poured a small taste for Geoff, and after Geoff had a taste, and acknowledged his approval with a slight nod of his head, the waiter poured a more generous portion in Meredith's glass followed by a serving for Geoff.

When the waiter turned to leave, Geoff picked up his glass and held it in Meredith's direction and said, "You take my breath away, M."

Meredith was speechless. She touched Geoff's glass with her own, and never releasing his eyes from hers, she said, "I love you." And, meant it. And, wished it.

• • •

They had not yet started on their dessert. The waiter had explained that they were to enjoy a specially prepared Tiramisu—an Italian creation of coffee-dipped ladyfingers layered with whipped eggs, sugar and mascarpone cheese. Puck had infused his version with bittersweet chocolate, he explained. He then opened a bottle of Cabernet Sauvignon saying, "Surprisingly, this Silver Oak cab goes great with chocolate, and I think you will thoroughly be happy with this most delicious ending to your meal."

Geoff was in the middle of profusely thanking their waiter when he flinched noticeably. Meredith had slipped her bare foot onto his crotch. As she slowly stroked him with the ball of her foot and with her toes, her face gave away nothing. She, too, thanked the waiter with sincerity. And, when he left, she slowly turned to face Geoff—her foot still lightly caressing him. "Can we talk about happy endings?" she inquired.

"Geoff half laughed and half sputtered, "Sure."

She slowly removed her foot, and picked up the small fork at the top of her place setting. Cutting the front point off her Tiramisu, she raised it to her lips and sensuously, with her lips and tongue, drew the delicate dessert into the soft folds of her mouth. With her eyes closed, she allowed this treat to literally melt. She slowly opened them. Geoff went to say something, but Meredith held up her hand to stop him once again. She gently picked up her wine glass, savored a sip, then, put it down.

"Tonight is your turn to be pleasured," she started. "I want to fulfill a few of your fantasies—just as you have done for me this afternoon." She got very serious. "Let me start by saying, what I experienced on that massage table with Dominique was both exquisite and erotic. I know you arranged that for me. She gave me your note. Only then was I able to relax and let the experience unfold."

Meredith took another sip of her wine, and Geoff did the same - as his mouth was getting quite dry, and he was finding himself in the early stages of arousal. "I want to tell you all that happened—as part of this journey with you is sharing everything. Do you want to hear?"

"Go on," Geoff said as he studied the light of the lantern dancing across her chest—giving artistic emphasis to her soft mounds while sparking rainbows off her new diamond necklace.

"She started by oiling my body with lavender, and kneading out my exhausted muscles. My neck and shoulders first - followed by my lower back and butt. By the time she had worked her way up from my feet, calves and hamstrings, my inner thighs were aching. I was scared at first, but knowing you had made this happen for me, I closed my eyes and let her explore. She kept saying how pretty I was, and that I was to relax and let myself be in the moment. She turned me over. Soon, she was touching me in a place I had never been touched before. She was applying gentle pressure just behind and below my belly button, and the stroking became more urgent. It took longer for me, but the orgasm was different, and maybe because I had never had a G-spot orgasm before—and had never been with another woman - it was extremely intense." Meredith was smiling as she remembered.

"Well, was it worth waiting for?" Geoff asked.

"I'm not quite done, Mr. G," she took a deep breath. "The feeling was so different, so satisfying, that I asked Dominique to show me how she had done it. "Without hesitating, she asked me to get off the table—which I did with very shaky legs. She untied her robe and let it fall to the ground. She then climbed up on the table, and knelt facing me. She asked me to oil her body. I squeezed the oil onto her shoulders and let it drip down her body. I hesitated, but she grasped my hands and placed them on her breasts. I worked her breasts slowly and softly—the oil making her nipples slippery and hard. She then guided my hand to her entrance. What I did next seemed so natural. I knew what would pleasure her in a way that only women would understand. As I slipped my fingers into her, her eyes shut and she moaned. I went for the same place where I thought she had been with me, but I was a little off. Dominique guided me until I felt a soft, but small, fleshy mound. She asked me to stroke it with two fingers—slowly. As our pace quickened, she took both her breasts in her hands and literally lost it. Like mine, her orgasm took her completely, and lingered. When, at last, her pleasure was over, she collapsed back onto the table."

Geoff could only shake his head and smile. "That makes me so happy, M. I love giving you new experiences. You know that."

She stopped him again, and said, "I know that, Geoff. You are a beautiful, self-assured, man. Another reason I am falling for you so. But, you must know: when Dominique had collapsed on the table, I climbed up with her. We kissed."

"I am so glad." He took a sip of his wine, and said, "So, you think you can show me how to do this for you?"

Meredith looked around, and found the Wolfgang Puck team busy in the kitchen cleaning up. She turned back to Geoff. Grabbing her glass of Perrier in her left hand, she poured a large portion of carbonated water on her right hand. Pulling her halter-top away from her, she slipped her wet hand inside her dress and caressed her left breast. She exhaled as her eyes hooded. Then she stood up and walked around behind him placing both hands flat against his chest. Leaning in, so that her wet breast grazed his neck while she slid her hands down to his lower abdomen, she whispered in his ear. "No vanilla sex for you, tonight."

She pulled away slowly—stopping to massage his shoulders. She leaned back down to his ear. "I can't wait to show you what I have learned."

Geoff leaned his head back, and they kissed upside-down. As the kiss grew more passionate, Geoff mouthed the words into her hungry lips, "I love you, too, Meredith."

Meredith pulled his chair back, and moved around to face him. She pulled her dress up so that she could straddle him. As she pressed against him, she could feel his excitement between her legs. Taking her hands and caressing both his cheeks she said, "Meet me in the classroom. Your lesson starts in fifteen minutes." Pulling his face to hers she kissed him greedily. In a second, she was gone.

Geoff's heart was racing. He let his passion calm before joining the Puck team in the kitchen as they were finishing their clean-up. He was glowingly complimentary and paid them a handsome tip. He said good-bye, and turned and re-entered this modern masterpiece.

Two things caught his eye. His Tiramisu sat uneaten still on their dinner table poolside. And, Meredith, clearly visible through the un-tinted glass wall, was slowly applying aloe lotion to her naked, and sunburned, body.

112

SUSIE

SHE WAS LARGELY INCOHERENT. SLURRING HER WORDS. ANGER; then tears. It was late afternoon. Geoff was at 42,000 feet, on his Gulfstream 550 getting caught up on emails and voice mail, as he raced on this short flight home to have dinner with his spouse. Before she had hung up on him yesterday, they had made arrangements for her to meet him at the airport, and they would go out to dinner, without the kids, and "talk." But, the unmistakably inebriated voice of his wife shocked him. Susie? Drunk? The message cue had said the call was at 3:37 PM, Sunday, an hour and a half ago.

"Geoff? Yeah, that Geoff. My *hus*band. What the fuck? " Her speech was slow, deliberate and slurred. "Never 'round anymore. Can't garden the lawn. Fucking can't even mow the yard. [laughing] Hi, baseball man-ger! Where ya been? Why are you so *such* a looooser? You. You have a wife, you know. You know her name? Shooshee. Shooshee Cam...er...on. WHAT'S going ON? HUH? OH, we're so bery busy big boy. Oh, Big Mister Cam...er...on and his *big secret trips.*" [deep breaths followed by soft crying; silence] "You think I dun-know. You're fucking MARY! Oh, little Miss Mary; Little Miss Finance Man-ger—has to go on all our little business trips. [crying harder] She smells so nice; so perfumey. You think she's purdy?" [hiccup; deep breaths; moaning] "I'm sick. Sick. Sick. Sick. Sick Sick. Fuck this." [more moaning; unintelligible babbling; then vomiting].

The line went dead.

• • •

The Gulfstream leveled over the tarmac at Oakland International Airport. Geoff had moved to the side of the aircraft where he could spy the private aviation terminal as they landed. He couldn't see anyone waiting on arrivals, but he doubted Susie would be there now. As Captain Mike pulled the jet into a space directly in front of the small terminal, there was no sign of his wife. And, his driver, Frank, was not there either.

Mike turned off the engines, and waited for them to spool down before entering the cabin. "You ready, Mr. Cameron?" Geoff was listening intently on a call with his back to him, but he swiveled and gave Mike the thumbs-up. Mike opened the cabin door and lowered the steps. He waited for Geoff for ten minutes while he completed his call. Geoff's luggage had been unloaded and placed inside the terminal, so when he emerged, Mike grabbed Geoff's briefcase and accompanied him inside.

"Can I call for a driver, Mr. C?"

"That won't be necessary, Mike. I already have. You have had a long day, today. Get home to that family of yours and enjoy a well-earned Monday and Tuesday off."

"Yes sir," Mike replied. He turned and walked back out to the aircraft to secure it before heading home.

Geoff sat in the small, deserted terminal, deep in his thoughts, awaiting his pick-up. He had lots on his mind. He was one hundred percent positive he had his story straight for Susie regarding his travel affairs. But a couple of things were bothering him. First, Susie said her friend saw him in "town."

He never was in town. He had gone straight from the airport to the Johnson Estate in La Quinta. He would have to play that part of the discussion by ear. And secondly, the email hacking was still unresolved and on his mind. Nothing more from Nick since yesterday, but he was anxious to meet with him on a variety of issues first thing in the morning. As he was jotting notes for that meeting, he heard a honk as his limo arrived. Grabbing his bags, he thought about how nice it was to have Frank. Frank was always on time, always helpful with his bags, and knew Geoff well enough to read his moods.

As Geoff got into the car, he gave his address in Tiburon to the driver. Soon they were off for his mystery marital reunion. Geoff wasn't sure quite what, or who, would greet him at home. When he pulled into his driveway, Susie's White Range Rover was there, and when he opened the front door, he was mobbed by all three of his kids. Lucy, Brooke and CJ were all laughing and talking at the same time. What was clear was that "Mommy" had the flu and was sleeping. Geoff suggested their favorite Mexican restaurant, and a huge cheer erupted.

"Let me freshen up and check on your mom. Let's leave in about a half hour?" he offered. There was no direct answer. They all dashed for their rooms as he made his way upstairs.

Geoff quietly opened the doors to their bedroom, and found Susie passed out on her side of the bed. He took his suitcase to his closet, and unpacked it himself leaving his tuxedo separated so that he could take it down to the car—and on to the dry-cleaners. He went into Susie's bathroom to check on things, and by-and-large, she had done a remarkable job getting sick without making too much of a mess. As Geoff cleaned a little vomit off the seat and the floor, he tried to remember any time when Susie was drunk. And sick? College? He just couldn't recall.

Geoff made his way back into the bedroom to the bed where he stood over Susie and just stared at her for a long time—deep in his own thoughts. His emotions ran wild and mixed. Great mother. Great corporate wife and partner. UBER community participant. But… No passion. No sex. No laughter of late. No happiness. Condescending. Judgmental. Critical. No lightheartedness. No sense of humor. No appreciation.

She was sound asleep. The peacefulness in her face was a relief to him. He turned and headed quietly for the door. He was so intent on tiptoeing out and closing the doors quietly, that he forgot his tuxedo.

But, as he exited the room there was one thing that Geoff knew for sure.

Susie didn't know who. But, she knew.

113

MEREDITH

I F THIS WAS THE SMALLER OF THE TWO JETS, MEREDITH COULDN'T have cared less. The force of the engines had pushed her back into her seat on takeoff, and now she was standing at the galley fixing herself a light salad.

She had embraced Geoff that morning, and held on tight to him for a very long time. She couldn't help the tears. She was scared and riddled with anxiety. Was it returning to her pitiful life in Grand Junction that bothered her so? Or, was it facing up to the reality of a failed marriage to a brutish psychopath—and the steps ahead of her to end it? Or was it leaving this miracle called Geoff Cameron? She didn't deserve him. She didn't deserve *this*. Would Geoff's interest in her fade—just as so much else had faded in her life?

Meredith brought her salad and a bottled Perrier with her to a table by the window. As she opened her water, she smiled to herself remembering last night and how she soaked her hand and slipped it inside her dress. Dominique was right. Dress, and act, in such a way that he will desire you all night. And, what about Dominique? A smile came to her face as she squirmed in her seat. What man would be so caring, and self-confidant, to arrange *that* experience for her?

Payback last night had been sweet. She closed her eyes and recalled the scene. She performing her first solo g-spot orgasm with him watching. Neither made it back to each other's arms before losing control. But, then she reciprocated with an erotic, and slow, anything-but-vanilla, sixty-nine session that ended with a traditional, and very different, orgasm for her than what she had just experienced. Both were sensational. If Geoff's pleasure could be measured by his engorgement and his verbal responses, Meredith was sure the evening had been a resounding success. They had fallen deep asleep wrapped in each other's arms.

• • •

The captain came on the radio. "Miss Meredith, we have about ten minutes before our decent into Grand Junction. Please stow any dishes and glassware into the galley washer drawers and make sure the doors are latched. Then if you can be seated, and affix your lap belt, we will be on the ground in twenty minutes."

She felt a rush of excitement, as she felt surprisingly at home in this environment. But, this scared her, too. It could all be over in an instant. She shook herself out of this dream, and forced herself to prepare for her e-entry.

As she buckled her seatbelt, and sat back in her seat, she started assembling her thoughts on picking up her car, charging her cell phone and picking up her messages. She was going to call Jess right away, and head straight there—and tell her everything. She badly wanted to share her plan with her. But, there was one thing that she couldn't have planned for.

Bobbie was meeting her plane.

PART III

THE HUNTED

114

BOBBIE

IT APPEARED, AT FIRST, TO BE A DISTANT WHINE THAT THEN GREW louder. Bobbie strained through his binoculars to get sight of the plane, but the day was cold and overcast. He could tell it was a jet—not a prop plane. It was so much like his life right now. He could hear and feel it all unfolding around him, and descending on top of him. But, he couldn't see it. It made him feel vulnerable, scared and angry. Not like hunting - when he was in ultimate control.

Bobbie had backed his truck in the parking lot of Private Aviation up against the fence that separated him from the tarmac. He was sitting on his lowered tailgate beside his truck. Numerous empty beer cans lay strewn behind him. Tommy had given him the ETA of the flight thanks to some timely and opportunistic information innocently intended for his app. And, Booker was $70 richer. The information on the flight to Oakland was useless except to confirm the mutual origin with this flight—and thus, the tryst.

The sound of the jet grew louder and closer, but he still couldn't see it. Then, it appeared—falling from the clouds above. He trained his binoculars on the Gulfstream. It was huge for a private aircraft. The CBC logo was unmistakable on the tail. As it flew above and past him, he worried that his intelligence was wrong, or that in some crazy way they had spotted him. But, just as the plane was retreating from sight, it banked hard to the left, and aligned itself with the runway. Bobbie witnessed it touch down and roll to a stop before it turned and headed back to the small terminal.

He jumped from the tailgate and climbed into the cab. He pulled to the far end of the parking lot. From the glove box he fetched a small paper-wrapped bundle the size of a fingernail. He opened it and poured the fluffy white contents on the center console. Using a razor blade, he chopped and arranged the powder into two parallel rows. From his pocket, he retrieved a short straw. Bobbie leaned down, and putting the straw in one nostril and holding the other closed, he snorted a line. He repeated with the other nostril ingesting it all. He blinked hard twice. Then headed for the terminal.

• • •

The Gulfstream quietly descended through the clouds. Captain John Bartlett had cleared his landing with the small control tower. He would fly two miles north of the runway at an altitude of 2,000 feet, bank hard into a tight 180-degree turn and land to the west. He had called ahead and made sure that Meredith's driver had been arranged and would be there to greet her. It was a chilly, gloomy day in southwestern Colorado, but the cloud ceiling was above them now. They touched down just three minutes behind schedule at 4:08 PM.

As the plane taxied, Meredith began to gather her things. Before she turned off her phone, she texted Geoff. "Safe in GJ. Thanks for the lift…in travel and in life. XXXOOOggg. ;-) M" She sent the message with a smile, turned off the phone and placed it in the padded bag that was left for her on the plane. She sealed it.

The plane came to smooth stop and the engines were turned off. Captain John exited the cockpit and smiled when he saw Meredith. The entire flight staff had grown accustomed to her unassuming charm and sunny personality. "Well, you're home, Miss Meredith. Let me grab a cart from the terminal and I will help you with your things. Why don't you stay right here? I won't be a minute."

"Sure. Thanks, John," she replied.

Two minutes later, John was back and starting to unload the aircraft - fetching her suitcase and all her bags from Rodeo Drive and Beverly Hills and placing them on the luggage cart. Meredith stepped off the plane into a cold blast of reality. It felt good to stretch, but she sure wished she had just landed back in Palm Springs. The two of them walked to the terminal in silence. Once inside the door, John said, "Looks like your driver is here."

Meredith, taking no notice, turned to John and gave him a warm hug. "Thank you for everything, John." And, she meant it.

Then she heard a familiar voice say, "I'll take 'em from here."

Meredith screamed involuntarily. John looked up to see a large muscular man in cowboy boots and jeans approach. She said, "What are you doing here?" The edge in her voice was very apparent.

"Taking you home, Honey," Bobbie said nicely. He turned to John, and introduced himself holding out his hand. "Hi, I'm Bob Edmonson. Meredith's husband." John grasped his hand, and the second he did, he wished he hadn't. Bobbie clamped down hard, and John winced in pain and tried to pull away. Bobbie held him tightly for two or three extra seconds than released him.

John stepped back a few steps, then said, "Nice to meet you too, Bob," although the expression on John's face clearly communicated disdain. Turning to Meredith, he said, "Is there anything I can do for you, Miss Meredith?"

"No. Thank you, John. I'll be fine." The look she gave him said otherwise.

"OK. Well, I'll be off then." John turned and headed back out the door towards his plane, but not until he turned to get a quick glimpse back at Meredith. And, her husband.

115

JESSICA

JESSICA HAD GONE INTO HER OFFICE, SUNDAY AFTERNOON, TO FINISH up a few things before heading to the market to pick up some dinner for her and her new roommate—and the requisite bottles of chilled Chardonnay. Meredith had been far less communicative on this trip, but nonetheless, had texted that she couldn't wait to see her and fill her in on all the details of her trip and her "plans." The last she had heard, she was in Beverly Hills, of all places, headed off to another secret getaway. This was all too exciting. And, as a struggling single mother, there was certainly a little pang of jealousy. But, Jess couldn't be happier for her friend who deserved a break from the hell she was living.

It was now 7:35 PM, and Jessica hadn't heard from her friend. She had fixed a yummy casserole for them to enjoy, and had sent Jasmine over to a friend's house so that they could curl up on the couch and catch up on all the "details." Jessica got up and turned off the oven, and placed the salad in the fridge. She poured herself another glass of wine, and dialed her friend, again. Nothing. It rang out and went to voice mail.

As it got later, she thought about calling that stranger, Nick George, who had delivered that first mysterious envelope to her office addressed to Meredith. He had left his contact details with her in case of an "emergency." But, for some reason, she didn't feel right about doing that now. Instead, she decided to take a drive. Where? She wasn't sure, but she had to do something.

116

MEREDITH

BOBBIE GRABBED THE CART AND STARTED PULLING IT OUTDOORS. The terminal was deserted on this late Sunday afternoon. Meredith didn't move and said, "Bobbie, I'm not going with you. Leave my things alone." He just laughed and continued out towards the parking lot. His truck was the only vehicle parked at the far end. Meredith took off after him.

"Bobbie, stop," she yelled. When she caught up with him, she grabbed him by the arm. "Please stop." She implored. He did.

He slowly turned around, and Meredith, dropping his arm, could see that Bobbie's eyes were blind with rage. She'd seen it before. And, she had always been able to talk him off his personal precipice. There was something else about him that she noticed, too. She couldn't quite place it, but this was a different Bobbie than the one she thought she knew.

"Oh, I'm going to stop all right," he said. "But not until I find out what is going on here." Before she could say anything, he yelled, "So, who, *Mrs. Edmonson*, is this guy who you are *fucking*?"

She tried to steady her thoughts and calm her outward demeanor. "Bobbie, it doesn't matter at this stage. You and I both know that this marriage is over."

"Over? *Over*? What do you mean, *over*? You are my wife, and we have a great life here in Grand Junction. For better or worse, remember? And, things are really starting to get a whole lot better."

Meredith dropped her head and shook it slowly in disbelief. Rather than replying directly, she fished into her purse to get her cell phone, but then realized she had none. Hers was in her car parked at the downtown office building where she had left it, and the other was now taxiing down the runway soon to be airborne. She had no choice.

"OK," she said quietly. "Let's go to a restaurant and talk."

"*Who. Are. You. FUCKING?*" he yelled. He was shaking with rage now. "We are going *HOME* to talk."

"No, Bobbie. We are not going home. I am not living there anymore, and I don't intend…"

Bobbie whirled around so suddenly that Meredith had no time to react. The back of Bobbie's fist struck her just below her nose on the right side of her face. The crunch was sickening. He knew he had broken her jaw. But what he didn't expect was how easily her face was torn open and the volume of blood that erupted from her mouth. Her eyes rolled back and she spiraled, like a limp ragdoll, falling to the concrete—her face taking the largest impact. She lay motionless on the ground.

Bobbie left her lying there while he loaded the bed of his truck with her things. He tore open every bag "admiring" all the contents. His rage welled up once more as the reality struck him that she was dressing for someone else. If he had only known the price…He picked up her remaining suitcase, and raised it high over his head with both arms, and hurled it with all his might at the back of his cab. The rear window shattered into a million shards.

He went and opened the passenger door. Then went back and hovered over the limp body—blood pooling under her face. With his boot he kicked her over so her vacant eyes were pointing up. Mixed in the blood on the ground were teeth and flesh.

He leaned down, and in one easy dead-lift, he put her lifeless body over his shoulder and walked her over to the open door. He crouched down and threw her on the front seat on top of the sea of broken glass. It occurred to him that the last time he had dealt with such an awkward beanbag of a person, he was putting clothing back on the HR Director, Janet Jacobs. This time, he didn't laugh even though the thought amused him. He slammed the door.

He walked around to the driver's side and climbed in. He opened the center consul and pulled out a Miller. He popped the top, and in one aggressive drag, emptied the entire beer before crushing the can and tossing it behind him through the now-vacated window into the bed of his truck.

"Don't fucking bleed on my car, Meredith," he growled. "You didn't tell me you were on your period." He belched loudly. "Hang on. We are going *home*."

117

JOHN

JOHN KNEW SOMETHING WAS TERRIBLY WRONG. THE LOOK ON MER-edith's face was as close as he could guess to panic and fear. As he walked out across the tarmac towards the Gulfstream, he thought about his options. Doing nothing was not one of them. He thought about radioing the larger G550 and alerting Geoff in flight, but he knew that Geoff couldn't do anything more than he could do on the ground. Then, he made a split decision. He dialed 911.

"911. What's your emergency?"

"My name is John Bartlett. I am a commercial aviator who just dropped off a female passenger at the Grand Junction private aviation terminal." John took some liberty with his next line. "I witnessed her being assaulted, and kidnapped, by a large white male."

"Can you describe the victim?"

"Yes. Female. Age: early thirties. Brunette. Ponytail. Wearing black jeans, black and white striped blouse and black leather jacket."

"How about the alleged attacker?"

"Male. White. Large; maybe 6'5", 250 pounds and very muscular. Tooled brown cowboy boots. Jeans. Brown and blue plaid lumberjack shirt. Week-old beard. They were headed for a large, raised, silver pickup truck in the private aviation parking lot."

"Please stay on the line while I call the local police." There was no background music—only deathly silence.

In what seemed like forever, she returned. "The Grand Junction Sheriff's Department is on their way. Thank you for calling 911." The line disconnected.

118

JESSICA

JESSICA STARTED HER CAR, AND WAS SHOCKED BY THE VOLUME OF the radio. How strange it was to realize that three hours ago, she was giddy with excitement to see her friend—her car laden with wine and groceries. She remembered cranking up the radio and singing at the top of her lungs, Peter Gabriel's "Back In the High Life" as she made her way home.

Now, she was panic stricken, cruising the streets of Grand Junction. She first went to the airport, but found the terminal and parking lot deserted. Then, she knew where she had to go.

She got on the freeway and headed to the far end of town. She had been to Bobbie's house many times before. The car could drive itself. Fifteen minutes later, she turned off the freeway and took a left at the intersection. A quick right put her in the older neighborhood where Bobbie and Meredith had their house. Jessica pulled up to a neighbor's home three houses away and killed her lights. She quietly got out of the car, and softly pushed her door closed until she could hear it latch. She didn't realize that she had left her cell phone on the car seat.

She walked softly towards the house, and when she got to the immediate neighbor's house she crossed their lawn and peeked through their bushes. She couldn't see much. It was dark, and it appeared there were no lights on in the house. She knelt to get a better view.

Then she heard something snap behind her. She shreaked as a large hand grabbed her by the arm. Her adrenaline coursed through her as she whirled strongly to try to break the grip, but was unsuccessful.

"What are you doing?" an angry voice shouted.

Jessica was speechless. When she was helped to her feet, and when she could turn around, she was weak with relief. It was not Bobbie. It was their neighbor who had seen her sneak through their yard. Jessica explained that she was worried about the Edmonson's, and had come to check up on them.

"Why not go to the front door and ring the bell?" the incredulous neighbor asked.

Jessica replied that she was worried about maybe some foul play and/or danger, and she was scared to approach the house directly.

"There has been no one living in that house for weeks. Coach Edmonson, right? We haven't seen him—or anyone—come and go from the property in quite some time."

Jessica thanked him profusely, and apologized repeatedly for alarming him. Then asked if he wouldn't mind accompanying her next door to have a quick look around. He was surprisingly happy to do so.

There was nothing to see. The house was clearly vacant, and as always was the case, was in need of some serious repair and attention. They shot flashlights into the gloomy interior. When they got to Bobbie and Meredith's bedroom, Jessica felt a little uneasy snooping there. But, there was nothing of interest there, either.

Jessica thanked the neighbor again, and promised to let him know if she found anything out. Then, she headed back to her car—much faster, and much noisier, than her way in.

When she got to her car, she started it, but before pulling away from the curb, she checked for phone messages. There was one voice mail from a number she didn't recognize. She hit play. What she heard next, chilled her.

"Hello. Jessica Stevens? This is Saint Mary's Medical Center—Intensive Care Unit..." Jessica started to hyperventilate. She listened to the rest of the message, and then got out of her car. She tried to control her breathing, and get her heart rate to settle. She tried to think clearly.

She paced the street enshrouded in that cold and clammy night. She stopped and hunched over placing her hands on her knees. She squeezed her eyes shut forcing tears to splash on the ground below. Jessica was shaking uncontrollably. She tipped her head back, and opened her eyes to the dark, damp, sky above. "Please, God. Please. Please. *Please.*"

"Let her *live.*"

119

GEOFF

EOFF FINISHED PACKING. MEREDITH HAD BEEN GONE SEVERAL hours already. She had driven off down the serpentine driveway in the Range Rover. Geoff had stayed behind. He gathered his laundry, and his remaining clean folded clothes, and arranged them tightly into his suitcase. Before closing up his bag, he decided to double-check the bathrooms. All was in order in his, but when he checked Meredith's, there was a red garment neatly hanging over a chair. There was a note pinned to it.

"Thought I would return the shirt you so generously loaned me in Aspen. Put it on. And smell me. ;-)"

It was his 49ers jersey. Geoff laughed out loud. He couldn't help himself. He picked it up and bunched it onto his face and inhaled deeply. The smell was unmistakable. Her favorite perfume, Allure, was mixed with a little Coppertone, a little chlorine—and a little Meredith. He closed his eyes, smiling.

He smelled it one more time before burying it deep within his dirty clothes. He closed his bag and zipped it up. Before leaving the room, he pulled out his cell phone.

> From: gquest100@hotmail.com
> Subject: Smell Me
> Date: December 7, 2014 at 4:07 PM PST
> To: mquest99@aol.com
> Found your little present. Couldn't have been a better gift in the
> world—except if you were back here with me in the flesh. Will NOT

wash that special jersey. It will remind me of you every day until we meet again. It won't be long. I promise.

G

He was hopeful of, and almost expected, an immediate, and flirty, reply. Her plane should have, long ago, dropped her off in Grand Junction. He put his phone in his back pocket as he wheeled his suitcase out to the carport and the Mercedes SUV.

A reply would never come.

120

JESSICA

JESSICA WAS IN HER CAR NOW RACING TO THE HOSPITAL. SHE FRAN-tically dialed their go-between, Nick George, for the third time in the last fifteen minutes. Again, she got his voice mail. She was exasperated. She choked out the words, "Nick, *please*, this is Jessica Stevens, Meredith's friend. Please call me! Something terrible has happened to Meredith."

There was nothing but silence.

Then she started texting as she raced down city streets to the freeway.

• • •

Nick had, uncharacteristically, turned off his phone. He and Stephanie lay naked, exhausted, and in a deep sleep on his bed high above the bay of San Francisco and the Golden Gate Bridge on that glorious, sun-draped, Sunday afternoon.

121

BOBBIE

BOBBIE WAS BREATHING HARD—PANTING LIKE A BEAST. HE CHARGED through the forest crashing through the high-country underbrush; his backpack unusually heavy. His bow and arrows were catching occasionally on the flora that seemed to reach out to grab him.

He stopped and quieted himself - listening intently. Nothing. He turned and kept running—tripping and stumbling frequently. He knew exactly where he was, and where he was going. He would be safe there.

• • •

"How in the fuck did a cop car show up right at the time I was leaving the airport?" he wondered again. The Sherriff had immediately turned on his lights, and tried to pull Bobbie over. He had run the plates and knew that the truck belonged to Coach Edmonson—who was a person of interest in the mysterious deaths of the District Superintendent and the HR Director.

The Sherriff had given good chase, and was a very skilled driver, but was no match for a four-wheeled drive, a labyrinth of dirt roads and a panicked, and experienced, navigator at the wheel. Bobbie swerved hard, left and right, as he bounced hard up the terrain to an unmarked trailhead. Meredith's lifeless body bounced and ricocheted, too—the razor-sharp glass shards tearing at her flesh.

Then he made a final right turn up towards his intended destination. Meredith's body slumped against his right leg before she dropped to the floor—pinning

Bobbie's foot to the accelerator. The truck lurched forward and slammed into a large pine tree. The impact smashed his face into the steering wheel.

He had screamed, "Shit!" just before impact, but the collision had not knocked him out. He felt blood coming from his nose, but his brain was clear. He jumped out of his truck and reached around in the truck bed for his backpack, his bow and his quiver of arrows. They were not there.

His eyes were wild as he scanned the immediate vicinity for his, now, priceless belongings. The contents of his truck bed had been strewn across the forest floor. It took him but a minute to locate what he would need for his survival. His backpack was thirty yards ahead of the truck in a gathering of leaves. It took him a while longer to find his bow and arrows, but he found them snagged in a nearby bush.

He slipped on the backpack and affixed his weaponry. He then froze. He could hear a car engine in the far distance. He ran back to the truck one last time. The front of it was wrapped around the pine tree and was still smoking and hissing. He looked in the driver's side window at the motionless, bloody, human form on the floor, and for once, could think of nothing to say.

He inhaled a large glob of phlegm and blood from the back of his throat, and coughed it into his mouth. Leaning his head in the window one last time, he expelled it into the direction of her face. He didn't wait around to see if it had hit his mark. He was no longer the hunter.

But that would change.

122

NICK

NICK AWOKE WITH A START. IT WAS DARK OUTSIDE. AFTERNOON HAD already turned to evening. The cacophony of twinkling lights below them was just starting to bloom. He gently kissed Stephanie's neck; she moaned softly and stirred. She rolled over and grabbed him again in a passionate embrace—which Nick did nothing to stop. But, then, he rolled over—instinctively checking the clock. What? 6:28? Boy, were they ever in deep REMS! He rubbed his temples to clear the delirious cobwebs. Had it been three hours? Sex with Stephanie had always been aggressive and fun—and exhausting. And weekend sex had the added bonus of a post-coital nap. But three hours was a first.

He sat on the side of the bed, turned on the bedside lamp and putting on his reading glasses, he scanned his text messages. Stephanie was instantly alert as she heard him say, "No. No. This can't be happening. Shit." Nick never swore. Then he started listening to his voice mails. Stephanie could make out a female's muffled voice, but not the words—although she tried.

Turning to him and sitting up in bed she said, "What's up?"

He kept staring at his screen in silence as he scrolled. And, without saying another word, he dashed into the bathroom to throw some cold water on his face. He said, as he was dressing, "I've got to get into the office. Seems one of our new employees in Grand Junction has a crisis."

"Personal or professional?" she inquired.

"I'm not sure, but it sounds serious." He was being purposely vague. He had put his Chief Operating Officer's hat back on. But going to sleep with his phone turned to mute was inexcusable. Particularly, this weekend.

"When did this all happen?" she asked as he was heading for the door.

"Over three hours ago. I've got to go, Steph. Make yourself at home. I'll be late."

He didn't wait for a reply.

123

GEOFF

THE KIDS WERE SCREAMING AND LAUGHING HAVING A TERRIFIC TIME with their dad at Paco Escobar's in downtown Tiburon. Geoff was having as much fun as the kids. He was getting a full update on all their activities, and all the school gossip. The waiter came by and took their dinner order. Geoff asked for another margarita just as he felt his phone buzz in his pocket. He kept laughing with the kids, but was now completely distracted. My God, it had taken her long enough!

He excused himself from the table, and said that he would be right back—leaving his rowdy kids behind. He slipped past the mariachi's - ducking under a swinging guitar, as they belted "Rancho Grande" to another loud and boisterous table. He loved this place. No wonder it had been a family favorite ever since they had moved here.

He made his way to a quiet corner by the bar, and opened his text messages. What would she say in reply? He could hardly wait—a smile coming to his lips. He looked down at the lighted screen, and his expression changed instantly. What he read forced adrenaline through his veins. It was from Nick.

"Call me. EMERGENCY. It's M."

• • •

Geoff fumbled with his phone, then dropped it. He felt sick to his stomach. He quickly picked it up and dialed Nick. "What's up? Talk to me."

Nick was panicked, and Geoff could feel it in his voice. "It's M. She's in the ICU at St. Mary's Medical Center in Grand Junction…"

"Go on," Geoff hurriedly urged.

"Assaulted. Everyone there thinks it was her estranged husband. From what I can gather, it's pretty bad, Geoff."

"Whom did you speak with? The hospital?""

"No, Meredith's best friend, Jessica—you know, her go-between—the one that I have been liaising with. She was hysterical."

"How bad is she?"

"Jessica said the doctors informed her that she was going into immediate surgery. There was hemorrhaging on her brain and significant blood loss. Her blood pressure was dangerously low. It's serious."

Geoff was uncharacteristically slow to respond.

"Geoff? Geoff, you there?" Nick begged.

"Yeah sorry. I, uh…shit; sorry." He stammered.

"Look Geoff, where are you?"

"I'm at Paco Escobar's in town with my kids."

"Go home and pack. Frank will be picking you up at the house 9:30 PM. Mike is filing the flight plan to Grand Junction as we speak. You're departing out of San Francisco International. That is where the plane will be waiting for you. Booker is with him, and will be flying the Long Ranger for local support and transportation if needed. He will be departing soon to get a head start on you guys."

"Thank you, Nick." Geoff let out a deep breath.

"Geoff?"

"Yeah."

"I want you to know something. I fucked up."

"We'll talk about it later. I've got to get going."

"No, Geoff, wait. Please."

"What?" Geoff was clearly short.

"This all happened over three hours ago."

"What do you mean: '*three hours* ago'?"

"I was asleep when Jessica called. I'm not sure what is happening there now. It may all be over."

"OK. We'll talk about it when I return."

Nick replied, "No, we can talk about it on the way. I'm going with you."

• • •

Booker thought twice about sending the flight plans to Tommy, the app engineer. He had typed out the origin and destination of the flights tonight—both his and the Gulfstream's—but he hesitated. He didn't know why. He guessed it was guilt over making money on a CBC emergency of some sort. It was late and he and Mike would be flying into the night—getting some serious overtime, and a bonus if all went well.

Booker went through his thorough pre-flight check. He was departing an hour and a half before Mr. Cameron and the jet. They would get to Grand Junction about the same time, and meet up at the terminal. He started his engines, and the big blade started it slow sweeping rotation. He checked his phone one last time, and saw the unsent message in his outbox. Without thinking, he hit "send."

124

SUSIE

SUSIE STIRRED. SHE COULD FAINTLY HEAR NOISE IN THE BEDROOM. No, it wasn't the bedroom. Geoff's closet? What time was it? She looked at her bedside Cartier clock. It was hard to read the dial with such dry and bloodshot eyes. Even the hands that glowed in the dark were small and blurry. "Geoff's home?" she strained her mind trying to figure out where she was and what was happening.

Then she felt it. The queasiness had returned. Her neck heated and started to sweat as her stomach churned. She could feel the bile rising and collecting in the back of her throat. She stumbled out of bed and headed straight to her bathroom where she shoved her head into the toilet. The spasms convulsed her.

Geoff could hear the painful retching in the other room. He quickly closed up his new casual carry-on bag and placed it on the top of the center island of drawers. Within seconds he was kneeling behind Susie, holding her hair back, as she suffered. He got a wet, cold, washcloth and swabbed her forehead, the back of her neck and her mouth. She started taking deep breaths, and the dry heaves mercifully abated for the time being. He helped her to her feet, and with an arm around her waist, he escorted her back to bed. He sat her down and gently laid her back onto her goose-down pillows. He kissed her forehead and said, "I'll be back in a few days."

She drowsily replied, very softly in a whisper, "OK, Honey. Thanks. We'll talk in the morning."

She was incapable of hearing a response. And, Geoff had said nothing.

He returned to his closet as his phone buzzed. Frank was outside. He opened his suitcase from his Palm Springs trip and pulled out his toiletries and repacked them into his new bag. He also grabbed one more item. The 49ers jersey.

On his way out, he checked on his kids. They were all still awake. He had told them on the way home from dinner that he had an unavoidable business emergency, and for them to look after their mom while he was away. He didn't know when he would be back. He kissed them all good-bye.

They all would say later that each of them had noticed a change in their father.

As for Susie, she couldn't say good-bye. She was passed out again. And was dreaming. She saw Geoff. Mowing the front lawn. And, she was smiling and waving.

125

JESSICA

THE TV WAS ON, AND IT WAS LATE. "I LOVE LUCY" WAS THE FEATURED broadcast, but Jessica couldn't hear what was being said or comprehend the laugh tracks in this very depressing waiting room. Jasmine was asleep, curled up on the sofa beside her with her head in her lap. She just sat there motionless - her eyes open and fixed on the wall ahead of her.

The door opened, and a man walked in. Jessica paid no attention. People had been in and out all night. The man, sat right next to her, and placed a hand softly on her shoulder. She involuntarily jerked, and Jazzy awoke with a start.

"Jasmine? It's me, Nick." He said quietly and calmly.

Jessica focused. Once she had recognized the voice and the face, she let her guard down and started to sob—putting her face into her hands—shaking her head from side to side. Nick put his arm around her and she turned and buried her head into his shoulder. "What are you doing here?" she choked into his shirt.

"I've actually come with Geoff. He wants to see Meredith as soon as he is able. But, he also wants to speak with you. Is that OK?"

Jessica thought for a while, then replied, "I'd rather speak to him in the morning. I'm exhausted, and very emotional. I'm not sure I am thinking very clearly tonight."

The waiting room door opened again, and another stranger entered. Jessica looked up and hesitated. There was no doubt in her mind who the man was. He was tall, very attractive, deeply tanned with longish, wavy, salt-and-pepper hair. He wore concern like a blanket, and he came straight up to them, and never taking his eyes off of her, he extended his large hand and said, "You must be Jess, Meredith's good friend."

Jessica nodded. "That's me."

Geoff replied kindly, "Thank you for everything. I mean it."

She kept nodding, unable to speak.

"May I go in and see her?"

"No. She is still in surgery."

"What?" Geoff was incredulous.

"The doctor said it would be rough, and given the nature of her injuries, he wasn't sure what he would find. He said as soon as he was finished he would come in and talk to me. That was what?" She looked at her watch. "Seven hours ago?"

Nick left the room, leaving Jessica with Geoff. Jasmine was back asleep on the couch. "Can I pour you a fresh cup of coffee?" he asked.

"Sure," she replied with emotional resignation.

They both went to the coffee bar and fixed their drinks. They sat down at a side table facing each other. Geoff's face emitted concern, but primarily, warmth and compassion. He took a sip of his coffee, and asked, "Who did this to Meredith?"

* * *

Two hours later, when the doctor walked in the door, Jessica was still answering questions about her friend and her friend's life. They both rose.

The doctor spoke first, "I'm sorry sir, but you are going to have to leave us alone for a few minutes."

Jessica answered immediately, "No, it's OK. Mr. Cameron here is a close family friend. He can stay."

Geoff didn't move. The doctor then said, "OK." He cleared his throat then proceeded. "I'm not going to sugar-coat this." He was speaking to Jessica. "She survived the surgery, but is in a medically-induced coma. She has sustained blunt-force trauma to her frontal lobe and has formed a challenging hematoma on her brain. Her broken jaw and facial lacerations are quite serious, too, but we had a plastic surgeon delicately suture her up after we wired her jaw shut. She will be in a coma, I am guessing, for at least three to four days."

Geoff asked, "When will she awake? What will her likely recovery look like?"

"It depends on her now," the doctor replied. "How her body can respond will be of primary importance. If she makes it through the next six to twelve hours, she has a better chance of...let me be blunt...surviving. Recovery? To what degree I can't say. It's still way too early. Survival first. She could manifest an infection or get pneumonia. The key here, though, is to urgently reduce the pressure on her brain, and that's what we will be focusing on intently. I'm sorry. I wish the news were better. One hour at a time here."

"Thank you, Doctor," Geoff said catching the doctor's eyes. "I just have to ask, what person could do such a thing to this beautiful woman?"

The doctor took a deep breath, and placed a hand on Geoff's shoulder. Looking first at Jessica, and then back at Geoff, hissed, "A monster."

126

BOBBIE

BOBBIE RACED HIS WAY, ZIG-ZAGGING, TO THE TOP OF THE RIDGE line. From there, he peered down into the dense valley below. This was one of his favorite local spots to hunt wild game, and his knowledge of the terrain would give him an advantage—for a time. He had to assume they had found his truck, and soon, the dogs would be on his trail. He had no time to lose.

It was dark. Night had fallen quite some time ago, and that would be to his near-term advantage. He had a photographic memory of this valley and the surrounding landscape. He made his way down carefully until he reached the stream at the bottom. Walking upstream about a half mile, he found the crossing area used regularly by hunters and hikers. He stepped into the fast moving water, and carefully made his way to the other side. Once there, he walked about 400 yards to a boulder wall at the end of a box canyon. There, he removed his shoes, and threw them high up into the rocky hills. He sat, and opened his backpack, and pulled out a new pair of hiking shoes—putting them on with a new pair of socks. He retraced his steps back to the stream and entered it exactly where he had gotten out. He smiled when he thought of the dogs, and their handlers, trying to follow his sent across the river and into the box canyon.

He was sorely tempted to circle back and climb the box canyon wall from behind. It would be like shooting helpless goldfish in a bowl. But, Bobbie had other plans for his twenty arrows. Instead, he clipped together his hiking poles, and stepped into the freezing stream where his scent would be lost. Gingerly, he made his way downstream for almost a mile. His feet were now numb from the frigid water, but Bobbie was used to being cold and uncomfortable. His pain threshold was very high—unusually so. It was one of his advantages in the wild.

He stepped out of the stream and onto a small pebble-laden beach at a bend. Sixty yards inland was a thicket of undergrowth where he could rest until daybreak. Then, he would make his assault up to the aerie, and the secret cave. There, he could eat, and think and plan.

127

GEOFF

THE DOCTOR HAD JUST LEFT, AND GEOFF WAS SEATED NEXT TO JES-
sica—the two of them were talking softly so as not to wake Jessica's daughter.
The door to the waiting room opened quietly and Nick walked in. He pulled a
seat over to them and sat listening respectfully as they spoke.

When there was a lull in the conversation, Nick said, "I booked rooms for
all of us at the hotel across the street. The Ritz Carlton it isn't, but it is clean,
comfortable and convenient. Jessica, I reserved a suite for you and Jasmine. It's
getting late. There's nothing else for us to do here tonight. We should get some
sleep and be back here first thing in the morning."

Geoff spoke immediately. "I'm staying here. You all go get some rest." They
both stood and nodded their understanding. But, then Geoff added, "Nick can I
speak with you a minute?"

Jessica went over to the couch where Jasmine lay sleeping. She nudged her
awake, and the two of them moved slowly for the door.

"Wait for me in the reception lobby, Jess," Nick said. "I'll walk with you to
the hotel."

Jessica gave him a weak thumbs-up and nodded her approval.

As the two departed, Geoff turned to Nick and said, "Get me the best tracker,
and sniper, this great country of ours has to offer. And, I want him, or her, or
both, here tomorrow by noon. Can you do that for me?"

"Yes sir," Nick responded earnestly.

"One more thing. Can you get me a hand gun?"

"Sure."

"A big one."

"Yes sir."

"By noon tomorrow?"

"Or sooner. See you in the morning."

128

SUSIE

IT WAS MONDAY MORNING, DECEMBER 8TH. IT WAS RHONDA'S BIRTH-
day, and Susie was sure that she expected presents, but at least cards, from
everyone in the spin class. Susie didn't have time. Maybe she would give her a
thank-you card for turning her on to her private investigator. That's where Susie
was headed right now.

Susie had a smashing headache. She was in a particularly foul mood. She had
barely been able to get the kids off to school this morning trying her best to seem
chipper and enthusiastic. The yard remained shabby, and there were dirty dishes
in the sink. Rosanne had been late, and Susie had threatened her with her job.
Only after some begging, did Susie acquiesce.

She had never been that drunk. She recalled virtually nothing. She remembered drinking vodka martini's yesterday afternoon until she was so unsteady that
she went to bed. And then, to the bathroom. Over and over again.

Geoff had come home, right? Yes, of course he had. The kids went out to
dinner with him to that lousy Mexican dive he likes so much. His unpacked bag
was in his closet. In fact, she had the whole thing in the back of her Range Rover.
She couldn't wait to dissect it with Trevor. Geoff's office had only said that he was
traveling on some sort of company emergency. Right.

• • •

"He's back in Grand Junction, Colorado right now," Trevor was saying. "Not
unusual given his recent acquisition there. But, what IS unusual is that he is at

the main hospital, Saint Mary's. Been there since late last night—or early this morning, I should say."

"How do you know all of this?" Susie was rubbing her temples—a large bottle of carbonated Evian by her side.

"Simple. I was alerted to his departure last night thanks to the bug you placed in his briefcase. When I saw him stop in Grand Junction, I called my contact there. We've been tailing him."

"Any idea why he is at the hospital? His office said it was a company emergency."

"Not sure. But what we do know is that he spent the night there. His COO, Nick, is with him, but Nick and a woman and a young girl departed together around 3:35 AM, and crossed the street and checked into the Roosevelt—an older, but nice, hotel. Earlier, our tail saw a doctor enter the room, and was there for about ten minutes. What I can tell you is that this, being a smaller hospital, the waiting room is shared—used for both the ICU," Trevor made sure to make eye contact with Susie, "and, Maternity."

Susie was silent, but nodded.

129

BOBBIE

I T WAS EARLY MONDAY MORNING, AND THE AIR WAS CRISP AND THE sky clear. The dreary weather of the past couple of days had lifted—much to his disappointment. Bobbie's lair was perfect. He had spent many a night there before, and Bobbie was comfortable and confident. It was a rare cave, high up on a ledge, large enough for him and his things, but also hidden by foliage. He had been here dozens of times and had never been discovered by humans, but occasionally by animals attracted by his scent.

There were three access points to his hideout. These would allow him an unusual choice of coming-and-going options as well as an emergency escape if needed. His new shoes would provide no familiar scent for the dogs.

He sat at the entrance to the cave where the light was best, and pulled out a folded piece of paper.

~~Don DeLatore - Superintendent~~

Charlie Fredericks—Principal

Hugh Preston—Lawyer

~~Janet Jacobs—Human Resources~~

~~Meredith Edmonson—Fuck Bitch~~

Only two left. Then, he could skip town and disappear into the wilds of Canada. There would be so much commotion over his wife's death, that the two remaining assholes would be easy targets. "Who do I hate more?" he asked himself. "Pretty equal. But, let's pay Chuckie a visit first."

"Always nice to leave the lawyer for last."

130

NICK

I T WAS NOW LATE MONDAY, AND HE AND GEOFF WERE IN A DARK BAR in a back booth speaking with a stocky, muscular man in his late thirties. He sported a crew-cut, crisp khaki pants, shined shoes and a tight, short-sleeve sport shirt—and an Air Force decorated leather jacket that now hung on a hook by their booth. Nick led the conversation. Geoff was listening intently.

"So Major Erikson, please give Mr. Cameron here a brief on your background."

"Yes sir." The military man turned to Geoff and addressed him directly. "Mr. Cameron, sir. My name is Major Edwin Erikson. I am a major in the US Marine Corps stationed out of Camp Pendleton, California, but currently on loan to the U.S. Air Force in Colorado Springs. I am an honors graduate with dual degrees from the U.S. Naval Academy in Annapolis, and earned my Navy Seal designation one year after graduation. I have served three decorated Seal tours in the Middle East as a sharp shooter, sniper and intelligence officer. Sir."

Geoff was impressed. "Do you have the time to help us?"

"Yes sir. I am on two-week leave between Cadet classes. If this assignment takes more time than that, I have failed my mission, sir."

Geoff glanced at Nick and nodded. He went to get up, but Nick stopped him. "Ed already has an update for you." Geoff lowered himself back into the booth.

Major Erikson spoke. "Sir. This hunter and fugitive is no stranger to the surrounding territory. And, from what I have already gathered, is no stranger to this town. He spends a significant amount of his free time in the wilderness as an accomplished bow hunter. I'm guessing, accurately I think, that after what he is accused of doing, he is somewhere out there in the woods hiding out. He would need provisions, so I have already contacted the three sporting goods stores in town, and asked to see their security videos."

"And, they shared that with you?" Geoff quizzed.

"It's hard to turn down a uniformed military officer. It's a small town. And, I can be quite persuasive, sir."

"Go on," Geoff prodded.

Major Erikson passed his iPhone over to Geoff after queuing up a video. "Press play."

As Geoff watched intently, the major said, "That's our man. Confirmed." Geoff nodded. It was the first time Geoff had had a glimpse of the man. "He is at Jeffrey's Rod and Gun buying typical supplies consistent with a prolonged stay in the wilderness. What is unusual, is that he is buying a new set of hiking footwear. No one would do that and risk blisters under such circumstances."

"Go on."

"By zooming in on the video, the store manager could identify the make and style of shoe that he purchased."

"So what?"

"Our fugitive is without wheels, so his immediate escape and whereabouts is in the immediate vicinity. If he's as clever as everyone says he is, he will do his best to divert the search through deception. That includes the dogs. Thus, the new shoes - with no clean scent. He will likely ditch his scent-laden old pair in a place that will throw the dogs off the trail, and he will wear his new shoes out."

"OK. I'm listening." Both Geoff and Nick were.

"I've got a duplicate pair of his shoes in my possession. The shoe has a unique tread pattern—easier to track than a wounded animal, sir."

Geoff smiled a rare grin for him in the last twenty-four hours. "What are you waiting for?"

"Nothing, sir. It's important to inform my superiors of my battle plan. That's all."

"One more thing, Major."

"Sir?"

"I want this bastard alive."

"I understand, sir. Given the circumstances and the mission environment, I will do my best. But, I will not compromise any further innocent life."

Geoff said, "Understood. Good luck. And, good hunting."

"And, sir?"

"Yes, Major?"

The three other bar patrons sitting near us? They're mine. I have brought them along for your security. They will not leave your side until this animal is apprehended."

"Thank you, Major. Very thorough of you."

"It wasn't me, sir." Looking to his left, he said, "Mr. George ordered them. They will be as inconspicuous as possible." Geoff looked at Nick and nodded approvingly.

The major spoke again, "One more thing. You are being tailed."

Geoff lifted his eyes in surprise. "That so?"

"Do you wish for me to disable this irritant before I head into the wilderness?"

"Please."

"Consider it done." The major stood and saluted, grabbed his coat and hurried out the door.

Geoff turned to his trusted friend. "Thanks, Nick. Well done. And, thanks for the gun."

131

GEOFF

IT WAS NOW TUESDAY NIGHT, AND GEOFF WAS SITTING QUIETLY IN the waiting room with Jessica. They had just had a light meal in the cafeteria, and were waiting for an update from the doctors. Meredith had survived the first forty-eight hours, but was still in a deep coma. At 8:45 PM the door pushed open, and a new doctor emerged. He extended his hand.

"Hi. I'm Doctor Russell. I am one of the evening ICU doctors here on call. I am here to give you an update on Mrs. Edmonson."

Geoff interrupted, "Who is in charge here?"

"For the whole hospital? That would be Dr. Raymond Gould."

"Can I speak with him?"

"No, that is not possible. He is home at the moment."

Geoff was clearly getting edgy. "So, let me understand. We have been here since late Sunday night, and it is now Tuesday night. And, while our friend has been in your care, we have neither been able to see her, nor have we had the pleasure of a visit from your chief of staff."

"I'm very sorry. The patient has been in intensive care and cannot see visitors due to the possible transmission of infections," he replied calmly. "Would you like an update on Mrs. Edmonson?"

Geoff took a deep breath and calmed himself. "I apologize, Dr...?"

"Russell"

"Got it. Dr. Russell, yes, we would appreciate an update on Mrs. Edmonson."

"Come with me."

132

SUSIE

SUSIE'S PHONE RANG. IT WAS WEDNESDAY MORNING. THE KIDS WERE already at school. Rosanne was downstairs cleaning and preparing lunch. She picked up her cell phone and answered, "Hello?"

"Hi Susie, this is Trevor. Have you heard from your husband?"

"Yes. As a matter of fact, twice. He confirmed he is in Grand Junction on business. What's up? Any updates?"

"First of all, you were supposed to let me know if, and when, you spoke, or made contact, with your husband."

"Sorry. I forgot."

"You are paying me a lot of money to find out what your husband is up to. While I would like to think I can break this on my own, I need a little more help from you."

"OK. Sorry."

"Look, Mrs. Cameron, we have tailed your husband, and as I have told you, we have ascertained that there is something considerably of interest to him at Saint Mary's Med Center."

"I know all this, already. Is this all you have for me?"

"Well no, actually. We were able check the patient logs for both ICU and Maternity. There were thirteen babies born Sunday night; two are still there. One was born prematurely, the other was born with a whole in his heart."

She couldn't help herself, "His?"

Yes, both the remaining babies are male. But in ICU, there were seven patients admitted Sunday. Three in an automobile accident, one motorcycle fatality, two recreational vehicle mishaps and one domestic violence case. None seem to be linked to your husband."

Susie asked, "If I may, what is the gender of the domestic violence victim?"

"Female. But she's a local. And, they know the perp: her husband. Not likely. So, we think this may be a paternity."

"But, his suspicious behavior didn't start nine months ago, Trevor." Susie was clearly getting frustrated.

Unflapped, Trevor deadpanned, "It may be a 'premie.'" Then without waiting for a reply, he continued, "This is really not what I am calling about. Your husband's tail was disabled, his camera smashed, his cell phone stomped on, and his tires slashed. Your husband is certainly aware he is now being followed and under surveillance. We may have to lay low for a few days."

"And THIS is what I have already paid you over $100,000 for? Good work." She disconnected.

133

CHARLIE

IT WAS 5:30 AM WEDNESDAY, AND CHARLIE FREDERICK'S ALARM clock woke him. He was so tired. It had been a late night last night. After the faculty meeting, the Granite High's Principal had joined his wife for one of their favorite dinners: pepperoni pizza and cold merlot at Pepe's. The meeting had gone well. There were still questions about their football coach and the future of the team. But this was faculty, not parents. It had largely been stress free.

Now he lay there in bed, next to his warm wife, debating as to whether he should get up, put on his sweats, and head out in the bitter morning chill. Or, reset his alarm for 7 AM, and catch a little more wonderful shut-eye. His stomach grumbled, and he took that as a sign of what he needed to do. He slid out of bed and went into the bathroom to change. When he was ready, he quietly tip-toed over to his wife's side of the bed, and softly kissed her on her cheek. She didn't stir.

In the kitchen, he poured himself a steaming traveler of coffee and added both sugar and cream. "Just like my wife: hot, blond and sweet," he said to himself smiling remembering their night last night. Charlie grabbed his briefcase with his other hand, and with difficulty, opened the front door and stepped outside. He had a change of clothes at the gym.

He took a deep breath of that fresh, ice-cold, mountain air and stepped off his porch to cross his lawn towards his car. Had it been light, he might have seen the steam rising from the nearby garden. He couldn't see a thing—unlike the quiet assailant behind the night-vision scope. Bobbie had one shot, he knew. It had to not only disable his prey, but also keep it from screaming. That left no option but a throat shot.

Bobbie loaded the arrow. He had picked one with wild boar blood already on it. Charlie boy was a big fucking pig, and this was going to be a fitting payback for his "paid vacation." He slowly pulled the gut-string back all the way under his chin. He placed the crosshairs where they needed to be. When Charlie stopped to pick up the morning paper, and stopped to scan the morning headlines. He was distantly aware of a rustling, and a whistling of air. The arrow struck savagely at his Adam's apple tearing open his windpipe. He shrieked in fear and panic, but no sound could be heard—just rasping from the gaping wound. His morning paper, coffee and briefcase went flying—the latter springing open on impact and the contents were picked up by the morning breeze, and carried away effortlessly down the street. His body twisted grotesquely and fell quietly to the lawn. Charlie was grasping helplessly at the arrow trying to remove it - thrashing on his dew-wet lawn.

The next thing the principal knew there was a large boot on his chest. He looked above him in horror at Coach Edmonson. "Chuckie! Can I call you, Chuckie?" Charlie's eyes were bulging with fright and suffocation. "Thanks for the vacation, you fucking pig." Now the boot was on his throat, and on the intruding arrow, pinning his head face up. Bobbie reached over his shoulder and fetched another arrow. Without saying a word, he threaded it onto the string, and pulled the bow back to its full taughtness. He then tipped it forward, and sighting the arrow to its target, he let it fly.

The arrow entered Charlie's left eye socket, traveled effortlessly through his brain matter and exited into the Frederick's front lawn and the earth below.

The arrow pinned him to the ground, and he was instantly brain dead, but that didn't stop his involuntary muscle spasms and jerks. Bobbie took his boot off Charlie's throat, and stepped back to admire the jerking. It was almost like he was running in place.

"Have a good workout, Chuckie. And, oh yeah, enjoy your permanent *unpaid* vacation."

And with that, Bobbie slipped back into the early morning darkness leaving his deadly arrows where they were. He wanted the entire community to know the identity of the killer. And, fear him.

Four down. *Two* to go. He had added another name to the list.

Game on.

134

GEOFF

HE HAD WITNESSED AND SEEN MANY THINGS IN HIS LIFE, BUT WHAT loomed in front of him left him speechless and breathless. He, Jessica and Dr. Russell all stood in front of a large picture window. The doctor was speaking, but Geoff heard none of it. What he saw through the glass brought such incapacitating sadness, anger and anxiety that he found himself grasping, unsuccessfully, with his sanity.

He took the doctor's word that the human being lying in the ventilator tent, with wires and tubes protruding everywhere, who was connected to machines that blinked, whirred, chimed and made jagged lines on screens, was Meredith. He moved forward, and placing both hands high on the glass, stammered, "Beautiful, beautiful, Meredith. Please come back to me." The tears running unabated down his grief-stricken face. As he dropped his head, he whispered, "Please."

The doctor placed his hand on Geoff's shoulder, this time to comfort him, and Jessica stood back and tried to absorb all of this, too. Geoff was inconsolable. Paying no attention to the doctor, he turned to Jessica, and it took a few seconds for him to catch his breath. He looked down to her, and his eyes were red and pooling. He never blinked as he locked eyes with her.

"I did this to her, Jess. She didn't deserve this. I am so, so, sorry." He then closed his eyes and bowed his head. "Dear sweet God, forgive me."

The entire south wing of the hospital could hear his anguished sobbing.

135

NICK

GEOFF HAD RECOVERED SOMEWHAT, AND WAS SITTING ACROSS THE table from Nick in the hotel restaurant. It was now Thursday. They had just ordered lunch. "How fast can it be done?"

Nick replied, "In Los Angeles, it will take two days. Denver, three."

Geoff thought a moment then said, "I'm thinking LA."

Nick responded, "I'm thinking Denver. It's far closer, less risk, and in the end, gives us far more control."

"Go with it. I trust your judgment. Just keep me apprised of the progress."

"Of course."

Nick changed the subject. "Any word from Major Erikson?"

"Crickets."

"What about them?" Nick was puzzled.

"Sorry. I meant 'silence.'" Geoff allowed himself a tired, nervous, smile.

Nick thought that was a small miracle. He had never seen his friend and business partner so devastated in his life. They had been at that table for two hours walking through the numerous deals and decisions that Geoff had to make, and this had been the first time in their working relationship that it seemed that Geoff just didn't care about his business. His head wasn't in this game. He was delegating nearly everything to his able support team, and had asked Nick to take over and supervise the results. He was flat. His eyes were weary and dull.

"The major said he would alert us as soon as he made contact. He has both our cell numbers," Nick assured. "The last I heard from him was last night late when you were at the hospital. He said he was on to something, but wouldn't tell me. He said he wanted to keep me arms-length on this deal—or something like that."

Geoff just nodded quietly. Finally, he said, "I like him. I only hope he is as good as his credentials."

His phone pinged. At first, he paid no attention to it. Then thirty seconds later, it pinged again. He picked up the phone, and Nick watched as his friend went from being completely disinterested to becoming fully alert. He jumped to his feet.

"What is it?" Nick asked.

Geoff handed him his cell phone so that Nick could read the two new texts. The first was from the ICU from Dr. Russell. "Please call me ASAP."

The second was from Jessica.

"Meredith is waking up."

136

HUGH

THE DISTRICT LAWYER, HUGH PRESTON, LIVED IN A LARGE COLONIAL home nestled in an aspen grove he had planted himself twenty-two years ago. He, and his wife Bonnie, had raised their three daughters there, and had given them a rich and memorable childhood in that exceptionally happy environment. They were all off to college or grad school now, which is why Hugh was still working. He would retire in three years. He had it all planned out.

It was 12:30 PM Thursday, and Hugh turned his car into the long driveway that led to his house. He loved coming home for lunch with Bonnie on Thursdays. It had been a ritual of theirs since their last daughter had left for the University of Colorado, Boulder.

He parked his car by the back kitchen door, and jumped out. The first thing he noticed was the window blinds were closed. He tried the door. Locked. What? He fumbled for his keys, and inadvertently dropped them on the porch. When he leaned down to pick them up, he heard the doorknob turn and the door open. Relieved, he looked up and smiled. Then froze.

"Come on in!" Coach Edmonson said with enthusiasm. "Bonnie and I were just hanging out together wondering when you were going to join us."

"What are you doing here, Robert?" Hugh demanded.

"Oh, I just decided to come by and pay a visit, and your wife was kind enough to invite me to lunch."

"Where is she?"

Bobbie turned his head and called over his shoulder, "Bonnie? Hugh is home! We can have lunch now!" Then lowering his voice, Bobbie said, "You know, your wife is a stickler for details."

Hugh sprinted past Bobbie, ran through the dining room and into the grand foyer.

Bobbie put his fingers in his ears and laughed. Then, he heard the blood-curdling scream. "Noooooooooooooooooooooo! Nooooooooooooooooooooo! NO! NO! NO! NO!"

The coach walked slowly through the house to join Hugh and his wife at the front of their home. When he got there, he found Hugh, curled up in a ball on the floor. Above him, hung his wife. She had been stripped, and garroted by a noose, and attached to the large, crystal chandelier. She was swinging and twisting slightly, but the horror of the scene was still unfolding. She looked like a bloated, life-sized, pincushion. There were sixteen arrows in her, some protruding all the way through her body. Her eyes were wide open and her mouth drooped open expelling saliva and blood.

Bobbie was now speaking warmly. "Hey, sorry, Hugh. I had to shoot her so many times, because she wouldn't stand still!" He started laughing uncontrollably. He choked out, "I tried to end it as quickly and painlessly, as I could, but she just wouldn't cooperate."

Then he stopped laughing. He left the lawyer alone, and went into the den. When he came out he had his bow, and the remaining two arrows. "Get up."

Hugh didn't move from his fetal position on the floor.

Bobbie walked over, and kicked him with the sharp toe of his cowboy boot. Hugh yelled out in agony. "GET UP!" Bobbie screamed.

Hugh struggled as he pulled himself up on all fours- panting. He remained there motionless like a dog.

Bobbie walked over and opened the front door. "Get out!" He demanded.

Hugh looked up at him pathetically, questioning his orders.

"I said…GET OUT!" When Hugh didn't move, Bobbie knelt down beside him and whispered in his ear, "Bonnie didn't want to play my game, either. But, I think you might be interested." He continued, "I'm giving you a five-minute head start. I promise not to leave you hanging, like Bonnie here. But, I need you to leave the house. You will be running for your life. I get two shots. If I miss, you live. If, I don't? You join Bonnie for dessert up at the Big House." Bobbie got up.

When Hugh still didn't rise from his all-fours crouch, Bobbie calmly said, "The clock is not your friend. Tic. Toc."

Hugh slowly and painstakingly rose, and stumbled for the open front door. His eyes, vacant. Once there, he slowly turned around and met Bobbie's dark eyes. "You fucking bastard. You will rot in hell."

Bobbie's response was calm and measured. He looked at his watch.

"Tic."

137

GEOFF

JESSICA WAS PACING AT THE FRONT ENTRANCE OF SAINT MARY'S when Geoff's car pulled up. The door opened before the car had come to a stop. Geoff jumped out as the driver was unclasping his seat belt. He was laser-focused on getting inside, and getting to Meredith, but Jessica stopped him. She grasped him with both hands just above each of his elbows, and turned him to face her. She said excitedly, "She's out of her coma. But, she's not awake, and not aware—at least that I know of. But, she is breathing on her own without the ventilator, and she has been removed from all the machines that were keeping her alive. She's heavily sedated."

"Is she going to be alright?"

Her reply didn't totally answer his question. "The doctor says that it's too early to tell. The swelling on her brain has receded, and they were able to surgically remove the hematoma. Her brain waves and vital signs are normal, but the doctor cautioned about being too optimistic."

Geoff shook his head in disbelief. "Can we see her?"

Jessica nodded, and said. "One at a time. And, each visitor has to register with the hospital. I've already registered you." She let go of him.

"Take me to her."

• • •

Geoff walked slowly into the room, and quietly knelt by her bed. He hadn't seen her, really, since she had driven away from their weekend together in La Quinta.

She had been wearing a light and breezy black and white striped silk blouse and he could see her ponytail blowing in the warm desert air as she walked to her loaded car. She had stopped, and turned before opening her door, and mouthed the words "I love you," then blew him a kiss. He had tapped his heart with his finger, then lifted it and pointed at her. No words were needed, but he sure now wished they had spoken that one last time.

Meredith's beautiful thick raven hair was gone. There was a large bandage wrapped around her head hiding the ugly laceration the surgeons had cut to reach the hematoma and relieve the pressure on her brain. Her right eye was shut and swollen. The entire right side of her face was puffy and purple. Her mouth was wired shut, and the facial wounds were deep—mostly still raw and bandaged. She had several IV's in her arm, a feeding tube, and she was still connected to a monitor that kept tabs on her heart rate and blood pressure. Her eyes were closed, but Geoff could see the gentle rise and fall of her chest as she breathed on her own. He took her hand.

"Hey," he said softly in her ear. "It's me. Geoff…with a G."

• • •

It had been over an hour, and Geoff had never let go of her hand. He just sat there and talked and talked. Occasionally, he would bring her hand to his face and hold it to his cheek. He had even disclosed his plans for their next trip together: Stanley, Idaho. A small log cabin in a field of wildflowers. They would picnic, fish, hike and explore, he told her. He couldn't wait to show her, he said, and much more.

He felt his phone buzz. Without letting go of her hand, he pulled his phone out and checked his messages. There were three from Susie. The last one saying "Have you called the gardeners, yet?"

Then he saw the one that had just come in. It was from Major Erikson.

"I've got him. He's alive." There was an address. And, directions to meet them in the backyard.

He nodded to himself, and put his phone back in his pocket. He pulled Meredith's soft hand across his chest so that it rested over his heart. Geoff leaned down to her ear, and whispered, "I'll be right back, Beautiful. Wait for me."

And with that, Geoff rose and quietly exited her room at the ICU. He slipped silently down the hall and out the back door. No one saw him leave; not Jessica, not Nick. And, not his bodyguards.

138

BOBBIE

ONE MISTAKE, AND THE TASK HAD BEEN MADE FAR EASIER, BUT NO less urgent. Major Erikson had tracked the footprints to Bobbie's cave. The treads were like blinking DNA markers leading right to the opening. His intention was to lay and wait high in an adjacent tree until the wolf came back to his lair. But, he took the opportunity to quickly search the cave before setting his trap.

The crumpled piece of paper read:

Don DeLatore - Superintendent

Charlie Fredericks—Principal

Hugh Preston—Lawyer

Janet Jacobs—Human Resources

Meredith Edmonson—Fuck Bitch

Now, he couldn't afford to wait around. He hoped he would make it there in time.

He didn't.

• • •

When Edwin Erikson arrived at the Fredericks' abode, he found the front door open, but did not enter the house. Instead he searched the surrounding property, his gun drawn, for possible dangers and/or traps. The front yard was easy to "clear" but the backyard opened to a wilderness area with no fencing or borders. He searched the perimeter, and soon found what he was looking for: the footprints.

Major Erikson followed these slowly and quietly—stopping quickly, and often, to listen for danger. He was surprised to find two sets of differing footprints heading in the same direction. He got to an open field, and the tracks led him right up to the edge of a cliff. Before looking over the precipice, he looked left, then right, scanning the surrounding overgrowth for anything amiss. All was quiet and still.

Edwin then looked over the cliff, and saw the crumpled body far below on the rocks. It was motionless. He had seen death so many times before that this sight neither shocked him nor repulsed him. But it did call him to action, and he redirected his attention back to the footprints.

It was then that his knee exploded. Edwin grimaced in agony as he looked down in horror at an arrow protruding from his leg. He crumpled to the ground loosing his grip on his weapon—the gun tumbling just out of reach to his right.

"Do not move," the voice said a ways behind him. Edwin heard footsteps crackling through the underbrush. Bobbie knelt quickly behind the major. Edwin froze as he felt the unmistakable cold, sharp, edge of a very large blade against his throat.

"Who are you?"

Major Erikson responded calmly, "I am the Fredericks' neighbor. I happened to be driving by the house and saw the front door open, so I stopped to check things out."

Did you find anything amiss?" Bobbie asked.

"No, not at all." Ed choked—his pain threshold clearly reached. "I closed the door, and to be honest, came back here to take a piss. The next thing I know I have a goddamned arrow through my knee."

Bobbie took stock of the situation, then replied, "Sure you were. You're a lying sack of shit. If you had to take a piss so bad, you'd have peed your pants." Bobbie pulled the knife across the side of the major's neck and cut deeply through his flesh. The major jerked uncontrollably and closed his eyes in pain.

Without moving the knife from the major's throat, he freed his victim's cell phone from his back pocket, and dropped it in front of him. "Unlock it," Bobbie demanded.

The major reached down slowly so as not to disturb the dagger at his throat. He did as he was told. "Now hand it to me slowly with your left hand."

Bobbie grasped the phone, and navigated the touch-screen quickly with his left hand to see all the recent calls and texts that had been sent. Bingo. Geoff Cameron.

"The Frederick's neighbor, huh?" Bobbie growled. He tossed the phone back on Edwin's lap. "You have one chance to save your life, you motherfucker, and what you do next determines if you live or if you die." Without waiting for a reply, he continued, "Seeing that I can't type at the moment, I need you to send Mr. Cameron a little short text that says you have caught me. Here. Alive. I want to see the message before you send it."

Edwin did as he was told. He held up the phone so that Bobbie could see the screen and its message.

"Thank you. Now you will live. In infamy."

The massive hunting knife first sliced through the major's windpipe. Bobbie was shocked at how muscular his prey's neck was, but compared to his prize buck, it went relatively quickly. The tearing of gristle and bone, combined with the gurgling of gushing blood made for a macabre intrusion into the peacefully grotesque scene that was the Frederick's back yard.

Once the head was separated from the body, Bobbie picked it up by the hair—it's short crew cut making it particularly difficult - and carried it to the back porch where he tossed it just outside the rear screen door. He then returned to the headless body, and placing his boot on the major's leg, with some effort, heaved his arrow free. Bobbie studied the arrow - the tip slightly damaged from the violent impact. He then smelled it. Smiling, he put the arrow, still dripping wet with the lifeblood of his prey, into the quiver on his back along with his only other remaining arrow.

Bobbie picked up the cell phone from the dirt nearby, and looked again at the message the major had typed. He hit "SEND." He then went over, and leaned the phone up against the detached head.

Leaving the body where it was, and the head and phone by the screened porch, Bobbie went back to his secret hiding place in the thick overgrowth behind the house. He crouched. He checked his bow and scope. And waited.

139

GEOFF

HE HAD NO IDEA WHERE HE WAS GOING, BUT THE ADDRESS ON THE text message was now the destination on Geoff's navigation. He hurtled through light traffic praying quietly that he wouldn't get pulled over by the local authorities. The message had said to meet them in the backyard.

He screeched to a stop at the curb. He checked his large .357 magnum handgun on the seat next to him making sure it was loaded and the safety was off. He jumped out of the car, and raced for the side gate that led to the rear of the house. He yelled for the major, but there was no reply. He yelled again.

Then his attention was drawn to what looked like a boulder sitting by the back door. He approached it quickly, but cautiously. What he discovered, he found hard to comprehend. A human head in a pool of dark red blood. Eyes open and bulging. Mouth gaping. The major. Geoff started shaking uncontrollably, as this scene, with him in it, was unfolding rapidly before his eyes. And, the phone? It was leaned up against the head. Jeff leaned down and picked it up, and the screen immediately came to life. On it was this message: "So you like fucking my wife?"

Geoff jerked his head up in sudden, vulnerable, panic, and franticly searched the backyard for something; anything. The arrow entered his thigh just below his crotch. He screamed and instantly fell to the ground clutching his leg. He had never before experienced such searing pain.

Bobbie stepped from his lair, and walked slowly, but deliberately, towards the man, moaning on the ground, writhing in pain. He kicked away Geoff's gun. Then he buried the toe of his large, tooled, cowboy boot deep into the solar plexus below Geoff's ribcage. The world went black.

140

BOBBIE

GEOFF BEGAN TO GAIN CONSCIOUSNESS SLOWLY AND PAINFULLY. When his eyes slitted open he was lying on the ground with his face in the dirt—a liquid pooled under his mouth. The pain in his leg was almost secondary to the damage inflicted to his midsection. He looked up. As his eyes cleared, he tried to focus on the large, unshaven, man with a toothpick in the corner of his mouth. He was holding up a piece of paper studying it intermittently with Geoff's face. Then he knelt down in the dirt next to Geoff, and took a large handful of Geoff's long wavy hair, and screwed his head upward towards him.

Bobbie then took the mysterious piece of paper and turned it around in front of Geoff's face. Geoff was panting hard, and again found it hard to focus. But, his vision cleared long enough for him to get a crystal glimpse of that paper. It was Meredith. And, him—Geoff. In the elevator. Kissing. His right hand inside her blouse.

Bobbie released his hold on Geoff's long locks, and his head dropped freely, and hard, back into the dirt. Bobbie stood, and with his boot, rolled Geoff over awkwardly onto his back—the arrow protruding through his thigh preventing him from lying flat. Geoff's head lolled limply from side to side. Bobbie pulled his bow from the ground, and reached back into his quiver, and pulled out his last remaining arrow—the one with the knee-damaged tip. He loaded it onto the bowstring and pulled it back to full taughtness. He moved his boot to Geoff's head—stilling it. He then leaned over, sighted Geoff's left eye, and hissed, "So. You like fucking my wife? Well, FUCK…"

There was a very loud POP that startled them both. Bobbie flinched, and the arrow released on its own. The hissing projectile tore into the dirt just grazing Geoff's head tearing open a gash just above his left ear. Blood was oozing to the ground.

Geoff was again unconscious. At his feet, the football coach was motionless. The bullet had entered the right side of his head, just below his temple. The hollow point projectile had taken off the entire right side of his face - the ragged, torn, meat and brain matter of the exit wound splayed wide across the Frederick's backyard steaming in the late afternoon chill.

141

NICK

NICK, AND THE THREE BODYGUARDS, RACED TO THE ADDRESS AS outlined in the same text sent to *both* Geoff and Nick. When they screeched to a halt at the property, they all jumped out of the car simultaneously, and raced for the same side gate Geoff had used ten minutes earlier.

The bodyguards, all trained snipers from the Marine Corps, entered first. Nick almost fell into them when they suddenly stopped, dropped to their knees and pointed their guns. The lead Marine yelled, "FREEZE! PUT DOWN YOUR GUN!"

The lone standing figure turned and slowly lowered his arm and dropped his weapon to the ground, then raised both his arms in surrender. The bodyguards never lowered their guns, but kept them trained on the assailant.

Nick was trying to make sense of the scene as he raced towards the bodies— the first of the four to arrive. He couldn't believe his eyes. There standing below the shooter was a body with its head blown virtually away, and his friend and boss, rolling on the ground, moaning with a head wound and an arrow protruding from his thigh.

As the Marine bodyguards approached with their guns trained, the lead shouted, "Identify yourself!"

The shooter appeared shaken, but waving his hands in front of him, exclaimed, "Please hold your fire. I am friendly. I killed the assailant as he was about to put an arrow through Mr. Cameron's head."

Nick broke in, "How in the world do you know Mr. Cameron? And, what are you doing here?"

He replied, "I am with a private investigator out of San Francisco..."

142

MEREDITH

THERE WAS A LARGE TEAM OF MEDICAL PRACTITIONERS SWARMING around the room. Meredith was awakening, and with that awakening came awareness. She was still quite sedated, but agitated. She knew enough to know she was in a hospital and in a lot of pain. She couldn't open her mouth past a small slit, but she was breathing. She didn't know how she had come to be there. As she wavered back and forth between sleep and consciousness, she dreamed.

She was swimming—floating freely underwater in a crystal-clear pool. There was someone she wanted to see, desperately. But, she didn't know exactly who. That person was important to her—that she knew for certain. But, this person… seemed just out of her reach.

The nurses finished checking all the vital signs taking copious notes on the clipboard attached by a cord at her feet. The doctor was making his own notations when Jessica slipped into the room. She stayed out of the way until they were finished cleaning the room. When they left, she approached the bed. Taking her hand, she said, "Hey, girlfriend. What 'cha been up to?"

Meredith stirred. She slowly turned her head towards the voice and opened her eyes. It took her a few moments, but then Jessica could see the recognition come to her face. And if eyes could smile, the grin was ear-to-ear. Meredith spoke through clenched, wired, teeth. "Jess."

"Hi, Mer." Then she brought forth a big smile, "Am I ever glad to see you."

"What happened to me? Where am I?" she hissed.

"You're at Saint Mary's. You've had a bad accident."

"What day is it?" Meredith said one word at a time.

"Thursday. You've been asleep since Sunday," Jessica said carefully.

"Asleep?" she was able to force out.

"Yes. You had a nasty fall and sustained a head injury that required surgery. The doctors sedated you so that you could recover as quickly as possible." She was careful not to use the word "coma."

Meredith nodded. Then she whispered, "I feel like a mess. Do you have a mirror? I at least want to comb my hair."

Jess now knelt very close to her friend, and said, "Listen, Mer. I just want to prepare you. You're here because you almost lost your life. The surgeries were serious and major. You are pretty beat up both from the accident and the surgeries. What you are going to see in that mirror of mine is going to shock you, OK?"

Again, Meredith nodded her understanding, but held her hand out. Jessica rummaged around in her handbag and pulled out a small mirror. She hesitated before handing it to her friend, but then, did. Meredith took it and held it. It didn't take long. The shriek came from the back of her throat and was muffled at her teeth. The mirror dropped on the bed and she closed her eyes tight - breathing heavily. Jess sat there and comforted her friend as best she could, but Meredith was inconsolable—her catastrophically damaged face was wet with tears.

Neither of them heard the door open.

143

GEOFF

ESSICA FELT A HAND ON HER SHOULDER, AND SHE JUMPED—STAR-
tling Meredith, too. They both looked in the same direction. A smile came
to Jessica's face, but Meredith's eyes were not clear—neither her vision nor her
memory. As with Jessica, it took some time. She squinted, and seemed to be
concentrating earnestly while this man joined Jessica by her side. He had a cane.

Jessica said, "I'm going to leave the two of you alone for a while, OK?"

Meredith looked up at her with panic, and violently shook her head from side
to side, but Jessica ignored her silent pleas. Jessica put a hand on this stranger's
arm, and said, "I'll be in the waiting room if you need me."

He replied kindly, "Thanks, Jess, but that won't be necessary. Why don't you
go home? Jazzy is really anxious to see you, I'm sure. Let me walk you out." He
arose and escorted her to the door and stepped outside in the hall.

When he had said the word, "Jazzy," a distant memory started to form. Then
the door reopened and this tall handsome man with wavy, salt-and-pepper, hair—
and a bandage on the side of his face - stepped in and closed the door behind
him. She never took her eyes off of him. He seemed so familiar. He pulled a chair
up next to her bed, and took her hand. She wanted to pull away, but something
prevented her.

Then he said, "Hey." He leaned over and kissed her softly on her good cheek.
"God, I missed you, M."

Her eyes grew wide with recognition. They were expressive and alive. She
could feel the veil lifting, and her heart flooding with joy. Then, tears followed,

and her eyes closed. He clasped her hand in his and softly stroked it—bringing it to his mouth occasionally to kiss it.

But then, just as instantly, the scene shifted and darkened. The tears stopped, and waves of shame washed over her. She decided, right then and there, that she wanted to die. She remembered what she had seen in the mirror.

Meredith turned her deformed, and misshapened, face away from Geoff, and tried to curl up into a ball, but the tubes and wires attached to her prevented it. She just wanted him to go away.

JUST AFTER

MIKE PARRISH RADIOED THE TOWER ASKING FOR PERMISSION TO land. The Tower had given him immediate emergency clearance to get priority landing on Runway 23R. Ground Control was awaiting their arrival and had cleared all taxiways to allow expedient movement to the Private Aviation terminal. Slowly, Mike pulled the gleaming Gulfstream 550 into a slow bank on its approach to San Francisco International Airport.

The plane was uncharacteristically full. Stephanie was on board to handle most of the logistics while Nick remained in Grand Junction for questioning with the local authorities. There were doctors, nurses and specialists making the journey with them to make sure their patient was comfortable. They would also accompany Meredith on her brief transfer flight to Stanford University Medical Center, in Palo Alto.

Geoff was alone with her now in the back stateroom which Nick had had converted into a medevac nerve center for Meredith's transport to the finest doctors in the world. Her jaw was now unwired, but the damaging, and deforming, injuries remained. Her face was not as swollen, but the black and blue bruising had now added yellow to its spectrum. Meredith tried to put her future out of her mind, and focus on each day, each minute, as it unfolded. She was petrified.

Geoff was talking to her. She allowed herself to glance his way, and smile a crooked smile. Then she put her head back on her pillows and rested her eyes. Geoff leaned over and kissed her softly on the mouth, making sure to not touch where she had been so badly injured. She delicately sighed.

"Did I ever tell you that I have a secret fetish for bald-headed girls?" he asked.

Meredith started laughing, and that sparkle returned to her eyes—then, she winced in pain grabbing her side.

"I am so sorry, M," Geoff said—serious now.

Meredith caught her breath until the pain passed. Then she turned to him and winked. "Let me be your first."

• • •

On the ground, the jet slowly maneuvered its way across the north end of the airport until it turned its final corner as the private terminal approached. Mike was shocked to see the throngs of spectators awaiting their arrival. He notified his passengers, on the PA system, that they had company.

CBC's pilot eased the Gulfstream, with its priceless cargo, to a designated spot on the tarmac adjacent to the Long Ranger helicopter. As Mike shut the engines down, three police cars and a paramedic raced out to greet them. Twelve officers jumped out and waited patiently by the aircraft door. They were joined by Booker.

The door lowered, and the stairs tapped to the ground. Two officers boarded. Then, one-by-one, the occupants stepped off the plane and down the stairs—led by Stephanie. She held a clipboard. The crowd at the terminal was getting loud and unruly. The pilots came out next followed by two CBC staff. Then there was a long delay.

Next off were the doctors and nurses who were all clearly focused on what was following them. At the bottom of the stairs, they gathered and turned around. The officers, assisted by two paramedics, extricated a stretcher from the belly of the aircraft. The opening was very narrow, and they struggled. Once the stretcher was out on the tarmac, they raised the legs, and reattached the IV's.

The one last to emerge, was the Chief Executive Officer of Cameron, Boone & Covington. Geoff limped down the stairs aided by his cane, his upper right thigh wrapped in a large bandage. He met up with his fellow passengers—now a small crowd gathered at the nose of the aircraft.

The spectators, seemingly in the hundreds, were now shouting questions. It was obvious the press was there in force, and had been alerted to something.

"Mr. Cameron. *Mr. CAMERON!* What, in your own words, happened in Colorado?"

"We heard there was a murder! Care to comment?"

"Who's the girl? Are you having an affair?"

The questions were being yelled over the top of each other. Geoff couldn't figure out what in the world they knew, and why they would be here to greet his plane. How could they have known when he was arriving? Geoff decided that he would just ignore them all. What he couldn't have known was that Bobbie's good friend, Tommy, from the Wrecking Crew was deep in the crowd, yelling at the top of his lungs, egging them on.

Geoff made a point to go to every person who was a part of this flight, and shook each of their hands—thanking them for their assistance and professionalism. Then he went over to Meredith, and took her right hand with his left so as not to lose his cane. "You ready?" he asked. She nodded softly. "Booker is here, too. He can't wait to see you." That brought a smile to her face.

"Let's do it," she said.

And with that small comfortable exchange, they headed for the helicopter. But first, they had to pass the throngs of people gathered at the terminal fencing.

• • •

Her voice was unmistakable—the shrill and the urgency repeating his name over and over again. When they got close to the fence, Geoff looked up. And there, in the very front row, was Susie. Her voice seemed to blend in with the shouted requests of the press, but Geoff answered neither. He made eye contact with his wife, and held it.

Then, looking back down to the stretcher, he took Meredith's hand, once again, and hobbled with her, and their medical team, to the helicopter that would fly his Meredith to the help she so desperately needed.

And, to the future they so desperately deserved.

ACKNOWLEDGEMENTS

THIS FIRST NOVEL HAS BEEN QUITE A JOURNEY. I SET OUT TO WRITE a book that I would love to read myself: a compelling love story and thriller, full of sex and violence, and short "punchy" chapters that each end with a surprise - inviting the reader to keep turning pages well into the night.

When I wrote my last words (before my extensive editing), I felt not only tremendous satisfaction, but also, sadness. The process of putting this fantasy into words was shear joy, and my time at the keyboard was literally "time going lightly."

And speaking of time at the keyboard, I would first like to thank the wonderful staff and patrons of the Manhattan Beach CA Public Library where 95% of the initial draft of this novel was written. Sitting at one of their desks, with a magnificent view of the Pacific Ocean, gave me the tranquil environment needed for my dream to unfold under my fingertips.

Eight wonderfully diverse readers volunteered to travel on this journey with me: four women and four men. I asked of them to be brutally honest, and they were. I greedily absorbed all of their advice. Profound thanks, first and foremost, to my lifelong friend, Nick George, who accompanied me at that fateful dinner with Meredith and Jessica in 2013, and who's name I stole for one of the main characters. He was my constant soulmate and almost-daily confidant on this project. To Sherry, a C-suite real estate executive and former colleague, whose encouragement and advice propelled me to seek realism over sensationalism. To Yana, a meticulously precise dentist, and relentless fact-checker, who kept this work "believable," and whose knowledge of Rodeo Drive played an important role in the telling of the shopping scenes in Beverly Hills. To Dennis, a respected lawyer and professional sports team president, who shares my love of "beach-read" thrillers and who, over the years, spent endless hours with me on a Kauai beach (while our families played), reading and kibitzing over our favorite novels and authors—helped to shape my novel. To Greg, a brother-in-arms colleague, who's regular phone calls encouraged me, but also warned me to "be careful."

Hopefully, I was. To Judith, a brilliant Swiss educator and engineer, who I met on a long flight to Shanghai, who's demands for "more" after reading each section kept me incredibly motivated. And, last but not least, to my fabulously gay friend, Anna P. Sunshine, whose input on some of the more intimate scenes were both humorous and priceless. I owe you all a debt of gratitude that can never be repaid.

One of the great joys for me in this journey has been to re-connect with a former colleague in my Fortune 200 days—Yolanda Harris, now CEO of The Keynote Group. Her advice, counsel and shear enthusiasm for this book that flowed from the moment she turned the last page, has been both inspirational and tremendously helpful.

At the outset of writing this book, I happened to be at a party with Jennie Nash—renowned book coach, author and Founder/Chief Creative Officer of Author Accelerator—and I mentioned that I was writing a book. She squealed, grabbed me, and said, "Let's talk!" Three hours later, we were still in the den "talking shop." Jennie is a friend, and her informal advice throughout, really helped—both in the process and in the writing. Her best piece of advice, in my opinion, was that the only critic you need to please is yourself—you have to love what you wrote. And I do. Thank you, Jennie. She also advised to NOT let your spouse read the book until it is finished…

So, to my spouse and three grown children, thanks for enabling me to write this novel - even though there were times of tremendous doubt. As my spouse recently explained, "I have known you intimately for over thirty years, and I never saw this coming. You? Writing a novel?"

The writing of this book has been another chapter of a life I am trying to live well. My children will now always be able to say that I was an international CEO of a Fortune 200 company, a successful international entrepreneur, an adventurer, a sports car enthusiast, an educator, a mentor, a trekker, a thrill-seeker, a devoted father and husband—and now, an author. And, what will they also forever be able say about me? "He was no Geoff Cameron."

And finally, to Meredith and Jessica: Two strangers I met at a dinner with my friend Nick in Grand Junction, Colorado. That carefree night gave me a glimmer of hope about a different journey—and, the beginning of a great story. I hope you both enjoy reading this novel as much as I had fun writing it. After all, it all started with you.

C. Lindsey Williams
September 18, 2018

CPSIA information can be obtained
at www.ICGtesting.com
Printed in the USA
LVHW060747250420
654423LV00008B/205/J